John Gilmore

Storm Warriors

Life-Boat Work on the Goodwin Sands

John Gilmore

Storm Warriors
Life-Boat Work on the Goodwin Sands

ISBN/EAN: 9783337413200

Printed in Europe, USA, Canada, Australia, Japan

Cover: Foto ©Andreas Hilbeck / pixelio.de

More available books at **www.hansebooks.com**

STORM WARRIORS;

OR,

Life-Boat Work

ON

THE GOODWIN SANDS.

BY THE

REV. JOHN GILMORE, M.A.,

RECTOR OF HOLY TRINITY, RAMSGATE; AUTHOR OF "THE RAMSGATE LIFE-BOAT,"
IN MACMILLAN'S MAGAZINE.

FOURTH THOUSAND.

LONDON:
MACMILLAN AND CO.
1875.

LONDON:

PRINTED BY WILLIAM CLOWES AND SONS,

STAMFORD STREET AND CHARING CROSS.

TO

THE MOST BELOVED MEMORY OF MY LATE FATHER,

JOHN GILMORE, COMMANDER, R.N.,

AND TO THE MOST BELOVED MEMORY OF
MY LATE ELDEST BROTHER,

ROBERT GRAHAM GILMORE, CAPT., R.N.R.,

TWO MOST BRAVE, AND SKILFUL, AND TRUE,
AND LOVING-HEARTED SAILORS,
WHO HAVE PASSED IN FAITH AND PEACE TO THE
HAVEN THAT THEY HUMBLY SOUGHT,
I INSCRIBE THIS WORK.

J. G.

PREFACE.

"O MAMMA, I do hope that we shall be wrecked on the Goodwin Sands, that we may be saved by the brave life-boat men!"

"You horrid boy, hold your tongue, do," replied the Mamma, who was anticipating, with some degree of nervousness, starting upon a voyage for Australia in about three weeks' time, and could scarcely be expected to enter to the full into her young son's very practical enthusiasm.

But within the last half hour the boy's shrill voice had been heard at the Ramsgate pier-head, among the cheers that welcomed the life-boat back from a night of toil and triumph on the Goodwin; and for the present, to be saved from a wreck by the life-boat men is to him one of the most delightful ideas on earth.

After reading an article in 'Macmillan's' of the life-boat men's doings, a brave English Admiral, then commanding a fleet, wrote—" My heart warms to the gallant fellows ; tell them so, and please give them the enclosed (a guinea each) from an English Admiral without mentioning my name."

A Kentish Squire, sending a donation of a guinea for each of the men wrote,—" To read the brave self-sacrificing doings of the Ramsgate life-boat men, makes me proud of the men of my county."

Other gentlemen wrote, and ladies wrote, and by-and-by we heard from Australia, America, South America, and also from other parts of the world came evidence, that English hearts, wherever they are, cannot but feel deeply as they read the simple narrative of such gallant deeds. "Your life-boat stories have undoubtedly helped on the good life-boat cause," said Mr. Lewis.

"The public have evinced considerable interest in those tales of life-boat work," said Mr. Macmillan ; and so the idea grew that I must write a book about the life-boat work on the Goodwin Sands.

A formidable idea this for a man with no " learned leisure," and quite unconscious of possessing any especial literary skill, or any especial literary ambition.

Certainly, I could have no difficulty in obtaining full and abundant particulars of the various adventures of the life-boat.

It was gravely said to a friend of mine,—"It is really very wrong of Mr. Gilmore, as a family man, to risk his life in the life-boat." I have been able to get all particulars without risking my life, and without, which is not much less to the point, lumbering up the boat with a useless hand; moreover, I doubt whether I should have had very keen powers of observation, while cold and exhausted and breathless, and clinging for very life to the thwarts, with the seas rushing over me, and tearing at me, striving to wash me out of the boat; which would have been my condition and very soon the condition of any unseasoned landsman who went to share the strife which the experienced boatmen often find it hard enough to endure.

I have managed better: I have had sometimes two, three, or four boatmen up to my house; and we have fought their battles over again; I questioning and cross-questioning, getting particulars from them, small as well as great.

"What did you do next?" To one such question, I remember the answer was—"Why then we handed the jar of rum round, for we were almost beaten to death."—"But with the seas running over the boat, and the boat full of water, it must have been salt-water grog very soon—how did you manage it?"—"Well, Sir, when there was a lull, a man just took a nip; then if there was a cry, ' Look out ! a sea !' he put the jar down between his legs, shoved his thumb in the hole, held on to the thwart with his other arm, then bent well over the jar and let the sea break on his back."

Thus getting them to recall incident after incident, I got the full details of each adventure ; and when we arrived at the more stirring scenes, it was very exciting work indeed; the men could scarcely sit in their chairs —their muscles worked, faces flushed, and most graphically they told their tales, I, not one whit less excited, taking notes as rapidly as possible.

Truly I must live to be an old man before I forget the hours I have spent in my study with Jarman, Hogben, and Reading, and R. Goldsmith, and Bill Penny, and Gorham, and Solly, and some other of my brave boatmen friends, as they have told me their many experiences and toils and dangers in life-boat work.

To Jarman especially do I owe thanks for his many graphic narratives ; he was coxswain of the boat for ten years, and during the time of most of the adventures related.

One difficulty I have had to contend with has been the comparative sameness in the ordinary life-boat services. I could have had nine narratives in one especial fortnight, for nine times was the life-boat out during that time ; but it has taken nearly ten years for me to find a sufficient number of narratives so varying in their chief incidents that the book should not of necessity be wearisome from repetition, and at the same time give a picture of the varied experiences and dangers of life-boat work.

I must leave my Readers to judge how far I have gained my object in the selection I have made.

As the few life-boat stories I have already published have been used to some extent in public Readings, Penny Readings, and on the like occasions, I have thought it well to make each story, as far as possible, complete in itself, although to effect this, some repetition of similar incidents has been unavoidable.

I come of a sailor family—this will account to landsmen for my seeming acquaintance with nautical matters ; I have never been to sea—this will explain to sailors the ignorance on such matters that they will not have much difficulty in detecting.

"God help the poor fellows at sea !"—"God protect and bless the life-boat men !" (humble, honest, hardworking and most generous and brave-hearted men as I well know full many of them to be) ;

"And God prosper the good Life-boat Institution, and advance its noble object !" that many a brave fellow may be spared to his family and home ; many a good man be plucked from death to be yet the joy and support of loved ones; and many a man, unfitted to meet death, be snatched from its jaws to live to repent and to seek that peace which he had formerly disregarded. With such prayers I launch my book. And may God further it to His glory, by making it instrumental in gaining yet increased sympathy with the already much-loved life-boat cause; thus blessing it to be one of the humble instruments, among many, in helping to work out the results for which, in our sailor-loving land, so many are ever ready to hope, to work, to pray.

One last word. The narratives related are, I firmly believe, as far as possible, strictly and literally true; I am positive the boatmen would not knowingly exaggerate in the least; and I have sought to tell the tales, incident by incident, what the men did, and what the men suffered, and what the men said—simply as they related each circumstance to me.

CONTENTS.

CONTENTS.

CHAPTER XXV.

CHAPTER XXVI.

CHAPTER XXVII.

CHAPTER XXVIII.

STORM WARRIORS.

CHAPTER I.

HOW THE SHIPWRECKED FARED IN DAYS OF OLD, AND THE GROWTH OF SYMPATHY ON THEIR BEHALF.

A worthy Quaker thus wrote:—"I expect to pass through this world but once; if, therefore, there can be any kindness I can show, or any good thing I can do to any fellow human being, let me do it now. Let me not defer or neglect it, for I shall not pass this way again."

BEFORE in fancy we man the Life-boat, and rush out into the storm, and have the salt spray dashing over us, and the wind singing like suppressed thunder in our ears—before we watch the gallant Storm Warriors of the present day, in their life-and-death struggle, charging in through the raging seas to the rescue of the shipwrecked, let us look back and see how the unfortunate by shipwreck fared in the old time, and then take a hasty glance or two, watching the gradual growth, from age to age, of sympathy for the distressed; humanity becoming more pronounced, and more practical; the progressive adaptation of Maritime

B

Law to the advancing tone of feeling; the gradual organization and development of that most noble Society, "The National Life-boat Institution," which has for its sole object the lessening of the dangers of the sea, and the saving of the shipwrecked; and, lastly, the progress and final triumph of the labours of science, in the invention of a life-boat which is able successfully to defy the efforts of the most raging storms.

The "good old days!" Those who sing too emphatically the glories of the "good old days" must either be influenced by the enchantment distance lends to the view, or guided by the wholesome proverb, "Let nothing, except that which is good, be spoken of the dead."

Human nature seems an inheritance unchanging in its properties, and it was in the old time much as it is now, capable of bringing forth fruit good or bad, in accordance with the training it received, or the associations by which it was surrounded. The old days were very far from being either very golden or very good, the strong arm was too often the strong law, and selfishness was far more likely to make the weak ones a prey for plunder, than was compassion to make them objects for assistance. There was a good deal of the Ishmael curse about the old feudal days; the Baron's hand was too ready to be against every man's, and every man's against his; to plunder and to pillage at all convenient opportunities, as well by sea as by land, seemed very much a leading institution.

In the thirteenth and fourteenth centuries Piracy

was almost openly recognized ; a foreign ship with a
rich cargo was too great a temptation for the free
sailors of those rough-and-ready days, and there was
in reality as much of the spirit of piracy in the rugged
justice by which it was endeavoured to suppress
the crimes, as in the crimes themselves.   Supposing
an act of piracy to have been committed, restitution was first demanded from the nation, or maritime
town, to which the pirate belonged ; and if satisfaction was not obtained, then the aggrieved party was
allowed to take out " Letters of Marque," and might
sally forth to all intents a pirate, to plunder any ship
sailing from the place to which the vessel which had
first robbed him belonged.   This system was acknowledged under the name of the " Right of Private
Reprisal ;" and so, what with pirates licensed and
unlicensed, ships seeking plunder without any discrimination, and ships seeking revenge without much,
Hallam might well write : " In the thirteenth and
fourteenth centuries, a rich vessel was never secure
from attack, and neither restitution nor punishment
of the criminals was to be obtained from Governments,
who sometimes feared the plunderer, and sometimes
connived at the offence."

To piracy was added the constant petty warfare
and feuds that were carried on between maritime
nations, and even between towns of the same nation.

Hallam quotes, " The Cinque Ports, and other
trading towns of England, were in a constant state of
hostility with their opposite neighbours during the
reigns of Edward I. and II. ; half the instruments of

Rymer might be quoted in proof of these conflicts, and of those with the mariners of Norway and Denmark."

Sometimes mutual envy produced frays between different English towns ; thus in the year 1254 the Winchilsea mariners attacked a Yarmouth galley, and killed some of her men.

The evil effects of this confusion of might with right, the anxiety occasioned by this constant warfare, and by these petty feuds, lingered longer on sea than on land ; and kept the morals of the seafaring population of the coasts at the lowest ebb ; and as one consequence, the plundering of vessels wrecked on the shores was in all parts of Europe carried on with as ruthless a hand, as was piracy and privateering afloat.

It may be somewhat interesting to consider the gradual progress of legislation with reference to this very terrible system and crime of wrecking ; and while doing so, we shall receive further proof of how the rough mastery of the strong over the weak crept into the Laws, and how full a development it had in such laws, as especially related to wrecks and wreckage.

It is hard in the present day to conceive how, in the name of any government making claim to the administration of justice, such a law could have been passed as that which existed prior to Henry I., which gave the king complete possession of all wrecked property : ownership on the part of the original possessor was supposed to have been lost by the action of the sea. Whether the law originated in that strong instinct for the appropriation of unconsidered trifles, which is rather a snare to all governments, or whether it was found necessary to make the king the owner of wreckage, in order to lessen the temptation to cause vessels to be wrecked, and their crews murdered for the sake of pillage, no unfrequent occurrence in those days, however it was, the law existed, and the ship-wrecked merchant might come struggling ashore upon a broken spar, and find the coast strewn with scat-tered but still valuable goods, so lately his, but now by law his no longer, any more than they belonged to the half dozen rude fishermen who stood watching the torn wreck, and dispersed cargo being wave-lifted high upon the beach.

Henry I., whose declining years were years of tender and deep sadness, on account of his own losses at sea, was somewhat more compassionate in his dealings with the unfortunate by shipwreck.

He decreed that a wreck or wrecked goods should not be considered lost to the owner, or become the property of the Crown, if any man escaped from the wreck with life to the shore.

Henry II. made a feeble enlargement of this scant degree of mercy—he expanded this saving clause, so that if either man or beast came ashore alive, the wreck and goods should still be considered as be-longing to the original possessors; but failing this, although the owner should be known beyond all possibility of doubt, all the saved property should belong to the king; so that in those old days, if a cat was supposed to have nine lives, it was quite sufficient to account for its being for so long a popular institution on board ship; for even a cat washing ashore, would become the owner's title-deeds to all of his property that the sea had spared.

Richard I. could be generous in things small as well as great; he could act nobly upon principle as well as upon impulse; it must have been, indeed, only natural to his open unselfish nature and high courage, to spurn the idea of robbing the robbed, of making the victim of the sea's destructive power the further victim of a king's greed; he was prepared to give his laws of chivalry a wide interpretation, and let them ordain succour for the distressed by the rage of waters, as well as for the distressed by the rage of men.

And so when about to take part in the third crusade, King Richard decreed, "For the love of God, and the health of his own soul, and the souls of his ancestors and successors, kings of England.

"That all persons escaping alive from a wreck should retain their goods; that wreck or wreckage should only be considered the property of the king when neither an owner, nor the heirs of a late owner, could be found for it."

For several centuries all European nations had for the foundation of their maritime laws, a certain code, called the Code of Oleron.

There is the usual veil of historical uncertainty clouding the origin of these laws, for while some authorities declare that Richard I. had nothing to do with them, others declare that they were completed and promulgated by Richard, at the Isle of Oleron, as he was returning from one of his crusades, and that

they had first and especial reference to the customs
on the coasts of some of his continental domains.

The Laws of Oleron contain thirty-seven articles,
and make very terrible statements as to the system
of wrecking, which in those days disgraced the then
civilized nations of the earth, while they show also,
that if sinners were then prepared to sin with a high
hand, that the authorities were prepared with no less
energy to inflict punishment for crime.

Some of the extracts from these laws are as utter
darkness compared with light, when you read them
beside extracts from the Life-boat journals of the
present day, suggesting as they do the customs of
the people as regards wrecking, and the scant mercy
that was shown to the shipwrecked.

Consider, for instance, the picture as given in the
following extracts from the old laws of Oleron :—

" An accursed custom prevailing in some parts,
inasmuch as a third or fourth part of the wrecks that
come ashore belong to the lord of the manor, where
the wrecks take place, and that pilots for profit from
these lords, and from the wrecks, like faithless and
treacherous villains, do purposely run the ships under
their care upon the rocks."

The Code declares, that the lords, and all who
assist in plundering the wreck shall be accursed,
excommunicated, and punished as robbers. " That all
false pilots shall suffer a most rigorous and merciless
death, and be hung on high gibbets."

" The wicked lords are to be tied to a post in the
middle of their own houses, which shall be set on fire

at all four corners, and burnt with all that shall be therein ; the goods being first confiscated for the benefit of the persons injured ; and the site of the houses shall be converted into places for the sale of hogs and swine."

But if this threat of burning the said wicked lords, and the wholesale confiscation and destruction of their houses and properties, had not sufficient terrors to control such hardened sinners, and if they, or others, were prepared to add murder to robbery, then the laws enacted—

" If people, more barbarous, cruel, and inhuman than mad dogs, murdered shipwrecked folk, they were to be plunged into the sea until half dead, and then drawn out and stoned to death."

Railway directors and others would scarcely like the enforcement of laws parallel to those which dealt with the carelessness of Pilots ; which provided, " That if negligence on the part of the Pilot caused shipwreck, he was to make good out of his own means the losses sustained, and if his means were not sufficient, then he should lose his head ;" it was meekly suggested; "that some care should be taken by the master and mariners," possibly as much for their own sakes as for the sake of the unfortunate pilot. " That they should be persuaded that the man had not the means to make good the loss, before they cut off his head."

The preamble of an Act of Parliament is generally the summary of the arguments for the necessity of the Bill.

The preamble of a Bill for the repression of crime, may be therefore taken as the expression of the national conviction, that such crimes exist at the time.

If so, during the reign of George II. human nature did not show itself to be one whit better than in earlier days, still were men equally capable of cruel selfishness and wrong, although civilization had done much to curb the outward expression of many of the former evils, and to control, to some extent, the open and virulent barbarities of still darker days.

For we find that the old laws, and barbarous modes of punishment, were not sufficient to cope with the strongly developed tendencies for wrecking, which showed themselves, in various ways, to be existent, and in full activity.

And therefore a new Act was passed, which recited—

"That notwithstanding the good and salutary laws now in being against plundering and destroying vessels in distress, and against taking away ship-wrecked, lost, and stranded goods, that still many wicked enormities had been committed to the disgrace of the nation." Therefore certain provisions were enacted, the bearing of which was as follows :—

Death was to be the punishment for the chief of these enormities, such as hanging out false lights for the purpose of bringing vessels into distress.

Death for those who killed, or prevented the escape of shipwrecked persons.

Death for stealing goods from a wreck, whether there be any living creature on board or not.

Acts of Parliament in following years felt the impress of the more merciful spirit of legislation which began to prevail. The punishment of death for theft from a wreck was reduced to imprisonment; while penal servitude for life was made the penalty for a new development of crime, namely, that of wilfully scuttling, or setting on fire, or wrecking a ship for the purpose of defrauding or damaging Insurance Offices or Owners.

The existing Merchant Shipping Act of 1854, and the amendments and additions to it, now form the Code by which all maritime questions are arranged; and most of the barbarities, cruelties, and wrongs which, for so many ages, added to the perils of the sea, both as to life and property, are now sufficiently guarded against.

But still a most subtle cruelty and fatal wrong is left almost altogether untouched, that of sending vessels to sea in an unseaworthy condition, as to hull, or spars, or sails, or rigging, or perhaps dangerously overladen; many a vessel only worthy of being utterly condemned, which no office would think for one moment of insuring, and that would scarcely pay for breaking up, is bought cheap, patched up, and sent, perhaps, to float up and down our coasts as a Collier, a sort of dingy coffin, only waiting to be entombed by the first heavy gale and raging sea in which she is caught, and then to go quickly down to her grave, carrying with her her crew, unless they have taken warning in time, and found some chance of escaping, which they are not slow to take advantage of, know-

ing the nature of the craft they are in ; but many a
brave sailor finds no escape, and feels no hope, when
once the heavy gale breaks on the crazy craft, and
thus dies a victim to one of the treacherous, and
permitted, and most fatal cruelties of our most
Christian and most enlightened age ; but this state
of things, we may well believe, will not be permitted
to last much longer ; the attention of the public
has been thoroughly aroused to the subject, more
especially by the zealous, energetic, and unselfish
action of Samuel Plimsol, Esq., M.P., who having the
welfare of the poor sailor most thoroughly at heart,
has attacked with every courage the still existing
abuses, arising chiefly from the deficiencies in our
Maritime Code, and all who have sympathy with the
sailor must wish him success, and who has not ? but it
is hard work to develop legislative action, even from
wide-spread national sympathy ; but the work is
commenced ; and as one result of his action, a Royal
Commission has been issued by Her Majesty. The
following is a synopsis of the opening instructions
of the Commission :—

VICTORIA R.

WHEREAS—We have deemed it expedient for
divers good causes and considerations that a
commission should forthwith issue to make
inquiry with regard to the alleged unseaworthi-
ness of British Registered Ships ; whether arising
from overloading, deck-loading, defective construction, form, equipment, machinery, age or

improper stowage; and also to inquire into the
present system of Marine Insurance; of the
alleged practice of undermanning ships; and also
to suggest any amendments in the law which
might remedy or lessen such evils as may be
found to have arisen from the matters afore-
said, &c., &c.   Given at our Court at St. James's
the 29th day of March, 1873, in the thirty-sixth
year of our reign.

> By our command,
> (Signed)   H. A. BRUCE.

We may now therefore have great hopes, that there
will be speedily some good result, from the spirited
manner in which this question of sending unseaworthy
vessels to sea has been brought before the public.

NOTE.—I have to thank a friend for Notes, which he kindly gave me,
of extracts which he made from books to which he had access in the
British Museum, referring to the Ancient Maritime Laws upon Wrecking.
My friend has, since this Chapter was first written, developed his Notes
into an Article, which he published in a periodical; I have, nevertheless, not refrained from giving the account, which I think my readers
may find interesting.

> J. G.

CHAPTER II.

WRECKERS.

"O father! I see a gleaming light;
   O say what may it be?"
But the father answered never a word!—
   A frozen corpse was he.

And ever the fitful gusts between
   A sound came from the land;
It was the sound of the trampling surf
   On the rocks and the hard sea-sand.

The breakers were right beneath her bows
   She drifted a dreary wreck,
And a whooping billow swept the crew
   Like icicles from her deck."
Longfellow.

"Perhaps some human kindness still
   May make amends for human ill."
Barry Cornwall.

As we have considered the growth of legislation upon the question of wrecking and wreckage, and contrasted the more civilized, but not perfect code, now existing, with the barbarous laws of days gone by, we may also, perhaps, well put in contrast the present character and action of our coast population, as a rule, with what they were in days more remote

Imagine a homeward-bound vessel some two hundred and fifty years ago, clumsy in build, awkward in rig, little fitted for battling with the gales of our stormy coast, but yet manned with strong stout-hearted men, who made their sturdy courage compensate for deficiency of other means; think of many perils overcome, a long weary voyage nearly ended, the crew rejoicing in thoughts of home, of home-love and home-rest, the headlands of dear Old England, loved by her sons no less then, than now, lying a dark line upon the horizon, the night growing apace, the breeze freshening, ever freshening, adding each moment a hoarser swell to the deep murmurs of its swift-following blasts; the ship scudding on, breasting the seas with her bluff bows, rising and pitching with the running waves which cover her with foam!

Look on land! keen eyes have watched the signs of the coming storm, men more greedy than the foulest vulture, "more inhuman than mad dogs," have cast most cruel and wistful glances seaward! yes, their eyes light up with the very light of hell, as they see in the dim distance the white sail of a struggling ship making towards the land!

And now try to imagine the scene, as the night falls, and the storm gathers, two or three ill-looking fellows drop in, say, to a low tavern standing in a by-lane that leads from the cliff to the beach, in some village on our south-western coast—soon muttered hints take form, and in low whispers the men talk over the chances of a wreck this wild night; they remember former gains, they talk over disappointments, when on similar nights of darkness, wildness, and storm, vessels discovered their danger too soon for them, and managed to weather the headlands of the bay.

The plot takes form; with many a deep and muttered curse, the murderous decision is taken, that if a vessel can be trapped to destruction, it shall be.

There is an old man of the party whose brow is furrowed with dread lines; he does not say much, but every now and then his eyes glare, and his features work as if convulsed; his comrades look at him, twice, and as a terrific squall shakes the house, a third time: silently he rises and leaves the inn; his mates now look away from him, as if quite unconscious as to what he is about; their stifled consciences cannot do much for them, but can give to each, just one faint half-realized sensation of shame.   Now in the pitch darkness of the night, with bowed head, and faltering steps, battling against the storm, the old man leads a white horse along the edge of the cliff, to the top of the horse's tail a lantern is tied, and the light sways with the movement of the horse, and in its movements seems not unlike the mast-head light of a vessel rocked by the motion of the sea.   A whisper has gone through the village, of a chance of something happening during the night, and most of the men and many of the women are on the alert, lurking in the caves beneath the cliff, or sheltered behind jutting pieces of rock.

The vessel makes in steadily for the land; the captain grows uneasy, and fears running into danger; he will put the vessel round, and try and battle his way out to sea.

The look-out man reports a dim light ahead;

What kind? and Whither away? He can make out
that it is a ship's light, for it is in motion. Yes, she
must be a vessel standing on in the same course as
that which they are on. It is all safe then, the captain
will stand in a little longer; when suddenly in the lull
of the storm a hoarse murmur is heard, surely the
sound of the sea beating upon rocks? yes! look, a white
gleam upon the water! Breakers ahead! Breakers
ahead! Oh! a very knell of doom; the cry rings
through the ship, Down, down with helm, round her to;
too late, too late! a crash, a shudder from stem to
stern of the stout ship; the shriek of many voices in
their agony, green seas sweeping over the vessel, and
soon, broken timbers, bales of cargo, and lifeless bodies
scattered along the beach, while the shattered remnant
of the hull is torn still further to pieces with each in-
sweep of the mighty seas, as they roll it to, and fro,
among the rocks. Fearful and crafty the smile that
darkened the dark face of the willing murderer, who
was leading the horse with the false light, as he heard
the crash of the vessel, and the shrieks of the drowning
crew, fearful the smiles that darkened the faces of the
men and women waiting on the beach, as they came
out from their places, ready to struggle and fight
among themselves for any spoil that might come
ashore; a homeward-bound ship from the Indies—great
good fortune, rich spoil—bale after bale is seized upon
by the wreckers, and dragged high upon the beach out
of the way of the surf—but see, a sailor clinging to a bit
of broken mast, with his last conscious effort he gains a
footing on the shore, staggers forward and falls. Is
he alive? not now! Why did that fearful old woman

kneel upon his chest, and cover his mouth with her cloak? Dead men tell no tales! claim no property!

Have such things been possible?

They have, and have been done; traditions of such dread tragedies still linger on the Cornish coast, and it is a matter of history that all around our shores miscreants were to be found, who were ready to sacrifice to their blood-thirsty avarice those whom the rage of water had spared.

Yes, and still many sailors find their worst enemies ashore, and know no danger so great as that of falling into the hands of their fellow-men; but not now in the small harbours or fishing-villages of the coast—not now among the seafaring population of our shores, must wretches capable of such deeds be looked for, but among the degraded quarters of our large maritime towns—among the land-sharks, who haunt the docks, the crimp-houses, the dens of infamy, the low taverns—there Jack may still be wrecked, and drugged, and robbed, and perhaps murdered. But even there darkness has not got it all its own way; for if there are many who are ready to ruin the reckless sailor, there are many others, thank God, who are ready to warn and aid him. Seamen's Churches, Bethels, Sailors' Homes, Sailors' Missionaries, and all sorts of benevolent institutions, seek to struggle with, and overcome, the bad effect of the many evils to which the sailor on shore is exposed.

And the sea-coasts where the Storm Warriors now gather tell a tale of hardihood, of courage, of endurance, and of skill, no less than the olden days could boast

C

of. But now courage is glorified by mercy, and hardihood by sympathy, and endurance is sustained, and skill and enterprise are quickened into action by the noblest feelings, and readiness for self-sacrifice, which can move the heart of man.

If our last pages have been gloomy in the picture they have given of what was frequently done not many generations ago, let us seek a contrast, which shall be as light to darkness, and compare with those scenes of old, a picture of that which happens month after month, and in the winter season week after week, and sometimes, almost day after day, on our own coasts in the present time.

A homeward-bound ship is rushing along, skimming the green seas, seeming to rejoice in the pride of her beauty, strength, and speed ; there is some fatal error or accident, and she comes suddenly to destruction. Many men are anxiously on the look-out ; they have been watching her closely from the shore, and eagerly preparing for action at the moment of the shipwreck, which for some time they have feared must happen. And now guns fire, and rockets flash, and the signals quickly given are quickly answered, and the Storm Warriors rush into action ; they are not now the Storm Pirates as was the case too often of old, they are the Storm Warriors ; their flashing lights tell of coming rescue, and do not lure to destruction ; for as the gallant life-boat men rush into all danger, make every effort, battling with mad waves and boiling surf, they fight under the noble banner of Mercy— THEIR MISSION IS TO SAVE.

CHAPTER III.

THE INVENTOR OF THE LIFE-BOAT.

"The most eloquent speaker, the most ingenious writer, and the most accomplished statesman cannot effect so much as the mere presence of the man who tempers his wisdom and his vigour with humanity."

Lavater.

WHAT dreams had Lionel Luken, coach-builder of London, in the year 1780, or thereabouts? The perils to machines, or coaches, in those days were many and varied; the roads were often rough, and dangerous enough to equal the pleasing variety and exciting accompaniments of a cross-country gallop; the bridges were very few, and the fords very many.

Did Lionel Luken lose coach, or customer, or both, in a rushing flood which overwhelmed some burdensome coach and unhappy travellers at one of these fords? and, thinking over the disaster sorrowfully, patiently, and profitably, as great minds and great hearts will think, did he conceive the idea of a coach warranted against sinking, with air-tight compartments? and then, expanding the idea, did the noble thought occur to him of building a boat that

C 2

would not merely float in the rush of a flood, but
that would defy the troubled waters of a raging sea?
And was it thus, that Lionel Luken gained unto himself the immortal honour of being the first inventor
of the Life-boat?

In whatever manner the idea presented itself to
him, and however it was developed in the mind of
the skilful and humane coach-builder, certain it is
that it seized him very thoroughly, and that he, being
one of the race of God's heroes, alike humane, brave,
and earnest, was not content to let his happy, his
blessed thought die barren of result, but made noble
and persevering efforts to bring his invention to a
successful issue. He had high courage, for his
courage was inspired by the great hope that his boat
might be the instrument of plucking many poor
sailors from dread peril, carrying them through
threatening seas, snatching them from the very jaws
of death, and of restoring them to their loving ones
in their loved homes. With this holy ambition,
Lionel Luken laboured nobly, as, urged by a like
ambition, many now labour nobly for the good life-
boat cause. But the old days were not days of quick
sympathy, or of ready enterprise, and Luken, although
supported, to a certain extent, by royalty, uselessly
clamoured at official doors, and sought public patron-
age in vain.

People seemed then to have no strong objection to
other people being drowned, just as they had no
strong prejudice against others suffering the tortures
of miserable prisons, the worst asylums, or any of the

many horrors which a more enlightened age has sought with some degree of success to lessen or remove.

In the year 1785 Luken took out a patent for a boat which, to a great extent, embodied almost all the more needful properties possessed by the present model life-boat ; he at the same time published a pamphlet ; " Upon the invention, principle, and construction of insubmergible boats." He suggested that such boats should be protected by bands of cork round their gunwales, that they should be rendered buoyant by the use of air-cases, especially at the bow and stern, and that they should be ballasted by an iron keel.

But even when the good man passed from theory to practice, and succeeded at Bamborough in getting a boat converted into a life-boat on the above principles, and when this boat proved a success, and saved many lives, even then he could obtain no support from the authorities in carrying out his grand object.

The story is told of a general who blamed a soldier for ducking at the sound of a cannon ball, saying that he had no business to be a soldier if he had the faintest objection to being shot. On the same principle, the first lord of the Admiralty, in his stern rejections of Luken's many efforts, may have considered that life-boats would interfere with a sailor's prerogative for being drowned ; and drowned indeed many of the poor fellows were—swept to destruction in sight of land, for winds were cruel, and rocks were hard, and seas wild, and ships frail, while benevolence slept, and the cries of the drowning did not reach official ears, and Luken's loud appeals on behalf of humanity were disregarded, and he, brave man, who had so long struggled, hoping against hope, became utterly disappointed that the movement, the importance of which he so realized, and for which he had so long laboured, did not become general.

Still he had the satisfaction of seeing his plan adopted in one or two places, in Shields especially, as we shall show ; and he had the great happiness of knowing that, time after time, lives were saved by the boats which were built after his model. He had done all that he could, and went on building coaches, not, we may presume, on life-boat principles ; and he tried somewhat to content himself, as he looked forward with hope for a time of greater enlightenment and sympathy, when he trusted that the seed he sowed, almost with tears, would bring its harvest of sheaves, and full of this faith, the good man devised an inscription for the stone which should mark his resting-place in a quiet country churchyard, simply stating, "That he was the Inventor of the first life-boat."

Honoured be the memory of Lionel Luken !

CHAPTER IV.

THE GROWTH OF THE LIFE-BOAT MOVEMENT.

"What is noble? 'tis the finer
    Portion of our mind and heart,
Linked to something still diviner
    Than mere language can impart;
Ever prompting—ever seeing
    Some improvement yet to plan;
To uplift our fellow-being,
    And, like man, to feel for Man."
                    C. Swain.

IF the ear were only as powerful to enable the mind to realize things heard, as the eye is powerful in enabling the mind to realize things seen, many reforms would have been worked out promptly, instead of having to wait year after year, sometimes almost generation after generation, while the mind of the public has had its sympathies but slowly awakened by the constant statement of some evil, and the unceasing demand for its remedy.

Thus it was, that a terrible scene of disaster and death, of which many were the agonized eye-witnesses, did more to urge forward the life-boat cause than had been effected by the report of many similar tragedies, which but few lookers on had seen occur.

It was in the year 1789, a tremendous gale of wind was raging at Newcastle ; thousands of the inhabitants were watching the wild sea as it foamed up at the entrance of the port, and they trembled as they saw vessel after vessel stagger on through the sweeping waves, running into the harbour for refuge.

One ship, the *Adventurer*, missed the entrance of the port, and was driven on to the rocks ; the seas rushed over her deck, and flew half-way up the masts ; the crew took refuge in the rigging, and the wreck was so near to the pier, that the horrified and terror-stricken people thronging there, could hear the cries for help, and even see the growing shade of the death agony upon the faces of the men, as they became more and more exhausted and faint from exposure to the heavy seas ; and then they saw one after another of the seamen torn from his hold and perish miserably ; and this within call of these thousands of spectators, who were full of grief and sympathy, but were unable even to attempt a rescue.

Brave men stood powerless, and as they were frantically appealed to, to try and save the drowning men, could only groan over the utter impossibility of rendering them any assistance ! Yes ! the daring, hardy, skilful sailors, wept with the weeping women, as they stood overwhelmed with helpless horror watching the most heart-rending scene.

Strong boats were there, ready to be manned, boats that had successfully battled with many a rough sea,

but they were *not life-boats*, and to go out into such a
mad boil of raging waves in any other kind of boat
than a life-boat, would have been certain death to all
the crew, without affording the faintest possibility of
help to the shipwrecked ; and thus, without help,
without hope, one after the other of the poor shipwrecked sailors, exhausted and faint, fell back into the
wild waves and perished : the vessel was speedily
torn to pieces, the crowd slowly and sorrowfully went
home ; soon the darkness of night shadowed the wild
sea and the saddened town, but the day's work was not
done—the tragedy was not without fruit, in more
senses than one, " the blood of the martyrs is the seed
of the church ;" the sympathies of the people were now
fully aroused ; meetings were at once held at South
Shields—a committee was formed—and premiums
were offered for the best life-boat.

William Wouldham, a painter, was one of the successful competitors ; he presented a model embracing
many excellent qualities ; Henry Greathead, a boat-
builder of South Shields, stood next on the list.

The various models presented were discussed—
their more excellent qualities selected—and from the
suggestions thus obtained, a model life-boat was
planned, from which, as a type, Greathead built a
boat, which, either from the fact that he improved
upon the model given to him, or because his name, as
its builder, was chiefly associated with it, became
known as Greathead's life-boat, and he gained the
honour of being its inventor—not but what the claims
of Wouldham were stoutly asserted ; and we may

believe by many accepted, for in the parish church of
St. Hilda, South Shields, a tombstone erected to the
memory of Wouldham bears at its head a model of
his life-boat, with the following inscription :—

> "Heaven genius scientific gave,
>   Surpassing vulgar boast, yet he from soil
>   So rich, no golden harvest reap'd, no wreath
>   Of laurel gleaned. None but the sailor's heart,
>   Nor that ingrate, of palm unfading this,
>   Till shipwrecks cease, or Life-boats cease to save."

Within the next fifteen years, or so, Greathead
built about thirty life-boats, eight of which were sent
to foreign countries. At last the life-boat cause was
wakened into life, but into no vigorous existence ; it
did not actually die, but lingered on with here and
there a spasm of vitality, as some local cause or
stirring advocate excited a momentary interest in the
question.

Life-boat stations were scattered at long intervals
round the coast, and boats of various designs, some
very good, were placed at a few of the more dangerous
positions on our shores.

The public was not altogether unprepared to move,
but was waiting for the needed impulse.

The whole cause, in spite of all its intrinsic merits
and great claims upon humanity, waited for the
coming man, and he was found in the person of Sir
William Hillary, Baronet, one of nature's real noblemen ;
his heart was great, as his arm was strong ; his love
for the sea was only equalled by his love for sailors ;
all that concerned their well-being excited his quick

sympathy and active interest, and his feelings were, as a matter of course, very sincere, and very earnest for the life-boat cause.

Sir W. Hillary lived at Douglas, in the Isle of Man. His sympathy for the sailor proved its vitality by being active and practical: he established Sailors' Homes, and in many ways sought their improvement and benefit; and when the hour of danger came, when the storms raged and lives were in peril, Sir William was the first, not only to encourage, but also to lead the boatmen to the rescue of the shipwrecked; he shrank from no danger, he shared all labour, and endured all hardship, and this to such an extent, that he was personally engaged in efforts by which more than three hundred lives were saved.

The following are some of the occasions in which Sir William's heroic efforts were blessed in their results to the saving of life :—

In the year 1825 Sir William, and the crews under him, rescued eighty-seven persons, sixty-two of these from the steamer *City of Glasgow;* eleven from the *Leopard* brig; and nine from the *Fancy* sloop.

In the year 1827 they saved seventeen lives. In 1830, four different crews were rescued, forty-three lives being saved; and in 1832 no fewer than fifty lives were saved from a passenger-ship.

The nature of the perils Sir William Hillary so nobly encountered, and the toils he shared, may be well illustrated by an account of the rescue of the crew of the *St. George.*

On the 29th of November, 1830, the mail steamer

St. George struck on St. Mary's rock, not far from Douglas. The captain had no boats to which he could trust in so violent a sea; he therefore cut away the mainmast, and endeavoured to construct a raft from its wreck, together with the spars which they had on board; but the seas proved too heavy for him to be able to do so, and he signalled his distress to the shore.

Sir William Hillary and a crew of twelve men at once manned the life-boat, and proceeded in the direction of the wreck; they found the steamer hard upon the rock, and surrounded by such a raging boil of surf that any attempt to rescue the unfortunate passengers and crew seemed almost impossible; nevertheless they were not the men to leave their fellow-creatures to perish without making an effort for their safety, at whatever risk that effort must be made; they therefore let the boat rush before the gale into the heart of the surf; here she was completely at the mercy of the wild and broken waves—her rudder was torn off, oar after oar was broken, until scarcely half the number were left—some of the air-tight compartments were strained and filled with water, and rendered useless, and to add to the dismay of the crew, one of the tremendous seas which rushed over the boat washed Sir William and three men overboard; it was only after the greatest difficulty that they were recovered, and, happily, without being much hurt; the life-boat was then hurled by the waves between the steamer and the rock, here the broken mainmast and other wreckage were being driven violently by the surf in all directions, so that the life-boat was in a very whirl-pool of danger.

The crew and passengers of the steamer thought, however, that they would be safer in the boat, in spite of the dread peril she was in, than on board the steamer, which was being torn and beaten to pieces, and they left the steamer for the boat ; the boat had then more than sixty persons on board ; and hour after hour her crew struggled in vain to get her out of the position of extreme danger, in which the force of the gale and the rush of the waves held them as in a vice ; every moment was one of very great hardship to all on board the boat, as the surf continually flew over them in volumes, and the danger of being crushed by the wreckage, that was tossing and leaping in the contest of the mad sea that raged around them, was incessant.

After nearly three hours of the hardest struggle, they managed to get the almost disabled boat a little clear from the rock and the wreck, but still they were unable to make any headway against the seas, or get beyond the circle of surf, when at length the sea, as if tired of sporting with its shattered prey, drove the boat so far beyond the range of the surf, that other boats were able to come to her assistance and all lives were saved.

Such was the nature of the perils and hardships that Sir William Hillary often readily and nobly encountered in his efforts to save life.

When, therefore, urged by the cruel necessities of the case, he pleaded for the life-boat cause, and illus-

trated his pleading by his own personal experience,
men began at last to listen to what he urged. He
described not only that the dangers of the shipwrecked were fearfully increased from want of due
means for their rescue, in the absence of boats properly
constructed to contend against the peculiar danger
arising from the raging seas and broken water which
generally surrounded a wreck, but he showed also
how, from the same cause, brave men too often rushed
to their death.

That in answer to the cry for rescue, men put to
sea, urged by the generous impulses of sympathy and
courage, went forth possessed of all the needed bravery,
the strength, the skill, the determination to perish or
to save : they did often perish, and did not save, because they needed the boats which could alone safely
contend with the dangers that they had to encounter.

Two members of Parliament, Mr. Thomas Wilson
and Mr. George Hibbert, were especially moved by
such a tale, told by such a man, out of a brave, loving,
full heart, and illustrated by such terrible experience,
and they gave Sir William their very hearty co-opera-
tion ; and these three men became, in the year 1825,
the founders of the " Royal National Institution for
the Preservation of Life from Shipwreck."

Sir W. Hillary undertook the formation of a branch
committee of the society for the Isle of Man, and so
fully succeeded that, by the year 1829, each of the
four harbours of the station possessed a life-boat.

Under the organization of this society, and with the
aid of some fourteen smaller, and local associations,

and notably with the assistance of " The Shipwrecked
Fishermen and Mariners' Royal Benevolent Society,"
which was instituted in the year 1839, and provided
seven life-boats on different parts of the coast, the
life-boat cause went on, doing much noble work, but
leaving very much more undone ; and very much that
was effected was not done in really the best way.

Thus the life-boat cause had prospered, the work
was becoming organised ; but still much was wanting ;
it needed some new and great stimulus—and in a few
years the stimulus came.

CHAPTER V.

THE INVENTION AND LAUNCHING OF THE PRIZE
LIFE-BOAT.

"In spite of rock and tempest's roar,
In spite of false lights on the shore,
Sail on, nor fear to breast the sea,
Our hearts, our hopes are all with thee;
Our hearts, our hopes, our prayers, our tears,
Our faith triumphant o'er our fears,
Are all with thee—are all with thee!
"The Ship of State."—Longfellow.

IN the year 1848, the Admiralty called for returns from
the various coastguard stations which gird the coast, as
to the condition of the life-boat service in their respective neighbourhoods; the results showed a state of
things very far from satisfactory. It appeared that
the number of life-boats was about one hundred, but
out of these, only fifty-five were reported as being in
good repair, and a great many of this number were
declared to be of such heavy construction, that very
much of their usefulness was sacrificed.

Twenty boats were reported as being only in fair

repair, and twenty-one boats were declared to be bad and unserviceable. From many stations came the reports of great loss of life from want of a boat. From Ballycotton, for instance, where a life-boat could be easily manned, and yet, sad to state, that within fifteen years no fewer than sixty-seven lives had been lost, no life-boat being there to effect a rescue.

The evidence for the necessity for further effort was also afforded, by the long distances which existed between many of the life-boat stations. Twenty-seven miles, thirty-three, forty-five, ninety-four, one hundred and forty-one, and one hundred and fifty-one miles being among such distances ; thus in various places the coast was left absolutely unprotected for many miles together.

Equally sad, and similar to that given by Sir W. Hillary, was the evidence as to the faulty construction of many of the boats, inasmuch as although they were a decided improvement upon the ordinary boat, yet they too often proved incompetent to contend against the rush of seas and broken water to which they were exposed ; from this cause the most painful tragedies frequently occurred, the loss of brave fellows who went out to save others from a dreadful death, and who through no lack of courage, of strength, or of skill, on their part, but from the faulty construction of the boat they were in, found one common grave with those whom they sought to rescue from the raging seas.

Thus one life-boat gained a most sad notoriety : on one occasion she drowned four of her crew ; on another occasion twelve ; and on a third, twenty men

D

were drowned out of her. A second, so called, life-boat lost on one occasion two men, on a second three men, and on a third all her crew; when she was most properly condemned as too dangerous to be of use.

A Scarborough life-boat lost sixteen men. At Dunbar, on the occasion of a man-of-war being wrecked, the life-boat in two trips saved forty-five men; on her third trip she upset, and nearly all who were in her were drowned; she was condemned, and for many years no life-boat at all was stationed there, although from time to time many lives were lost.

Thus we find that in the year 1850 life-boat work was no unknown work. Life-boat societies had done much, and were doing much. Life-boats had been stationed in various localities during the preceding half century, and there were at the date mentioned seventy-five life-boats in England, eight in Scotland, and eight in Ireland; but nearly one-half of these were, from one cause or another, more or less unserviceable; and many of the most exposed parts of the coast were still unprovided with life-boats. In that year, 1850, there were six hundred and eighty-one wrecks : the loss of life was about seven hundred and eighty-four, including a crew of eleven men, whose boat upset one stormy November night, they having put off to the assistance of a vessel in distress.

It was evident that the life-boat system was not sufficiently developed or general, and there was, moreover, no universally approved model of a boat in which all boatmen might have confidence; this latter

consideration was especially brought before the notice
of the public by an accident which occurred to the
Newcastle life-boat, the sad particulars of which are
given in the following extracts from a letter written
December 14th, 1849, by the then treasurer of the
life-boat "Friend of the Ports of Newcastle-upon-
Tyne and South Shields," Mr. R. Anderson.

"The life-boats of the Port of Newcastle, stationed
at the entrance of the Tyne in North and South
Shields, have been for about sixty years instrumental
in saving the crews of those vessels which have been
unfortunately stranded at the entrance of the port.
No correct account was kept of the exact number so
rescued from danger previous to the year 1841, but
since then four hundred and sixty-six persons have
been brought ashore from sixty-two vessels.

"On the morning of the fatal accident, the *Betsy*,
of Littlehampton, laden with salt, was stranded on the
hard sand ; and the receding tide left her among
heavy breakers, with a heavy ebb-tide running past
her.

"The life-boat was launched about 9 A.M., and being
manned by twenty-four pilots, immediately proceeded
to the vessel ; and, having hailed her, and given
instructions to the people on board to prepare two
ropes ready to throw to them, they waited for a little
time between the ship and the shore for the ropes to
be got ready, then they again proceeded to the vessel,
and succeeded in getting alongside ; the rope from
the after end of the vessel was received into the boat ;
the rope from the fore end had just been received and

reeved in the ring at the stern, and a few fathoms hauled
into the boat ; and the shipwrecked men were preparing
to descend, when a terrific knot of sea recoiling from
the resistance it met at the vessel's bow, threw the
bow of the boat up over end, and the bow-rope not
holding, the boat was driven in that position, with all
her crew thrown into the stern, astern of the vessel,
into the rapid ebb-tide, which running into her,
caused the boat to capsize, and all the men were
washed into the sea ; they were carried away by the
tide.

"The accident was seen from the shore, and immediately the second life-boat was launched from
South Shields, and, with seventeen pilots on board,
proceeded with all possible despatch to the assistance of the crew of the former boat ; they found and
rescued three, one had succeeded in getting on board
the brig, and thus only four out of the twenty-four
were saved.

" Nor were the crew of the stranded vessel forgotten ;
the third life-boat from North Shields was launched ;
and notwithstanding the appalling accident, a crew
of seventeen brave fellows manned her instantly, and
proceeded alongside the *Betsy*, and brought all her
crew, and the one pilot who succeeded in getting
on board her, safely ashore.

"The first life-boat which had turned end-over-end
was washed ashore bottom up ; her great want was
the self-righting principle."

Urged by the necessities of the case, which became
daily more apparent, the Duke of Northumberland,

President of the National Life-boat Society, organized
a plan by which the intellect and experience of the
world at large should be encouraged to invent
a life-boat, which should be on all points as perfect
as possible.

His Grace offered a premium of one hundred
guineas for the best model of a life-boat. The
defects of the existing boats were pointed out as
a guide to inventors, they being chiefly :

" 1. They do not upright themselves in the event
of being upset.

" 2. That they are too heavy to be readily launched
or transported along the coast in case of need.

" 3. That they do not free themselves from water
fast enough.

" 4. That they are very expensive."

A committee was formed to examine, and report
upon the models.

The offer of His Grace, and the conditions of
the competition, were published in October 1850, and
no expense or pains were spared in making them
known.

The interest and excitement produced by the notice
were deeply and widely felt ; the challenge was
accepted by great numbers of people—amateurs, to
whom to invent a life-boat seemed a laudable and
holy ambition, vied with the boat-builders who had
thoughts of professional reputation to give a spur to
their humanity—speedily in all parts of England, and
in many other parts of the world, busy minds and
skilful hands were at work.

In due time models came teeming in upon the committee in almost overwhelming numbers.

Not content with asking for models of life-boats, the committee also asked for information upon certain defined points, the models sent in numbered no fewer than two hundred and eighty, while the answers to inquiries were sufficient to fill five folio volumes of manuscript. As for the models, every possible form and every possible principle seemed to find its illustration.

There were boats designed upon the principle of Pontoons, of Catamarans, of Rafts, Steamers, Paddle-box Boats, North Country Cobles—every possible modification of the whaleboat, and of the ordinary boat; boats made of wood, of tin, of galvanized corrugated iron, boats with cork linings, with air-boxes, with water-ballast, with no ballast, tubular boats, boats a series of tubs, a series of boxes; to be propelled by oars, by sails, by paddle-wheels, by screws, to be worked by hand power, by steam power, by atmospheric air.

The Committee might well feel overwhelmed at such a perfect rush of ideas and designs thus suggested for their consideration; and as they began to go into details, they found it almost impossible to decide which model was best, where the elements of excellency were so varied and so numerous, especially as they found that so large a number of the boats presented such excellent combinations of different good qualities.

The committee therefore deemed it necessary to

organize a regular competitive examination, assigning marks to different necessary qualifications, that they might thus be able to arrange the boats presented in an order of merit, dependent upon their respective combination of good qualities.

The following is the list of qualities that were required in the boats, with the number of marks apportioned to each.

1st Quality.	Rowing boat in all weathers	20
2nd ,,	Sailing boat in all weathers	18
3rd ,,	Sea boat, *i.e.*, stability, safety, buoyancy forward for launching through surf	10
4th ,,	Means of freeing boat from water readily . .	8
5th ,,	Extra buoyancy nature, amount, distribution, mode of application	7
6th ,,	Power of self-righting	9
7th ,,	Suitableness for beaching	4
8th ,,	Room for, and power of carrying passengers .	6
9th ,,	Moderate weight for transport along shore .	3
10th ,,	Protection from injury to bottom . . .	3
11th ,,	Ballast, as iron 1, water 2, cork 3 . . .	6
12th ,,	Access to stem and stern	3
13th ,,	Tumbler heads for securing warps . . .	2
14th ,,	Fenders, life-lines, &c.	1

With their mode of examination thus fully organized, the Committee patiently and carefully set about their interesting task, and after much labour it was decided that the model presented by Mr. James Beeching, of Great Yarmouth, possessed the best combination of necessary qualifications, and to it was awarded eighty-six out of the one hundred marks ; and the inventor had the gratification of receiving the following letters from the Duke of Northumberland, and from the Chairman of the Life-boat Committee :—

Alnwick Castle,
SIR, *13th August,* 1851.

It gives me much pleasure to send you a cheque for £105, as the prize for the best model of a life-boat.

And I must thank you for the assistance you have given me and the Society for Saving Life from Shipwreck by that model, which will enable us to establish a better life-boat on the coast than those at present in use.

Yours, &c.,
NORTHUMBERLAND.

To Mr. James Beeching.

Somerset House, London,
SIR, *14th August,* 1851.

I have the gratification to acquaint you that the Committee appointed to examine the life-boat models sent to Somerset House, to compete for the premium offered by His Grace the Duke of Northumberland for the best model of a life-boat, have awarded the prize to your model.

I am therefore directed by His Grace to transmit to you the enclosed cheque for £105, and the report of the Committee upon which the award was founded.

Yours, &c.,
J. WASHINGTON, R.N.,
Chairman of the Committee.

To Mr. James Beeching.

A fine boat, called the *Northumberland*, was speedily

built by Mr. Beeching, and she immediately commenced a more memorable career than has ever fallen
to the lot of any other boat—the stormy petrel of the
sea—the pioneer of a work not more glorious than
much which had been attempted, but which crowned
almost every brave effort with abundant success, where
science aided sympathy with all the fruits of her skill,
so that the double cry of agony, where on the one
hand there was lamentation for the shipwrecked and
lost, and on the other a cry, if possible, even more
piteous still, for those who perished in their efforts to
save the shipwrecked—a cry that had been too often
heard, was soon almost to cease from the land.

The early passage in the history of the *Northumberland* seemed to suggest that hers was to be
a holiday existence, her career commenced with a
round of triumphant display and popularity. She
visited various parts of the coast, and all her properties
were displayed, creating everywhere confidence in her
powers, and enthusiasm at the thought of the stimulus
to be given to the great work of saving life from
shipwreck, by the possession of such a noble and
efficient boat.

There was a great gathering at Ramsgate to witness
the first public trial the boat was to be put through ;
naval officers, elder brethren of the Trinity House,
scientific men of all services were interested deeply in
the series of experiments to which she was to be sub-
jected, for they all fully realized how the question of
life or death to thousands, yea, in the course of time, to
tens of thousands, was involved in the problem, as to

whether any boat could be found competent to resist all the fury of a raging and broken sea.

The *Northumberland* was manned, and first her stability was to be tested; all her crew stood and jumped upon one gunwale, but failed to upset her; her self-righting property was next to be tried; they brought her under a crane, and passing a rope from her mast round her bottom, gradually hauled her over, and she was bottom up; they let go the strain on the rope, and in five seconds she had righted herself, and in twenty seconds more she had emptied herself of water. Again she was to be turned over, and this time fresh interest was to be excited in the experiment, as Mr. Samuel Beeching, the son of the inventor and builder of the boat, determined to show his confidence in her powers by being in her when she was upset: slowly the strain is again put upon the rope under-running the boat, and she gradually turns over, Mr. Beeching clinging to the centre thwart the while; a moment's suspense, the boat is keel up, and the brave man out of sight—scarcely time for a pang of fear, when the boat comes round with a throb, and the man is seen standing on the thwart, cheering in answer to the cheers with which the success of the experiment and his re-appearance are greeted.

Now for a trial at sea, among the bright leaping waves, which seem full of playfulness and glee, as if ready to greet her merrily, and to whisper no word of the many deadly conflicts she must wage with them in coming days, ere she shall snatch the spoil of human life from their rage and strength.

Strong arms are at the oars, the good ash staves bend, and away she shoots through the waves, holding her own successfully as other boats race with her.

Her sailing powers must be tried, and a revenue-cutter accepts her challenge; both bowl along with a fresh breeze bellying their sails, and the life-boat behaves well and bravely, and proves also a success under sail.

The breeze freshens, and there is a great bubble of leaping surf in the broken water in the angle of the pier; an ordinary boat would speedily be swamped there; but there the life-boat rides on the tumbling seas like a thing of life; every experiment increases the confidence that her crew and the lookers-on feel in the boat.

Seaward now for a sterner trial, and on the field where her numerous future contests are to be fought, and her numerous victories gained; out and away where the rolling seas break in upon the Goodwin Sands, and where they fret into surf as they are checked in their race, and make the sea white with the foam of their falling crests; away into the tumbling seas, running the gauntlet of the leaping waves; away, and away, she speeds round the north end of the Sands, then steers for the North Foreland, until all her crew are perfectly delighted with her powers, and return to describe the trip, and how she behaved, and the confidence they have in her, that they would not hesitate to go in her into any broken water whatever.

Great is the congratulation and gladness among the naval and scientific men who are watching the experiments, and many thank God, that at last the problem is solved—that a boat is found able to defy the broken surf and raging waves—a fit and safe instrument in the hands of the brave-hearted boatmen, who are ever ready to do and dare all that is possible, in their efforts to save life from shipwreck.

The crew that went out in the boat made the following report :—

To the Harbour Commissioners.

" This is to certify that we have this day been to sea in the *Northumberland* prize life-boat, and have had every opportunity of proving her sailing qualities ; she has also been through a great deal of broken water and heavy sea, and we consider her, in the true sense of the word, perfectly qualified to encounter any bad weather when occasion might require her services, and we should be quite willing to go in her to any vessel in distress at any time."

The prize life-boat was purchased in December, 1851, for £250, by the Trinity Board, for the use of the Royal Harbour at Ramsgate, with the dread Goodwin Sands for her special cruising ground.

The trial of the life-boat became an especial feature at the various regattas held round the coast. The interest in her became very general, and a great move was given to the life-boat cause.

At Teignmouth they determined that the trial should be of a very practical and somewhat sensational nature—a capsize out at sea ! At eleven o'clock one stormy morning the signal was given to man the life-boat. In about one quarter of an hour she was making her way out to sea, and then her crew endeavoured to capsize her; they had tried in vain to do so in smooth water, would she defy their efforts in a rough tumble of sea and heavy weather? They set all her sails and manœuvred in every way to upset her, but without effect, when, while she was heeling over almost on her broadside, with all her sails full, the crew, at a given signal, jumped on her lee-gunwale, and down on her broadside she went; her sails were let go, and she righted at once, only two of her crew were thrown out of her, and these, with their cork jackets on, were bobbing up and down quite happily among the waves; they were soon picked up, and the boat speedily on her way again, the men more pleased and confident than ever in her wonderful powers.

But the National Life Boat Institution was not quite contented with the prize life-boat; she had gained eighty-six marks out of the one hundred in the competition of models; she was near perfection, but still could be improved upon; and as the great aim of the Society was to obtain a perfect boat, they would naturally not be content with anything less than this desired perfection, a boat that should satisfy the judges to the full in every particular, and thus merit the whole one hundred marks, instead of the eighty-six.

Mr. Peake, the then assistant master-shipwright at the Royal Dockyard at Woolwich, was appealed to. He made the matter his especial study. He took the prize-boat as his model, and combining with it some of the best qualities of the other boats, constructed a boat not differing much, or in any essential point, from the prize one, but yet sufficiently an improvement upon it to be pronounced as far as possible perfect on all points ; and it was at once adopted by the National Life Boat Institution as the standard model life-boat.

The life-boat cause was now to know no further stay in its onward course, the Committee was formed of thoroughly earnest and warm-hearted men—men full of practical knowledge and warm sympathy. Moreover, the Institution was blessed with as able and indefatigable a Secretary as Institution ever rejoiced in, this in the person of Mr. Richard Lewis, Barrister-at-Law ; the appeal to the public for sympathy and assistance was general, and generally acknowledged.

The Society told of dangerous headlands, of treacherous sands and tides all round the coast, of shipwrecks frequent, and deaths often occurring for want of a life-boat, and of life-boats, faultless in construction, only waiting the time when the Committee should have the means to place them where needed ; the funds grew as the wants were realized, and the heart of the nation was warmed to the noble cause ; the wreck-chart still showed a dismal circumference of casualties round the coast, marking dangerous points where many vessels had been lost ; but the inner line of defence began also to show itself on the map, and the marks of the life-boat stations began year by year to confront more regularly the signs of places where danger and shipwreck were most frequent.

But more of this, and the noble Life-boat Society, in the closing chapter of the book. It is time that we

launched our life-boat for its real work. The waves are
roaring on the Goodwin, the life-boat is at her moorings in the harbour of Ramsgate, the brave boatmen—
Storm Warriors indeed—are on the watch, hour after
hour through the stormy night walking the Pier, and
giving keen glances to where the Goodwin Sands are
white with the churning seething waves that leap
high, and plunge and foam amid the treacherous shoals
and banks. Look! a flash is seen; listen, in a few
seconds, yes, there is the throb and boom of a distant
gun, a rocket cleaves the darkness; and now the cry—
Man the life-boat! Man the life-boat! Seaward Ho!
Seaward Ho! But now in a boat efficient on all
points, whose only career shall be to save, and not to
add victim to victim, as she herself is overcome by the
rage of the sea.

CHAPTER VI.

THE RAMSGATE LIFE-BOAT AT WORK.—STORM WARRIORS TO THE RESCUE.

> " Ye mariners of England,
>   That guard our native seas ;
> Whose flag has braved a thousand years
>   The battle and the breeze !
> Your glorious standard launch again
>   To match another foe ;
> And sweep through the deep,
>   While the stormy winds do blow,
> While the battle rages loud and long
>   And the stormy winds do blow."

IT was a Sunday night, in the month of February, a few years ago, the anxious boatmen, who kept a diligent watch, shrugged their shoulders as they cast keen glances to windward, and declared that it was going to be a very dirty night.

Heavy masses of cloud skirted the horizon as the sun set ; and as the night drew on, violent gusts of wind swept along, accompanied by snow-squalls.

It was a dangerous time for vessels in the Channel, and it proved fatal to one at least.

Before the light broke on Monday morning, the Margate lugger *Eclipse* put out to sea to cruise round the shoals and sands in the neighbourhood of Margate, on the look out for the victims of any disasters that might have occurred during the night.

The crew soon discovered that a vessel was ashore on the Margate Sands, and directly made for her. She proved to be the Spanish brig *Samaritano* of one hundred and seventy tons, bound from Antwerp to Santander, and laden with a valuable and miscellaneous cargo.

Her crew consisted of the captain, Modesto Crispo, and eleven men ; it was during a violent squall of wind and snow that the vessel was driven on the Sands, at about half-past five in the morning ; the crew attempted to get away from the vessel in the boats, but in vain, the oars were broken in the attempt, and the boats stove in.

The lugger *Eclipse*, as she was running for the brig, spoke a Whitstable fishing-smack, and borrowed two of her men and her boat. They boarded the brig as the tide went down, and hoped to be able to get her off the Sands at the next high water. For this purpose, six Margate boatmen and the two Whitstable men were left on board.

But with the rising tide, the gale came on again in all its fury, and the boatmen had speedily to give up every hope of saving the vessel. They hoisted their boat on board to prevent her being swamped by the seas which were breaking heavily, and all hands began to feel that it was becoming a question, not of saving

E

the vessel, but of saving their own lives. The sea rushed furiously over the wreck, lifting her, and then letting her fall with crushing violence upon the sands. Her timbers did not long withstand this trial of their strength ; a hole was quickly knocked in her side, she filled with water, and settled down upon the sand.

The waves began now to break with great force over the deck ; the lugger's boat was speedily knocked to pieces and swept overboard ; the hatches were forced up, and some of the cargo which floated on the deck was at once washed away. The brig began to roll and labour fearfully, as wave after wave broke against her, with a force that shook her from stem to stern and threatened to throw her bodily upon her broadside ; the men, fearing this, cut the weather-rigging of the main mast, and the mast soon broke off short with a great crash, and went over the side.

All hands now took refuge in the fore-rigging ; nineteen men had then no other hope between them and a terrible death than the few shrouds of the shaking mast.

The wind beat against the poor fellows with hurricane force ; each wave that broke against the vessel sprang up in columns of foam and drenched them to the skin ; the air was full of spray and sleet, which froze upon them as it fell.

The Margate boatmen were there, but the Margate lugger could not have lived five minutes in the sea that surrounded the vessel ; the Whitstable smack would have been wrecked at once, if she had attempted to get near the wreck, and thus the poor fellows, caught in a trap, had to be left by their comrades to their

fate, their only chance of escape being the possibility
of a life-boat coming to their rescue, and this before
their frail support should yield to the rush of wind
and sea.

And resting in this hope they waited hour after
hour, clinging to the shrouds of the tottering mast;
but no help came, until one and all despaired of life.

In the meanwhile, news of the wreck had spread
like wildfire through Margate. In spite of the gale,
and the blinding snow squalls, many of the inhabitants
struggled to the cliff, and with spy-glasses tried to
penetrate the scud, or to gain in the breaks of the
storm some glimpses of the wreck.

As soon as the peril the crew of the brig were in
was known, the smaller of the two Margate life-boats
was manned and made to the rescue. As she sailed out
into the storm, the seas broke over her and filled her;
this her gallant crew heeded little at first, for they had
every confidence in her powers to ride safely through
any storm, that her air-tight compartments would prevent her from sinking; but to the astonishment of the
men they found that the boat was rapidly losing her
buoyancy, and fast becoming unmanageable; indeed
she was filling with water, which came up to the men's
waists. The air-tight boxes had evidently filled;
and they remembered, too late, that the valves, with
which each box is provided to let out any water that
may leak in, had been left unscrewed in the excitement
of starting. Their boat, with the air-tight compartments filled with water, virtually ceased to be a
life-boat, and her crew had to struggle for their own

safety. Although then within a quarter of a mile of the brig, there was no help for it, they could make no farther way against the storm ; the boat was unmanageable, and the only chance of life left to the boatmen themselves, was to run her ashore on the nearest part of the coast. It was doubtful whether they would be able to succeed even in this ; and it was not until they had battled for four hours with the sea and gale, that they were able to get ashore in Westgate Bay.

There the coastguard were ready to receive them, and did their best to revive the exhausted men. As soon as it was discovered at Margate that the first life-boat was disabled, the large life-boat, the *Friend of all Nations*, was got ready with every speed, and with much trouble dragged round to the lee side of the pier, where it was launched. Away she started, her brave crew doing all they could to battle with the gale, and force their way out to the wreck ; but all their efforts were in vain ; the tremendous wind was right against them ; the sea completely overpowered them, and prevented their beating to windward ; the tiller gave way, and after a hard struggle her crew had also to give up the attempt, and this life-boat in turn was driven ashore about one mile from the town. With both their life-boats wrecked, the Margate men almost gave up all hopes of saving the crew of the vessel and the men that were left on board ; but this should not be the case until every possible effort had been made ; but it was with small hope for the ship-wrecked, and with much apprehension for the boats themselves, that the people watched two luggers—the *Nelson* and the *Lively*—undaunted by the fate of the life-boats, stagger out mid the sweeping seas to the rescue.

The fate of one lugger, the *Nelson*, was soon settled ; a fearful squall of wind caught her before she had got many hundred yards clear of the pier ; it swept her foremast out of her, and her crew had to make every possible effort to avoid being driven on the rocks, and there wrecked.

The *Lively* was more fortunate ; she beat her way out to sea, but found so heavy a surf breaking over the Sands, that it was evidently impossible to cross them, or to get near the wreck.

The Margate people became full of despair, and many a bitter tear was shed for sympathy and for personal loss as they watched the wreck, and thought of the poor fellows perishing slowly before their eyes, apparently without any possibility of being saved.

A rumour spread among the crowd that the lieutenant of the coastguard had sent an express off to Ramsgate, for the Ramsgate steamer and life-boat ; but this scarcely afforded any hope, as it was thought impossible that the steamer and life-boat could make their way round the North Foreland in the teeth of so tremendous a gale, or that, if they did so, it was supposed impossible that either the ship could hold together, or the crew live, exposed as they were in the rigging, during the time it would of necessity take the steamer and boat to get to them.

We now change the scene to Ramsgate.

From an early hour on the Monday morning, groups of boatmen assembled on the pier at Ramsgate; they were occasionally joined by some of the more hardy among the townsmen, or by a stray visitor, attracted by the wild scene that the storm presented.

The boatmen could faintly discern, in the intervals between the snow-squalls, a few vessels in the distance, running before the gale, and they were keenly on the watch for signals of distress, that they might hasten to the rescue.

But no such signal was given.

Every now and then, as the wind boomed by, some landsmen suggested that it was the report of a gun from one, or other, of the three light-vessels, which guard the dangerous Goodwin Sands; but the boatmen shook their heads, and those who with spyglasses kept a look-out in the direction of the light-vessels confirmed them in their disbelief.

About nine o'clock, tidings came to Ramsgate that a brig was ashore on the Woolpack Sands off Margate. It was, of course, concluded that the two Margate life-boats would go to the rescue; and although there was much anxiety and excitement as to the result of the attempt the Margate boatmen would certainly make, no one had the least idea that the services of the Ramsgate life-boat would be required. But shortly after twelve a coastguard man from Margate hastened breathless to the pier, and to the harbour-master's office, saying, in answer to eager inquiries as he hurried on, that the two Margate life-boats had been wrecked, and that the Ramsgate boat was wanted.

The harbour-master immediately gave orders, " Man the life-boat."

No sooner had the words passed from his lips than the boatmen, who had crowded round the door in anticipation of the order, rushed away to the boat.

First come, first in ; not a moment's hesitation, not a thought of further clothing ; they will go as they are, rather than not go at all. The news rapidly spreads ; each boatman as he heard it, hastily snatched up his bag of waterproof overalls, and south-wester cap, and rushed down to the boat ; and for some time boatman after boatman was to be seen racing down the pier, hoping to find a place still vacant ; if the race had been to save their lives, rather than to risk them, it would hardly have been more hotly contested.

Some of those who had won the race and were in the boat, were ill prepared with clothing for the hardships they would have to endure, for if they had not their waterproofs at hand they did not delay to get them, fearing that the crew might be made up before they got to the boat. But these men were supplied by the generosity of their disappointed friends, who had come down better prepared, but too late for the enterprise ; the famous cork jackets were thrown into the boat and at once put on by the men.

The powerful steam-tug, well named the *Aid*, that belongs to the harbour, and has her steam up night and day ready for any emergency that may arise,

speedily got her steam to full power, and with her
brave and skilful master, Daniel Reading, in command, took the boat in tow, and together they made
their way out of the harbour. James Hogben, who,
with Reading, has been in many a wild scene of
danger, was coxswain, and steered and commanded
the life-boat.

It was nearly low water at the time, but the force
of the gale was such as to send a good deal of spray
dashing over the pier; the snow fell in blinding
squalls, and drifted and eddied in every protected
nook and corner. It was hard work for the excited
crowd of people, who had assembled to see the life-
boat start, to battle their way through the drifts and
against the wind, snow, and foam to the head of the
pier; but there at last they gathered, and many a
one felt his heart fail as the steamer and boat cleared
the protection of the pier, and encountered the first
rush of wind and sea outside. "She seemed to go
out under water," said one old fellow; "I would not
have gone out in her for the universe." And those
who did not know the heroism and determination that
such scenes call forth in the breasts of the boatmen,
could not help wondering much at the eagerness
which had been displayed to get a place in the boat
—and this although the hardy fellows knew that the
two Margate life-boats had been wrecked in the attempt to get the short distance which separated the
wreck from Margate; while they would have to
battle their way through the gale for ten or twelve
miles before they could get even in sight of the vessel.

It says nothing against the daring or skill of the Margate boatmen, that they failed. In such a gale they could not get to windward against wind and tide, success therefore was almost impossible without the aid of steam ; with a steam-boat to tow them into position for dashing in upon the Sands, the Margate boats would in all probability have succeeded ; without such assistance the Ramsgate boat would have certainly failed. As soon as the steamer and boat got clear of the Ramsgate pier, they felt the full force of the storm, and it seemed almost doubtful whether they could make any progress against it. They slowly worked their way out of the full strength of the tide, as it swept round the head of the pier, and then began to move ahead a little more rapidly, and were soon ploughing their way through a perfect sea of foam.

The steamer with its engines working full power, plunged heavily along ; wave after wave broke over its bows, sent its spray flying over the funnel and mast, and deluged the deck with a tide of water, which, as it rushed aft, gave the men enough to do to hold on.

The life-boat was towing astern with fifty fathom of five-inch hawser out, an enormously strong rope about the thickness of a man's wrist. Her crew already experienced the dangers and discomforts, that they were ready to endure, perhaps, for many hours, and without a murmur, in order to save life.

There was anxiety and fear, but the one thought of anxiety and fear was, as to whether they could possibly be in time to save the lives of the poor fellows, who must, for so many hours, have been clinging to a shattered wreck. It would be hard to give a description to enable one to realize the position of the men in the boat, as they were being towed along by the steamer. The use of a life-boat is, that it will float and live, where other boats would of necessity be swamped, upset, and founder; they are made for, and generally only used on, occasions of extreme danger and peril, for terrible storms and wild seas.

The water flows into the boat, and over it, and it still floats: some huge wave will break over it, and for a moment bury it, but it rises in its buoyancy and shakes itself free; beaten down on its broadside by the waves and wind, it struggles hard, and soon rises again on an upright keel, and defies them to do their worst; and even if some mighty breaker should come rushing along, catch her in its curling arms, and bodily upset her, only for a few seconds would the triumph last, the boat would speedily right again, sitting like an ark of refuge in the boiling sea of foam, while her crew, up-held by their cork jackets, would be floating and struggling around her, until one after another would manage to regain her sides, and clamber in over her low gunwale at the waist, and shortly she would be speeding away again on her life errand. Such were the qualities of the noble boat, which we are watching, while she is urging her way through the dismal seas, while a dozen poor fellows, some nine or ten miles off, are hanging to the shaking shrouds of a tottering mast, the waves that are breaking over them threatening every moment to be their tomb.

Away! away, then, brave boat! gallant crew! God grant you good progress!

Since the moment of clearing the pier, the waves that broke over the boat filled her time after time, and did everything but drown her. The men were up to their knees in water; they bent forward as much as they could, each with a firm hold upon the boat.

The spray and waves rushed over them, and as they beat continuously upon their backs, although they could not penetrate their waterproof clothing, still they chilled them to the bone, for, as the spray fell, it froze, indeed so bitter was the cold that the men's mittens were frozen to their hands.

After a tremendous struggle the steamer seemed to be making head against the storm; they were well clear of the pier and getting on gallantly. They made their way through the Cud Channel, and had passed between the black and white buoys, so well known to Ramsgate visitors, when a fearful sea came heading towards them. It met and broke over the steamer, buried her in foam, and swept along.

The life-boat rose to it, for a moment hung with her bows high in air, and then as she felt the strain of the tow-rope, plunged bodily into the wave, and was almost altogether under water; the men were nearly washed out of her, but at that moment the tow-rope broke, the wave threw the boat back with a jerk, and as the strain of the rope suddenly ceased, the boat fell across the seas which swept in rapid succession over her, and seemed completely at their mercy. Oars out! oars out! was the cry, and the men, as soon as they could get breath, got them out, and began to make every effort to get the boat round again, head to wind, but in vain, the waves tossed the oars up, the wind caught the blades, and it was as much as the men could do to keep them in their hands. The gale was too heavy for them, and they drifted rapidly before wind and tide towards the Brake Shoal, which was directly under their lee, and over which the seas were rushing with great violence. But the steamer, which throughout was handled most admirably, both as regards skill and bravery, was put round as swiftly as possible, and very cleverly brought within a few yards to windward of the boat, as she lay athwart the sea.

The men on board the steamer threw a hauling line on board the boat to which was attached a bran new hawser, and again took the boat in tow.

The tide was still flowing, and as it rose, the wind came up in heavier and heavier gusts, bringing with it a blinding snow and sleet, which, with the spray, still freezing as it fell, swept over the boat, till the men looked, as one said at the time, like a body of ice.

The men could not look to windward for the drifting snow and blinding seas which were continually rushing over them, they only knew that the strong steamer was plunging along, taking all as it came, for they felt the strain on the rope; thus they realized that each moment's suffering and peril brought them nearer to their poor perishing fellow-sailors; and not one heart failed, not one repented of winning the race to the life-boat.

Off Broadstairs, they suddenly felt the way of the boat stop. The rope broken again, was the first thought of all; but on looking round as they were enabled to do, as the boat was no longer being dragged through the seas; they discovered to their utter dismay that the steamer had stopped; they thought that her machinery had broken down, and at once despaired of saving the lives of the shipwrecked, for with the wind as it was, it would be long hours before they could beat up against the gale, and get to the Sands, on which they were told the wreck lay; a moment's suspense and they discovered, to their gladness, that the steamer had merely stopped to let out more cable, fearful that it might break again in the struggle that was before them, as they fought their way round the North Foreland.

Another hour's hard struggle, and they reached the North Foreland. There the sea was running tremendously high—the gale was still increasing; the snow, sleet, and spray, rushed by with hurricane speed.

Although it was only early in the afternoon, the air was so darkened by the storm that it seemed a dull twilight. The captain of the boat was steering; he peered out between his collar and cap, but looked in vain for the steamer. He knew that she was all right, for the rope kept taught; but many times, although she was only a hundred yards ahead, he could see nothing of her, still less able were the men on board the steamer to see the life-boat.

Often did they anxiously look astern, and watch for a break in the drift and scud to see that she was all

right ; for although there could be no doubt as to the
strain upon the rope, she might be towing along
bottom up, or have all her men washed out of her, for
all they could tell. The master of the steamer
watched the seas, which broke over the *Aid*, making
her stagger again, as they rushed towards the life-
boat, and several times the fear that she was gone
came over him. But steamer and life-boat still
battled successfully against the storm.

As soon as they were round the North Foreland,
the snow squall cleared and they sighted Margate ; all
anxiously looked for the wreck, but nothing of her
could they see. They saw a lugger riding just clear
of the pier, with foremast gone, and anchor down to
prevent her being driven ashore by the gale. They
next sighted the Margate life-boat driven ashore
and abandoned in Westgate Bay, looking a complete
wreck, the waves beating over her. A little beyond.
this they caught sight of the second life-boat, also
washed ashore ; and then they learnt to realize to the
full the gallant efforts that had been made to save the
shipwrecked, and the destruction that had been
wrought as effort after effort had been overcome by
the fury of the storm. But where was the wreck ?
Had she been beaten to pieces, all lives lost, and were
they too late ? A heavy mass of cloud and snow-
storm rolled on to windward of them in the direction
of the Sands off Margate, and they could not make
out any signs of the wreck there.

There was just a chance that it was the Woolpack
Sand that she was on. They thought it the more

likely, as the first intelligence of the wreck that came
to Ramsgate declared that such was the case ; and
accordingly they determined to make for the Woolpack Sand, which was about three miles farther on ;
they had scarcely decided upon this, when, providentially, there was a break in the drift of the snow to
windward, and they suddenly caught sight of the
wreck.   But for this sudden clearance in the storm
they would, as we have said, have proceeded farther on,
and some hours must have passed before they could
have found out their mistake and got back again, and
by that time every soul of the poor shipwrecked crew
must have perished.

The master of the steamer made out the flag of
distress flying in the rigging of the vessel, the ensign
union downwards ; she, doubtlessly, was the wreck of
which they were in search.

But still it was a question how they could get
to her, for she was on the other side of the Sand.
To tow the boat round the Sand would take a long
time in the face of such a gale ; and for the boat
to make across the Sand seemed almost impossible, so tremendous was the sea that was running
over it.

Nevertheless there was no hesitation on the part of
the life-boat crew.   It seemed a forlorn hope, a very
rushing upon destruction, to attempt to force the boat
under canvas through such a surf and sea ; but they
looked at the tottering wreck ; they felt how any
moment might be the last to the poor fellows clinging
to her, and they could not bear to think of the delay

that would be occasioned by their going round the Sands.

Without hesitation, therefore, they cast off the tow-rope, and were about setting sail, when they found that the tide was running so furiously that they must be towed at least three miles to the eastward before they would be sufficiently far to windward to make certain of fetching the wreck.

It was a hard struggle to get the tow-rope on board again, tossed about as they were by the tumbling seas, and a bitter disappointment to all, that an hour, or more, of their precious time must be consumed before they could possibly get to the rescue of their endangered brother seamen; but there was no help for it, and away again they went in tow of the steamer. The snow-squall came on again, and they lost sight of the wreck, but all kept an anxious look-out, and now and then, in a break in the squall, they could catch a glimpse of her. They could see that she was almost buried in the waves which broke over her in great clouds of foam, and again many and weary were the doubts and speculations, as to whether any on board of her could still be alive. For twenty minutes or so they battled steadily on against wind and tide.

The gale, which had been increasing since the morning, came on heavier than ever, and roared like thunder over head; the sea was running so furiously and meeting the life-boat with such tremendous force that the men had to cling on their hardest not to be washed out of her, and at last the new tow-rope could no

longer resist the increasing strain, and suddenly parted
with a tremendous jerk ; there was no thought of
picking up the·cable again—they could stand no further delay, and one and all of her crew rejoiced to
hear the captain of the life-boat give orders to set
sail.

CHAPTER VII.

THE RESCUE OF THE CREW OF THE "SAMARITANO," AND THE RETURN.

> Now set the teeth, and stretch the nostril wide ;
> Hold hard the breath, and bend up every spirit
> To his full height !   On, on, you noble English,
> Whose blood is set from fathers of war-proof !
> Fathers that, like so many Alexanders,
> Have, in these parts, from morn till even fought.
> "King Henry V."—*Shakespeare.*

HARDER still the gale, and the rush of the sea and the blinding snow. The storm was at its height. As the life-boat headed for the Sands, a darkness, as of night, seemed to settle down upon the men ; they could scarcely see each other ; but on through the raging sea and blinding storm they drove the gallant boat. As they approached the shallow water, the high part of the Sand, where the heaviest waves were breaking, they could see spreading itself before them, standing out in the gloom, a white, gleaming, barrier wall of foam ; for there as the rushing waves broke, they clasned together in their recoil, and mounted up in columns of foam, their heavier volume falling, and their crests caught by the wind and carried away in white streaming clouds of spray, while the fearful roar of the beat of the waves could be heard above the gale.

But still straight for the breakers the men made. No faltering, no hesitation, brows knit, teeth clenched, hands ready, and hearts firm, and into it with a cheer.

The boat, although under the smallest sail she could carry—a double reefed fore-sail and mizen—was driven on by the hurricane force of the wind, on through the outer range of breakers she plunged, and then came indeed a struggle for life.

The waves no longer rolled on in foaming ranks, but leapt, and clashed, and battled together in a raging boil of sea. They broke over the boat, the surf poured in first on one side of the boat, and then on the other, as she rolled to starboard and port, wildly tossed from side to side. Some waves rushed bodily over the boat, threatening to sweep every man out of her. Look out, my men! hold on! hold on! was the cry. When they saw some huge breaker heading towards them like an advancing wall, then the men threw themselves breast down on the thwart, curled their legs under it, clasped it with all their force with both arms, held their breath hard, and clung on for very life against the tear and wrestle of the wave, while the rush of water poured over their backs and heads, and buried them in its flood. Down, down, beneath the weight of the water, the men and

F 2

boat sank ; but only for a moment ; the splendid boat
rose in her buoyancy, and freed herself of the seas,
which for a moment had overcome her and buried her,
and her crew breathed again ; and a struggling cry of
triumph rises from them. Well done, old boat! well
done! all right! all right! Yes, all hands here, no
one washed out of her; and with a quick glance of
mutual congratulation they look at each other, and
rejoice that all are safe, scarce time for a word.
"Now she goes through it, now she's forging ahead!
keep a tight hold, my boys!" A moment's lull, as
she glided on the crest of some huge wave, or only
smaller ones tried their strength against her ; then
again the monster fellows came heading on, again the
warning cry was given ; look out! hold on! hold on!
and the men crouched, and clung, and struggled for
their lives, while the wild waves rushed over the boat.

Thus until they got clear of the Sands the fearful
struggle was again and again repeated ; but at last
it was for a time over, they had burst through the belt
of raging surf and got again into deep water. They
had then only the huge rolling waves and less broken
tumble of sea to contend with ; this, in such a
furious gale of wind, was bad enough, and almost more
than any other kind of boat could have endured, but
little in comparison to what they had just gone
through, and escaped from.

The boat was now put before the wind, and every
man in her was on the look-out for the wreck. For
a time it remained so thick that there was no
possibility of finding her, when again a second time a

sudden break in the storm revealed her : she was about half a mile to leeward.

They shifted the foresail with great difficulty, and again made in for the Sands towards the vessel. The appearance of the wreck as they approached her made even the stoutest among them shudder.

She had settled down by the stern in the Sands, the uplifted bow being the only part of the hull that was to be seen ; the sea was making a clear breach over her.

The mainmast was gone, her foresail, and foretop-sail were blown adrift, and great columns of foam were mounting up, flying over her foremast and bow. They saw a Margate lugger lying at anchor just clear of the Sands, and made close to her. As they shot by they could just make out, mid the roar of the storm, a loud hail, eight of our men on board ! and on they flew, and in a few minutes were in a sea that would instantly have swamped the lugger, noble and power-ful boat though she was.

Approaching the wreck, it was with terrible anxiety they strained their sight, trying to discover if there were still any men left in the tangled mass of rigging, over which the sea was breaking so furiously. By degrees they made them out. " I see a man's head, look ! one is waving his arm."—" I make out two ! three ! why the rigging is full of the poor fellows ;" and with a cheer of triumph, at being yet in time, the life-boat crew settled to their work.

The wreck of the mainmast, and the tremendous wash of sea over the vessel, prevented their going to the lee of the wreck. This increased their danger tenfold, as the result proved.

When about forty yards from the wreck, they lowered their sails, and cast the anchor over the side. The moment for which the boat had so gallantly battled for four hours, and the shipwrecked had waited almost in despair for eight hours, had at last arrived.

No cheering! no shouting in the boat now, no whisper beyond the necessary orders; the risk and suspense are too terrible! yard by yard, the cable is cautiously payed out, and the great rolling seas are allowed to carry the boat, little by little, nearer to the vessel. The waves break over the boat, for a moment bury it, and then as the sea rushes on, and breaks upon the wreck, the spray, flying up, hides the men lashed to the rigging from the boatman's sight. They hoist up a corner of the sail to let the boat sheer in; all are ready; a huge wave lifts them. Pay out the cable! sharp, men! sharp! the coxswain shouts; belay all! The cable was let go a few yards by the run, and the boat is alongside the wreck. With a cry, three men jump into the boat and are saved! All hands to the cable! haul in hand over hand, for your lives, men, quick, the coxswain cries; for he sees a tremendous wave rushing in swiftly upon them. They haul in the cable, draw the boat a little from the wreck, the wave passes and breaks over the vessel; if the life-boat had been alongside she would have been dashed against the wreck, and perhaps capsized, or washed over, and utterly destroyed. Again the men watch the waves, and as they see a few smallei ones approaching, let the cable run again, and get alongside; this time they are able to remain a little longer by the vessel; and one after another, thirteen cf the shipwrecked men unlash themselves from the rigging and jump into the boat, when again they draw away from the vessel in all haste, and avoid threatened destruction.

"Are they all saved?" No! three of the vessel's crew, Spaniards, are still left in the rigging; they seem almost dead, and scarcely able to unlash themselves, and crawl down the shrouds and await the return of the boat.

Again the boat is alongside, and this time the peril is greater than ever. They must place the boat close to the vessel, for the men are too weak to make any spring to reach her; they must remain alongside for a longer time, for two life-boatmen must get on to the wreck and lift the men on board; but, as before, they go coolly, quietly, and determinedly to work; the cable is veered out, the sail manœuvred to make the boat sheer, and again she is alongside; the men are seized by their arms and clothing, and dragged into the boat.

The last one left is the cabin-boy; he seems entangled in the rigging. The poor little fellow had a canvas bag of trinkets and things, he was taking as presents to the loved ones at home, and all through the howling storm, the rush and beat of the waves, as he held on exhausted and half dead to the shrouds, he still thought of those loved friends, and clung to the canvas bag.

God only knows whether the loved ones at home were thinking of, and praying for him, and whether it was in answer to their prayers and those of many others that the life-boat then rode alongside that wreck, an ark of safety mid the raging seas.

They shout, the boy lingers still, his half-dead hands cannot free the bag from the entangled rigging. A moment and all are lost ; a boatman makes a spring, seizes the lad with a strong grasp, and tears him down from the rigging into the boat—too late, too late; they cannot get away from the vessel ; a tremendous wave rushes on : hold hard all, hold anchor ! hold cable ! give but a yard, and all are lost ! The boat lifts, is washed into the fore-rigging, the sea passes, and she settles down again upon an even keel ! Thank God ! If one stray rope of all the torn and tangled rigging of the vessel had caught the boat's rigging, or one of her spars—if the boat's keel or cork fenders had caught in the shattered gunwale, she would have turned over, and every man in her been shaken into the sea to speedy and certain death. Thank God, it is not so, and once more they are safe.

The boat is very crowded ; she has her own crew of thirteen on board, six of the Margate boatmen and two Whitstable fishermen, who were left on the vessel, the captain, mate, eight seamen and the boy ; thus, thirty-two souls in all form her precious freight.

The life-boatmen at once, without a second's delay, haul in the cable as fast as possible, and draw up to the anchor to get clear of the wreck, for they must get some distance away before they dare let go their

cable, or with the wind and seas setting directly
towards the vessel they would be driven upon her,
unless they had plenty of room to sail by her.

An anxious time it is, as they draw up to the
anchor; at last they are pretty clear, and hoist the
sail to draw still farther away before they let go.

There is no thought of getting the anchor up in
such a gale and sea.

" She draws away," cries the captain of the boat,
" pay out the cable; stand by to cut it; pass the hatchet
forward; cut the cable, quick, my men, quick." There
is a moment's delay, a delay by which indeed all their
lives are saved; a few strong blows with the hatchet,
and the cable would have been parted. A boatman
takes out his knife, and begins gashing away at the
hawser. Already one strand out of the three, which
form·the strong rope, is severed; when a fearful gust
of wind sweeps by, the boat heels over almost on her
side—a crash is heard, and the mast and sail are
blown clean out of the boat.

Never was a moment of greater peril. Away in
the rush of the wave the boat is carried straight for
the wreck; the cable is payed out and is slack; they
haul it in as fast as they can, but on they are carried swiftly, apparently to certain destruction. Let
them hit the wreck full, and the next wave must throw
the boat bodily upon it, and all her crew will be swept
at once into the sea; let them but touch the wreck,
and the risk is fearful; on they are carried, the stem of
the boat just grazes the bow of the vessel, they must
be capsized by the bowsprit and entangled in the wreck-

age; some of the crew are ready for a spring into the bowsprit to prolong their lives a few minutes, the others are all steadily, eagerly, quietly, hauling in upon the cable might and main, as the only chance of safety to the boat and crew ; one moment more and all are gone, one more haul upon the cable, a fathom or so comes in by the run, and at that moment it mercifully taughtens and holds ; all may yet be safe : another yard or two and the boat would have been dashed to pieces.

They again haul in the cable, and draw the boat away as rapidly as they can from the wreck, but they do it with a terrible dread, for they remember the cut strand of the rope. Will the remaining two strands hold ? The strain is fearful, each time that the boat lifts to a wave, the cable tightens and jerks, and they think it breaking ; but it still holds, and a thrill of joy passes through the heart of all, as they hear that the cut part of the rope is safely in the boat.

But the danger is not even yet over : all this time the mast and sail have been dragging over the side of the boat ; it is with great difficulty that they get them on board.

The mast had been broken short off about three feet from the heel.

They chop a new heel to it, and rig it up as speedily as they can, but it takes long to do so ; for the boat is lying in the trough of the sea, and the waves are constantly breaking over her ; moreover, she is so crowded that the men can scarcely move, and the gale is blowing as hard as ever.

For the poor Spaniards, as they cling to each other, the terrors of death seem scarcely passed away ; they know nothing of the properties of the life-boat, and cannot believe that it will live long in such a sea. As the waves beat over the boat and fill it, they imagine that she will founder, and each time that the great rolling seas launch themselves at her they cling to each other, expecting that she will capsize; besides, the poor fellows' nerves are not in a very good state ; for eight hours they have been in great danger, for a large portion of that time in momentary expectation of death, during the four hours they were lashed to the rigging of the wreck, with the life nearly beaten and frozen out of them by the constant rush of sea and of spray, and by the bitter wind.

One of the Spaniards seeing a life-belt lying down, which one of the crew had thrown off in the hurry of his work, sits upon it by way of making himself doubly safe. But the work goes on. At last the mast is fitted and raised. No unnecessary word is spoken all this time, for the life and death struggle is not yet over ; nor, indeed, can it be before they are well away from the neighbourhood of the wreck. Now, as they hoist the sail, the boat gradually draws away ; the cable is again payed out little by little ; as soon as they are well clear of the vessel they cut it, and away they sail. The terrible suspense is over when each moment was a moment of fearful risk. It had lasted from the time when they let go the anchor to the time when they got clear of the vessel—about one hour. The men could now breathe freely, their faces

brighten, and from one and all there arises sponta-
neously a pealing cheer. They are no longer face to
face with death, and thankfully and joyfully they sail
away from the sands, the breakers, and the wreck.

The gale was still at its height, but the peril they
were in then seemed nothing to what they had gone
through, and had happily left behind. In the great
reaction of feeling, the freezing cold and sleet, the
driving wind, and foam, and sea, were all forgotten ;
and they felt as light-hearted as if they were out on
a pleasant summer's cruize. They could at last look
round and see who they had in the boat, speak
hearty words of congratulation to the Margate and
Whitstable men, some of whom they knew, and
strive by a good deal of broken English, and slaps on
the back, and shaking of hands, to cheer up the
Spanish sailors, and to let them know how glad they
are to have saved them. They then proceeded in
search of the steamer, which, after casting the life-
boat adrift, made for shelter to the back of the Hook
Sand, not far from the Reculvers, and there waited,
her crew anxiously on the look-out for the return of
the life-boat.

As they were making for the steamer, the lugger
Eclipse came in chase to hear whether they had
succeeded in saving all hands, and especially, whether
all the men of her crew were saved. They welcomed
the glad tidings with three cheers for the life-boat
crew, and made in for the land. Soon after, the
Whitstable smack made towards them upon a similar
errand, and her crew were equally rejoiced to hear

that their ship-mates with all hands were safe. It was too rough, a great deal, for the men to be taken on board the smack ; and so she, after speaking them, tacked in for the land.

The night was coming on apace ; it was not until they had run three or four miles that they sighted the steamer ; and when they got alongside her it was a difficult matter to get the saved crew on board. The sea was raging, and the gale blowing as much as ever, and the steamer rolled and pitched heavily ; the poor shipwrecked fellows were too exhausted to spring for the steamer as the opportunities occurred, and had to be almost lifted on board, one poor fellow being hauled on board by a rope. Again the boat was taken in tow, almost all her crew remaining in her, and they commenced their return home. The night was very dark and clear ; the sea and gale had lost none of their force ; and until the steamer and boat had got well round the North Foreland, the struggle to get back was just as great as it had been to get there.

Once round the Foreland the wind was well on the quarter, and they made easier way ; light after light opened to them ; Kingsgate and Broadstairs were passed, and at last the Ramsgate pier-head light shone out with its bright welcome, and the men began to feel that their work was nearly over.

A telegram had been sent from Margate in the afternoon, stating that the Ramsgate life-boat had been seen to save the crew ; but nothing more had been heard. The boatmen had calculated the time when they thought the steamer and life-boat might both be back; and the fearful violence of the storm suggested some sad occasion for the delay. As hour after hour grew on, the anxiety increased; real alarm was beginning to be felt by all, and a keen watch was kept for the first appearance of the steamer and boat round the edge of the cliff.

As the tide went down, and the sea broke less heavily over the pier, the men could venture farther along it, until, by the time of the boat's return, they were enabled to assemble at the end of the pier, and there a large and anxious crowd gathered. The anxiety of all was increased by the suggestions and speculations of disasters, which always present themselves at a time of suspense and apprehension; and so, when the steamer was announced with the life-boat in tow, the reaction was great, and the watchers shouted for very joy.

And as the "Storm Warriors" entered the harbour waving the strong right arms that had worked so well, and shouted, "All saved!" "All saved!" and the flags of triumph were seen flying out in the gale. Cheer after cheer broke from the crowd as they welcomed home from the dread battle-field those who had fought and conquered, and now bore with them as trophies of their victory, nineteen men; fellow-sailors, whose lives had been saved from a terrible and certain death. And many cheered again as they thought of the number who would have had life-long cause to mourn, if these poor fellows had perished. Parents, wives, children—what a group they would seem if they could be pictured watching the saved ones return ; what words, and looks, and tears of thanks where feelings are too deep for words, for the Storm Warriors, and for the life-boat cause, and for the generous English people who placed such boats at the disposal of such brave hearts and strong hands— of men ready to dare all and to do all that men can do to rescue the perishing from death.

Think only of the group that may possibly welcome back the little pale, exhausted cabin-boy, their hearts as warm as his, their love as deep as his—as his, which made that little canvas bag full of simple presents so dear to him that he held to it through all the many hours of the storm ; that made it his first thought when the wild seas rushed over the vessel, and the crew had to take to the rigging ; love that made him, when grown men thought only of their own lives, rush to his chest and seize his treasure, and all through the wild gale cling to it ; cling to it still, though the winds in their bitter cold froze him through and through, and the seas beat over him hour after hour. Think of the faces that may have seemed to peer at him out of the darkness of the storm. A loving-hearted father ready to thank him for the tobacco-box ; a mother for that wonderful brooch ; a little dark-eyed brother for the knife with four blades, and a little sister for the little very blue-eyed doll with such rosy cheeks. No, he could not let the bag go, and so it nearly cost him his life, and by the delay his clinging to it caused, nearly cost all the brave men their lives also ; but the good God would not let so much simple love work so much disaster,

and the loving ones shall see him again, and perhaps
he will stand, and perhaps each of his fellow-sailors
will stand, in the centre of some tearful group,
who again and again will weep, and thank God,
as they are told of the wreck, and the hours of peril,
and the waiting for death, and the hopeless despair,
and the strange wonderful boat that came in through
the storm ; and how they were saved, when they
never thought to see home again. And often shall
the brave boatmen be blessed and thanked by
grateful hearts, and the life-boat cause not forgotten.
I repeat the picture that we may learn to think
much of the sailor's arrival home, as well of his
being saved from the wreck, and thus learn to
appreciate the more the value and the mercy of
life-boat work.

But to return. The Spanish sailors had, by the
time they reached the harbour, somewhat recovered
under the care of the life-boat crew, and were further
well cared for, and supplied with clothes by the
care of the Spanish consul. And the hardy English
boatmen did not take long to recover from their
exposure and fatigues, fearful as they had been.

The Spanish captain, in speaking of the rescue,
was almost overcome by his feelings of gratitude
and wonder. He had quite made up his mind for
death ; he felt that the wreck could not by any
possibility hold together much longer ; every moment
he expected a final crash ; and all his experience
taught him that it was impossible for any boat
to come to their rescue in such a fearful sea. His

experience of the life-boat was new, and not easily to be forgotten.

He had a painting made of the rescue to take with him and show to the Spanish Government. It is pleasing to be able to wind up this story with stating, that the English Board of Control acknowledged the bravery and exertions of the men engaged in the rescue, by presenting to each of them 2*l.* and a medal, and that the Spanish Government also gratefully acknowledged the heroic exertions of the men, by granting to each a medal and 3*l.*

CHAPTER VIII.

A NIGHT ON THE GOODWIN SANDS.

"God help the poor fellows at sea !"
Far away inland, when tempests blow
  Wild through the dark'ning night,
We list to the roar of the winds as they go
  On their hurricane steeds to the fight ;
For the hosts of the storm-king are gathering fast
  Where the white-crested waters flee,
And our heart breathes this prayer, as he rushes past,
On the wings of the northern howling blast,—
  "God help the poor fellows at sea !"

C. T.

"GOD have mercy upon the poor fellows at sea !"
Household words these, in English homes, however
far inland the homes may be ; and although near
these homes the sea may have no better representa-
tive than a sedge choked river, or canal, along which
slow barges urge a lazy way.

For when the storm-wrack darkens the sky, and
gales are abroad, seaward fly the sympathies of
English hearts, and the prayer is uttered, and in many
cases, in this sea-loving island of ours, with very
special reference to some loved and absent sailor.
It is those, however, who live near the sea-shore, and

watch the warfare going on in all its terrible reality, that learn the more truly to realize the fearful nature of the struggles for life that go on round our coasts; and who learn as the wild gales rave to find an answer to the murmurings of the fierce blast, in the prayer, "God have mercy upon the poor fellows at sea;" and this especially as they welcome ashore, as wrested from death, some rescued sailor, or mourn over those who have found a sudden grave almost within call of land.

It is a pretty picture enough from Ramsgate Pier, when fifty or a hundred sail are in sight within two or three miles of land, and the day is sunny, and the sea bright, and a good wholesome breeze is bowling along; but anxious withal, when the clouds are gathering, and the fleet of vessels are seeking to make the best of their way to find shelter in the Downs: and a south-westerly gale moans up, and the last of the fleet are caught by it, and have to anchor in exposed places, and you watch them riding heavily, making bad weather, the seas every now and then flying over them. It is winter time, and the weather stormy; day after day brings into the harbour fresh evidences of the deadly contest that rages out at sea —vessels towed in disabled, with bulwarks washed away, masts over the side, bows stove in, or leaky, having been in collision, touched the ground or been struck by a sea; who at such times can withhold their interest or sympathy? the veriest landsmen grow excited, and make daily pilgrimages to the pier, to see how the vessels under repairs are getting on, or what new disasters have occurred.

But it is at night-time especially that your thoughts take a more solemn and anxious turn. As you settle down by the fireside for a quiet evening, you remember the ugly appearance the sky had some two or three hours before, when you stood watching the scene from the end of the pier. You felt that mischief was brewing, as the gusts of wind swept by with increasing force, and you looked out upon a troubled sea that every minute seemed to grow more white and raging.

The Downs anchorage was full of shipping; a few vessels had parted their cables, and had to run for it, while the luggers, heavily laden with chains and anchors, staggered out of the harbour to supply them : other ships made for the harbour ; you almost shuddered as you looked down upon them from the pier, and saw them in the grasp of the sea, rolling and plunging, with the waves surging over their bows. Another minute's battle with the tide, you heard the orders shouted out, you saw the men rushing to obey them—the pilot steady at the wheel, and you could scarce forbear a cheer as ship after ship shot by the pier-head and found refuge in the harbour.

Altogether it was a wild exciting scene, and you cannot shake off the effect—the wind rushes and moans by, a minute before it was raging over the sea.

The muffled roaring sound that is heard, is that of the waves breaking at the foot of the cliff. From the windows can be seen, gleaming out in the darkness, the bright lights of the Goodwin light-ships, which guard those fatal sands—sands so fatal, that when the graves give up their dead, few churchyards will

render such an account as theirs, not only as to the
number of the dead, but also that the Sands are a
battle-field which entombs the brave and strong, who
go down quick to their grave, quick from the full tide
of life and strength, from the eager stern deadly contest in which, to the last, all their strong energies
were fully engaged.

Men who, a few hours before, were reckless and
merry, anticipating no danger and ready to laugh at the
thought of death ; who, if homeward bound, were full
of joy as they seemed almost to stand upon the threshold of their homes ; or by whom, if outward bound, the
kisses of their wives, which seemed still to linger on
their cheeks, and the soft clasping arms of their little
ones, which seemed still to hang about their necks,
were only to be forgotten in the few hours of terrible
life struggle with the storm, and then again to be
keenly remembered in the last gasping moment, ere
the Goodwin Sands should find them a grave almost
within the shadow of their homes.

There is a sudden report ; surely the firing of a gun,
a wreck, a vessel on the Sands—watch, yes, there ! A
rocket streams up from one of the light-vessels, and
the gun and the rocket five minutes after, form the
signal that calls to the life-boat for assistance. The
breakers on the Sands could be clearly seen from the
shore during the day, as they rose and fell like fitful
volumes of white eddying smoke, breaking up the
clear line of the horizon, and tracing the Sands in
broken broad leaping outlines of foam.

Yes ! and now, amid those terrible breakers, some-

where out in the darkness, within five or six miles,
near that bright light, there are twenty, thirty, fifty,
you know not how many, of your fellow-creatures,
struggling for their lives.

Ah! listen to the storm blast, with what dread
force it rushes by, what a dirge it seems to moan; and
well it may, for if the gale lasts only a few hours, and
there is no rescue, the morning may be bright and
fair and calm, and the sea as smooth as a lake, but
nothing of either ship or crew shall any more be seen.

But, thank God! there will be a rescue! You know
that already brave hearts have determined to attempt
it; that strong ready hands are already at work in
cool, quick, preparation; that, almost before you
could urge your way against the tempest down to the
head of the pier, the steamer and life-boat will have
fought their way out against the storm and darkness
upon their errand of mercy.

"God have mercy upon the poor fellows at sea;
upon the shipwrecked in their dismal peril; upon the
brave Storm Warriors speeding out in danger and
hardship!" this is the prayer that indeed often finds
utterance, when the sleeper is awakened in the dark
hours of the night by the howling of the wind or the
boom of the signal gun. And at Ramsgate the prayer
may be uttered fervently indeed by those, who, when
they hear the signal of distress, know that the endangered vessel is experiencing all the dread dangers
of the Goodwin Sands, for the vessels wrecked upon
them have indeed, if the weather is bad, but a poor
prospect of ever sailing the broad seas again.

The Goodwin is a quick-sand, and it is this, as well as the tremendous sea that beats upon it in heavy weather, that makes it so terribly fatal to vessels that get stranded on it.

At low tide a portion of the sand is dry, and hard, and firm, and can be walked on for a distance of about four or five miles; but as the water again flows over any part of it, that part becomes, as the sailors say, "all alive," soft and quick, and ready to suck in anything that lodges upon it. Suppose a vessel to run on with a falling tide, where the sand shelves, or is steep, the water leaves the bow and the sand there gets hard; the water still flows under the stern, and the sand there remains soft a longer time; down the stern sinks lower and lower; the vessel soon breaks her back, or works herself deeper and deeper by the stern; as the water rises she fills and works and still sinks deeper in the sand every roll she gives, until at high tide she is, perhaps, completely buried, or only her topmasts are seen above water.

Other vessels, if the sea is heavy, begin to beat heavily, and soon break up.

Lifted up on the swell of a huge wave, as it breaks and flies away in surf and foam, the vessel thumps down with all its weight upon the sands, the timbers give and strain, the seams open; she soon ceases, as she fills with water, to rise upon the wave; great gaps are torn from the bulwarks; the decks burst open with the air seeking to escape from the hold, and as the sea rushes over the vessel, each roll she gives wrenches her more and more; the masts fall over the side;

her cargo floats and washes away, and speedily, even in a few hours, she is in a torn and shattered condition, completely wrecked and destroyed. The broken hull is full of water and lurches heavily to and fro with each wave, rolls and slightly lifts and works, until it has made a deep bed in the Sands in which it is soon completely buried—so that many vessels have run upon the Sands in the early night, and scarcely a vestige of them been seen in the morning.

By way of illustration, let me tell what happened one dark stormy night some few years back. The harbour steam-tug *Aid* and the life-boat had started from Ramsgate early in the day, to try and get to the *Northern Belle*, a fine American barque, which was ashore not far from Kingsgate ; but the force of the gale and tide was so tremendous, that they could not make way against it, and were driven back to Ramsgate—there to wait until the tide turned, or the wind moderated.

About two in the morning, while they were making ready for another attempt to reach the *Northern Belle*, rockets were fired from one of the Goodwin light-vessels, showing that some vessel was in distress on the Sands. They hastened at once to afford assistance, and got to the edge of the Sands shortly after three in the morning. Up and down they cruised, but could see no signs of any vessel.

They waited until it was daylight, and then saw the upper portion of the lower mast of a steamer standing out of the water. They made towards it, but found no one was left, and no signs of any wreck floating about to which a human being could cling.

They concluded, that almost immediately upon striking, the vessel must have broken up, sunk, and been buried in the quick-sand. Poor fellows! poor fellows! a sharp, sudden death: would that the vessel had held together a little longer. Away, then, now for the *Northern Belle.*

They had not made much way ahead when the captain of the *Aid* sees a large life-buoy floating near. "Ease her," he cries, and the way of the steamer slackens. "God knows but what that life-buoy may be of use to some of us." The helmsman steers for it; a sailor makes a hasty dart at it with a boat-hook, misses it, and starts back appalled from a vision of staring eyes, and matted hair, and wildly tossed arms. They shout to the life-boat crew, and they in turn steer for the buoy; the bowman grasps at it, catches it, but cannot lift it, his cry of horror startles the whole crew, and some spring to his help; they lift the buoy and bring to the surface three dead bodies that are tied to it by ropes round their waists. Slowly and carefully, one by one, the crew lift them on board, and lay them out under the sail.

The *Violet*, passenger steamer, had left Ostend about eleven the previous night; at two in the morning she struck on the Goodwin Sands; a little after three there was no one left on board to answer the signals of the steam-boat that had come to their rescue, and show their position; at seven there was nothing to be seen of the steamer, crew, or passengers, but a portion of one mast, the life-buoy, and the three pale corpses sleeping their long last sleep under the life-boat sail. Such are the Goodwin Sands.

It was a storm-ridden November day, the weather was very threatening throughout; it was blowing hard, with occasional squalls from the east-north-east, and a heavy sea running. At high tide the sea broke over the east pier. As the waves beat upon it and dashed over in clouds of foam, the pier looked from the east cliff like a heavy battery of guns in full play. The boatmen had been on the look-out all day, but there had been no signs of their services being required; still, they hung about the pier until long after dark.

At last they were straggling home, leaving only those on the pier who had determined to watch during the night, when suddenly some thought that they saw a flash of light. A few seconds of doubt, and the report of the gun decided the matter.

At once there was a rush for the life-boat. She was moored in the stream about thirty yards from the pier. In a few minutes they had unmoored her, and got her alongside; her crew was already more than made up; some had put off to her in small boats, others had sprung into her when she came within a few feet of the pier. She was over-manned, and the two last in had to turn out.

In the meantime, a rocket had been fired from the light vessel. Many had been on the look-out for it, to decide beyond all doubt, which of the three light-vessels had fired the gun. It proved to have been the North Sands Head vessel that had signalled.

The cork jackets were thrown into the boat, the oars and ropes overhauled, all things seen to be right, and the men in their places and ready for their start in a comparatively few minutes. The crew of the steam-tug *Aid* had not been less active. Immediately upon the first signal, her shrill steam-whistle resounded through the harbour, calling on board those of her crew who were on shore, and her steam, which is always up, was rapidly got to full power, and in less than half an hour from the time of the firing of the first gun she was gallantly steaming out of the harbour with the life-boat in tow. As she went out a rocket streamed up from the pier head. It was the answer to the signal of the light vessel, and told that assistance was on the way.

Off they went, ploughing their way through a heavy cross sea, which frequently swept completely over the boat.

The tide was running strongly, and the wind right ahead ; it was hard work breasting both sea and wind in the face of such a gale ; but they bravely persevered, and gradually made head-way.

They steered right for the Goodwin, and having approached it, as near as they dare take the steamer, they worked their way through a heavy sea along the edge of the Sands, on the look-out for the vessel in distress.

At last they make her out, and, as they approach, find two Broadstairs luggers riding at anchor outside the Sands.

The Broadstairs men had heard the signal, and the

wind and tide being in their favour, they soon ran down to the neighbourhood of the wreck. On making to the vessel, the Ramsgate men find her to be a fine-looking brig, almost high and dry upon the Sands.

Her masts and rigging are all right ; the moon, which has broken through the clouds, shines upon her clean new copper ; and, so far, she seems to have received but little damage.

A grand thing for all hands, for owners, under-writers, crew and boatmen, the men think, if they can only get her safely off when the tide rises, and bring her into harbour ; a fine vessel and perhaps valuable cargo saved, and a pretty bit of salvage, which will be well earned and nobody should grudge, for the boat-men have to live, as well as to save life.

Efforts have already been made for the vessel's relief. The *Dreadnought* lugger had brought with her a small twenty-five feet life-boat. The *Little Dreadnought*, and this boat with five hands, had succeeded in getting alongside the brig.

The steamer slips the hawser of the Ramsgate boat, and anchors almost abreast of the vessel, with sixty fathom of chain out.

There is a heavy rolling sea, but much less than there has been, as the tide has fallen considerably. The life-boat makes in for the brig, carries on through the surf and breakers, and when within forty fathoms of the vessel, lowers the sail, throws the anchor over-board, and veers alongside. The captain and some of the men remain in the boat, to fend her off from the sides of the vessel, for although it is shallow water, the tide is running over the Sands like a sluice, and it requires great care to prevent the boat getting her side stove in. The rest of her crew climb on board the brig. Her captain had, until then, hoped to get his vessel off, as the tide rose, without assistance, and had refused the aid of the Broadstairs men ; but now he realizes the danger that his vessel is in, and very gladly accepts the assistance that is offered.

One of his crew speaks a little English, and through him the captain employs the crew of the life-boat and the Broadstairs men, to get his ship off the Sands.

CHAPTER IX.

THE WRECK ABANDONED, AND THE LIFE-BOAT DESPAIRED OF.

"Alone upon the leaping billows, lo!
What fearful image works its way? A ship!
Shapeless and wild . . .
Her sails dishevell'd, and her massy form
Disfigured, yet tremendously sublime:
Prowless and helmless through the waves she rocks,
And writhes, as if in agony! Like her,
Who to the last, amid o'erwhelming foes,
Sinks with a bloody struggle into death,—
The vessel combats with the battling waves,
Then fiercely dives below! the thunders roll
Her requiem, and whirlwinds howl for joy!"

Crabbe.

THE boatmen, as soon as they get on board the brig, find that she is in a very perilous position, but have hopes of getting her off.

At all events they will try very hard for it. She is a fine new and strongly-built Portuguese brig, belonging to Lisbon, and bound from Newcastle to Rio, with coals and iron. Her crew consists of the captain, the mate, ten men, and a boy.

She is head on to the Sand, but the Sand does not shelve much, and her keel is pretty even. The wind is still blowing very strongly and right astern. The tide is on the turn, and will flow quickly: there is no time to be lost; the first effort must be to prevent the brig driving further on the Sand.

With this object in view the boatmen get an anchor out astern as quickly as possible; they rig out tackles on the foreyard, and hoist the bower anchor on deck; they then slew the yard round, and get the anchor as far aft as they can; then shift the tackles to the main yard, and lift the anchor well to the stern; shackle the chain cable on, get it all clear for running out, try the pumps to see that they work; and then wait until the tide makes sufficiently to enable the steamer, which draws six feet of water, to get a little nearer.

They hope that the steamer will be able to back close enough to them, to get a rope on board fastened to the flukes of the brig's anchor, and to drag the anchor out, and drop it about one hundred fathoms astern of the vessel. All hands will then go to the windlass, keep a strain upon the cable, and each time the vessel lifts, heave with a will—the steamer, with a hundred and twenty fathoms of nine-inch cable out, towing hard all the time. By these means they expect to be able, gradually, to work the vessel off the Sands.

But they soon lose all hope of doing this; it is about one o'clock in the morning; the moon has gone down; heavy showers of rain fall; it is pitch dark and very squally; the gale is evidently freshening again; a heavy swell comes up before the wind, and as the tide flows under the brig she begins to work

very much, for now the heavy waves roll in over the
sand, and she lifts, and falls with shocks that make the
masts tremble and the decks gape open.

The boatmen begin to fear the worst.   The life-boat
is alongside, with seven hands in her ; she is afloat in
the basin that the brig has worked in the sands, and
it takes all the efforts of the men on board to prevent
her getting under the side of the vessel and being
crushed.

The wind increases as the tide flows, and the brig
works with great violence, now, as she rolls and careens
over upon her bilge, she threatens to fall upon, and
destroy the life-boat.   The captain of the boat hails
the men on the brig to come on board the boat, and
get away from the side of the vessel as fast as they
can.   The boatmen try to explain the danger to the
Portuguese, but they cannot understand.   Hail, after
hail, comes from the boat, for every moment increases
the peril, but the Portuguese captain still refuses to
leave his vessel.   Any moment may be too late ; the
boatmen are almost ready to try and force the Portuguese over the side, but they cannot persuade them
to stir ; and as they will not desert them, they also
wait on ; wait on while the ship rolls, and works, and
groans, while the seas fly over her, and at any moment
she may break up.   Suddenly a loud sharp crack, like
a crashing of thunder, peals through the ship.

The boatmen jump on the gunwale, ready to spring
for the life-boat, for she may be breaking in half ; no,
but one of her large timbers has snapt like a pipe-
stem, and others will soon follow.

The Portuguese sailors make a rush to get what things they can on deck; altogether they fill eight sea-chests with their clothes. These are quickly lowered into the life-boat. Her captain does not like having her hampered with so much baggage, but cannot refuse the poor fellows, at least, a chance of saving their kit. The surf flies over the brig, and boils up all around her. The life-boat is deluged with spray, and her lights are washed out; the vessel still lifts and thumps and rolls with the force of the sea. Time after time the snapping and rending of her breaking timbers are heard; at each heave she wrenches and cracks and groans in all directions—she is breaking up fast. Make haste, make haste! for your lives be as quick as you can! The chests are all lowered, the boy is handed into the boat, the Portuguese sailors follow, the boatmen spring after them, and the brig is abandoned.

We have said that it was about one o'clock in the morning when the squalls came on again, with heavy rain and thick darkness. The steamer had remained at anchor, waiting for the tide to rise, when, with the water deeper, she would be able to get nearer the brig. But as the gale freshens there is a dangerous broken sea where she is riding, and she begins to pitch very heavily. She paddles gently ahead to ease her cable, but it is soon evident to the men on board her, that if they are to get their anchor at all they must make haste about it.

They heave it up, and lay to for the life-boat.

The sea increases so rapidly that the *Dreadnought*

II

lugger is almost swamped, and has to cut her cable without attempting to save her anchor, and to make with all speed before the gale for Ramsgate. The *Petrel* lugger springs her mast, which is fished with great difficulty, and she, too, makes the best of her way to the harbour.

The wind continues to increase, the gale is again at its height, and a fearful sea running. Wave after wave breaks over the steamer's decks, but she is an excellent boat, strongly built and powerful; and her captain and crew are well used to rough work.

Head to wind and steaming half power, she holds her own against the wind, and keeps, as far as her crew can judge, in the neighbourhood of the wreck and of the life-boat. As time passes, and the crew of the steamer can see nothing of the boat, they get anxious. The wreck must have been abandoned long before this; has the boat been unable to get away from her? is the boat swamped or stove? and are all lost? They signalize again and again, but in vain; they can obtain no answer. They cruize up and down as near the edge of the Sands as they dare, hoping to fall in with the boat. Now they make in one direction, and now in another, as in their eagerness and apprehension the roar of the storm shapes itself into cries of distress, or as a darker shadow on the sea leads them into the hope that at last they have found the lost boat. All hands keep steadfastly on the look-out, and get greatly excited; the storm becomes truly terrible; but they forget their own peril and hardships

in their great anxiety for the safety of the crew of the
life-boat, and of the poor fellows who were on the
wreck.

Their anxiety becomes insupportable, heightened
as it is by the horrors of the night.

Through the thick darkness, the bright light of the
Goodwin light-vessel shines out like a star. With a
faint hope the crew of the steamer wrestle their way
through the storm and speak the light-vessel.

" Have you seen anything of the life-boat ?" the
captain of the steamer shouts out. "Nothing! nothing!"
is the answer. It seems to confirm all their fears, and
they hasten back again to their old cruising ground—
they will not lessen their exertions, or lose any chance
of rendering assistance to their comrades. It is still
pitch-dark, and the storm rages on—the hours creep
by, O how slowly !

How they long for the light ! All hands still on the
watch ! and as the first grey light of dawning comes,
it is with straining eye-balls they seek to penetrate
the twilight, and find some signs of their lost comrades.
It is almost broad daylight before they can even find
out the place where the wreck was lying.

With all speed, but little hope, they make for it ;
and then indeed their great dread seems realized.
The brig is completely broken up, literally torn to
pieces. They can see great masses of timber, and
tangled rigging, but no signs of life. Nearer and
nearer they go and wait for the broad daylight ; but
still nothing is to be seen, but shattered pieces of
wreck, moored fast by the matted rigging to the

buried remains of the hull, and tossing and heaving in the surf.

Some of the men fancy they can see fragments of the life-boat heaving about with the other wreckage, but whether it is so or not, the end seems the same, and after one last careful but fruitless look around, to see whether there are any signs of the life-boat elsewhere on the Sands, sadly they turn the steamer's head away from the dreary fatal Goodwin, and make for the harbour.

They grieve for brave comrades tried in many scenes of danger, and think with faint hearts of the melancholy report they have to give, and it is but little consolation to them in the face of so great a loss, to remember that they, at all events, have done all in their power, and that they have nothing to reproach themselves with.

To return to the life-boat men; all hands have deserted the brig, and there are now in the life-boat thirteen Portuguese sailors, five Broadstairs boatmen, and her ordinary crew, consisting of thirteen Ramsgate boatmen, altogether thirty-one souls. The small *Dreadnought* life-boat has been swung against the brig by the force of the tide, and is so damaged that no one dares venture in her. The tide is rising fast, the gale blowing as hard as ever, the surf running very high and breaking over the vessel, so that one constant torrent of spray and foam is falling with no light weight, or small volume, upon the life-boat which is under the lee of the brig, and the men have no protection from the falling sheets of spray. The

vessel is rolling heavily, she has worked a bed in the
sands, which the run of tide has somewhat enlarged,
and in this she half floats, rolling from side to side
with fearful rapidity and violence.

The life-boat is afloat within the circle of the bed ;
the brig threatens to roll over her. " Shove and haul
off, quick! Shove and haul off," are the orders.   Some
with oars, pushing against the brig, others hauling
might and main upon the brig's hawser, they manage
to pull the boat two or three yards up towards the
boat's anchor, and to get her a little farther off from
the side of the brig. Now she grounds heavily upon the
edge of the basin that has been worked in the sand by the
brig. " Strain every muscle, men ; now, or never ! now,
or never ! for your lives pull !" and pull and strain they
did. No! not one inch will the life-boat stir ; she falls
over on her side, the surf and seas sweep over her, the
men cling to the thwarts and gunwale ; all but her
own crew give up all thoughts of hope ; but they know
the capabilities of the boat and do not lose heart—
Crash ! the brig heaves, and crushes down upon her
bilge ; again and again she half lifts upon an even
keel and rolls, and lurches from side to side ; each
time that she falls to leeward, she comes more and
more over and nearer to the boat.

This is the danger that may well make the stoutest
heart quail.   The boat is aground — helplessly
aground ; her crew can see through the darkness of
the night the yards and masts of the brig swaying
over their heads ; now tossing high in the air as
the brig rights, and now falling nearer and nearer

to them, sweeping down over their heads, swaying
and rending in the air, the blocks, and ropes, and torn
fragments of sails, flying wildly in all directions. Let
but one of the swaying yards but hit the boat, she
must be crushed and all lost. The men crouch down
closer and closer, clinging to the thwarts as the brig
falls to them ; casting dread glances at the approaching yards ; all right once more ; another pull at the
cable—hard, men, hard ; over again comes the brig ;
stick to it, men, stick to it, my men ; crushed or drowned
it will be soon over if we cannot move the boat ;
another pull, all together ; again, and again, they make
desperate efforts to stir the boat, but she will not
move one inch ; they must wait, and if needs be, wait
their doom ; and as they wait the danger each moment
increases.

It is a fearful time of suspense, this waiting aground
on the dread Goodwin, in the darkness and wildness of the storm, half dead with cold and the
ceaseless rush of surf over them, and watching in
the shadowy darkness the swaying masts of the
rolling brig, swinging nearer and nearer, and how will
this question of life and death be decided ? Which
will happen first ? will the tide flow sufficiently to
float them, or will the brig crush them with her
masts and yards before they can get beyond her
reach.

The men can do nothing more in the dark wild night
and terrible danger ; each minute seems an hour ; they
almost forget to try and protect themselves from the
wind and spray, and they watch the brig as if spell-

bound, as she rolls nearer and nearer; each moment
the position gets more desperate.

Any one hit? as the flying blocks hanging from the
yard-arms rattle over the heads of the men in the boat.
No! but a few feet nearer and we should all have
been crushed—a turn or two more and we shall be
finished. There is a stir among the men; the moment
seems come; they prepare for the last struggle. Some
are getting ready to spring for the flying rigging of
the brig, as it sways over their heads, hoping thus to
get on board the wreck if the life-boat is crushed up.
"Stick to the boat, men! stick to the boat, men, it's
our only chance," the coxswain cries out, "the brig must
soon go to pieces, while we may yet get clear; stick to
the boat!" And the brig, which had quivered while
lying on her side as if coming bodily over, while the
dark yards hovered over the crouching men, lifted
again, and once more the men breathe with a sigh of
relief; for that time they quite expected the boat to
be crushed and pinned where she lay.

At this moment the boat trembles beneath them,
lifts a little on the swell of the tide that is beginning
to reach her, and grounds again.

It is like a word of life to the men, and instantly
all are on the alert, they get all their strength on the
hawser, and as the boat lifts again, and comes a little
more on an even keel, they draw her a yard or two
nearer to her anchor, but not any farther from the
brig, and over again the brig slowly rolls; again
and again they make desperate efforts to get beyond
the reach of her dark side, and swinging yards

and masts, but it is long before they can do so : at last they succeed as the water flows still more, and now they ride to their anchor a few yards beyond the reach of the brig, which they watch break up, and listen to the groaning and rending of her timbers, and the flapping of her torn sail and tangled rigging. Both the wind and tide are setting with all their force right upon the Sands, and the captain of the boat sees what is before them ; where they are now at anchor will soon be one wild rage of broken sea. To get away from the sand in the face of the fierce gale and tide is impossible ; and so there is no alternative, they must beat right across the Sands, and this in the wild fearful gale, and terrible sea, and pitch dark night, and what the danger of this is, only those who know the Goodwin Sands, and the dread seas that sweep over them, can at all imagine.

They ride at anchor for some time, waiting for the tide to rise sufficiently for them to get over the Sands. They see the lights of the steamer shining in the distance, outside the broken and shallow water ; but there is no hope of assistance from her : their lanterns are washed out, they cannot signalize ; and if they could, the steamer could not approach them.

The sea is breaking furiously over them. Time after time the boat fills as the broken waves wash clean over her, but instantly she empties herself again, and rises to her water-line. The gale sweeps by more fiercely than ever. The men are nearly washed out of the boat, and worse still, the anchor begins to drag. The tide has made a little, and they are being driven each moment nearer to the wreck; there may be water enough to take them clear; at all events, there is no help for it, they must risk it. "Hoist the foresail; stand by to cut the cable. All clear."—"Ay, Ay!"— "Away then."

And the boat quickly heads round, and then, under the power of the gale and tide, leaps forward, flies along; but only for a few yards, when, with a tremendous jerk, she grounds upon the Sands. The crew look up, and their hearts almost fail them, as they find that they are again within reach of the brig.

Her top-gallant masts are swaying about, her yards swing within a few feet of them, her sails which have blown loose and are in ribbons, beat and flap like thunder over their heads. Their position seems worse than ever; but they are not this time kept long in suspense. A huge breaker comes foaming along; its white crest gleams out in the darkness high above them, a moment's warning, it breaks over them and swamps them, but all are clinging might and main to the boat.

Another breaker comes streaming along; it swamps them again in passing, but now the volume of the wave seizes the boat, up it seems to swing it in its mighty arms, and to bodily hurl it forward; and then the boat crashes down on the Sands as the wave breaks, and grounds them with a shock that would have torn every man out of her, if they had not been holding on.

But one great peril is passed; the mighty swing of the huge waves has carried them yards forward, and

they are clear of the wreck ; but at that moment they
are threatened with another danger almost as terrible.
The small *Dreadnought* life-boat has been in tow
all this time ; it has not been wise to have her in tow,
but she belongs to the Broadstairs boatmen, and
neither they nor the Ramsgate boatmen like to abandon her.

As the Ramsgate boat now grounds, the smaller
boat comes bow on to her, sweeps round, and gets
under her side ; the two boats roll and crash together ;
each roll the larger one gives, each lift of the sea, she
comes heavily down on the other boat ; the crash and
crack of timbers are heard ; which boat is it that is
breaking up ? Both, if this continues, must be very
speedily destroyed. Some of the men get out the
oars and boat-hooks, and push for their very lives,
thrusting and striving their utmost to free the
Dreadnought, which is so dangerously thumping and
crashing under the quarter of the larger boat. It is a
terrible struggle in that boiling sea, with the surf
breaking over them. But all their efforts seem in
vain, the boats still crash and roll together ; one of
them is breaking up fast. "Oars in," shouts the
coxswain ; "over the side half-a-dozen of you—take
your feet to her ;" and some of the brave fellows spring
over, clinging to the rail of the deck of the high air-
boxes that are at the bow and stern of the Ramsgate
life-boat. Again and again, all together, a fierce
struggle, but without success ; a big wave comes rolling
on, it washes over them, but as the larger boat lifts,
the men blindly thrust out with their feet, and the

Dreadnought is pushed clear. The men scramble, or are dragged back into the Ramsgate boat; the tow-rope is cut, and the *Dreadnought*, almost a wreck, is swept away by the tide, and is lost in the darkness, while, most mercifully, the Ramsgate boat still remains uninjured.

A third time they are providentially saved from what seemed almost like certain death; and yet they have only commenced the beginning of their troubles, for is there not before them the long range of sands, with the broken fierce waves and raging surf, and many a fragment of wreck, like sunken rocks studded here and there, upon any one of which, if they strike, it must be death to them all?

The boat is still aground upon the ridge of sand. She lifts, and is swept round, and grounds again broadside to the sea, which makes a clean breach over her. The Portuguese are all clinging together under the lee of the foresail, and there is no getting them to move. The crew are holding on where they can; sometimes buried in the water, often with only their heads out. The captain is standing up in the stern, holding on by the mizen-mast; sometimes he can see nothing of the men as the surf sweeps over them. He orders the chests to be thrown overboard, but most of them are already washed away; the rest are unlashed from their fastenings, and lifted as the men can get at them, and the next wave carries them away. Heavy masses of cloud darken the sky; the rain falls in torrents; it is bitterly cold; the men can do nothing but hold on; the tide rises gradually;

suddenly the boat lifts again ; it is caught by the
driving sea, and is flung forward.   There is no
keeping her straight, the water is too broken ; her
stern frees itself before the bow, and round she
swings ; her bow lifts a little ; onward she goes a few
yards, and grounds again by the stern ; round sweeps
the bow, and with another jerk she comes broadside
on the Sands again, lurching over on her side, with the
terrible surf making a clean sweep over the waist.   It
is a struggle for the men to get their breath, the spray
beats over them in such clouds.   This happens time
after time.   The captain calls the men aft, that the
boat may be lightened in the bow, and thus be more
likely to keep straight.   Most of the boatmen come
to the stern, but the Portuguese will not move, and
even some of the boatmen are so exhausted with the
violent exertions they have made, and by the beating
of the waves, that they are almost unconscious, and
only able to cling to the gunwale and thwarts of the
boat with an iron, nervous grasp, and are thus just
able to save themselves from being washed out of
her.   As the coxswain notices their exhausted state,
he expects each time as the big waves wash over
them to see some of them leave go their hold and be
carried away ; and although he makes as light of it
as he can, and tries to cheer them up, he himself has
very small hope of ever seeing land again.

The sands on the sea shore, if there has been any
surf, appear at low tide uneven with the ridges or
ripples the waves have left on them.   On the Good-
wins, where the force of the sea is in every way

multiplied, and the waves break and the tide rushes
with tenfold power, the little sand ripples of the
smoother shore become ridges of two or three feet
high.

It is on these ridges that the life-boat so continually grounds. As the tide rises she is swept from
one to the other by the long sweeping waves ; she is
swung round and round in the swirl of the cross-
seas and rapid tide, thumping and jerking heavily
each time that she strands. All this is in the midst
of darkness, of bitter cold, and of a raging wind, surf,
and sea, until the hardship and peril are almost too
much to be borne, and some of the men feel dying in
the boat.

One old boatman afterwards thus described his feelings. "Well, sir, perhaps my friends were right when
they said I hadn't ought to have gone out—that I was
too old for that sort of work "—he was then about sixty
years of age—" but, you see, when there is life to be
saved, it makes one feel young again ; and I've always
felt I have had a call to save life when I could ; and I
wasn't going to hang back then ; and I stood it better
than some of them after all. I did my work on board
the brig, and when she was so near falling over us,
and when the *Dreadnought* life-boat seemed knocking our bottom out, I got on as well as any of them ;
but when we got to beating, and grubbing over the
Sands, swinging round and round, and grounding every
few yards with a jerk that bruised us sadly, and almost
tore our arms out from the sockets—no sooner washed
off one ridge, and beginning to hope that the boat was

clear, than she thumped upon another harder than ever, and all the time the wash of the surf nearly carrying us out of the boat—it was truly almost too much for any man to stand. There was a young fellow holding on next to me; I saw his head begin to drop, and that he was getting faint, and going to give over; and when the boat filled with water, and the waves went over his head, he scarcely cared to struggle free. I tried to cheer him a bit, and keep his spirits up. He just clung to the thwart like a drowning man. Poor fellow, he never did a day's work after that night, and died in a few months.

"Well, I couldn't do anything with him, and I thought that it didn't matter much, for I felt it must soon all be over; that it couldn't be long before the boat would be knocked to pieces. So I took my life-belt off, that I might have it over all the quicker; for I knew that there would be no chance whatever of life if the boat once went, and I would have it over all the quicker, for I didn't want to be beating about those sands alive or dead longer than I could help; the sooner I went to the bottom, the better, I thought. When once all hope of life was over—and that time seemed close upon us every moment—some of us kept shouting, just cheering ourselves and one another up, as well as we could; but I had to give that up, and I remember hearing the captain crying out, 'We will see Ramsgate yet again, my men, if we steer clear of old wrecks.' And then I heard the Portuguese lad crying, and I remember that I began to think that it was a terrible dream, and pinched

myself to see if I was really awake ; and I began to
feel very strange and insensible. I didn't feel afraid
of death, for, you see, I hadn't left it to such times as
that to prepare to meet my God. And if ever I spent
hours in prayer, be sure I spent them in prayer that
night. And I just seemed going off in a kind of dead
faint, and felt very dream-like, and as if I couldn't
hold on any longer ; and as I felt this I thought, in a
feeble sort of way, of my friends ashore, and bid them
good-bye like, for I knew that I should be soon
washed out of the boat, when I looked up, and the
surf was curling up both sides of the boat, and I
was going to throw myself down on the thwart, that
the seas might beat upon my back, and I should
never have lifted it up again, when I saw a bright
star. The clouds had broken a little, and there was
that blessed beautiful star shining out. Yes, truly it
was a blessed beautiful star to me ; as it caught my
eye it seemed, in my weak state, to lay a strange hold
upon me ; to gather all my attention, and to call me
back to life again. And I began to have a little
thought about seeing my home again, and that I
wasn't going to be called away just yet. And I
straightened myself up a little, and laid a firmer hold
upon the boat, and lifted my head to look for the
star after each time the seas beat over us, and I kept
my eye upon it whenever I could ; and I cannot
explain how it was, but looking for and watching that
star kept me up, and when I got ashore, I seemed at
first not much worse than the best of them. But for
seven whole days after that I lost my speech, and lay

like a log upon my bed ; and I was ill a long time—
indeed, have never been right since, and I suppose at
my age I never shall get over it.   But what is more,
I believe something of the same sort may be said of
most of those that were in the boat that night.   One
poor young fellow is dead, another has been subject
to fits ever since, and not any of us quite the men we
were before, and no wonder when you think what we
passed through.

"I cannot describe it, and you cannot, neither can
any one else ; but when you say you've beat and
thumped over those sands, almost yard by yard, in a
fearful storm on a winter's night, and live to tell the
tale, why it seems to me about the next thing to
saying that you've been dead, and brought to life
again."

The coxswain of the life-boat, brave Isaac Jarman,
was chosen for that position for his fortitude, skill,
and daring, and well did he sustain his character that
night, never for one moment losing his presence of
mind, and doing his utmost to cheer the men up.
The crew consisted of hardy, daring fellows, ready to
face any danger, to go out in any storm, and to do
battle with the wildest seas ; but the horrors of that
night were almost too much for the most iron nerves.

The fierce freezing wind, the almost pitch darkness,
the terrible surf, and beating waves, and the men
unable to do anything for their safety ; the boat driven,
almost hurled, by the force of the waves from sand
ridge to sand ridge, and apparently breaking up
beneath them each time she lifted on the surf and

crushed down again upon the Sands, besides the danger of her getting foul of any old wrecks—how all this was lived through seemed miraculous. Time after time there was a cry of " Now she breaks up! she can't stand this! all over at last!" Another such thump, and she is done for, and then the boat would writhe, almost on her beam ends, while the waves beat over, until she was again lifted and thrown forward to crash down and ground again ; and all this lasted for about two hours, as almost yard by yard they beat from ridge to ridge over the sands.

Suddenly the swinging and beating of the boat cease ; she is in a very heavy sea, but she answers her helm and keeps her head straight. At last they have got over the Sands and into deep water ; the danger is passed, and they are saved. With new hopes comes new life. Some can scarcely realize their comparative safety, and still keep their firm hold upon the boat, expecting each second another terrible lurch and jerk upon the Sands, and the heavy rush and wash of the seas. No : that is all over, and the boat, in spite of her tremendous knocking about, is sound, and sails buoyantly and well.

The crew quickly get further sail upon her, and she makes way before the gale to the westward. The Portuguese sailors lift their heads. They have been clinging together and to the boat, crouching down under the lee of the foresail during the time of beating over the Sands ; they notice the stir among the boatmen, and that the terrible jerking and thumping of the boat and the rush of sea over her have ceased ;

I

and they also learn that the worst is passed, and that the danger is at an end.

Long since did they despair of life ; and their surprise and joy now know no bounds. Bravely on goes the life-boat, making for the westward. The Portuguese are very busy in earnest consultation. The poor fellows have lost their kit, and only possess the things they have on, and a few pounds that they have with them. Soon it becomes evident what the consultation has been about. "Coxswain!" one of the boatmen cries out, "they want to give us all their money!"

"Yes! yes!" said the interpreter, in broken English, "you have saved our lives! Thank you! thank you! but all we have is yours; it is not much, but you take it between you ;" and he held out the money. It was about 17*l.*

"I, for one, won't touch any of it," said the coxswain of the boat. "Nor I !" "Nor I !" others added ; put your money up."

The brave fellows will not take a farthing from brother sailors, whom they know to be poor, much like themselves ; and in a few words they make them understand this, and how glad they are to have saved them.

The life-boat makes good way, and soon runs across the Sands through the Trinity Swatch Way, and, without further adventure, she reaches the harbour about five o'clock in the morning. The crew of the brig are placed under the care of the Portuguese Consul, and the boatmen go to their homes, to feel for

many a long day the effects of the fatigues and perils
of that terrible night.

During all this time the steamer has been cruising
up and down the edge of the Sands, vainly searching
for any trace of the life-boat; and soon after daylight
she made, as has been already described, for the
harbour.   Her captain and crew are half broken-
hearted, and scarcely know how they shall be able to
tell the tale of the terrible calamity that seems so
certainly to have happened.   Suddenly, as the mouth
of the harbour opens to them, they see the life-boat.
They stare with amazement, and can scarcely believe
their eyes.   "Astonished," said the captain of the
steamer, describing his feelings, "that I was; never so
much so in my life, as when I stood looking at that boat.
I could have shouted and cried for very wonder and
joy; you might have knocked me down with a straw."
Thus the captain of the steamer described his feelings.
It was the same with all the crew; and as the steamer
shot round the pier and heard that all were saved, and
the life-boatmen all right, the good news seemed
to more than repay them for the dangers and anxieties
of the night.

Thus did the crew of the gallant life-boat and of the
steamer help to earn that night the noble reputation
that belongs to our boatmen and sailors at large—
testimony to which was given, on one occasion, by
a foreign captain, who said, "Ah! we may always
know whether it is upon the English coast that we are
wrecked, by the efforts that are made for our rescue."

CHAPTER X.

SIGNALS OF DISTRESS—OUT IN THE STORM.

> " And the coming wind did roar more loud,
> And the sails did sigh like sedge ;
> And the rain poured down from one black cloud,
> The moon was at its edge.
> The thick black cloud was cleft, and still
> The moon was at its side ;
> Like water shot from some high crag,
> The lightning fell with never a jag,
> A river steep and wide."
>
> *Coleridge.*

WILD weather on land! wild weather at sea! fear
and trembling, and earnest prayers, in many a quiet
home, for loved ones at sea, who must be within reach
of the gale that hurries so fiercely by.

How impressive it is to lie awake listening to the
storm—to hear the rush of the wind, now moaning in
the chimney, now thundering at the windows against
which the rain beats and hurtles ; to fancy or to feel
that the house trembles shaken in the rude power
of the blast, or, if near the sea-shore, to hear the
waves breaking on the beach, a half-suppressed
tumultuous uproar, like the faintly heard riot of a

distant angry mob. To get farther to sea in one's thoughts, and to picture a noble ship with close-reefed topsails running before the gale, or beating away from the dread neighbourhood of dangerous sands or coast, while the pilot, anxious and watchful, and the crew, eager and alert, peer through the darkness to catch the welcome guidance of some bright warning light, or are on the watch to detect the fainter light of some ship that is steering her course perilously near ; the passengers all the time wistful and anxious, asking many questions, and receiving cheering answers, but given with that unreality of tone that makes the hearer fear the sound, more than he can believe the sense ; or to imagine a vessel at anchor, the cables swinging out at their full length, the sails all closely furled, but the gale beating against the hull, and masts, and yards, with a power that threatens to sweep the ship and her living freight to a speedy destruction ; to picture the ship lifting, and pitching, and surging, in a cloud of spray, the hungry waves leaping at it, as if to devour it before its time, the anchors yielding foot by foot, or the cable giving, and the hungry sands waiting in a terrible rage of foam and sea under the lee.

In the morning to look from tall cliffs upon a golden beach, upon the fretting surf that lines it, upon the sea bright with sunshine, smooth browed, but like a great giant rolling his huge limbs in uneasy sleep ; quick with great billows rising and falling in restless heavy long lines of waves. Then to look at the distant Goodwin Sands, and to watch the white leaping surf, fangs in the jaws of death, still gnashing

and mumbling after their midnight meal, in which
they ravened perhaps on a goodly ship, and mangled
many brave sailors, and weeping women and trembling wondering children ; unless their victims were
snatched from their grasp by the brave Storm
Warriors who rush into their midst in the very fiercest
of their strife, and wrestle with them for their prey.

Such pictures are often suggested by the midnight
gale, and such after-scenes are witnessed in the morning's calm at Ramsgate, as at many another spot on
the bold coast of our sea-girt island home, where each
howling wind that rushes on breathes the trumpet-
blast that calls to the struggle of life and death.

It was a tempestuous wintry day early in December,
a few years ago, when the scenes occurred which the
following will be an attempt to describe :

During the whole of the day the wind has been
blowing hard from the west-north-west. The weather
has been very unsettled for some little time, squally
with the cloud-scud low, and swiftly flying past ; now
the weather is becoming worse, and the blasts are
more frequent and more fierce, rapidly growing into
a heavy gale. The Fitzroy's signal hangs ominously
from the flag-staff, giving a warning of the dangerous
winds which may be expected.

The Downs anchorage is crowded with shipping,
so much so, that the lights of the vessels anchored
there throw a glare upon the darkness of the night,
such as is shed by the lights of a populous town.

Every now and then a vessel leaves the fleet, and,
running before the gale, seeks surer refuge ; or perhaps

a homeward-bound ship swiftly threads her way
through the crowd of vessels, the crew half rejoicing
in the gale, which at every blast bears them nearer
home.

On Ramsgate Pier rumours of disasters at sea, bring
the watchful lookers on together in anxious gossip ;
many partially disabled vessels have already found
refuge in the harbour, and now a schooner is brought
in by some Broadstairs boatmen.   When they boarded
her in answer to her signals of distress, they found
that the mate with a woman and child alone remained
on board.   The schooner had been in collision during
the previous night, and whether the rest of her crew
had escaped to the other vessel, or had been lost
overboard, was left a matter of dread uncertainty.

As it is a stirring sight to see the vessels making
through the heavy seas for the harbour, so it is an
exciting, and withal a gallant, sight to watch the
luggers heavily freighted with anchors and chains, to
supply vessels that have slipped their cables, bearing
away bravely in all the rush of the storm, upon their
errands of daring enterprise.

The afternoon creeps on ; it is half-past three, a puff
of smoke is seen coming from the Gull light-ship, but
the wind is too strong, and in the wrong direction, for
the report of the gun to be heard.   The signal is,
however, at once accepted, and soon the steamer and
the life-boat are away in the storm.

They make for the light-vessel to learn for what,
and in which direction their services are required.   A
squall of thick rain hides the Downs and the south

end of the Goodwin Sands from view. Suddenly the
squall clears away, passing rapidly to windward, and
now from the pier and cliff, although not yet from the
lower level of the steamer's deck, or from the life-boat,
the vessel that is in danger is seen.

A large light schooner has driven from her anchorage, and is now dragging perilously near the Goodwin
Sands. She is too near, with the wind as it is, to have
any chance of escaping by slipping her cable and sailing clear of the Sands ; she is driving fast, and the
large flag, that she has hoisted as a signal of distress,
can be very distinctly seen from the cliff. The
watchers on shore, by taking her bearings, see how
rapidly she is dragging her anchors and nearing her
doom ; and the nature of the tremendous sea she is in
is also very evident.

She is light, buoyant, and lifts to every wave ; she
looks like a gallant charger taking a succession of
desperate leaps, as first her bow is thrown high in the
air, and she then rides for a moment high upon the
top of the wave, and then again her stern is thrown
high, and her bow is almost buried as the huge short
wave passes under her. Repeatedly those who are
watching her from the shore, have their fears aroused
that her straining cables have at last parted, and that
she is in full career for the waiting deadly Sands. It
is an alarming sight. The lookers-on from the cliff
only take their eyes off her to look occasionally at the
steamer and life-boat as they are making their way to
her rescue.

The steamer rolls and plunges on—nothing daunted,

nothing disturbed, by all the buffeting she gets ; the
life-boat rises like a cork to every wave, and plunges
through the crests as she feels the drag of the steamer,
while the foam spreads out on either side like a fan,
and the scud and spray fly over her in a cloud.

The steamer and life-boat make their way to the
Gull Lightship, where they learn that a schooner has
been seen in distress, bearing south-south-west, supposed to be on the South Sand Head.

On through the giant seas and driving surf, in the very
teeth of the gale, they make gallant way, and are about
to take up a position from which the life-boat can dash
in through the broken water to the rescue of the crew.

A large Deal lugger is beating up to windward from
the neighbourhood of the Sands, they speak her, and
learn that she has rescued the crew of the schooner.

The lugger, one of the finest of all the noble boats
that sail from Deal beach, had, some time before the
schooner got into such a dangerous position, sheered
alongside her, at no slight risk, and as she shot by,
the crew had jumped into her, forgetting in their
hurry and excitement the flag of distress which they
had left flying high, pleading still, and not in vain, for
help that was no longer needed. Nothing can be
done for the schooner ; driving fast, she soon begins to
thump on the Sands ; darkness settles down upon her,
the fierce waves have her for their prey, and in the
morning not one remaining fragment of her is to be
seen ; she has been torn utterly to pieces, and what
the tide has not swept away, the Sands have completely
buried.

The steamer and life-boat, when they leave the
schooner to her fate, make for a barque, which, with
main and mizen masts cut away, seems, although she
is in great danger, to have a chance of weathering the
storm.

The wind is too heavy, and the tide too strong, for
the steamer to be able to tow her into a safer
position ; her crew have already made their escape,
and she is left in turn, but not, as it proves, to meet
the fate of the schooner, for she successfully rides out
the gale.

A further cruise round the Sands, to see if their
services are required by any distressed vessel, and
they make again for Ramsgate, which they reach
about half-past six. The steamer and life-boat are
moored, ready for any fresh call which may be made
for their services, the probability of which seems very
great, and all the men remain on the alert.

In such a storm anxious watchers are on the look-
out at all the stations round the coast. Boatmen
under the protection of boat-houses, or boats, or
grouped together at friendly corners, are keeping a
steadfast watch upon the seas. One or two every now
and then take a few strides into the open for a wider
range of view, and then back again to cover. The
coastguard-men, sheltered in nooks of the cliff, or
behind rocks, or breasting the storm on the drear
Sands as they walk their solitary beat, peer out into
the darkness watching for those signals from the sea—
the gun flash, or the gleam of the rocket, which while
they speak hope to the imperilled, tell to those

on shore of lives in danger—of those who must speedily be rescued, or must die.

Or the watchers listen for the dull throb of the signal gun, the sign of wild warfare, and struggles for life mid the charges and conflicts of breaking waves and dashing seas, a signal that the waiting Storm Warriors instantly accept, and rush into the contest to snatch their dying brethren from the arms of the enemy that is too strong for them.

Sometimes the telegraph wires speed the message of distress along the coast, as happened one stormy New Year's Eve, when a ship was seen off Deal beach in almost a blaze of light, burning tar-barrels, and firing rockets to tell of her distress ; an intervening fog seemed to prevent the look-out on board the light-vessel seeing her, and some boatmen on Deal beach, who could not possibly get their boats off the sands in the face of the strong gale blowing straight on shore, put their halfpence together to pay for a telegraph message—the messages were dearer then than they are now—and sent their swiftest runner to telegraph to Ramsgate ; and after all, there was some unfortunate mistake, and fatal delay, and a telegram at last sent for further particulars, which was answered with a demand for urgent speed, and away then flew steamer and life-boat, and they neared the wreck, and rounded to, to send the life-boat in, when some of the boatmen thought they heard an agonising shriek, and others thought it was only the wail of the storm ; but they looked, and the great green seas swept over the wreck, turned her right over, and she

was seen no more, and twenty-eight lives went to
their account. A piteous New Year's tale it was
that was told next morning ; a boat's crew got away
from the ship soon after she struck, and battling
through the broken seas, made way before the wind
to Dover, and they told the story, that the lost vessel
had picked up a shipwrecked crew, who were thus
a second time wrecked, and at the second time
lost ; and that more of the crew would have come
away in the boat, and in other boats, but it was a
great risk, and there was a Deal pilot on board
who pointed out the danger; and said that the
Ramsgate life-boat was certain to be out to their
rescue, they might be sure of her ; and so they stayed
and lighted tar-barrel after tar-barrel, and fired rocket
after rocket ; and when the sea washed their signal
fires out, and swept the decks, they took to the
rigging, and waited for the life-boat ; and as they
waited the poor Deal pilot could watch the light
on the beach, by the house where slept his wife
and eight children, who were to call him husband—
father—no more.

The life-boat men scarcely liked to speak of the
agony and disappointment it was to them to be thus
just too late ; no fault of theirs, poor fellows ; they
would, if they could, have sooner swum to the wreck,
if that were of any use, than have been too late to
save the poor perishing lives.

There was an official inquiry into the matter made
by the authorities in London, and it was decided that
no one was to blame ; that it was one of those unfortu-

nate occurrences which never would have happened, like many others, if people could only be as wise before an event as they are after, and which no one could regret more than those who were in any way the unfortunate, and of course most unintentional, agents of bringing it about.

And now to proceed with the adventures of the life-boat on the night in question.

About a quarter past eight in the evening, the harbour-master of Ramsgate receives a telegram. It tells its tale in its own short way, and the harbour-master learns that round the stormy North Foreland, some miles to westward of Margate, the *Prince's* light-ship is firing guns and rockets, and that the *Tongue* light-ship is repeating the signals.

The vigilant coastguard-man who had first noticed the signals hurried to Margate with the tidings ; but there the fine life-boats are powerless to help. The wind is blowing a hurricane from west-north-west, and drives such a tremendous sea upon the shore that no boat whatever could possibly get off and work its way out to sea ; it would merely be rolled back upon the beach in the attempt.

The coastguard at Margate at once saw how impossible it would be to render the required aid from Margate, and hastened to send a telegram to Ramsgate calling for help. The harbour-master there receives it, and now hurried action at once takes the place of wistful anxious waiting.

For hours the steamer and life-boat have quietly rested in the sheltered harbour, lifting gently to the small waves that have been playing against their sides. The men for hours have been gazing out into the darkness, watching for signals, and listening to the roar of the gale, and to the murmur and tumult of the tumbling waves. The expected challenge comes. Ready! all ready! is the answer, and they rush to action at once, without waiting for one moment to consider whether a challenge to such strife should, or should not, be accepted.

They know the hardships and peril of the work upon which they are called; but they know the other side of the question also; and it would make many comparatively useless lives as noble as are the lives of many of these poor boatmen, if all would only consider the result of good work, as well as the labour, and forget the trouble, or personal hardships of the labour, in the keen hope to realize the desired result. And these boatmen, as they have been crouching down under shelter of the pier wall, watching the progress of the storm, have had many a memory, and many a vision, to occupy their thoughts and stir their anxious courage; memories of brave fellows plucked from the very grasp of death; and visions of that which they well know how to picture; brother sailors perhaps clinging to the spars of a shattered wreck, while the wild waves leap around and only a few fragments of creaking yielding timber shield the poor men from their fury, and from death.

They know the power of the waves to tear the strongest ships to pieces in a few hours, and are ready, all ready, for any stern deadly wrestle with the fury of

the storm, for the rescue of those who stand in such
dread need of help.

The order is given, and the usual rush to the life-
boat takes place.

The regular Ramsgate boatmen have not, this
time, the race for the boat all to themselves ; the
Adder revenue-cutter is in the harbour, and two
of her men get into the life-boat, and with ten boatmen and the coxswain, the crew is made up. The
men on board the steam-tug *Aid* are prompt as
usual, and within half-an-hour from the giving of the
order the steamer and life-boat are out to the rescue,
again fighting their way through broken seas, and
breasting the full fury of the gale.

Imagine the picture that was shrouded in the thick
darkness of that wild night.

The steamer is strong and powerfully built, and
has never failed in any of her struggles with the
storm, but has in every part worked true and well ;
and this when failure in crank, rod, or rivet, might
have been death to many lives. Seek to imagine
this brave little steamer at her perilous work. Thrown
up and down like a plaything by the mighty sea, now
half buried in the wash of surf, or poised for a
moment on the broad crest of a huge wave, and again
shooting bows under into the trough, rolling and
pitching and staggering in the storm, but still battling
on true to her purpose. Still onward and onward
she goes ; the beat of the paddles, the roar of the
steam-pipe, the throb of the engines, mingling with
the hoarse blast of the gale, and the lash and hiss of

the surf and fleeting spray; while to the watchers on shore, her light flitting here and there as she rolls and tosses, alone tell of her progress.

The life-boat is almost burrowing her way through the spray and foam. Each man bends low on his seat, and holds fast by thwart or gunwale. The wind has changed, and the boat is being towed in the face of the gale and sea, and does not ride over the waves as easily as she would if she were under canvas only, but is dragged on and on, plunging through the crests of the seas. "It was just like as if a fire-engine was playing upon my back, not in a steady stream, but with a great burst of water at every pump," said one of the men whose station was in the bow.

It is a wild sea; the waves and surf that break against the bows of the big ships that are at anchor in the Downs send their spray flying high, almost to the topmast heads; so it may well be imagined how the heavy seas nearly smother the steamer and life-boat as they breast all their force, heading against the gale. Now the waves rush over the bow, and again a cross wave catches the side of the boat, throws her almost on her side, sweeps bodily over her; while she pitches and rolls with a motion quick as that of a plunging horse. But the men know her well, and trust her thoroughly; and with a firm hold and stout hearts they resolutely journey onwards.

Now, the wind veers a little, and the high cliffs somewhat break its force, and the men feel less the power of the gale; but still the wind is almost directly ahead, and the ebb tide is running against them with great strength. Every yard of advance is won by a struggle with the seas, as the steamer *Aid* pants and beats her way onward. But still it is won, and all hands are content. At last they get round the North Foreland, and begin to feel that they are nearing the scene of action.

The rain ceases, and the clouds of flying scud lift a little. It is still pitch dark, but free from mist and rain—clear dark, as they call it.

The men see the Margate Pier, and the town lights, which shine out steadily and clearly ; and it seems to them a strange contrast as they look from their rough post of danger, action, and hardship, upon the town resting in quiet peace, unconscious of the storm.

They make for the *Tongue* light-ship, which is stationed about nine miles from Margate. Every five minutes the darkness of the horizon is broken by the flash of a rocket which is thrown up by the light-ship. It goes flying up against the gale, and bursting, gives a moment's gleam as its stars caught by the fierce wind, pass away, floating in a short stream of light to leeward. The steamer's crew make for the light-ship, looking anxiously the while in all directions for any signal which may guide them more directly to the vessel in distress ; but they see none, and so speed on towards the light-ship.

As the steamer passes her on the lee side, as slowly and as near as possible, the coxswain is told that signals had been seen from the high part of the Shingle sand bank, supposed to be from a large vessel in distress.

K

The life-boat in turn sheers near the light-vessel in passing, and hears the same report.

Again they urge their way, struggling onward in the gale; but they can see no sign of a vessel, and no vestige of a wreck.

Perilous and anxious is the work as they feel their way along the very edge of the dangerous Sands; the roar of the gale is too great for any cries of distress to be heard. The hull of the vessel may be overrun with the seas, and the crew, clinging to the masts or rigging, be utterly unable to give any signals by firing guns or rockets, or by showing lights; and the night is so dark, that from the life-boat they can only see a few yards ahead. The men are most anxiously on the look-out; each time that the boat rises high upon a sea, they try their utmost to peer through the darkness by which they are surrounded. No! the breakers gleam white, and the steamer's light is tossing to and fro with every pitch and roll of the vessel; but nothing more can they make out. And the anxiety of the men, both on board the steamer and the life-boat, becomes greater and greater; they do not like to leave the neighbourhood of the Sands without thoroughly examining it, fearing that in doing so they may leave behind them, to a despair rendered more terrible, and to a death rendered more bitter by the false hopes that had been excited, some poor fellows clinging desperately to a few fragments of trembling wreck. But still they can see nothing and can hear nothing of either wreck or crew; either the vessel must have gone utterly to pieces, or the men on board the *Tongue* light-ship have been mistaken in the position of the signals they have seen.

As the men are listening intensely for the faintest signal or cry of distress, they fancy that they hear the booming of a distant gun, fired at intervals. Now in a lull in the storm they hear it more distinctly, and see in the far distance the flashing of a rocket-light. Watching and listening still, they soon discover that the *Prince's* and *Girdler* light-ships are at the same time repeating signals of distress. They must give up their present search, and hasten to the rescue where such urgent demands are being made for their help. Their consolation is, that at all events they can do nothing more in the utter darkness in searching for the wreck, which they have been already so long looking for in vain ; and before daylight, or soon after, they can probably be back to resume their search after having, as they hope, done good work in the interval. At all events, they must be off ; and off they go, leaving, as it proved, a crew of storm-beaten men in as desperate a position as it was well possible for men to be. They think it best to make for the *Prince's* light-ship first, and on arriving there they are told that a large ship has been seen making signals. They think that she is on the Girdler Sands, but she may be on the Shingles. Away again in the darkness they speed on their noble mission. At last they plainly discern a light on the south part of the Shingles ; they make for it, but only to be again disappointed. It is the light of the steam tug *Friend of all Nations*, which is lying-to under the lee of

K 2

the Shingles to be protected from the rush of the
seas. But here they are somewhat repaid for their
efforts, for they learn beyond doubt that the vessel in
distress is a large ship on the Girdler Sands ; and
more than this, that another large ship, disabled and
in great distress, had been seen driving down the
Deeps, a very narrow channel between the Shingle
and the Long Sand. It must have been signals
from this latter vessel which had been seen by the
men on board the *Tongue* light-ship. They are
unwilling to pass on their way to the Girdler without
making an effort to find the vessel which had been
seen in such great distress, and which, in every probability, had gone ashore somewhere in the neighbourhood. So they make a cruise in the direction of the
Deeps. They search narrowly, but in vain, and at
last hurry away as the Girdler light-ship still
continues to fire heavy guns. At last their long,
persevering, and hazardous search is crowned with
success. Upon nearing the Girdler light-ship, they
see on the Sands the flare of blazing tar-barrels ; they
know these must be the signals made by the vessel
that has run on the Sands. At once every man forgets
all about his many hours of exposure to wet, cold,
and exertion, and wakens up to full strength and
vigour ; and all begin at once to make preparations
for going into the rescue.

The steamer is obliged to steer clear of the broken
water, not only because of the danger of grounding,
but also because of the wildness of the seas as
they break upon the Sands, as their surf would be

quite sufficient to sweep her decks and swamp her. She skirts the breakers and tows the life-boat well to windward. The men on board the boat watch their opportunity ; and as soon as they find themselves in the right position for reaching the wreck, they cast off the tow-rope, and the wind and sea at once swing the boat's head round, and she plunges into the midst of the broken water which is rushing over the Sands.

It is a desperate strife of waters, and into the very thick of the fray, straight as an arrow, the boat rushes. The strength of the gale is so great, the men only dare to hoist a close-reefed foresail ; but swiftly it bears the boat along. At times the boat is so overrun with broken water and surf that the men can scarcely breathe. They, however, cling resolutely to the boat, and again and again she shakes herself free of water, and the men straighten themselves for a moment, draw a few long breaths, when again they meet a tangle of broken waves. Down into the trough of the troubled seas the boat plunges, and over her and her crew the waves again rush in all directions ; and thus she undauntedly works her way to the wreck.

CHAPTER XI.

THE EMIGRANT SHIP.

> Borne upon the ocean's foam,
> Far from native land and home,
> Midnight's curtain, dense with wrath,
> Brooding o'er our venturous path.
> While the mountain wave is rolling,
> And the ship's bell faintly tolling :
> Saviour ! on the boisterous sea,
> Bid us rest secure in Thee."
>
> *L. H. Sigourney.*

IT is one o'clock in the morning; the moon gleams but through the gulfs in the dark deep clouds which sweep swiftly across her path.

The men see a large ship hard and fast on the Sands and in a perfect boil of waters. The tremendous seas surge around her, and as they wildly leap against her shake her from stem to stern; the spray is flying over her in great sheets, and mingles with the dark masses of smoke, which rise in thick clouds from the flaming tar-barrels, while smoke and spray are swept swiftly to leeward by the force of the wind. The vessel is making all possible signals of distress; the

fierce gale has driven her, at each lift of the sea, higher
and higher upon the Sands, until she has reached the
highest part, and there has grounded fast. As the tide
fell the waves could no longer lift the ship, and let
her crash down upon the sand, else long since she
would have been utterly broken to pieces.

The boat makes in for the ship, the people on
board see her, and cries and cheers of joy greet her
approach. The foresail is lowered, the anchor thrown
overboard, and the boat fast sheers in towards the
vessel, which they find to be an emigrant ship crowded
with passengers.

The cable goes out by the run, and is too soon
exhausted, for with a jerk it brings the boat up within
sixty feet of the vessel. As the poor emigrants see
the boat stop short, their cries for help are frantic, and
sound dismally in the boatmen's ears, as slowly and
laborously they haul in the cable, and with much
troube get up their anchor, before making another
attempt to get alongside the ship. In the meantime
they answer the cries of the people with shouts to
encourage them, and the moon shining out, the emi-
grantssee that they are not deserted. The sea is so
heavy, and the boat's anchor has taken so firm a hold,
that it is a long time before they can get it up ; at
last they succeed, and now sail within fifty fathoms of
the vessel, before they heave the anchor overboard
again.

It is necessary if they are to windward of a vessel
to let the anchor down as far as possible from her,
that they may get plenty of sea-room when they haul

up to it again, so that when they set sail they may have space enough to sail clear of the vessel upon which the seas would throw the boat bodily, if they did not allow themselves room to steer a course which shall be clear of her.

They let the cable out gradually and drop alongside; they get a hawser from the bow, and another from the stern of the vessel, and by these they are enabled to keep the boat moderately well in position, the man on board hauling and veering on the ropes, and upon the boat's cable attached to the anchor, so as to keep the boat sufficiently near without letting her strike against the sides of the vessel, and this, in the broken seas and rapid tide, is a matter of no small difficulty. The ship is the *Fusilier*, bound from London to Australia; her captain and pilot shout out to the men on board the boat, "How many can you carry? we have more than one hundred souls on board, more than sixty women and children." And it is with no little dismay that the terrified passengers look down upon the boat half buried in spray, and wonder how she could by any possibility be the means of rescuing such a crowd of people. The men answer from the boat that they have a seamer near, and that they will take off the passengers and crew in parties to her. Two of the life-boat men, as the boat lifts on the top of a sea, make a spring, catch hold of the man-ropes and climb on board the ship. "Who comes here?" shouts the captain, as the two boatmen, clad in their oilskin overalls, with their cork belts on, and pale and half exhausted with their

long battling with wind and sea, jump from the
bulwarks amid the excited passengers who crowd the
deck. "Two men from the life-boat," is the reply,
and the passengers throng round them, seize them by
the hands, and some even cling to them with an
energy of fear, that requires considerable force to
overcome. The light from the ship's lamps and the
faint moonlight reveal the mass of people on board,
and the terrible state of exhaustion and fear that
most of them are in ; some are deadly pale and terror-
stricken, their eyes wildly staring, and trembling in
every limb ; some are in a fainting condition, and are.
supported by friends, who half forget their own terrors
in their efforts to console the sufferers who seem to
need it most; the wild shrieks of some of the poor
women pierce the gale, while others of the passengers
are quiet and resigned, but their pale and firm looks
and clasped hands suggest the depth of the emotions
that they are at such pains to control. It has been a
long long night of terror and most anxious suspense,
and many of those who have held up bravely during
its hours of danger and almost of despair, now break
down at the crisis of the life-boat's arrival. But the
night has not been one of unreasoning fear with all.
There are those on board who, filled with a calm
heroism, have by their example of holy faith exerted
great influence for good among their fellow-passengers
—one woman especially, who has been for some time
employed by a religious society in London, visiting
among the poor, proves herself well fitted for scenes
of danger and distress. Gathering many around her,

she read and prayed with them ; and often as the
wild blasts shook the vessel to the keel, there mingled
with the roar of the storm the strains of hymns, and
many poor creatures gathered consolation and confidence as they were led to look, from their own
perfect helplessness and weakness, to the Almighty
arm of a loving God ; and many, who had already
learnt to know and to feel those truths which take the
sting from death, were encouraged to draw nearer to
place their full reliance upon the sufficient atonement
of Him who has declared, " I am the resurrection, and
the life : he that believeth in me, though he were
dead, yet shall he live : and he that believeth in me
shall never die." Thus there was light in the darkness
and songs in the night, and the voice speaking mid
the tempest said, " Peace, be still ;" and many felt,
although the warring elements still raged, a calm,
which recklessness may assume, but which faith alone
can give at such an hour. This is no fancy sketch,
no effort to drag in a bit of attempted pathos.
One hundred immortal souls were momentarily
expecting the summons which should launch them into
eternity ; and a most terrible shade in the tragic
picture it would indeed have been, had not any of
that throng been prepared for the summons by the
exercise of earnest humble faith—if by all of them
the expected messenger, who seemed to linger minute
by minute upon the threshold, was dreaded only
with a despairing fear, as the King of Terrors, if not
any were prepared to welcome him calmly as the
messenger of Peace.

But now the life-boat men are upon the deck—a prospect of safety dawns upon all—a wild scene of excitement for a moment prevails, and there is a rush made for the gangway of the ship. Mothers shriek for their children; husbands strive to push their wives through the throng, and children are trodden down in the rush.

It is a few moments before the excitement ceases, and the captain can exercise any authority; but the emigrants, checked for a minute, regain self-control, fall back from the side of the vessel, and await for orders.

"How many will the life-boat carry?" the captain asks the life-boat men. "Between twenty and thirty at each trip," is the answer. "There is a very nasty dangerous sea and surf over the Sands, if too crowded we may get some washed out of her."

It is at once decided, as a matter of course, that the women and children shall be taken first, and the crew prepare to get them into the boat.

Two sailors are slung in bow-lines over the side of the vessel to help the women down. The boat ranges to and fro in the rush of the tide, the men do their utmost to check its sheering, hauling and easing in turn the hawsers which are passed from the ship to the bow and stern of the boat, but there is no keeping her for one moment steady; now she veers right away from the vessel as far as the cable will let her, and again comes in upon a rush of sea as if to crush herself against the wreck; up she is lifted on the crest of a wave to almost the level of the ship's deck, and down again plunges as the wave passes, many feet below, and leaves a deep and dismal gulf of tumbled sea and foam between her and the ship.

It is a terrible scene ; the crowd of helpless frightened people, and the comparatively small boat, tossed wildly in the rage of maddened waves, their one hope of rescue ; and it is dangerous and difficult work getting the people into the boat ; it would have been quite difficult and dangerous enough if all had been active and resolute sailors accustomed to scenes of danger, but how much more so, when a large proportion of those to be saved are helpless women, some aged and infirm !

The women who are mothers are called first ; one is led to the gangway, and shrinks back from the scene before her. The boat is lifted up on a big wave, the men stand on the thwarts with outstretched arms, ready to catch her if she falls, but the next moment the boat drops into the wild waste of water many feet below, and is half covered with a rush of foam.

No wonder that the poor woman shrieks with terror, and seeks to struggle back on to the deck of the vessel ; no time for persuasion, she is urged forcibly over the gangway, and now hangs in mid-air, held by the two men who are suspended over the side by ropes ; as the boat rises again, the boatmen, who stand ready to catch her, cry, " Let go !" The two men do so, but the woman, in her terror, clings to one with a frantic grasp, and the next moment, as the boat falls away from the side of the vessel—oh ! must she not fall into the sea ? for the man to whom she is clinging cannot hold her as she is ; one of the active prompt boatmen sees her danger, makes a spring, grasps her by the heel, drags her from her hold, catches her in his arms in her fall, and both of them roll over into the boat, their fall broken by the men who stand ready to catch them.   The half insensible woman is quickly passed to the stern of the boat and thus she is saved.   Now, they are ready again, for all are anxious that not a moment shall be lost ; the number to be rescued, and the time that must of necessity be occupied in going to and from the steamer, makes every minute a question of life and death.

Again, up the boat rises ; the woman who is being urged forward makes a half spring, and is got into the boat without much trouble.

The next time the boat rises she does not come well alongside, she rather falls short and sheers off. A woman is being held over the side by the two men : " Don't let go, Jack ; don't let go !" the woman struggles, the position of the men is so awkward that they cannot hold her firmly, and she is struggling from their grasp, while the mad waves leap below, and if she falls she must at once be swept away by them, and down she does fall, but at that moment the boat sheers in again, just enough to enable one of the men to grasp the clothes of the woman and to drag her, as she falls, on to the side of the boat, and she too is saved.

Again to work ; another woman, she is sobbing, and cries out piteously, " Oh ! don't shake me ; be careful,

don't hurt me!" Poor creature! she is very near her
confinement; downs she falls from the hands of the
men who are holding her into the arms of the boatmen,
and rolls over into the bottom of the boat. Some of
the husbands on board throw blankets down to the
poor half-dressed women in the boat; the blankets are
rolled into bundles that the wind may not carry them
away. Some of the women in the boat are crying
aloud for their children; a passenger rushes frantically to the gangway, cries, " Here, here!" and thrusts
a big bundle into the hands of one of the sailors, who
supposes it to be merely a blanket which the man
intends for his wife in the boat. " Here, Bill, catch!"
the sailor shouts and throws the bundle to a boatman
who is standing up in the boat; he just succeeds in
catching it, as it is in the point of falling into the sea,
and is thunderstruck to hear a baby's cry proceed
from it, while there is a shriek from a woman, "My
child! my child!" as she springs forward, and
snatches it from him, which tells, indeed, of the
greatness of the danger through which the poor little
thing has passed. In spite of all the boatmen's care
and labour the boat every now and then lurches
with a tremendous thump against the ship's side, and
would be stove in but for the massive cork fenders
which surround her, and still she is leaping and tossing
about; now high as the main chains of the ship, now
low in the trough of a big sea, the hollow of which is
so deep that it leaves but little water between the
bottom of the boat and the sands; but with all eager
haste the men work on, and at last, after many hair-

breadth escapes, and some heavy falls, thirty women
and children are got on board, and the boat is declared
to be full.

The boatmen cast off the hawsers from her bow and
stern, and begin to haul in hard upon the cable.
They draw the boat up to the anchor with much
difficulty, for as the range of cable gets shorter, the
boat jerks and pitches a great deal in the rush of the
short waves, and in the swing of the tide. The
anchor is up at last ; the sails are hoisted ; the boat
feels her helm, gathers way swiftly, and shoots clear of
the ship. A faint and half-hearted cheer greets them
as they pass astern of the vessel ; the remaining
passengers watch them with wistful and somewhat
anxious glances as they plunge on through sea and
foam. Away the boat bounds before the fierce gale—
on through the flying surf and boiling sea—on,
although the waves leap over her and fill her with
their spray.

Buoyantly she rises and shakes herself free, staggering as a cross wave mid the broken water dashes
itself against her bows ; tossing her stern high as she
climbs the waves' tall crests, then pitching almost bows
under as the rolling waves pass under her stern ; and
lurching heavily on her side as she sinks into the
trough of the sea. It is, in spite of their hope, a dread
time for the poor women and children on board her,
with those whom they love as themselves, left, they
almost fear, to perish on the wreck, and while to
themselves death at every moment seems very near ;
trembling with cold and excitement, they crowd to

gether, and hold on to the boat, to each other, to anything ; it is hard to think of safety while the boiling seas foam so fiercely around, ready, it seems, at any moment to overwhelm and bury the boat in their fierce waves. And the poor women take a more convulsive and firm grasp, as every now and then the men see a giant cross sea heading towards them, and give a quick warning cry—" Hold on !" and the sea comes with a clean sweep over the boat, almost washing them out of her.

The steamer, as has been said, towed the life-boat well to windward, that she might have a fair wind before which to run in for the wreck, but as soon as the life-boat left the steamer, away she speeded round to the other side of the Sands, to leeward of the wreck, that the boat might again have a fair wind to her as she comes from the wreck, and she now lays to, awaiting the boat's return.

On she comes ; the broken water is now passed ; the air is full of scud and spray, but the cross seas overrun her no longer ; she is in deep water, and the exhausted emigrants begin to raise their heads and look about them ; they could not have endured that continual breaking of the waves and rush of water over them much longer ; how their hearts lift with joy as they hear the cheering voices of the men, and have the lights of the steamer pointed out to them, shining bright and near !

Thus, with thirty women and children, their first sheave of the harvest to be gathered from death, the life-boat men run their boat alongside the *Aid*

The steamer is put athwart the seas, to form a break-water for the boat, which comes under her lee; the roll of the steamer, the pitching of the boat, the wild wind and sea, with the darkness of the night only faintly broken by the light of the steamer's lanterns, render it a somewhat difficult matter to get the women out of the boat. As the boat rises the men lift up a woman and steady her for a moment on the gunwale, two men on the steamer catch her by the arms as she comes up within reach, and she is dragged up the side on to the deck. There is here also no time for ceremony; a moment's hesitation, and the poor creature might have a limb crushed between the steamer and the boat. As each woman is thus got on deck, two men half lead half carry her to the cabin below.

One woman struggles to get back to the boat, crying for her child, the men do not understand her in the roar of the gale, and she is gently forced below; again the rolled-up blanket appears, it is handed into the steamer, and is about to be dropped upon the deck, when half-a-dozen voices shout out, "There is a baby in the blanket!" and it is carried down into the cabin, and received by the poor weeping mother with a great outburst of joy.

"God bless you! God bless you!" she exclaims to the man, and then blesses and praises God out of the abundant fulness of her heart.

Some of the poor women are completely overcome by the reaction which takes possession of them now that they find themselves in safety; they had been

comparatively calm and resigned during their hours
of hardship and danger ; now they realise the nature
of the peril to which they have been exposed, and in
which many whom they love are still placed. Some
throw themselves on the cabin floor, weeping and
sobbing ; some cling to the sailors, begging and en-
treating them to save their husbands and children
who are on board the wreck ; while others can do
little else than offer up some simple form of prayer
and praise to God.

Instantly that the boat is freed from her passengers
she drops astern of the steamer, and is towed round
the sands, to get again into position to make a second
trip to the vessel ; and when the straining cable is let
go, and her sail hoisted, she heads round, gathers way,
and bounds in like a greyhound through the troubled
sea towards the wreck. A slant of wind comes and
drives her from her course, and she fails in reaching
the ship, and makes for the open water. The steamer
speedily picks her up, tows her into a more favourable
position, and the boat soon gets again alongside the
vessel.

There are still on board more women and children
than will fill the boat, and they have to leave some
half-a-dozen behind. All the old difficulties in
getting the women down the side of the vessel into
the life-boat are repeated, although the wind has now
fallen a little. They make for the steamer, and as
each new comer is handed down into the cabin, the
anxiety of those who are eagerly looking for some
loved one is great indeed, and the meetings again,

after so dread a separation, are naturally very affecting.

For the third time the boat makes to the ship, and now brings away the remaining passengers. The cabin of the steamer is full of women and children in every stage of exhaustion and excitement ; and they are all very thankful to God for the full answer vouchsafed to the earnest prayers of the previous night.

It has taken more than three hours to get the emigrants on board the steamer ; there has been additional delay created by the boat twice failing to reach the ship, but this very delay, which at the time seemed so unfortunate, was, under God's providence, the means of saving further life.

The life-boat again makes for the *Fusilier* to see what the crew of the vessel will do, whether they will abandon the vessel at once, or wait to see the result of a change in the weather which seems to promise. They get alongside ; the gale has gone down very considerably, and the tide has been falling fast for some time. The ship being light, has not received so much injury from the thumping on the ground as they anticipated ; and, as she is high up on the sands, the tide has left her the sooner, so that she has settled down in shallow water, and there is now, therefore, no immediate danger ; although, should the wind get up with the returning tide, she may be very speedily beaten to pieces.

The captain of the ship thinks that if the wind goes down she may possibly be got off at the next high tide, as she has not been much knocked about ; but while he is unwilling to abandon the vessel while there is a chance of her being rescued, he feels the greatness of the risk, and wishes the life-boat to remain alongside him. It is nearly day-light ; the night is clear, and the wind still blowing very hard, although the fierceness of the gale seems expended.

The life-boat makes her way to the steamer, and takes orders to be given at Ramsgate to send luggers with anchors and cables, that every effort may be made to get the ship off, if the weather continues to moderate. The boat then returns and lies by the ship, while the steamer, heavily freighted with rescued emigrants, makes the best of her way towards Ramsgate.

CHAPTER XII.

THE RESCUE OF THE CREW OF THE "DEMERARA," AND THE EMIGRANTS' WELCOME TO RAMSGATE.

"Eternal Father, strong to save,
Whose arm hath bound the restless wave,
Who bid'st the mighty ocean deep
Its own appointed limits keep ;
O hear us when we cry to Thee
For those in peril on the sea."

Hymn.

"Now we must leave our fatherland,
And wander far o'er ocean's foam ;
Broken is kinship's dearest band,
Forsaken stands our ancient home.

"But one will ever with us go,
Through busiest day and stillest night ;
The heavens above, the deeps below,
Stand all unveiled before his sight."

Hymn.

THE emigrants describe their perils to the men on board the steamer, and mention that during the previous evening, while their ship was driving, and some time before she struck, they saw a large ship in great distress, and drifting fast in the direction of the Sands, but that as darkness set in, they lost sight of her.

The crew of the steamer keep a sharp look-out for this vessel, or for any signs of her. She is evidently the one of which they had already heard, and of which they had been in search before they discovered the *Fusilier*.

After some time they discover part of a mast and other wreckage entangled in the Sands, and can only conclude that the vessel has gone utterly to pieces, with the loss of all hands, during the night; they must speed on, and get the poor emigrants cared for on shore with all possible haste. But for the delay that had been occasioned, the steamer would have been far on its way to Ramsgate by this time, while it was yet too dark for them to see any distance; now in the grey light that increases rapidly they can search for any other signs of wreckage. As they proceed down the Prince's channel, and get near to the light-vessel, they see the small remnant of a wreck, which they think may be the bowsprit and jib-boom of a vessel dismasted and on her beam ends; they get nearer to her, and find that she is well over on the north-east side of the Girdler or Shingle Sands. Some of the crew wish to launch the steam tug's small life-boat, eighteen feet long, and make in through the surf to the wreck, to which they think they can see some of the crew clinging; but it is considered too great a risk to take so small a boat through such a broken sea, and it is agreed that they had better go back for the large life-boat.

They put back, and passing to leeward of the *Fusilier*, strike the flag half-mast high, as a sign that the boat is to join them. This she speedily does, and they together make for the newly-found wreck ; as they approach her, they can see that she is a vessel on her beam ends, with only her foremast standing. The life-boat makes in for her; the men wonder greatly that the vessel has held together so long, for she is broken and torn almost to pieces ; the copper is peeled off her bottom, the timbers are started, rent, and twisted ; the planking is wrenched off, almost all the cargo is washed out of the shattered hull, and here, and there, the light is to be seen through her bottom ;· there remains now little more than the skeleton of the ship that a few hours before, taut and trim, had buoyantly bounded over the seas ; and where was her gallant crew that had so bravely sailed her then ? The foremast, feebly held in position by a remnant of the deck, lies stretched a few feet above the water. The crew and pilot have been lashed to it for many hours, and have, for that time, seemed to be trembling over a fearful and yawning grave ; the heavy waves foam up and beat against the hull, and the doomed ship is, bit by bit, being torn further to pieces. The crew, as they cling on, hear the timbers creaking and snapping ; the deck was blown up as the water covered it, by the force of the confined air, and its fragments have been swept away in the swift tide.

The heavy waves make a greater and greater breach over the ship ; at times the ship lifts a little from the mere force of the blows given by the tremendous seas ; at any moment the foremast may break off short, and the wreck be rolled right over. The mast quivers at every shake and heave of the wreck ; the fierce tide rushes five feet beneath where the trembling sailors cling, over whom the waves are continually breaking. An hour passes, and the men are to their wonder still spared ; another and another hour, but they have no means of giving any signals of distress, and there seems no room whatever for hope. How can there be ? they ask each other. Suddenly they make out a steamer's lights in the distance, and watch them with a wistful curiosity ; to their astonishment the steamer seems to make directly for them, and then to cruise backwards and forwards within a few hundred feet of them.

A few of the trembling sailors shout out once or twice, but the rest smile grimly at the idea of any voice being heard, even a few yards off, in the roar of such a gale.

They watch the steamer's lights in a very agony of suspense, but without any hope that they themselves can be discovered in the darkness.

They see a smaller light some distance astern of the steamer, and imagine it to be that of a life-boat. As they hopelessly watch the movement of the vessels, they hear the dull throb of heavy guns from the distant light-ships. They see the faint flashes of light from the rockets : they know that these signals are calling to the steamer and life-boat to speed on elsewhere, to the rescue of other drowning ones ; yes, the steamer, in answer to these signals, is leaving them, and abandoning her vain search, and with a deepening despair they watch her lights grow fainter and fainter, and at last disappear in the distance. So they are left alone in their desolation, while the wild winds roar and the hungry waves rage around them.

The moon goes down, the darkness deepens, the gale rushes by more furiously than ever ; then comes a slight lull, and a faint light streaks the horizon. They tighten their grasp upon the trembling mast and torn rigging, and speak a few words of hope.

They may yet witness another sun-rise ; for in the dull grey light of the early dawn they can see faintly a steamer in the distance. She is approaching, but her course will hardly bring her near enough to discover them, lying as they are up on one torn mast only just out of the water. How intensely they watch her ! and many an earnest beseeching prayer is uplifted, and from some hearts that were withal not much accustomed to prayer. Eagerly ! eagerly ! they watch her ! How some feebly speak words of hope, while others will not be aroused out of their despair ! Thank God ! she changes her course, and makes in directly for the Sands, upon the edge of which their frail wreck rests. They may all begin to hope again, and joy comes in upon them like a flood. They shout aloud, and wave a rag of canvas, the only means of signalling that is left to them. The steamer sees them, she dips her flag as a signal that they are seen ; and then, to the unspeakable horror of the poor men, slowly turns round, and steams away full speed in the direction from which she came. An agony of fear again comes over the poor fellows ; they feel that they cannot be altogether deserted. Upon reflection, they see that no ordinary boat could live through the surf which separates them from the steamer; and the steamer would only have been herself wrecked if she had come any nearer the Sands. She must have gone for a life-boat. How long will she be away? They shudder as the creaking mast trembles beneath them; and look with heart dread at the yawning gulf of wild waters which gapes a few feet below; and they cannot but have a dismal fear that the steamer on her return with assistance, may find no vestige left either of them, or of the remnant of wreck to which they cling.

A short time, which however seems long indeed to them in their great suspense, and they again see the steamer, and soon they can make out, to their great joy, that she has the life-boat in tow. Still the flying surf beats upon them, and drives them, with its sheer weight, still closer to the mast; still the water rages around, while they cling with all desperate energy to the quivering shrouds; they are cold, and drenched, and exhausted, but they are full of hope; their hearts are lightened, their strength seems to return, the long hours during which they have seemed hopelessly face to face with death are passed, for the life-boat is near, and her gallant crew are speeding to their rescue.

The life-boat comes swiftly on, running before the still heavy gale; now rising like a cork to the mounting seas, or plunging boldly through the surf and broken water. Her men forget the long night-struggle of fatigue and danger through which they have passed ; much noble, self-denying, and dangerous work have they done, but they have still noble work to do—more lives to save, by the help of God—and with cool determination they cheerfully proceed to their new labours.

They find the water more and more broken as they near the ship ; the waves are flying high over the lost vessel ; the ebb-tide is running strongly. From the breaking seas, and from the position of the wreck, now on her broadside with her keel to windward, they cannot anchor on the windward side and let the boat drop gradually in upon the wreck, their only chance is to run with the wind abeam right in upon the fore-rigging. It is true that there is considerable danger in this, but at such times the life-boat men cannot stop to calculate danger, and must be ready oftentimes to risk their own lives in their attempts to save the lives of others. They, therefore, charge in straight amid the floating wreckage, and the boat hits hard upon the iron windlass, which is still hanging to the deck of the vessel.

A rope is thrown round the fore-rigging, and the group of exhausted sailors shout with joy as they greet the glad friendly faces of the life-boat men coming in upon them out of the storm of desolation that rages around. The crew, sixteen in number, including the pilot and a boy of about eleven years of age, are to the last extent exhausted and feeble, and slowly drop one by one from the mast into the boat, and leave to its fate the last storm-torn fragment of the *Demerara*, which has been for so many hours their only hope.

"Oars out, and pull hard ; let us get clear of all this wreckage before we have a hole knocked in the boat's bottom," and every boatman strains his hardest ; soon they are clear ; now a moment's delay ere they hoist the sail, and a great shaking of hands all round, and warm greetings, and heartfelt thanks from the saved ones, and the boat's sail is again hoisted, and away they make through the surf.

It is now nearly ten o'clock in the morning ; they soon reach the steamer, which is waiting to leeward. The emigrants have been watching the movements of the boat with the keenest interest ; their feelings of sympathy are moved to their very depths, by the fact of their having passed so lately through similar scenes of danger and rescue.

They crowd the deck, and shout after shout greets the boat ; the women cheer at the top of their voices, and welcome, with outstretched arms, alike the rescued and the rescuers.

One warm-hearted Irishwoman seizes the coxswain's hands in both hers, and shakes them with might and main, sobbing out, as the tears roll down her cheeks, "I'll pray the Holy Father for you the longest day that I live."

The steamer is literally crowded with rescued people ; the cabins are given up to the women and children, and the poor people half forget their present misery in great thankfulness for their safety ; they are wet and cold, and trembling with excitement and

with the effects of their long hours of fear and exposure ; the cabin is small and crowded to the extreme ;
the steamer rolls and pitches tremendously, as she
makes her way through the cross seas which still run
high and broken, though the height of the tempest is
past.

It is no unusual occurrence for a crowd of people
to be grouped at the pier-head, watching with interest
for the appearance of one of the many steamers which,
with flags flying in token of goodly freight, and with
gay appearance, as fitly betokens holiday time, makes
swiftly for the harbour ; but with a deeper interest
than ever is excited by such holiday scenes is the
steamer waited for now.

It is one of those bright, genial winter mornings of
which Ramsgate has so goodly a share. Many persons have been attracted to the pier to take, on that
pleasant promenade, a good instalment of the fresh
breeze, and to watch the sea, bright with sunshine, and
the waves glistening and flashing in their turmoil of
unrest.

Intelligence spreads that the steamer and life-boat
have been away all night, and are now every minute
expected to round the Point and appear in sight.

Great is the feeling of gladness, and deep the
satisfaction, as the gallant *Aid* appears with her
flags flying, and flags flying too at the life-boat's
mast-heads, telling the glad tale of successful effort.
The crowd rejoices greatly in the good work done ;
and as the steamer comes nearer it is seen that never
on a summer's day did steamer bear a fuller freight

of holiday-seekers than does the *Aid* now bear of those who have been rescued from deadly peril.

From the pier the crowd look down upon the multitude on board, and feel that that throng of fellow-beings have been just snatched from death, and a thrill of wonder and gladness passes through the on-lookers, and combines with that half formed sense of fear, which a realization of danger recently escaped either by ourselves, or by others, always gives.

The crowd waves, and shouts, and hurrahs, and gives every sign of glad welcome and hearty congratulation, and as the steamer sweeps round the pier-head, the pale upturned faces of one hundred and twenty rescued men, women, and children, smile back a glad acknowledgment of the welcome so warmly given. It is a scene almost overpowering in the deep feeling that it produces. The emigrants land ; they toil weakly up the steps to the pier, all bearing signs of the dangers and hardships through which they have passed.

Some are barely clothed, some have blankets wrapped round them, and all are weary and worn and faint with cold and wet and long suspense. There are aged women among the emigrants ; some who had been unwilling to be left behind when those most dear to them were about to seek their fortunes abroad ; others had been sent for by their friends, and to them the thoughts of the terrors and trials of a sea-voyage had been overcome by the longing to see, once again before they died, the faces so long loved and so much missed ; to see perhaps the grand-children upon whom, although they had never looked, yet they had thought of until they had become almost part of their daily life. It is piteous to see these aged women totter from the steamer to the pier.

And young men and young women are of the number ; they, crowded in the race at home, determined to seek in a wider field to make better way.

Here a poor stricken woman looks wistfully upon the white face and almost closed eyes of the baby in her husband's arms. This is the child that was so nearly lost overboard as it was thrown into the boat wrapped up in a blanket ; the mother's fears were not realised—the baby speedily recovered.

It now becomes the glad office of the people of Ramsgate to bestir themselves on behalf of those suddenly thrown upon their charity.

The agent of the Shipwrecked Fishermen and Mariners' Society at once takes charge of the sailors. Accommodation is found for the emigrants in houses near the pier, and a plentiful meal at once supplied ; many of the residents busy themselves most heartily ; clothes, dresses, coats, boots, and all necessary garments are most liberally given ; the people are ready to *spoil* themselves on behalf of the poor emigrants.

And thus warmed, fed, clothed and consoled by the heartfelt sympathy that is so evidently and practically manifested, the poor emigrants recover in a wonderfully short space of time from the state of physical and nervous exhaustion to which they had been reduced ; but they are never likely to forget the terrors of the night, or the debt of gratitude they owe to the gallant Ramsgate life-boat men, who so nobly effected their rescue.

Subscriptions in the meantime have been raised in the town to pay all expenses, and to put into the hands of the poor emigrants some little ready money.

One of the shipping agents has telegraphed to the owners of the ship, and been empowered to provide the emigrants all needed board and lodging; he does so, and on the next morning forwards them to London. A crowd of Ramsgate people bid them good-bye at the station, and receive grateful acknowledgments of the kindness and sympathy that have been shown, and they from their hearts wish their poor friends God speed.

The emigrants were cared for in London by the owners of the *Fusilier*. The weather moderating the morning after the wreck, the emigrants' things were got out of the vessel and sent on to them; and the owners of the *Fusilier* soon obtained another ship, in which they forwarded their passengers, and they had a prosperous voyage to Melbourne.

The *Fusilier* was ultimately got off the Sands, but no vestige of the *Demerara* was ever again seen.

CHAPTER XIII.

THE WRECK OF THE "MARY"—GALES ABROAD.

"Yet more ! the billows and the depths have more !
　High hearts and brave are gathered to thy breast !
They hear not now the booming waters roar,
　The battle-thunders will not break their rest.
Keep thy red gold and gems, thou stormy grave !
Give back the true and brave !"
Mrs. Hemans.

THE year was fast dying out.   Inland the wild winds did little to disturb the progress of Christmas preparations, or the happiness of Christmas gatherings.   The blasts swept ragingly along, and the last of the dead leaves were torn from the withering branches.   The stalwart trees battled sturdily in the woods ; but many a stout veteran that had long laughed at storms, at last was bowed in the grasp of the gale, and fell prostrate, or, like a fainting giant, leant with arms all abroad against his fellow-strugglers in the strife.

In the towns there was much wondering gossip at the force of the wind, and here and there some trivial disasters to record ; but for all its rage and bluster, the gale did not gather on shore many trophies of its

M

strength, and swept moaningly out to sea, to find in
the yielding waters a more ready ally, as it would
visit with its wrath man and his works.

The brave ships that were caught by the gale were
prepared to accept the accustomed challenge. It
overtook the tall vessels, and then the swelling sails
garnered the force of the wind and held it captive,
and made it speed the swift ship along.

It fell with its full strength upon the stout ships
riding at anchor, and moaned through the shaking
rigging, and by the swaying masts and yards, while
the groaning cables shuddered in every link, and the
strong anchors grappled the ground with a tighter
and tighter grasp, and held the good ships safe, in
spite of the raging wind and rush of sea, safe from
the greedy waiting sands, or cruel rocks.

Thus on the tempest-lashed ocean all was life, and
energy, and conflict ; and the dying year, as its
closing hours sped away, had at sea the howling winds
and seething waves to sing its dirge, and storm weary
sailors, and storm-beaten ships to mark its close.

Ships from the Thames, from the east coasts of
England and Scotland, from all northern Europe—
ships sailing under every flag, and bound to all ports,
gathered day by day in the Downs anchorage, where
they waited for the strong south-westerly gales to give
place to a more favourable slant of wind, that they
might pursue their way down Channel ; but still the
strong adverse winds prevailed. But while the outward-bound ships were thus obliged to halt in their
course, the homeward-bound ships came foamingly

along, their masts bending like whips under the small
spread of canvas they were alone able to carry.   Like
white-winged gulls they fled over the leaping seas,
and threaded their way through the crowded anchorage of the Downs.

The careless sailors laughed at the heavy blasts of
wind which in their force only hurried the good ship
on, and thus gave the crews a better prospect of
realising their hopes of being in Old England on the
near Christmas tide, to spend it with their friends on
shore, and share in, and by their presence greatly add
to, all the pleasures of the season.

But the smaller vessels at anchor in the Downs
began to ride uneasily, the force of the gale fell on
them with unchecked fury, the swift tide pressed them
sore, and raging seas broke over them again and
again.   Their anchors began to drag ; the breakers on
the Goodwin Sands leapt and foamed dangerously
near to leeward ; there was also danger of collision if
their anchors continued to drag, the ships in the
Downs being so crowded together.   Yes, there must
be a flight from the Downs on the part of many of
the smaller craft.   Some vessels make for Ramsgate
harbour, not many, as the charges are now so high
and restrictive as almost to make it cease from being
a harbour of refuge.   Other vessels make for an
anchorage round the North Foreland ; a dangerous
experiment this, as it frequently happens that a
sudden lull comes in the southerly gale, and in a short
time the wind chops right round, and begins to blow
from the northward harder than ever.   It was so on

M 2

the occasion of which we are writing. If a strong fort,
under which a fleet was anchored for protection,
suddenly fell into the hands of the enemy, a greater
change would not be wrought in the position, as to the
safety of the vessels, than is occasioned by this sudden
shift of wind to the vessels in the Margate Roads.
The high cliffs which have been their shield now
become their deadly peril. It had been desirable to
gain their shelter, it is now a necessity to escape from
their neighbourhood as soon as possible. And so, on
this occasion, as the wind chopped round all was at
once astir; some ships succeeded in regaining their
anchors, others had no time or power to do so; some
were driven ashore; twenty or thirty vessels had to
slip their cables, and as, with no anchors on board,
the captains did not dare to remain in the neighbourhood of the Sands or land, these vessels were
hauled on a wind, and like a flock of weary frightened
birds went staggering out into the North Sea.* The
hovelling-luggers from Ramsgate, Margate, Deal, and
Broadstairs are out during the gale; they go in chase
of the ships that have fled from their anchorage; they
place men on board such vessels as need them, either
to act as pilots, or to assist the weary crews. Some
of the luggers receive orders to fetch anchors and
cables for such vessels as have lost theirs, and away
they go plunging and speeding through the seas,
making for the nearest port where they can find agents
to supply them; and then out again with all speed,
heavily laden, with anchors and chains, in search of

* See note at end of chapter.

the vessels which have employed them, and which have, likely enough, been driven by the force of the gale, far from the position in which the luggers left them.

At midnight the gale gathers increased force ; the dark heavy clouds seem to settle lower and lower, and as the snow-squalls sweep by, the air and sea seem one confused mass of flying foam and snow.

The storm rages at Ramsgate Pier with all its fury ; the pier stands an advanced fortress unmoved by the fierce attack of the waves, and it is well manned by brave boatmen, the reserved guard of the storm— Storm Warriors ready to sally forth to rescue life at the first signal of danger.   One or two waggons, heavily laden with chains, and trucks with anchors, are being drawn down the pier by the struggling horses, the spray in heavy volumes washing over all.

Luggers in the harbour, and alongside the pier, are rolling and pitching in the rough tumble of the miniature sea that the gale arouses even there.

An anchor is hanging from the crane, a lugger beneath it is tossing up and down ; the men are doing their utmost to guide the anchor in its descent into the boat as she plunges about ; it is perilous work for all hands ; it seems a marvel that it can be done without staving in the boat, or crushing the men.

A group of boatmen are crouching under shelter of the wall of the pier, near the life-boat ; the night wears away—it is three o'clock in the morning.

A boatman makes his way to the pier-head ; he finds the coxswain of the life-boat on the look-out.

" Well, Jarman, a heavy gale this."

" A heavy gale indeed, Gorham ; it is blowing great guns and no mistake—a terrific sea, too ; just the night for our work, and I shall not be surprised if some is cut out for us, and pretty stiff too, before the morning."

" Likely enough, it is a sort of touch-and-go night for the Goodwin. I noticed before dark several vessels riding in the Gulls ; now the wind has cast in so heavily from the north, it will go hard with some of them, I fear.

" Yes, I noticed them ; they must have a bad time of it now ; it is to be hoped that the anchors will hold ; it will be almost sudden death for any poor fellows whose ships touch the Goodwin to-night ; why, with the sea that must be now raging there, it would take in a ship almost at a mouthful."

" True enough, coxswain ; I have been very anxious about them all night—cannot help thinking about them." And it is supposed that the boatman's fears were very terribly justified. One vessel was wrecked in the way we are about to tell ; and very grave fears were felt as to the fate of several others ; when the morning came, not one of the vessels that had been noticed the evening before as being anchored in such a dangerous position was to be seen, and yet it was almost certain that not any of them could have got away in safety.

Fishing-smacks that had been lying-to not far from the North Foreland saw the fleet of vessels driven from the Margate Roads, and afterwards saw several of them flying signals of distress, and

apparently in a sinking condition; but from the
extraordinary force of the gale, the fishermen could
render no assistance, and the weather was too dark
and thick for the signals for help to be seen from the
light-vessels, or from the shore; moreover, a good deal
of wreckage was seen floating about in the morning,
and the mast-head of one vessel was discovered
standing out of the water upon the Goodwin, the last
seen relic of some unknown ship and crew.

Among the vessels observed during the afternoon
to be at anchor in a very perilous position in the Gull
Stream, and making very bad weather of it, was the
Mary, a schooner of about 170 tons; she had been a
Dutch galliott, had a cargo of coals on board, and
was bound from Shields to Dieppe.

There was one fine young man on board, David
Fullarton. Life seemed more especially dear to him,
as he was engaged to be married; the arrangements
for the wedding had been made; he had been busy in
preparing a home; and a short voyage from Shields to
Dieppe and back, would do something towards the
expenses, and he would not be long away; and so there
were bright memories to look back upon, bright hopes
before him; but this terrible storm seems to cover all
with its shadow. As soon as darkness sets in, and the
gale shows signs of increasing in force, Fullarton
becomes very anxious, and keenly alive to the danger
the schooner is in; time after time he entreats the
captain to have the masts cut away, that the vessel
may ride more easily, and be less exposed to the fury
of the wind. "Do! captain, pray do! for the sake of

our lives let it be done ! we are dragging our anchors—
we are fast driving on the Sands ;" and again he begs
the captain to signal for assistance. " Why not ! why
not ? you will do it too late, captain, too late !" the
poor fellow cries in his restlessness and distress.

The night grows on, and its terrors multiply ; the
intense darkness, the wild sea, the howling winds
moaning and wailing through the rigging, the hoarse
roar and thunder of the breakers raging on the near
Goodwin Sands.

At last, the captain feels that the schooner is in
great danger, and orders the crew to set a tar-barrel
on fire ; they hasten to do so—Fullarton working with
eager haste ; but the wash of the sea over it and the
heavy wind will not let it burn ; they fill the barrel
with tow and tar, and grease, and at last get it to
flare up with a fierce flame that resists the storm ;
the watch on board the Gull light-ship had noticed
before dark the danger of the vessel, and had been
keenly on the look-out in her direction for signals of
distress ; on Ramsgate Pier, also, an anxious look-out
had been kept for some hours, the boatmen expecting
disasters in that quarter.

It is a little before four in the morning ; the men on
board the light-vessel see the signal of distress, and
fire a gun and send up a rocket to convey to the shore
the tidings that help is wanted.

The boatmen at once commence preparations with
all energy, they arouse the men asleep in the watch-
house on the pier, a man hurries to give the harbour-
master notice, the crew of the steamer *Aid* get ready

for sea, the harbour-master hurries down the pier and gives the men orders to start on their merciful and perilous errand.

Away they go in the teeth of the hurricane, clearing their way through the leaping foaming waves and the clouds of heavy spray.

The town and harbour lights gleam out in the darkness, but there is no looking back for them on the part of the men, and there may be none ; until by God's mercy, their work is successfully finished, and then doubly will the lights shine out a glad welcome on their triumphant return home.

The lights they now look for are the beacon fires of warfare ; calls to conflict and peril ; guides into the thickest of the dread battle-field.   As the life-boat lifts on the curl of a wave, the crew see the flickering flame of the signal-fire that is burning so fiercely in the tar-barrel on the wreck ; they make in for the signal at once, pass through the Cud channel ; snow-squalls come sweeping by, adding to the cold and darkness, and shutting out from their view all lights on the Sands ; the men are eager and excited in their quick sympathy for the shipwrecked crew—eager to brave all the dangers of the lashing seas which they know must be leaping and tearing about the wreck. And they well realize the deadly peril the poor shipwrecked seamen must be in, and think little in their struggle onward of all the hardships they themselves are enduring.

For about forty minutes they battle their way, and then find themselves near the wreck ; the signal flame from the burning tar-barrel leaps, and flickers, and burns low, and is almost extinguished by the spray; the life-boatmen watch it anxiously, for they know that if the crew of the vessel cannot succeed in keeping it alight, it will be almost impossible for them to find the vessel in the darkness of the night; the crew of the schooner also feel this to be the case, and bring clothes and bedding, and all the tar and oil they can get at, and by great exertions manage to keep the fire burning.

NOTE.—*Extract from Newspaper.*—"Five vessels wrecked off Margate :—On Friday evening there were about one hundred and fifty vessels anchored in the Margate and North Foreland Roads, where they were sheltered from a south-westerly gale. Suddenly, about one o'clock on Saturday morning, a violent gale sprung from the north-east, and the vessels in the Roads were compelled to slip their anchors and seek the nearest shelter. Rockets and flares were seen displayed in all directions from the numerous distressed vessels. The Broadstairs life-boat and the Margate life-boat, the *Quiver*, put to sea. Four vessels were driven ashore, three in the Main, and one in Margate Bay, and the crews of three were saved by the Broadstairs life-boat. Another vessel was run down off the North Foreland, and it is reported that another has gone to pieces on the Tongue Sand, and, it is feared, with all hands."

CHAPTER XIV.

THE WRECK OF THE "MARY"—A STRUGGLE FOR DEAR LIFE.

"Sleep on ; thy corse is far away,
 But love bewails thee yet ;
For thee the heart wrung sigh is breathed,
 And lovely eyes are wet."

G. D. Prentice.

"Now, my men, make ready !" the coxswain cries ; "we've got our work before us."

The night is wild, and dark, and bitter, blinding snow, and sleet, and storm-wrack rush along on the wings of the gale.

The Sands are alive with the rolling breakers, the fierce dash and seethe of the waves upon them add to the roar of the tempest ; never was a battlefield more full of raging foes than is that into the midst of which our Storm Warriors are about to rush ; never was band of men more beset by foes, more helplessly, hopelessly beset, than are the crew of the *Mary ;* how shall they be plucked from the midst of ten thousand raging waves ? any one of which would swamp an ordinary boat ; it can only by any possibility be done by such a boat as the life-boat, and only by such men as the life-boatmen.

And now the men settle to their work.

The mainsail and mizen are already close reefed, they are got ready for instant hoisting. The steamer lashes through the seas towing the boat farther to windward, the hawser is let go, the men hoist the sails as fast as they can in the leaping rolling boat; she feels the force of the blast, lays over on her side, down with the helm, she rights, her head comes round, and in through the boiling seas she makes for the wreck.

Each boatman has his life-belt on, and as the seas break more fiercely over the boat, the men twist the life-lines round their arms, so that if some huge wave, rushing over the boat, should wrench them from their hold, and wash them out of the boat, or that the boat should upset in the curl of a breaker, that they may have the better chance of getting back to her.

Each time that the boat lifts on the top of a wave they can make out the signal-fire on board the wreck, as the boat falls in the trough of a sea they speed swirling along, through a very gauntlet of hungry waves which leap upon her, as wolves would leap upon a strong horse; but she throws them off, as the horse might the wolves in the impetus of his speed and power.

" Ready in the bow ?"

"Ay! Ay!"

" Ready all ?"

" All ready."

" We are nearing the wreck," a plunge forward on a

big wave, and the dismasted vessel is seen only a few fathoms off.

"Over with the anchor, down with the mainsail; keep up the mizen, to let the boat sheer, and now for the wreck."

The life-boatmen are near enough to her to see by the fitful blaze of the tar-barrel that she is a small schooner, with a high stern, and that she is totally dismasted, and they recognise the Dutch-looking craft that they had watched during the afternoon; they catch the gleam of the pale faces of the crew, who are clinging to the gunwale.

Poor fellows! how they gaze out in the darkness; death, death, so near from the raging storm, from their sinking ship, from the terrible Sands on which the wreck of their vessel will be torn piecemeal by the strong fierce waves in so short a time.

How they cry out with hope, as they first catch sight of the lights that are shining out in the gloom, and drawing nearer and nearer! it may be only the lights of some vessel as badly off as they are : they will not think so ; they are on the Goodwin, the signals have been made, and answered from Ramsgate; if the life-boat can save them, they will be saved, and this small light dancing so wildly in the storm, and drawing nearer out of the dread darkness of the wild night, may be the light of the life-boat, and they will not despair.

It *must* be the life-boat! no other boat could come in through the seas as that boat has done; and now as she nears, the light is reflected on her blue-and-white sides, and they hear the men shout, and the poor fellows pass from despair to hope, and cling harder than ever to the gunwale of the wreck, as the seas wash over them.

On board the life-boat they veer out the cable rapidly; many fathoms run out, but still they seem to get no nearer the wreck, on the contrary, the wreck is getting farther and farther from them.

As the life-boatmen made the vessel out in the darkness, they supposed her to be hard and fast on the Sands, and as they neared, and could see how the waves were beating over her, this appeared still more to be the case, but it proves not to be so; the tide is much higher than usual, and the wreck, with two long lengths of chain-cable dragging over her bows, is drifting over the top of the Sands, and with the force of the gale, and in the strength of the tide, drifts faster than the men on board the boat are able to veer out the cable.

"Hold on the cable, the wreck is drifting, we must up anchor; to it, my men, hard and fast as you can."

This getting in the life-boat cable and anchor is terrible work; the wild seas are literally raging over the boat; it was bad enough when the boat was under weigh, running before the wind, bounding along with the waves in their flight, and thus escaping much of their fury.

But now the boat is head to the seas, she meets them as they rush on with all their force, and she wrenches and jerks at the cable with a power that threatens to tear her to pieces.

As many men as can lay hold of the cable do so;

they cling on to the boat with their legs round the
thwarts ; they give the hawser a couple of turns round
the bollard—a timber head in the fore part of the boat
used for towing purposes ; a huge wave passes ; the
boat falls in the trough of the sea ; as she falls the
strain of the cable lessens ; " Haul, and with a will, my
men, haul !" they get a fathom or two of cable in ; the
curling crest of a broken wave falls on board, almost
smothering the men, and filling the boat ; she droops
and staggers under the weight of water ; the men in
her as they cling to the thwarts are up to their necks,
the air-tight compartments in the boat lift her, the
valves in the floor open, she empties herself in a few
seconds ; a huge short wave curls on, she rises to it,
buoyant as ever ; it catches her under the bows, throws
her high in the air, as if it would turn her end-over-
end ; the men cling to the hawser for a breathless
moment ; it checks the boat, the wave breaks over the
boat in a cloud of spray and foam ; the boat drops ; the
men shake their heads free of the water ; again a loud
shout from the coxswain ; " Haul, haul, your hardest,
my men, hand over hand !" they get in a few more
feet of the strong rope, and so much nearer to their
anchor ; and then hold on with straining muscles for
another dread struggle with the next huge sea ;
hardly time for a few quick breaths, and here the sea
comes, like a terrible monster, with shaking mane and
gnashing teeth ; it foams along, gleaming out of the
darkness and straightly leaps upon them ; and thus
amid all the wild turmoil of the raging breakers, with
the boat thrown violently here and there in the might

of the seas, with the waves breaking over her in such
quick succession that the men can scarcely find time to
breathe, does the fight go on in order to recover the
anchor and cable ; the men had no thought of themselves ; they had but to cut the cable and run before
the gale, and the fierce strife would be over ; no ! they
must, at all costs, recover the anchor and cable, or
they will not be able to save the crew, and they will
fight and wrestle for it to the end.   At last the cable
shortens, another pull and the boat is right over the
anchor, she lifts on a sea, the anchor is torn from its
hold, and lifts with her : in with it, make it fast, hoist
the sails, the boat's head pays round, and she is again
steered for the wreck.   As the boat runs before the
wind and seas, the men, who are thoroughly exhausted, have a few minutes of comparative rest.

The time occupied by the life-boat men in recovering their anchor has been a dread time indeed,
for the poor shipwrecked crew.

With their shattered and slowly-sinking vessel
staggering and shuddering beneath their feet, the
heavy seas thundering against her and breaking over
her, each one threatening to be the final one which
shall sweep them all to destruction ; the men seemed
to be each moment on the verge of death.

The storm howls around them, their only ray of hope
proceeds from the life-boat light, which shines feebly
through the mist, and suddenly the boat has halted
short in her course towards them ; why, they can scarcely
understand ; but one thing they are sure of, that it is
no failing courage on the part of the men ; it is im-

possible that they should be left to perish in their distress.

Their one effort now is to keep the tar-barrel in full blaze, and cruelly the wind and seas seem to do their utmost to destroy this their last hope, and leave them without the signal which alone can guide the life-boat to their rescue.

Fullarton, poor fellow, is working with an excited energy, burning in the barrel everything that he can lay hands on, that is at all likely to feed the flame.

He had left home a few days before, so full of hope and joy, and glad anticipation ; they had had bad weather, and anxious watches, and sleepless nights since they sailed, and now the poor fellow is almost overwrought by work and watching, and broken down with dread anxiety. " It is not for myself so much, not for myself, as for my poor girl," he says to his mates ; they, kind fellows, amid their own cares and anxieties, and memories, and fears, do what they can to cheer him up.

Now as the life-boat comes rushing in through the seething seas, and breaks out from the darkness into the light of the fire which they succeed in keeping burning on the deck of the schooner, it is Fullarton's voice that is heard in piercing tones above the roar of the gale. " Be as quick as you can ! be as quick as you can ! we are sinking fast."

Yes ! it is very evident that the vessel must soon founder ; the wild seas are rushing over her ; her deck is almost level with the surface of the water ; at any

N

moment she may refuse to lift to the rise of the sea, and with one plunge sink bodily down.

The coxswain of the life-boat sees that the schooner is still drifting, and decides upon not anchoring the boat, but tries to run alongside the wreck, which is being kept head to the seas and wind by the drag of her chains. The boat runs alongside within a few feet; the grappling-irons are thrown on board, they catch in the gunwale of the wreck, the boatmen take turns with the lines round the thwarts, and begin to haul the boat slowly up to the wreck; it is hazardous work, for she is deeply laden with coals, and is half full of water; she is buried in the seas, and labouring very heavily; the men are afraid that in the rush of some cross sea the boat will be tossed bodily on to the wreck.

The boat lifts up on the crest of a towering wave; there is a tremendous strain upon the stout grappling-lines, a moment's lull in the rush of the broken water. "Haul in hard upon the lines, get her alongside, now, my men; sharp, my men!" the coxswain shouts; and then to the vessel's crew: "Be ready to jump directly we are near enough!" "Aye! Aye! all right, all right!" the crew cry, excitedly, and crouch ready to spring upon the gunwale, and over into the boat. "Be ready all! be ready all!" the coxswain again cries, as he tries to sheer the boat near enough for the men to jump on board. "Now! now! Stop! hold on, hold on all for your lives!" A tremendous breaker comes gliding on like a dark snow-crowned wall, deluges the men with the foam and spray that flies from its crest, lifts the boat in its strong grasp, the grappling-lines snap like threads, and the boat is swept on in the rush of the wave far away from the wreck; the boatmen look back, and in the glare of the signal-fire they can see the pale white faces of the despairing and terrified sailors, and as the boat is driven on through the dark wild seas, the cries of the poor fellows can be for some time heard penetrating the tumult of the storm.

Before the boat was driven away from the vessel, at the moment of the ropes parting, the coxswain, seeing that the boat would be carried away, shouted at the pitch of his voice, "Have ropes ready!" the crew heard the words; and are consoled in the depth of their disappointment; they know that they are not to be deserted, that while ship and life-boat both last, attempt after attempt will be made for their rescue. But how long will the wreck float under them? this is the terrible question, and they call out, and this is the cry that the boatmen hear indistinctly: "We are sinking fast! We are sinking fast!"

The swirl of the sea and the tide, and the force of the gale, drive the boat far away to leeward; the men hoist her sails again, heave her to, and then try to stay her, and make in again directly for the wreck; but she misses stays, as the seas come rushing over her, and they have to wear her round. They battle on, and are speedily ready for their third attempt, thankful to find that the poor labouring wreck is still afloat.

They run the boat close under the schooner's port-quarter; the sailors are all ready with the required ropes; they throw one on board the boat, and the men in the boat succeed in throwing two strong lines on board the wreck; once more the order is to haul in close alongside.

And again the boatmen see the white faces of the almost drowned and exhausted men light up with hope. Fullarton especially is full of joy in the reaction of his feelings; he almost feels saved, and is very excited. Cautiously the boatmen work, doing their utmost to prevent the boat being dashed against the wreck; now they are just alongside; two minutes more, and all are saved; no, a heavy sea comes foaming along, and as it breaks fills the boat and rushes over the ship, which staggers under its weight; the ropes which fasten the boat to the ship, jerk and wrench, but still hold; the boat lifts, clears herself of water, the men breathe again. Another tremendous wave comes rushing along, another, and then several in quick succession; the men cling with all their force to the thwarts; heavy volumes of water beat down upon their backs; the boat plunges, and is wrestled here and there in the strong tumult of the waves; the ropes seem ready to tear the masts and thwarts to which they are fastened out of the boat; at last one rope parts; another gives the moment after; the boat rises on the crest of a wave, she heels over, the third rope breaks under the tremendous strain, the boat springs forward and is torn away from the vessel, and is rapidly swept away under her stern; a loud shriek is heard, it is from poor Fullarton; the boatmen see him

as he stands between them and the glare of the flame;
he throws up his clasped hands in despair; the next
moment he wildly rushes along the deck, for a second
balances himself on the gunwale, crouches and springs
with all his force towards the boat—a heavy thud; he
hits the bow of the boat as she is driving away stern
first; a cry from the boatmen, " Man overboard !" as
he sinks a huge wave rolls over him, and bears
the boat farther away; Jarman, the coxswain, seizes a
life-buoy and jumps upon a thwart ready to throw it to
the man when he rises; a blast of wind catches Jarman,
nearly tumbles him overboard, and throws him down
into the bottom of the boat, wrenching the life-buoy
from his hand; the drowning sailor is again lost to
sight in the trough of the sea; he is swimming and
struggling hard, but the boat, although without sails,
is being driven faster than he can swim; the men see
his wild desperate efforts, as he plunges and springs
forward with outspread arms as if to grasp at the boat;
he is lifted high on the crest of a wave; it curls him
over, and with a cry he falls head first, and is buried
in the trough of the sea; once more they make out
his figure· as he springs up on the top of a wave
between them and the signal-fire; once again they
hear his cry of despair, and he is lost to them, and to
all dear to him on earth for ever.

It is all over in a few seconds; the hardy boatmen
shudder and feel sick at heart: so suddenly, so
terribly, so swiftly has the strong man died; and to
see their brother sailor thus perish within a few yards
of them, beaten under by the boiling waves so quickly

that they were utterly powerless to aid, is indeed, terrible to all. But not a moment is to be lost, any one of the mad seas which rush so continually over the wreck may founder her with its weight, or sweep the exhausted men out of her. The wreck cannot by any possibility float much longer; how can the men be saved? The life-boat is now right astern of the vessel, which is drifting slowly towards them; the seas run with such violence, swaying the wreck in one direction and the boat in another, that it is evidently useless to attempt to fasten the boat alongside the wreck, and the coxswain determines to adopt a new plan. The boat is right astern of the wreck, which is slowly drifting towards them; the coxswain of the boat will anchor the boat right in her path, and try to sheer alongside as she drifts past, and thus get the crew out of her. "Over with the anchor; veer out as little cable as she will ride to; hold on, stand ready all!"—and they anxiously watch the approach of the wreck.

On the wreck comes straight for them; the boat's mizen sail is hauled flat to help the boat sheer out of the ship's way; they must manage skilfully or she will drive right over the life-boat; the helm is put hard up; the mizen catches the wind; the boat sheers, the wreck just misses her; the boat is close to her starboard quarter. Down helm, and the boat sheers in close alongside, the men in the bow pay out the cable quickly to let the boat float alongside the ship, "Jump when we near!" they cry to the crew; "jump for it! be steady, but do not lose a chance!" a sea throws the boat within a yard of the wreck, three men spring on board ; a moment, and the next rush of sea sweeps the boat away and buries them all in foam. As the sea overruns the boat, the boatmen cling to the sailors who have sprung on board, to prevent their being washed out of her. "Have we got all?" "No, only three, one is left!" "Look out, then, my men; in we go again! the lee-tide is running very strongly—the cable is paying out fast."—"There is only about ten fathom of cable left," the men in the bow shout to the coxswain; he sheers the boat in, they can just make out the figure of a man at the stern of the vessel; they cry out to him: "Be ready; 'tis your last chance; you must jump for your life; we shall hardly have time to come in again;" they close in alongside; a heavy sea knocks down the men in the bow who are paying out the rope; at that moment the man on the wreck makes a desperate leap for the boat, he falls among the men; the end of the cable runs out into the sea. "Rope gone!" is the cry, but the man is saved; the ship is on the point of sinking, and they at once lose sight of her in the dark night. It is the captain who is last on board the boat; he looks round with thankfulness upon the life-boatmen and upon his saved crew: "But where is Fullarton?" he asks. "The man who jumped for the boat when the ropes parted."

"He fell short of the boat, and we could not save him," is the sad answer.

"Poor fellow, poor fellow! he was so terribly anxious, he could not wait. Oh! that he had only waited with us! but he was almost in despair before the boat came, and seeing you break away the second time was too much for him." And afterwards he told them the drowned sailor's piteous story—what a good fellow he was, and that it was because he was to be married upon his return home that he was so anxious, and felt life to be doubly dear to him.

It is about seven o'clock in the morning ; the day breaks wild and cold, and dismal as weather can well be. The faint light of the dawn scarcely makes its way through the thick clouds of flying spray and foam and half-frozen snow that drive fiercely along.

A dread suggestive picture as witnessed from the cliffs on shore is that of the Goodwin Sands in a storm—the raging mountains of white surf springing high in the air, and breaking into clouds of spray, and the waves racing along the Sands in foaming rollers, strong to sweep anything before them : to watch this from the shore at a distance of six miles is enough to make one shudder, so terrible a picture does it give of wild, hungry, irresistible power and rage, but what must it be for those who have to encounter this turbulent sea in the very thick of its strife ; in a boat almost buried by the waves, clinging to the thwarts, the life half beaten out of them ; and yet, hour after hour enduring all hardship, and sternly battling with all resistance—and all this the men in the life-boat have yet to endure.

The boat is on the top of the south end of the Sand, and in the fiercest strife of the wild sea, a foaming wilderness of water all around them ; the waves seem mad in the very fury of their contest ; they rear up and clash together with a roar and hiss; rush swiftly on; recoil as swiftly back; now meet others in their full onward swoop and contend for mastery; leap high in angry curling crests, then fall with thunder tones, but only to form in serried ranks, and rush swiftly again into the wild race and conflict.

No ordinary boat could endure this for a minute, the first of these mad curling waves would engulf her at once; the life-boat alone can contend with such broken battling seas, and come out a victor from the strife.

The men crowd aft that the boat may run better before the gale; they put oars out on each quarter to help the boat steer, and to prevent her broaching to, for if she does, the curl of the wave is so strong that she will be rolled over, and probably many of her crew and passengers lost, for although she would right again directly, all could not expect to get back to her in such a sea; she is full of water; the seas break over her in such quick succession, that she has no time to free herself, but she bounds on, and on, and soon, but not without much danger, the men escape from the broken water and reach the outer part of the Sand.

The boat is now put under fore-sail and mizen, both close reefed, hauled to the wind and pressed through the seas, to be certain of making the land, from which the gale is blowing so strongly.

The boat heels over under the pressure of her canvas, one gunwale is buried in the seas; the rescued men have never been in a life-boat before, and feel much alarmed.

"Ah! Geordie, man," says the captain to the mate,

"this is queer sort of sailing; it's sailing under water altogether;" and the men afterwards confessed, that not knowing what a life-boat could do, they expected every moment that she would capsize, and felt themselves in almost as much danger in the boat as they had been on board the wreck. It takes the boat about an hour and a half of this hard driving through the seas to beat up against the gale and get near to the land; the men then find themselves not far from the South Foreland light, between Deal and Dover. The ships in the Downs are many of them in great danger, driving from their anchorage, and some with signals of distress flying.

An English man-of-war is at anchor there; as the life-boat flies under her stern, the men on deck give a hearty cheer in honour of the Warriors of the Goodwin Sands. A large Dutch ship is next passed, all her crew crowd aft, and with much energy they also cheer the brave boatmen.

Some large Deal luggers are cruising about; the men on board see with much surprise the flag flying at the life-boat mast-head, telling the tale of triumph, that a crew had been rescued; for they declared in speaking about it afterwards, that they thought it a mere impossibility to get a crew off the Goodwin in such a night, and through such a terrific sea.

The life-boatmen begin to be uneasy about the steamer; they saw her last about five in the morning, with the Goodwin Sands close under her lee, and facing the full force of the gale.

They think that she will have run down the Sands

and be waiting for them ; they put the boat about, and
run out a little, hoping to meet her ; after they have
laid-to for about half an hour, waiting for the steamer,
a heavy squall strikes the boat, and carries away her
mizen-mast ; they at once wear her head round to the
land, and run into St. Margaret's Bay.   The men fear
that if they leave the protection of the high cliffs, the
boat, as she is now partially disabled, may be blown
over on the French coast by the force of the gale, and
they therefore run down under the cliffs to Dover.
Here they find further evidence of the terrible nature of
the gale; ships are being towed into the harbour disabled ; the sea is making a clean breach over the cross
wall ; part of the esplanade has been washed away, and
the mail packets have been driven back in distress ;
hundreds of people, hiding in sheltered places, are
watching the fury of the sea ; they have for some time
seen, with much interest, the gallant life-boat, with her
flag flying, making for the harbour, and many come
down the pier to welcome her.   The life-boat, as she
shoots round the head of the pier, meets the strong wind
in all its force ; she has lost her mizen-mast, anchor,
cables, and has scarcely a spare fathom of rope left; she is .
fast being driven out again to sea, when they manage
to get a rope to her from the pier, and many willing
hands clap on, and tow her slowly along ; in the meantime the harbour-master sends the steam-tug to her
help, and the boat is soon safely moored in the inner
harbour, and the men who have for so many hours
encountered such great hardship and peril are once
more upon dry land.

The shipwrecked crew are well cared for by the agent of the Shipwrecked Mariners' Society ; the life-boatmen go to the Sailors' Home, and under the influence of a hearty welcome and substantial cheer, speedily recover from the effects of their long exposure and fatigue.

The coxswain hastens to telegraph to the authorities at Ramsgate the safe arrival of the life-boat at Dover, and there is great satisfaction felt there at the assurance of the boat's safety.

While the life-boat was in among the breakers, battling with the seas, and disentombing, we may almost say, the terrified sailors from the hungry grave which yawned around them, the steamer kept her ground, as near as possible to where the captain thought the life-boat was at work, and just clear of the surf.

They waited hour after hour, but no signal came from that fierce battle-field ; the hoarse blast of the storm, the many-voiced roar of waters, overwhelmed all other sound ; the darkness of the night, the clouds of sleet and foam engulfed all in gloom. The crew of the steamer waited on in much anxiety, and not free from great peril.

The daylight broke, a grey flood of misty light rolled back the greater darkness, but they could see no signs of the life-boat ; they could make out by-and-by a few spars tossing wildly among the leaping seas and a tangled portion of wreck ; they steam in as near to it as they dare, and with their glasses watch closely every shadow, or spar, or mass of wreckage, but see no signs of life ; the sea is silent as to the fate of the crew, and after a careful and vain search, the captain of the steamer, feeling sure that if the lifeboat has succeeded in getting clear of the Sands, she must have been forced by the gale to run to Dover for shelter, he determines to make the best of his way there. Jarman, the life-boat coxswain, sees the steamer making for the harbour, and hastens to the pierhead ; one wave of his arm tells the whole story of success and safety.

The crew of the life-boat and of the steamer alike realize the responsibility of their work, that it is indeed one of life and death—that they must not be out of the way when wanted if they can help it ; for that any delay may be fatal to some dying crew, who are perhaps straining their eyes in vain searchings for their one earthly hope, the life-boat.

All hands at once prepare for their return to Ramsgate ; back round the stormy South Foreland again ; and home to be greeted, as such conquering heroes should be greeted, with smiles of welcome from hundreds of faces brightening up with hearty sympathy, and with ringing cheers that tell alike of admiration for courage, and of gladness for their return ; cheers that know no reserve, as they welcome those who come triumphant from the battle-field—cheers for those who come not from death-dealing, in however good a cause, but from life-saving—leaving none to echo their shouts of victory with the wailings of defeat.

The following letter will prove an apt and not uninteresting conclusion to the story, as it expresses the deep gratitude of the men who were saved, and gives in simple heartfelt language their tribute of thanks, and their declaration of admiration for the gallant and self-denying efforts by which their rescue from otherwise certain death had been so nobly effected.

> "119 *Church St., North Shields.*
> *Capt. Shaw, Harbour-master, Ramsgate.*

"DEAR SIR,

"I, the undersigned master, and likewise the crew of the *Mary*, which were saved by the gallant coxswain, Mr. Jarman, and his crew on the morning of the 21st inst., which I do believe to be unrivalled, for my idea is they used every effort to save the young man which was drowned, but it was in vain ; we all beg to return a vote of thanks to Mr. Jarman and his crew ; likewise to you, dear sir, which has everything in such order and discipline for the rescue of life ; and may the Lord bless them all, and look over them, when trying their uttermost efforts to rescue their fellow-men from a watery grave !

I cannot express my feelings good enough to reward the brave fellows' attendance. My love to them all, and I will make a letter appear in the public press after I get myself settled, therefore I beg to conclude."

> "From your grateful Friend,

> "WILLIAM FOREMAN, Master.
> "C. H. MOORE, Mate.
> "JOSEPH COLLINS, Carpenter.
> "THOMAS ATCHINSON, A. B."

To which letter the harbour-master returned answer, stating how gratifying it was to all connected with the life-boat and steam-tug that such gallant and skilful exertions should have reaped such success ; the sympathy and great regret that was felt for the loss of their young shipmate ; and that there were at Ramsgate, at all times both by day and night, gallant boatmen ready and willing to risk their lives when called upon to perform such perilous undertakings.

And, readers, can we do better than often, and especially when gales are abroad, echo the prayer offered for the life-boatmen by the rescued master of the *Mary*.—" The Lord bless them all, and look over them when trying to rescue their fellow-men from a watery grave !"

CHAPTER XV.

DEAL BEACH.

"Then courage, all brave mariners,
    And never be dismay'd,
While we have bold adventurers,
    We ne'er shall want a trade ;
Our merchants will employ us
    To fetch them wealth, we know ;
Then be bold—work for gold,
    When the stormy winds do blow."

M. Parker.

FEW places in the world, if any, have proved the
scene of more daring sailor-life than Deal beach.
Generation after generation of boatmen have passed
away, having spent their lives, from early boyhood,
in continuous strife with the swift tide, strong seas,
and rolling surf that race through the channels off
Deal, and break upon the Goodwin, or upon the Shingle
beach.

Other antagonists the old days used to provide,
and the young men's hands grew hard with handling
the bow, or spear, or javelin, or the musket, cutlass, or
boarding-pike, as well as with handling the tiller and
the ropes.

In the days of old, the Northern Sea Kings were, to the east coast of England, like clouds on the horizon, ever threatening a storm, but without any indication as to where the storm would break.

The coast of Kent was especially open to their attacks; they came down like wolves on the fold; a bright sunny morning, a bowling northerly breeze, a few specks on the horizon standing out darkly with the clear dawn behind them.

A few hours, and the Norsemen were at work; a fishing-village, wrecked and half buried in ruins, some of its stout defenders lying gashed and ghastly among its smoking embers; trembling fugitives still hurrying inland with a few of their lighter and more treasured goods, and the marauders holding swift and triumphant debauch upon the shore, as with rude cries of mirth and victory, they prepare to start seaward again before time can be found to gather forces to make any attack upon them, or any efforts can be made to regain the plunder the hardy robbers have obtained, or to revenge the slaughter they have worked.

The Romans, when they were lords of the land, felt the necessity of resisting these roving Sea Kings in a determined and organised manner; they formed nine military stations along the coast, and placed all under the command of an officer, to whom they gave the sounding title of Count of the Saxon Shore.

Four of these stations were in Kent—Reculver, Richborough, Dover, and Lymne. Remains of the Roman fortifications still bear witness that they were intended in defence from an enemy whose power was not lightly esteemed.

This military organisation of the Romans was afterwards developed into the establishment of the Cinque Ports and their respective members, the jurisdiction of which embraced a coast line from Reculver to Hastings.

The inhabitants of the Cinque Ports well earned and fully obtained great honour in the old days. The free men of the ports were styled barons, and held rank among the nobility of the kingdom. They stood the vanguard of defence against all England's continental enemies, and their service is thus described by Mr. Boys in his 'History of Sandwich' :

"The inhabitants were always on the watch to prevent invasion ; their militia were in constant readiness for action, and their vessels stout and warlike, so that, in Edward the First's time, they alone equipped a fleet of one hundred sail, and gave such a blow to the maritime power of France as to clear the Channel of those restless and insidious invaders. The state depended upon them for the safety of its coast-line and towns, and their services went by no means unrewarded ; an encouragement they had always been accustomed to receive, and this for commercial as well as for warlike enterprise, as by the wisdom of our Saxon ancestors, a merchant who had at his own expense three times freighted vessels with home produce was entitled to the rank of thane or baron. The Barons of the Cinque Ports walked in procession at the coronations of the kings and queens, and at the feast of the coronation had an especial table allotted to them in Westminster Hall at the right of the king; this privilege was preserved up to the time of the coronation of George the Third."

All this is evident and sufficient testimony of the nature and extent of the services of our coast heroes in defence of their country; and still the enterprise and daring continue, and bold, vigilant warfare goes on, although defence against a foreign foe has long ceased to be its first consideration. In later times, indeed, the revenue officers unfortunately, and to no small extent, took the place of the foreign foe in the minds and labours of by no means a few of the boatmen and inhabitants of these towns situated so conveniently adjacent to the Continent; and the enterprise and labours of the boatmen were no less daring, if less patriotic than in former days, and smuggling was elevated into as organized a business as fishing is now: one writer rather quaintly remarks, "Yet even this smuggling is not without its utility, for however the revenue may suffer, it gives birth to a very intrepid race of seamen, who are of the greatest service in relieving others from the dangers which befall shipping on this coast in bad weather."

Certainly the boatmen of Deal beach are not now, and probably never have been, surpassed for skill and daring.

If they can by any possibility get their famous luggers out to sea, no hurricane daunts them; their splendid boats glide over the seas, escaping the broken water—now high on the wave, now buried in the trough—and look like so many strong-winged gulls, as they seem almost to play with the storm.

Falconer, in his 'Shipwreck,' pays the following tribute to the skill and courage of the boatmen:

> " Where e'er in ambush lurks the fatal sands,
>   They claim the danger, proud of skilful bands!
>   For while, with darkling course, the vessels sweep
>   The winding shore, or plough the faithless deep;
>   Or bar, or shelf, the watery path they sound
>   With dexterous arm, sagacious of the ground.
>   Ceaseless they combat every hostile wind,
>   Wheeling in mazy track with course inclined;
>   Expert to moor where terrors line the road,
>   Or win the anchor from its dark abode."

Let us take a peep at Deal beach, and try to realize some of the scenes that are there to be witnessed.

Suppose a fine clear winter's day. A gentle south-westerly breeze has been blowing on and off for several days; many ships have found their way out of the Thames, or have beaten down helped by the tides from the North Sea, and having reached the Downs there ride safely at anchor; the ships-boats, or the galley punts, as the small Deal boats are called, are doing the little work that is to be done, and the large luggers are drawn high upon the beach.

The boatmen are lounging about the beach here and there, or they are smoothing the shingle down with shovels, where the tide has heaped it up, to give the luggers a fair run down into the sea in the event of their being wanted; tanned sails are spread abroad upon the shingle drying, women hang about knitting

and watching the ships at anchor for any signal for a
boat ; at times there is a move down the beach to
help a boat that is coming ashore out of the surf and
to drag it up high and dry.

The wind gets a slant to the south-east as the tide
ebbs, and at once all are alert in the fleet of ships at
anchor in the Downs, that have been waiting for a fair
breeze.   There is a hurry to the beach of all officers,
sailors, or passengers that may be ashore ; the last
supply of fresh provisions is taken on board those
ships on which the Captain can afford to be luxurious :
you can hear the orders shouted, the capstans at work ;
jibs are set, topsails loosened, the anchors got up and
catted, the sails let fall, and away the ships go down
Channel ; a fresh northerly breeze bowls along and
lasts some days, the outward bound ships go flying
through the Downs with top-gallant sails set ; and
except that they land a few pilots, there is nothing
whatever for the Deal men to do.

At last a change of weather promises, the homeward-
bound are to have a turn ; the outward-bound must
anchor in the Downs and wait a while.   The French
coast shows out clearly, the gulls are whirling about
uttering shrill plaintive cries ; the boatmen watch the
sunset, greyish white streaky clouds are gathering in
the west, the sun looks *sheer*, is the boatmen's word for
it, and as the long rays of light break through the
clouds—ah ! yes, we shall have a change of wind and
weather.   "The sun is setting up his backstays."
"Bright *skies* make dirty ways ;" and before daylight
closes the men overhaul their luggers and see that

everything is ready for a sudden start, should their services be needed.

A mizzling rain comes on, the wind is round to the westward and freshening ; some of the vessels which have been among the last to pass Deal bound to the southward, give up the hope of getting down Channel in the face of the freshening breeze, and return to find anchorage in the Downs.

It is a likely night for work, and the boatmen get ready for a cruise ; everything is prepared to launch one of the large luggers ; she is now drawn up high upon the beach ; her crew of fifteen men hasten to get ready for sea. It is a dark and squally winter's morning, about one o'clock ; fourteen of the men are now on board, each at his station ; one man stands ready to cut the lashing of the stop which holds the boat in position on the ways ; they wait till a squall passes ; the word is given, the lashing cut, the man springs to the gunwale of the boat, and climbs on board. Scarcely has he tumbled over the side when the boat rushes down the greased ways and is launched into the surf ; the mizen is already set, the foresail is hoisted with all speed, and the boat speeds on her way seaward.

As the day comes the breeze freshens, and many luggers are cruising about, speaking the vessels at anchor, or the vessels running through the Downs, ready to offer any assistance in their power ; upon some of the vessels they put men to pilot them into Ramsgate harbour, or round the North Foreland into the Margate Roads.

Or if the wind has blown heavily, there will be

generally some vessels that have lost their anchors and cables, and the boatmen will receive orders to supply fresh ones.

There is sometimes a degree of surprise expressed at the amount claimed by a boat's crew for taking an anchor and cable off to a vessel in distress ; it requires some knowledge of the work to appreciate its danger, and how hardly and well the money awarded is generally earned.

Consider, as an example, the case of the *Albion* lugger, as it happened during the gale, some of the incidents of which we are about to relate.

The *Albion* during her cruise meets with a vessel which is driving before the increasing storm ; she has lost both her anchors and cables, and the lugger receives orders to supply her from the shore ; the hardy crew receive the order gladly, put the lugger round, and beat through the heavy seas, making for Deal. They have to force the boat against wind and tide, and much skill is required to prevent her being filled by the rising seas which sweep around her ; now she rushes upon the beach, the surf breaks over her and half fills her with water ; with a tremendous thump and shake, she strikes the shore with her iron keel.

As the wave which bore the lugger in upon the beach recedes, a man springs overboard from the bow with a rope in his hand ; many catch hold of the rope, and haul their hardest to keep the boat straight, head on to the beach ; there is a stem strap—a chain running through a hole in the front part of the keel ; a boatman watches his opportunity, and as a wave sweeps back, rushes down and passes a rope through the loop of the strap ; the other end of this rope is fastened to a powerful capstan, which is placed high up on the beach. "Man the capstan ! Heave with a will," and the strong men strain at the capstan bars until the capstan creaks again. There is no starting the lugger; she is so full of water from the surf breaking on the beach, that she is too heavy for the men at one capstan to move her ; ropes are led down from two other capstans, and rove through a snatch block fastened to a boat on the beach ; all put out their strength, round they tramp with a "ho ! heave ho !" and slowly the lugger travels up the beach, and is safe from the roll of the breakers. The men get the water out of her, haul her higher up on to a swivel platform, turn her round head to the sea, and the leading hands hurry away to inquire about an anchor and cable. The agent supplies them with such as seem suitable for the size of the vessel, and which will perhaps weigh together about seven tons.

There is no small amount of labour attached to getting the anchor and chain cable on board the lugger, but in a short time all are again ready for sea.

The gale has rapidly increased in force, and a frightful surf is running on the beach ; the roar of the breakers on the shingle, the howling of the storm, the gleam of white foam, shining out of the mist and gloom, all picture the wildness of the storm, but the undaunted boatmen do not hesitate ; all is ready, the signal given, the boat rushes down the steep ways, and is launched into the sea. A breaking wave rolls in

swiftly, it meets the bow of the lugger in its rush, fills
her ; for a moment the big boat runs under water, and
then is lifted and twisted like a toy in the grasp of
the sea, and is thrown in the heave of the wave
broadside on to the beach ; a cry of horror from all
on shore, and a rush down to aid the crew, who are all
—there are fifteen of them—struggling in the surf ;
now the men are washed up by the wave, and feel the
ground, and stagger forward ; now they are caught
again by a breaker and rolled over ; it is for each of
them a terrible battle with the fierce seas ; here, one
gets on his feet and stumbles forward, he is caught by
the men on shore and dragged up the beach ; there, a
man is lying struggling on the shingle, trying in vain
to rise, exhausted and confused ; two men seize his
collar and pull him forward a yard or two, then get
him to his feet, and he escapes the next wave, which
would have washed him out to sea again. Now all the
men seem to be saved ; names are shouted—do all
answer ? no ! there is one missing ; all rush to the
water's edge, and gaze into the darkness ; eagerly
watching each shadow mid the surf ; there he is ! no !
yes it is ! there lifting on the surf ; there rolling over :
" Quick, quick, form a line !" and the brave boatmen
grasp each other's hands with iron strength and form a
chain, the lowest of the four or five men at the sea end
of the chain being in the water ; the waves battle with
them, but sturdily they persevere ; at last the body is
within the reach of the seaward man, he grasps it, the
men are dragged up the beach, and the poor insensible
man is carried ashore. Alive ? or dead ? they cannot

say, and with a great fear in their hearts they carry
him hurriedly up the beach, and soon, to the great joy
of all, he gives signs of life, and gradually recovers.

In the meanwhile the poor boatmen on the beach
have nothing that they can do, but watch their fine
boat, which was worth five hundred pounds, being torn,
and hammered to pieces in the surf, plank after plank
is wrenched from her, now with a loud crash she is
broken in half, the two halves part, the anchor and
cable fall through her, they can see part of the fore-
peak with one side torn away, floating in the breakers ;
soon that also is rent to pieces, and nothing but
fragments of the boat float in the surf, or are strewn
about the beach, and the boatmen, heavy-hearted, but
thankful that they have escaped with their lives,
go slowly to their homes, to rest for a few hours, and
recruit their strength, and then to be ready to form
part of the crew of any other boat, and at the first
summons to rush out again to the encounter with the
stormiest seas.

In a narrative of adventure and conflict with the
seas that rage over the Goodwin Sands, it would not
be well to refrain from bearing testimony to how
readily, how gallantly, the men of Deal, of Broadstairs,
of Walmer, and of Kingsdown, as well as of Ramsgate,
man their respective life-boats, whenever the call is
made for their services, and race out to the scene of
action, full of hardihood, of skill, of courage—true
Storm Warriors, ever ready to dare all and do all that
they may rescue the drowning from a watery grave.

CHAPTER XVI.

TIE LOSS OF THE "LINDA," AND THE RACE TO THE RESCUE.

> "A sudden crash, the mast is gone,
>   And with it goes all hope ;
> No longer can the fated crew
>   With the surging waters cope.
>
> "Now they commit their souls to God,
>   As men about to die ;
> For vain seems all the help of man
>   In this extremity.
>
> G. Ward.

AT daylight, in the morning after the destruction of the *Albion* lugger, the weather grows worse and worse; the grey misty gloom that hangs over the sea is scarcely broken by the swift gleams of light that find a faint way through the fast drifting clouds.

And the weather continues to grow more tempestuous still as the night grows on. Many ships come scudding northward before the gale ; they make the South Sand Head light, and steer their course for the narrow Gull channel that runs between the Goodwin and Brake Sands. The South Sands Head light-ship is moored at the southern extremity of the Goodwin Sands; it is about three miles from the South Foreland light.

In thick misty weather, which so often prevails in the Channel during westerly gales in winter time, it is often very difficult for vessels to make either of these lights.

And as the edge of the Goodwin Sands is very steep at this part, and has deep water close to it, keeping the lead going scarcely affords sufficient protection, for between two casts of the lead a vessel running fast may well pass out of deep water on to the Sands, and there be lost.

So it often happens that vessels running through the Downs in such weather, suddenly find themselves in a position of great peril.

On the night in question, the men on board the light-ship keep an especially vigilant watch, as the darkness of the night adds to the gloom which spreads its folds over the raging sea, and the direction and force of the wind, and the many ships that are flying before the gale, suggest the probability of disaster.

About midnight, the men on watch make out, in the lift of the mist, a fine brig not far from them, driving before the gale, and making straight for the Sands; the alarm is given, and a gun at once fired to give the unfortunate crew warning of their danger.

The look-out men fancy, by the changing of the position of the brig's lights, that the crew are making an effort to alter the vessel's course, and to weather the Sands; but it is too late! nothing can save her! The crew of the light-ship lose sight of her in the darkness, and make all ready to signal for the life-boat to come to the rescue of her crew; they wait a minute or two, watching, in the direction they think the brig must strike, for the usual signals of distress, and almost immediately see the bright flare of a tar-barrel; they fire a signal-gun from the light-ship, and its warning voice booms loudly above the storm; then they send up rockets; the shipwrecked are thus encouraged to hope, while the ready boatmen on shore are called to action.

The signals are seen at the Walmer life-boat station, one mile from Deal; and at the Kingsdown station, three miles from Deal; at both places the call is promptly and eagerly obeyed; the life-boats are got ready with all haste; they are speedily manned and launched, and struggle their way through the boiling surf, which is rolling upon the beach. They spread all the canvas they can stagger under, and the two boats fly before the gale straight for the light-ship; there they learn the position in which the signals of distress were seen, and cruise round the edge of the Goodwin in all the fierce tumble of sea, and skirt the ring of surf which marks where the rollers are breaking with terrible force upon the Sands; but they can obtain no guide, no clue to where the wreck is; no signal light shines out of that drear darkness pleading for help, and no sound can the men hear, listen as they will, other than the ceaseless roar of the storm. Still the brave boatmen will not abandon the search, and for some hours the boats continue their vain efforts.

The crew of the Kingsdown boat determine at last

that further search is useless, and as it is not possible
for them to beat back to their distant station in the
teeth of the gale, they run for Ramsgate, arriving
there just before dawn. The Walmer boat continues
cruising in the neighbourhood of the Sands until after
daylight, when her crew, seeing no signs of the wreck,
also determine to make for the shore.

The seas have been steadily increasing in violence,
and are now running very high, and as they curl and
break, the crest of each wave is caught by the fierce
wind, and dispersed in a cloud of spray.

Bravely the boat sails on through the troubled seas;
she is constantly overrun by the waves, and filled with
water, but each time she speedily regains all her
buoyancy, and bounds on over the seas. The men
have almost too much confidence in her, as if no
amount of sea and wind could possibly capsize her;
they carry on a press of canvas, until the stout masts
bend and the ropes strain again, and they make the
sheet fast; but now a fierce huge wave comes rushing
along, catches the boat broadside on, lifts the boat
high on its crest, and then completely curls her over
and passes, leaving the boat capsized, and all the men
struggling in the water.

But it is however only a passing victory, after all,
that the sea can boast over the life-boat; at once
she rights herself, gets rid of the water that fills her,
and rides upon the seas as bravely as ever.

Happily all the men have on their cork jackets, and
in them they float breast high; never was there such
a wild dance as they now seem to dance; tossed

high and poised for a moment on the cone of a leaping wave, again engulfed in the hollow trough of a sea, with a wall of tumbling water all around ; rising and falling in quick succession, their arms beating broken time as they struggle to swim towards the boat, which begins to drift fast away ; it is fortunate that some of the men have retained hold of the life-lines, the ends of which are fastened to the boat, by these they haul themselves alongside her, and all soon succeed in getting on board.

Away again through the Downs, across the high rolling seas, making for the shore, but their troubles are not yet at an end ; a blast of wind, fiercer than its fellows, strikes the sail, the boat careens over ; at that moment a huge wave leaps on the boat, strikes it with such force and so high, that it fills the sail with water and drives the boat bodily over, and the second time she is capsized, and the men, before they have recovered from the exhaustion caused by their former struggle, are the second time plunged into the sea, to find themselves battling for their lives with the waves. The cork jackets keep them afloat as before, but the waves run over them, and they are almost smothered in clouds of foam, until they are thoroughly worn out by the rush and beat of the seas which break over their heads. Up and down, tumbling here and there in the turmoil of the seas, pale and gasping for breath, almost too faint to make any struggle to regain the boat, becoming rapidly unconscious ; this time the wild dance mid the raging seas becomes truly too much like a dance of death.

Happily a powerful Deal lugger is near the scene
of the disaster; her crew at once do their best to pick
up and return to the life-boat those of the men who
are themselves unable to gain it.

The life-boat, self-righted, is floating high on the
waves quite ready for action as soon as her crew
can again take charge of her, and speed her on in
her course.

The men are, at last, all once more on board, the
boat is again got under weigh, and speeds safely to
the land.

But how, all this while, fared the unfortunate crew
of the vessel, in the vain effort to render assistance to
whom the life-boat men had incurred such hardship
and peril.

The unfortunate ship was the brig *Linda:* the
captain fancied the ship was in a safe course, free from
any immediate danger; the storm fog was too thick
for them to see the land, or any of the numerous
signal lights that guard the coast, but they kept the
lead going, and sped on before the gale; suddenly all
hands are alike startled and terrified by the loud
report of a gun fired quite close to them, and at
seeing the light of a light-vessel very near; they at
once realize their danger, for they know that the dread
Goodwin Sands must be right under their lee; with
frantic haste they attempt to wear the ship, but it is
too late; as she feels the helm she plunges in among
the surf, crashes upon the Sands, and the great seas
begin to fly over her; the ship must be lost, it is
beyond all hope that she can be saved; is there any

hope for the crew ?   They will not despair, or be lost
without making what small efforts they are able to
obtain assistance ; they know, from the violence with
which the ship rises and thumps upon the Sands, that
she must very speedily go to pieces.   They get a
tar-barrel, fill it with canvas, grease, and rags, light it,
and have the satisfaction of seeing it flare up with a
brilliant flame ; that, at all events, must sufficiently
penetrate the surrounding darkness and gloom to
make known their distress to the neighbouring light-
vessel.

Again, and almost immediately, they hear the loud
boom of the gun ; but as previously it seemed to them
the signal of death, so now it affords them a faint—a
very faint hope ; rockets too are fired by the light-
vessel ; surely the signals will be heard and seen on
shore, and the life-boat will come out in search of
them ; but where will they be then ?   There is no time
—no time ; the seas are washing over the deck, the
fierce fire of the tar-barrel is at once extinguished, and
the men hasten to take refuge from the sweeping seas
in the cross-trees and shrouds of the masts.   Seven
men spring to the foremast shrouds, and climb to the
cross-trees, the captain and four men cling to the
mainmast ; time after time the vessel lifts and falls
with a crash that wrenches her from stem to stern,
and makes all her timbers groan and rend, and nearly
shakes the sailors from their hold.   Now the ship
begins to work and writhe, the timbers break with
loud reports, planks are wrenched from her side in the
fierce tear of the sea, stout iron bolts are torn from

P

their hold and twisted like so much thread—the ship
is breaking up fast ; the masts sway about, the men
have to hold on their hardest to prevent being shaken
into the sea, so are they tossed and swung about in
the roll of the mast and the sway of the vessel.
Each wave leaping higher than those that have gone
before, seems to claim them for its prey ; everything
on the deck is swept away ; the deck itself opens, the
water gets down into the hold, and soon the deck
breaks up, and pieces float away in the wash of the
sea ; the bulwarks are torn off, and now a piece of the
side of the vessel is wrenched away ; the vessel must
be torn to fragments in a few short minutes, and
death seems very near to all the crew.

A tremendous wave rushes over the wreck, a crash
louder than a thunder peal ; the foremast has broken
off close to the deck, it falls over ; a few loud despairing cries, and the seven poor fellows who clung to the
mast are hurled into the sea, and are at once lost in
the wild rage of water.

The five men on the mainmast shudder in their
terror and despair, and cling closer and closer to the
mast as it sways and jerks from side to side ; there
may be a few minutes yet to live ; they think of home
and wife and children, and hold on the more convulsively while the seas break over them with increasing
violence ; it takes but a short time, and the wreck
beneath them seems in absolute fragments ; the poop-
deck is wrenched up, and a large piece of it is torn away;
at the next sea the wreck heels over, the mainmast is
carried away, and the captain and the four men are

hurled from it into the sea; the captain is thrown against a large fragment of deck with such force that both his legs are broken; he, however, manages to hold on to the piece of wreck, the other four men are also swept to it, and there cling; they find themselves surrounded by the hundred fragments of wreck into which the stout brig has been so rapidly torn.

The tide sweeps away the piece of deck to which the five men are so desperately clinging—away from the scene of the sad, swift, tragedy, and, by God's mercy, into an eddy of the current away from the surf and breakers which are thundering down in all their fury upon the Sands, and which would have swept the poor sailors at once to destruction if their frail raft had come within their reach. Away in the rough but not now broken seas the men are borne, their only hope the shattered, heaving piece of wreck that forms their raft; the horrors of the dark night are added to by the roar of the breakers as they crash down upon the Sands, and the poor sailors know not but that at any moment they may be met by some fresh eddy of the swift tide, and swept into the midst of that fatal surf. The fierce gale howls over them, the men are exhausted and hopeless, but they manage to lash the captain to the piece of wreck, his two broken legs make him faint and sick with agony; and on and on they float during the long dreary hours of the night.

They pass the Gull light-ship, watch its bright and, to them, mocking light, then they are carried to

the north-east of the Sands; there they meet the
changing tide, and it sets them to the southward, and,
to their great joy, away from the fatal Goodwin,
away in the direction of Calais, the seas still wash
over them. The agony of the captain is almost
unendurable, as every wash of the sea, every heave of
the frail piece of wreck jars his broken legs ; the men
have their nails torn from their fingers with the desperate
energy with which they clutch the smooth timbers of
the piece of deck on which they are lying.   Hour
after hour passes, and for fifteen hours they thus float
about, cold and wet, and wounded, and faint with
hunger and thirst ; the poor fellows become almost
unconscious, and can only just manage to hold on
mechanically to their frail support; the morning
passes, and they have no energy to look for a
passing sail, and no means of signalling if they saw
one.

Suddenly a loud shout surprises them, and they lift
their heads and see, with boundless joy, a large cutter
almost alongside the raft ; they seem called back from
death, and begin to arouse themselves from the swoon
into which they were all so rapidly sinking.

The cutter is a pilot-boat from Antwerp ; they are
got on board her not without much difficulty, so helpless are they, and so high is the sea still running ;
the kind-hearted Belgians have every pity for the
most miserable condition of the poor men, and do all
they can to restore them ; as soon as possible the
pilots land them at Deal, and they are taken to the
hospital and receive all possible medical care and

attention; they soon revive, the captain's broken limbs are set, and he ultimately recovers ; and while they mourn over the sad loss of their comrades, they cannot feel too much wonder, or be too deeply thankful, for their own most marvellous escape.

CHAPTER XVII.

THE RESCUE OF THE CREW OF THE "AMOOR."

" No wild hurrahs accompany
    The deeds these men do dare ;
No beat of drum, no martial strain,
    No spirit stirring air.

" But in the cold and darksome night
    They combat with the blast ;
And gain, by dint of hardihood,
    The victory at last.

" Then let us pay the honour due
    To such devoted strife ;
Where gallant men so nobly risk
    For fellow men their life."

G. Ward.

WE left, in our last chapter, the Kingsdown life-boat making for Ramsgate harbour, and the Walmer life-boat, after a couple of upsets, making for Deal beach. The Kingsdown boat reached Ramsgate about seven o'clock in the morning, the gale still blowing very heavily.

Shortly after seven o'clock signals are heard from the Gull light-ship; and the coxswain of the Ramsgate

life-boat receives orders from the harbour-master
to proceed at once to sea,—the steamer as usual
taking her in tow: the sea is very heavy, and the air
thick with rain and spray. The steamer and life-boat
work their way out through the storm, and find a brig
riding at anchor in the Gull stream, not far from the
light-ship; she has a flag hoisted at her peak as a signal,
and they make for her; the crew tell them, that shortly
before, in a lift in the storm, they saw a ship on the
north-west spit of the Goodwin; the life-boat cruises
in the direction pointed out, but the crew can see
nothing of the wrecked vessel, so they proceed to the
Gull light-ship, hoping there to obtain further information. The men find the crew of the light-ship anxiously
watching for their approach; they crowd aft as the
steamer and life-boat passes under the stern of the
vessel, and make signals to describe the position of the
wreck; the boatmen soon discover it, and as soon as
they have been towed into the right position for so
doing, slip from the steamer, and make in for the
stranded vessel.

It is now nearly low tide. As they approach, they
find that the wreck is high and dry on a ridge of sand:
nearer still, and they see a man walking towards them
on the sand, waving a large shawl; the life-boat is
steered towards him, and choosing a place where the
surf is breaking with less force, they run the boat on
to the sands; three of the crew jump overboard and
wade through the surf; they join the man on the Sands,
and make for the wreck; the heavy seas have driven
the Sands into high ridges, and the gullies between

these are waist-deep and full of running water, with
the sand soft and quick at the bottom ; through these
deep gullies the men have to wade.

Arriving at the wreck, they find it to be that of a
brigantine, named the *Amoor*. At about eleven
o'clock of the night previous, in the dark mist and
heavy gale, she had run on the Sands at nearly high
tide, the sea immediately ran over the vessel, and the
crew had no time to make a single signal of distress,
but had directly to climb up into the main rigging to
prevent being washed overboard. Fortunately the
ship was stem on to the Sands, with her stern to the
wind and tide, and she kept straight—and as she was
laden with coals, she kept upright on her keel. As
the tide rose, the waves in their rush lifted the wreck
and carried her gradually on and on, letting her fall
after each lift with a heavy shock that made it difficult
for the men to retain their hold. Then the seas broke
over her so heavily that the men feared that they
would be washed even from their position in the main
rigging, and managed to get on to the foremast ; here
they found more shelter. For about four miles did
the ship thus beat over the Sands, and the men felt,
with a great and deep thankfulness, that if they had
had the guidance of her themselves, they could not
have kept her more straight in her course along the
narrow high ridge of the sand than she was kept by
God's providence, for if the vessel had been carried to
the right or to the left of that narrow ridge of sand,
she would have got into deep water, and then must
have sunk immediately, so much was her hull shattered,

and all her crew would of necessity have been at once drowned.

But the agony of mind and the suspense endured this time by the men was something terrible. They could scarcely feel any hope that the wreck would long sustain the terrible shocks that she was receiving. They looked down upon the mad waves as they raced by, and each one seemed a ready grave; there was nothing to be done, no fierce struggle for life, which in its excitement should lessen the terrors of the apparently approaching death, only to cling on and wait in the darkness.

And now they feel that the end must soon come, for they hear the surf roaring near; it is roaring on the edge of the Sands, the waves rushing in from the deep water and breaking upon the Sands, and this right in the path along which their vessel is being driven yard by yard. A little more and she must be plunged in this surf, and then a few yards, and she must sink in deep water; and as thousands upon thousands have earnestly prayed that they might be kept off these deadly sands, so these poor sailors now earnestly seek that they may be left on them, until daylight comes, and their pitiable position may be seen, and they have a chance of being saved.

They are now within a quarter of a mile of the end of the sand, but the tide is falling rapidly, and the wreck lifts less and less; at last, to the great joy of all her crew, she grounds heavily and ceases to lift. She is swung round broadside to the tide, and falls over on her side, and then works and crashes almost to pieces.

The water now soon leaves her, and she becomes high
and dry, and speedily the men can leave the wreck
and stand upon the sand ; the surf rages around them
at a short distance; it is only for a few hours that where
they now stand will be dry, and then the sea will rage
over the sand again with all its fury. The captain is
a bold, active determined man ; he will throw away no
chance of safety ; something must be done before the
return of tide, and he will lose no time. The captain
and crew can form no opinion as to where they are ; the
vessel is an absolute wreck, beaten by this time almost
to fragments, they have no means of signalling their
distress, and it seems that their only chance will be
to make a raft out of the many shattered pieces of
timber that are hanging about the wreck ; the boats
have long since been destroyed and washed away.
The shipwrecked crew have only their knives to work
with, but they commence with all energy, wrenching
away the broken timbers from the deck and sides of
the vessel, cutting away the ropes, lashing the timbers
together.   But with their utmost efforts they can make
but slow progress, and they feel that their raft, when
as hastily completed, as it must be, will be but a frail
support in the rage of waters with which it will have to
contend, as soon as the sea again beats over the Sands ;
but still on that dry knoll of sand, in almost pitch
darkness, with the wind howling by them, and the
roar of the breaking waves all around, the men work
on and on.   The poor storm-beaten, wearied men, feel
faint and exhausted, but spare no labour, slack no
energy, for the tide will turn with the dawn, and then,

as an enemy creeping up to destroy them, will, in its speedy advance, give them short time for labour, and scant mercy, when it once seizes them as its prey. The dawn has broken, the tide is rising, and each man is inspired to fresh exertions. Suddenly, they are all startled by the loud report of a gun, fired at no great distance from them. What is it? What is it? they all cry. Soon a rocket goes whizzing up into the grey misty clouds. Is it a signal from some unfortunate vessel in distress similar to that which they are in? At all events that feeling of intense and hopeless solitude which almost overcame them, seemed disturbed, and whilst they eagerly work on, they at the same time keep a sharp look out in the direction from which the signals have been given; they are soon able to make out that it is a light-vessel that is signalling; this fills them with hope; they must have been seen by the watch on board, and it is on their account that the signal must have been made; but still they will not abate any of their efforts, the life-boat may not be able to reach them, or she may not be out in time to save them; at all events, with the tide creeping up as it is, they will not lose a chance, and go on busily constructing the raft. They have made considerable progress, having lashed a good many spars crosswise, and pieces of bulwark over them, when they discover a steamer's smoke not far off, and soon after make out a boat, which must be a life-boat, making in over the seas towards them; one man makes for the edge of the Sands, and soon the boat grounds not far from him, and three boatmen wade towards him.

The boatmen, when they reach the raft, find the men getting some provisions on to it, but all the stores have been under water during the night, and are spoilt. The joy of the shipwrecked men at the arrival of the boatmen is intense. "Thank God! that you have come," said the captain ; " I did not at all expect that any of us would have been alive this morning."

A strange meeting it seems, in that wild stormy morning, there, on the centre of the Goodwin Sands, where the waves had raged so furiously a few hours before, and would in a few hours rage so furiously again ; there, where the shipwrecked had expected to die a tragical death, the sailors and the boatmen stand greeting each other ; the life-boatmen rejoicing almost as much at being there ready to save the poor sailors, as they are at the prospect of being saved ; the ship's crew look down upon their raft, and feel indeed what a poor protection it must have proved in the storm which they would have had to encounter.

The crew of the wrecked vessel, now that the excitement of working with such fierce energy at the raft is over, begin to feel the reaction, and feel thoroughly exhausted, and look so worn and weather beaten, as if the death shade, which had seemed to hover over them for so many hours, had left its impress upon the countenance of each.

A few more words of greeting and thankfulness between the castaways and the rescuers, and all prepare to find their way across the Sands to the life-boat. The life-boatmen first climb on board the wreck, to see if they can find any small things which they

can save for the men, but every moveable thing seems
to have been washed out of the vessel ; they find the
cabin broken and crushed up, but manage to drag a
few of the captain's clothes out of it ; they find a dog
on board, which they save. And now all turn their
backs upon the wreck.

The shipwrecked sailors have become very feeble,
and some of them are scarcely able to drag their limbs
along, and require to be held up on both sides as they
wade through the shallow channels of water, many of
which they have to cross on their way to the boat.

They hurry on as fast as they can, for the weather
is very uncertain, and a mist or snow-squall coming
on would put them in the greatest possible peril, for
they would in that case very speedily be lost among
the gullies, which are half filled with water, and which
stretch in all directions across the Sands at low water ;
and the boatmen know what it would be to be lost
there ; with the sand getting soft and quick beneath
their feet as the tide rose, and with the narrowing belt
of surf each moment drawing nearer and nearer, there
to wander hopelessly for a short time, then to be
scarcely able to move as the sands grew quick, and
then to fall an easy prey to the fierce sweep of the
first breaker that rolled in upon them. It is no
wonder that the boatmen look with dread upon the
increasing gloom of the morning, and hurry the men
on as much as possible ; they make out the life-boat,
and with much difficulty and exertion they get to the
edge of the Sands.

The life-boat is at anchor with ten fathoms of chain

out ; the heavy breakers are rolling in and lifting her
with such violence as they sweep on, that at each lift
she drags her anchor, and beats further and further
over the spit of sand upon which the waves are ex-
pending their first fury.   The surf flies over the boat,
fills her, and then rages on in clouds of foam.   The
men on board are anxiously looking for the return of
their comrades with the shipwrecked crew, and greatly
rejoice as they see the groups of men struggling across
the Sands to the boat.   They soon make out how exhausted the shipwrecked men are, and feel that it will
be very hard work for them to wade through the surf
to the boat.   Some of the boatmen get life lines ready
to throw to any that may be overpowered and thrown
down by the wind and tide, others jump overboard to
go to the assistance of the enfeebled sailors.   It is
bitterly cold, and the water, as they wade through
it, feels as if it would freeze them through and
through ; they bring off the shipwrecked crew one by
one, the more exhausted of them being supported on
both sides between two life-boat men ; at last all are
on board, but they cannot yet leave the sands ; they
must wait until the water is high enough to float the
life-boat over the ridge which surrounds her.   All are
shivering with cold and wet ; they crouch in the boat
and protect themselves as well as they can from the
flying surf ; a long weary hour is thus passed ; the tide
rises sufficiently, sail is set, and the life-boat makes
for the steam-boat, and is greeted with cheers—cheers
that are heartily answered.   The shipwrecked sailors,
who had had during the night no hope of again giving

a cry of joy on earth, join in as lustily as they can, in that cry which, sounding over the wild seas, tells of noble deeds in struggling to save life, and of happy and most blessed results. That although the storm still swept furiously by, and although the waves still rushed madly around the shipwrecked, that they were now safe in the safety afforded by the noble life-boat. So safe, indeed, that it was not too soon for the poor sailors to rejoice in their rescue, and to express with heartfelt cheer their gratitude to the brave men who had rescued them from their position of deadly peril.

The steamer does not take long in towing the boat to Ramsgate, where all receive the usual warm greeting, and the shipwrecked the needful care.

The crew of the wrecked vessel, the *Amoor* of Elswick, are Germans; their consul takes care of them, and sends them to the Sailors' Home.

They proved so thankful for the rescue effected, that they wrote to their home authorities, and the life-boat men soon received from the Grand Duke of Mecklenburg Schwerin an expression of gratitude and admiration for their conduct, accompanied by a Silver Medal, a Certificate of Merit, and ten shillings each man.

CHAPTER XVIII.

THE RESCUE OF THE CREW OF THE "EFFORT"— THE DANGERS OF HOVELLING.

"All where the eye delights, yet dreads to roam,
  The breaking billows cast the flying foam
  Upon the billows rising ; all the deep
  Is restless change ; the waves so swelled and steep,
  Breaking and sinking ; and the sunken swells,
  Not one, one moment, in its station dwells.

Crabbe.

THE famous old life-boat *Northumberland* had done her work, and had done it nobly and well. Staunch, and true, she had breasted the hardest gales, stemmed the fiercest seas, and had been the means of rescuing hundreds of perishing men, women, and children from that which, without her, and the brave hearts and strong hands that sailed her, must have been swift, certain, and terrible death ; but at last her time had come—weather beaten, wrenched, and worn, with her thousand battles with the gales, she was condemned as being no longer to be intrusted with the precious lives that she contained, as she went forth to contend with the wild seas that rage over the Goodwin Sands.

The *Bradford*, a very powerful and excellent boat presented to the Life-boat Institution by the good people of Bradford, and by the Institution appointed to Ramsgate, had not yet been sent down, and a smaller boat called the *Little Friend* was occupying her place for the time.

But it was a clear fine morning, with the waves fretting and fuming somewhat, but dancing and gleaming brightly in the sunshine ; it had been squally during the night, and at times had blown very hard, but the morning promised better, and the life-boat was rocking gently at her moorings, no one thinking it likely that her services would be required for some time.

But the boatmen must be doing something, if only drawing their bow at a venture, and now the *Champion* is getting ready for sea ; she is one of the Ramsgate hovelling-luggers, a noble boat of twenty-two tons, fit for any weather.   In summer time she is fitted as a pleasure-boat, and, as such, takes many a holiday cruise ; but now she is in winter gear, and ready for rougher scenes and harder work.

The more threatening and heavy the weather, the greater the probability of disaster occurring, or having occurred, then the more ready are her crew to work their way out to the Goodwin Sands, and to cruise round them on the look-out for vessels in distress ; they dare not take the lugger into the broken water—there a life-boat alone can live ; but still she is a grand sea-boat, one that will stagger on with a ship's heavy anchor and chain on board, through weather bad enough for anything—a boat that is well

Q

suited for the hard and dangerous service which employs her during the winter months.

Her crew consists of ten men; the men get no regular pay, but any salvage or reward for services they may obtain is divided into fourteen shares: the boat takes three and a half shares for her owners, one half share goes to the provision account, as the crew when on board are supplied by the owners with provisions, and one share is given to each of the men —this is the ordinary arrangement. Complaints are sometimes made of the amounts charged by these men for services rendered; but the cases of a good hovel are few and far between; and often the luggers put out to sea, night after night, throughout a stormy winter, hanging about the Sands, in wind and rain, and snow and mists, the men half frozen with the cold, and half smothered with the flying surf and spray, and often week after week they thus suffer and endure, and do not make a penny-piece each man; working their hardest, without any other result, than that of getting more and more into debt at home, and almost tempted to become disheartened with it all, hardly able to hope against hope; then at last, perhaps, comes a chance—a big ship is on the tail of a sand bank; they render assistance and get her off; if she had remained there another tide she would probably have been knocked to pieces: they have saved thousands of pounds' worth of property; and the captain, and the owners, and the underwriters, all look aghast, and cry out with indignation, when they ask perhaps a sum that will give them ten or fifteen pounds a man—do something to pay the scores that have been growing month after month, something to requite them for the weary watching, and labour, and suffering, that they have had so many weeks in vain.

No! let those who grumble at the demands made on such occasions, feel fully assured that they know many easier, more pleasant, and more profitable ways of making money, than by hovering around the Goodwin Sands throughout the nights of a stormy winter, on the look-out for vessels in distress. The following tale will illustrate, in its simple narration of actual facts, some of the dangers to which the men are exposed when on such service.

On the morning in question a haze floated over the Goodwin Sands, preventing anything being made out from the shore; wherever the haze lifted a little, the men on the look-out on the pier closely watched the break in it with their glasses; for the channels on either side of the Sands are so narrow and the tides so strong, that it is an easy matter for a ship-master to lose his bearings in thick weather, and to run his ship on the Sands.

A squall passes over the Sands, driving the mists before it, and the men on the pier make out that a vessel is ashore on the Goodwin; she is completely on her broadside, and the boatmen, looking through powerful glasses, can see that men are walking about on the side of the wreck. The harbour-master is immediately informed; he knows that the *Champion* lugger is out there, but the surf may be too great for her to be able to render assistance, and he gives

Q 2

directions that the life-boat shall be at once manned. The steamer soon takes the life-boat in tow, and they proceed through a comparatively smooth sea to the vessel. Upon arriving there, they find that the *Champion* lugger has succeeded in sending in her small boat, and in taking the men off the wreck.

But as the boat makes off to the lugger's she loses an oar, and the tide is running with such strength that the boat's crew cannot stem it, and are driven back in the direction of the Sands ; the life-boat men see the danger the boat will get into if she is carried into the broken water, and at once give chase.

The men on board the lugger's boat are, not unnaturally, anxious to have the honour of saving the crew without the assistance of the life-boat, and they persevere in their efforts to reach the lugger ; suddenly the wind flies round to the north-east, and a heavy squall sweeps along accompanied with snow and sleet ; it becomes very thick and dark, the lugger's men think the squall will soon pass, and although their boat is only sixteen feet long, and has eleven men on board, they still work away striving to get back to the lugger. But the wind increases in force, and the sea begins to make rapidly, the little boat gets into shallow water and thumps heavily on the edge of the sand ; then the boatmen and the shipwrecked crew realize the danger they are in. The wrecked sailors begin to shout to the life-boat men to come to their help, and the boat's crew see that they cannot get away from the Sands by themselves ; in fact, that without the aid of the life-boat they must all then

and there perish, and they are glad to make for the
life-boat with all speed.   The sailors and some of the
boat's crew get on board the life-boat, two or three
hands remain in the small boat, which is taken in tow
by the life-boat, and they start in search of the
steamer; but the weather becomes more and more
thick, and they can see nothing of her; in fact, can
only see a few yards before them.   Now to their
dismay they find that they have come away without
a compass, and the wind has shifted so frequently and
rapidly, that they cannot guess at its direction, and
therefore cannot tell which way to steer; they are on
the top of the Sands, and in very shallow water, and the
boat often touches the ground with a great jerk as she
sails along.   Now, and again, she grounds bow on and
is swung round and round by the tide.   The tide as it
is low water runs through so many channels and swatch
ways that its direction does not at all help the men to
tell the course they are steering; and so, as a mere
matter of guess-work, and that they may keep the
boat's head in one direction, they put her on the wind,
and after being beaten about a good deal by the broken
seas, succeed in getting into deep water; but not until
they have been entangled for four hours among the
Sands.

After sailing for about half an hour, they discover
the Gull light looming red out of the thick mist.   They
then soon make out the *Champion*, and put her crew on
board her.   The lugger's men want the shipwrecked
crew to accompany them, but they are too content
with the life-boat, and refuse to move; the steamer

comes up and takes the life-boat in tow. Again the wrecked sailors cannot be persuaded to leave the life-boat for her, and as soon as the boat is in tow, and they are well under weigh, the wrecked sailors begin to tell their tale.

" The name of our wrecked vessel is the *Effort;* it is now several days since we sailed from the Forth, bound for Rotterdam, and ever since we have had a a terrible time of it, nothing but gale after gale, the wind flying about in all directions, until you can guess we were pretty well tired of all this beating about in the North Sea ; what with the wind driving us first in one direction and then in another—what with contrary tides and thick weather—we soon lost our reckoning, and must have been caught in the lee drift of the tide, and thus got carried on to the Goodwin Sands. We grounded heavily, at once felt the danger we were in, and hoisted lamps as signals of distress, but we knew that these could not be made out at any distance in such thick weather, and hurried to get a tar-barrel on deck to set fire to it, and make a good blaze; but our vessel was very light—she rolled from side to side almost yard arms under, and suddenly capsized altogether. At once, and with difficulty, we made for the weather-rigging, and were glad to find that not any of the crew were lost as she fell over. We lashed ourselves to the rigging. We knew to our great joy that the tide was falling; had it been rising we must have very soon been overrun by it, the vessel broken up, and every man of us lost. We were in danger enough as it was, for the brig soon after she capsized

was caught by the tide, and worked round with her
deck towards the seas; and as the heavy seas broke
over her and came rushing up the deck, they fell on
us with terrible weight, and beat us and crushed us
against the ship's rail, so that we were forced to unlash
ourselves from the rigging, and what to do we did not
know, till one of us said, 'Our only chance is to lash
the end of the ropes round our waists, and let go the
rigging as the waves come,' and so we did; and
terrible work it was. As the waves came we slackened
the ropes and went away a little with them, and as
they passed, half smothered as we were, hauled ourselves back to the rigging and held on a bit; and
then, when the next wave came, we let go, and were all
adrift in the wash again; our hands were almost torn
to pieces with the strain on the ropes, and grasping at
the side of the vessel." And they shewed where their
hands were torn, with the nails almost drawn from
the finger ends. "You see, too, how our clothes were
nearly dragged off us; it was indeed an awful time.
We encouraged each other as well as we could, but
soon became too exhausted to speak much, and just
went struggling on. The topmast heads were right
down in the Sands, and every moment we expected the
masts would break off short, and then the vessel
would have rolled over, and it would have been death
to us at once—but while there was life there was hope,
and so we held on, just hoping against hope, and so
we would not despair, but seemed to gather a little bit
of courage, again and again struggling to prolong,
for a few minutes, the life of which we saw so little

chance of at last saving ; but the tide was still falling,
and if we could only live through all the wash of the
sea, until it had gone down a bit, there was just one
more chance for us.

"Well, we stood it for about two hours, I should
think, the seas breaking over us continually, when we
began to feel that they were getting less heavy, and
ran less and less up the deck, and over the vessel.
And at last, although half dead with breathlessness
and fatigue, from the exertion and the constant rush
of the waves over us, we were able to drag ourselves
up on to the broadside of the vessel, and then we
threw ourselves down full length, to try and recover
our strength a little."

It was with no slight degree of interest and sympathy that the life-boat men listened to the tale of the
poor fellows ; three of whom were married men, and
they described how the thoughts of the loved ones at
home, while it added to their agony, yet nerved them
time after time to fresh efforts to struggle free from
the seas that overran them.

One man grew very excited as they told the dismal
story. His limbs and features worked, the horrors of
the past night came upon him in all their force, and as
the waves dashed over the life-boat, he fancied himself
again being washed off the side of the wreck, and
springing up he shouted, "Let me drown myself, let me
drown myself, I can stand it no longer !" and tried to
throw himself into the sea. Three men seized him, held
him down and tried to pacify him, but still he struggled,
shouting,—"I cannot stand it ! I cannot stand it ! let

me go! let me go!" He soon became somewhat
quieter, from exhaustion, but the men did not feel it
safe to let go their hold upon him, until they got into
the harbour.

It was now about half-past four in the afternoon,
and the life-boat work for the day was done, the shipwrecked crew staggered to the Sailors' Home; wondering much to find themselves still alive, after the
dread perils, and terrible struggles, and exhaustion,
of the previous night.

CHAPTER XIX.

THE HOVELLERS, OR SALVORS, SAVED.
THE "PRINCESS ALICE" HOVELLING LUGGER.

> " When they who to the sea go down,
>   And in the waters ply their toil,
> Are lifted on the surge's crown,
>   And plunged where seething eddies boil,
>
> " Then with Thy mercies ever new,
>   Thy servants set from peril free ;
> And bring them, Pilot wise and true,
>   Unto the port where they would be."
>
> *Hymn.*

No sooner has the life-boat started in the morning, in answer to the signal from the Goodwin light-vessel, than the master of the *Princess Alice* gathers a crew of twelve men, and follows as fast as possible in the wake of the life-boat.

A fine south-westerly breeze is blowing and the noble lugger bowls along at a great speed, and reaches the neighbourhood of the Sands about a mile and a half behind the life-boat. The lugger brings to an anchor just outside the Sands, and her crew, finding that the weather has somewhat

moderated, and that the sea has gone down with the
tide, determine to send six of their men in their small
boat into the wreck, to see if they can save any cargo
or rigging ; the men get to the wreck without much
difficulty, and find her right over on her broadside,
with her yard-arms buried some feet in the Sands ;
the top-gallant mast is gone ; her rigging and all her
top-hamper, a tangled mass, is floating and washing
about in a deep hole which the eddy of the waves,
beating against the wreck, has worked.

The men climb on to the side of the vessel, and
then lower themselves down from the weather-rigging
across the deck, which is lying almost upright on its
side, that they may look into the hold ; the hatches
are off, and they find that the hold is quite empty,
everything washed out ; it is difficult to get into the
captain's cabin, as the vessel is completely on her side,
or there may be things there worth saving ; they will
see to it by-and-by, and now they proceed at once to
save what rigging they can.   The three men on the
vessel get their knives and choppers to work, and
commence cutting away, when suddenly it begins to
get dark, a heavy squall threatens, and a storm of
snow and hail comes driving along before the wind.

The men in the boat shout out, "It begins to look
bad ; do you not think that we had better be leaving,
and get out of this ?"

But the men busy in the rigging are somewhat
excited over their work, and answer back, "It is only a
squall, a mere spoon drift, and will soon work round ;"
the wind, however, rapidly increases, and sweeps

by in such violent gusts, that the men on the ship's side are nearly blinded with the snow, and can no longer hold on against the wind; well! they are willing to work hard and risk much, to save what they can from the hungry Goodwin Sands, even if that which they save will give them only a few shillings a man; but if they cannot, they cannot; it is not the first time, by very many, that they have returned with nothing but danger and labour for their pains.

"Look sharp, men, look sharp; do you want to drown us all?" "Come down at once," is the cry from the boat; and the men lower themselves down over the slippery side of the vessel, into the small boat, which is leaping and tossing about in the waves which begin to surge up with some violence.

"Now, men, oars out and away with a will; I doubt we have left it quite long enough." "Aye! Aye! too long, I fear." "Well! time enough to think that when we find it so." "Which way are you going?" they ask the coxswain. "I don't suppose there is much choice, there will be less surf running at the back of the Sand, and the lugger is sure to expect us to come out there, now that the sea has got up; so round with her, and pull hard."

And away, as for their lives, the men pull, the little boat seethes through the troubled water, urged by her powerful crew; and they soon near the edge of the Sand, and are making for deep water. "Easy all, men! do you hear that?" And to their dismay, they hear the surf beating heavily, right ahead of them

"Didn't I tell you so?" "Hold your tongue—our work is to get out of this, not to grumble while in it." "Right enough then, and I am your man; but what next?"

"Pull ahead a little, and let's look at them;" and doing so, they see huge waves rolling in out of the deep water upon the shallow Sands, mounting up, curling over, and breaking, washing back, meeting other breakers foaming up against them; in fact, a sea of raging water surrounding the Sands; a sea in which their little boat would be swamped at once, and in which, indeed, no ordinary boat could float, and only a life-boat could possibly pass through.

As they mount on a wave they can see the lugger, riding safely just outside the surf, only a quarter of a mile off, waiting for them; but that quarter of a mile it is impossible for them to pass, and equally impossible for the lugger to get any nearer to them.

"Well, my men, there is no help for it here; we cannot get off the Sands this way, that's certain."

The seas begin to break heavily over the boat; the men keep her head to the waves, or she would be at once rolled over, so rapidly is the swell setting in; as it is, she begins to fill with water, and they have to continue bailing her; they must let her drift back, pulling easy to keep her head straight, and each wave carries them some distance further from the edge of the Sand. As soon as they get clear of the rollers and the surf, they rest on their oars, and consult what is to be done; it all seems very hopeless, but it is no good waiting where they are; and so they determine to return again to the wreck, as to their only place of safety, and this indeed but for a very short time.

They get to the wreck, and lay under shelter of her hull, not knowing what to do ; never did men seem in more terrible plight, the wreck could afford but the scantiest shelter to the crew who hopelessly clung to her the night before ; then the tide was falling, but now the tide is rising ; each moment the great rollers that are rushing in upon the Sands break nearer and nearer ; soon they will rush over the wreck, cover her completely, and rend and tear her to fragments. What can be done ? To remain where they are is certain death, to attempt to escape in their small open boat seems death, equally certain. Well, it is better to die doing than to die waiting ; but never have men held consultation under more apparently hopeless circumstances ; the boat the men are in is the boat the *Princess Alice* generally carries on her deck, between the masts ; she is about eighteen feet long, and four broad, fine boat enough for her size ; but she seems more than sufficiently filled by the six powerful men who are in her, and if she should be caught in the roll of one of the big waves, she will at once be capsized, or fill with water, and sink, leaving her crew but a few gasping moments of vain struggle with the boiling seas.

And the seas rage round them every moment nearer and nearer. Some of the men think that if they can drag the boat for about a mile over the crown of the part of the Sands that is still dry, and thus get out to windward of the North-west Spit,

that they may find more shelter there for a time,
and if they do find it somewhat smoother there, will
perhaps be able to work their way through the surf;
but upon a snow-squall, which for a time had darkened
all around them, clearing away, they find that the
breakers are throwing up as much surf there as anywhere else, and all hope of rescue in that direction is
gone ; and the conviction settles down upon them all,
that there seems indeed no possibility of escape ; but
still they kept cool, and quiet, and undaunted, prepared
to do their utmost, calmly and skilfully, up to the last
moment, letting no chance go by; at all events, they
will stop where they are no longer, as the breaking
seas are closing in upon them fast.

The Goodwin Sands are about nine miles long ; in
the middle of them there is at low water a large lake,
which is called on the chart " Trinity Bay," but which
is known to the boatmen as the In-sand ; the men
row in the direction of this lake, and row over the
sand-banks which surround it, as soon as the tide
has flowed sufficiently to enable them to do so ;
now they find themselves in completely smooth water,
and are safe ; but for how long ? a short hour or so,
for the hungry waves are following them up fast, still
higher and higher comes the tide, and a furious surf
begins to rage over the banks that for a time protect
the lake.

Well do the men know how short a time of rest
remains to them ; they hear the beat of the heavy
waves thundering near, they see the gleam of the surf,
the sea begins to boil up around them, the circle of

safety gets each moment more narrow, their dread
ruthless enemy is on them again, and the men brace
themselves for a life-and-death struggle, for with such
a struggle they are face to face.

" Now, my men, to it again! look out all !" and
each man grasps his oar hard, fixes his eye upon the
steersman, James Penny, watches his every sign, and
listens to his every word ; for in the struggle that
is before them any mistake may be at once fatal to
all.

The big waves roll in, fast following each other, and
the boat meets each one head on, and rises to it ; the
surf flies over the men, and into the boat ; " Bale away,
Penny ! bale away ! or she will swamp !"—and fast
the steersman bales ; he has one hand on the tiller,
and is watching the direction of every wave, and
shouting to the men, on which side to ease, on which
to pull a little harder, to keep the boat's head straight
to the waves ; for if but one wave catches the boat on the
side it will roll her over at once, and all must perish ;
they must row sometimes harder in a lull, sometimes
gently when a high roller comes, to avoid its breaking
upon them, or to prevent their burying the boat's bow
in its steep side.

The coxswain sees a tremendous wave rolling on ; a
few smaller ones come first ; up the boat flies, down
again, again mounts high, and again falls down ;
" Steady all, look out, half a stroke hard starboard side,
easy port, now easy all—easy all ;" the men stop pulling,
and lay their oars flat on the water to steady the boat,
the great wave rolls on, the boat's bow is tossed high,

nearly on end, the men lean back as far as possible,
but can scarcely keep their seats, or prevent being
thrown bodily forward upon the coxswain ; the boat
falls with a heavy plunge ; there is a moment's lull.
" Now a stroke, or two, my men ;" and they gently press
the boat forward and make a little way ; "Easy all, head
her to it, here she comes," and up again they mount
upon the crest of a wave, and are again nearly turned
end-over-end, but, happily, fall on an even keel as the
wave passes, and at once prepare themselves to meet
the next sea, and thus meeting wave after wave, over-
coming danger after danger, they go drifting slowly
with the tide.   The men do not dare at any time to
pull hard for fear of rowing the boat under, they make
therefore but little way ahead, not more than half a
mile, or so, an hour, but they are carried slowly by
the tide down Trinity Bay in the direction of the
Downs.

The boat has been nearly full of water all this time,
from the surf and spray that have broken into her, but
she happily has a belt of cork round her, underneath
the thwarts, or she must have long since been swamped,
but this, with the constant baling of the coxswain, has
kept her afloat.

The men have been able to remain in the bay until
the tide has risen greatly, and it is now high water over
the Sands, and the water being deeper, the seas do not
break nearly as heavily as before ; they are mounting
seas, not running seas.   The mounting sea swells up
and comes pushing along, like a hill of water, steep
on both sides ; its crest is caught by the wind and is

R

driven away in clouds of spray and foam, but a boat meeting it has time to rise, and float over it; but a running sea is much more dangerous; its base is caught and retarded by the Sands; it comes along, its sides steep as a wall, its crest curling more and more over until it breaks, and the upper portion of the wave falls with a mighty crash, with perhaps tons of water in its volume; it would be impossible for any boat but a life-boat to contend for a moment with such a rushing breaking sea as this, and the little boat the six men are in, with its heavy freight, would be swamped, beaten under water and rolled over by the first such sea she met; but if the men can only steer clear of these breakers, and keep the boat's head so as to meet the mounting seas bow on, and manage to bale her constantly so as to keep her a little free from water, they may live through it all yet; with this hope they labour on steadily, bravely, and hour after hour they thus contend with the storm; the boat is now coming to the worst of the water—to the steep edge of the Sand—and the men feel that, for a time, the danger must increase, and all brace themselves up again, prepared for any further effort, or care, that may be required.

The steersman, who has been steering and baling the boat for about four hours, suddenly lets the bowl with which he is baling fly from his hand; he gives a cry of horror, the men cannot help repeating it, for is not this likely to be a death-stroke to them all? The men at once realize the dread increase of danger this misfortune creates.

To keep the boat afloat without baling is impossible ;
the surf breaks into her continually ; the men cannot
bale with their southwesters, for they must keep
rowing ; they require both hands, and to exert all their
strength to free their oars from the seas, and to keep
the blades from being blown up into the air, as the
force of the gale catches them ; while the steersman
must of necessity keep one hand on the tiller ; and
all must continue labouring without one moment's
cessation to keep the boat's head straight to the seas.

Most happily the bowl is a wooden one, and there it
is floating a few yards from them ; they watch it
wistfully, as they, and it, are tossed up and down by
the quick waves ; back the boat down upon the bowl
they cannot, for it is on their broadside, and drifting
away on the tide faster than they are floating : it would
seem, that it must be an easy matter to pick up a bowl
that is floating only a few yards from the boat ; but
not so now, for every moment, racing swiftly after
each other, the waves come rushing on.   It is strange
as they watch the bowl to feel that their lives depend
upon their recovering it, and yet how likely they are
to perish in the attempt, and thus the men casting
anxious glances at the bowl keep steadily to their
work ; they allow no word of fear or discouragement
to be spoken ; they must have mind, nerve, and muscle
in full play ; if a word of hopelessness is let fall, " Don't
speak like that—don't speak like that, stick to your
oar !" they must be words of encouragement, or no
words at all, and in grim silence, except for the few
words of direction shouted out by the coxswain, the

R 2

men wait their fate. Suddenly the coxswain cries, " Here is a lull, round with her, sharp !" The men on the starboard side give a mighty pull ; the men on the port back their hardest ; one pull all together, the bowl is within reach ; the coxswain grasps it with a hasty snatch ! " Round ! round, with her quick, quick !" and the eager men get her head straight to the seas again; before the waves have time to catch the boat broad-side on and roll it over. All breathe again ; they have another chance of life. Thank God ! thank God !

They now pass away from the Sands and get into the Gull stream, but the wind has chopped round and continues to blow a fierce gale ; the sea is running very high and broken ; and in that rough sea they are still in extreme danger on account of the smallness of their boat, and so many men being in her, and they have to proceed with the greatest care and caution.

As they get into the Gull stream they see vessel after vessel running with close-reefed topsails before the gale ; the boatmen hail them but they get no answer : one little sloop affords them slight hope, for she is evidently altering her course, but after a moment's apparent hesitation, away she goes again before the gale, and abandons them to their fate. The captain of the little vessel related afterwards, how in the height of the storm he saw some poor fellows in a small boat, and had a great wish to try and save them, but the sea was running so high that he felt it was impossible to heave his vessel to, and so had to leave them, and that they must have been driven on the Sands and lost. This sloop was about a quarter of a

mile from the boat, and the men do not again get as
near to any other ship, and as vessel after vessel
passes, and the night begins to grow dark, the position
of the men becomes more and more hopeless—and
they all feel that if no vessel picks them up, they
must soon be blown in again upon the Sands, and
there perish.

All of the men, except one, are married ; the man in
the bow has a wife and five children, and it is his
thoughts of them that keep him nerved to his work,
for although weak, exhausted, and almost fainting, he
still sticks to his oar and feebly paddles on ; the only
single man in the boat is his brother-in-law ; and his
mind keeps running as much upon what his sister will
do, as a widow with five children, as it does upon the
thoughts of his own probable fate ; and so although
the men will not permit themselves to lament or
bemoan their almost certain fate, for fear of weakening
their own nerves or discouraging each other, each has
his solemn conviction of what must soon happen, and
is in his own breast thinking of death, and bidding
" Good-bye," to the loved ones who are resting those
few miles away.

The Downs had been full of ships at the commence-
ment of the storm, but as the wind increased in violence
and blew right through, the anchorage was no longer
safe, and vessel after vessel slipped her cable and ran
before the gale ; until at last only one vessel, a large
American ship, remains at anchor. The boatmen
make her out when they are about half a mile from
her, and find, to their great joy, that she is almost

directly in the path in which they are drifting; to get
alongside her is their last hope, for although the tide
is now carrying them against the wind and from the
Sands, the tide will very soon turn, and then with the
tide, and before the wind, they will be swept with
terrible speed right in upon the Sands, and must there
at once perish, and it will be impossible for them to
row against the tide, as all their efforts will still be
required to keep the boat bow on to the seas.

Whenever, after the passing of a few of the largest of
the waves, there comes a comparative lull, or smooth,
and they dare press the boat, they pull a few strokes
and shoot ahead, and thus manage to get exactly in
the path of the American ship.

As they drop slowly towards her they shout time
after time, but cannot make themselves heard; and it
is getting too dusk for them to be seen at any distance;
the seas are running alongside the ship almost gunwale
high, and it is impossible to get nearer to her than
within fifty yards. Hail after hail the men give, still
they get no answer; they can see a man on the poop,
but he evidently neither sees nor hears them, and their
last chance seems slipping away, for they are fast
drifting past the vessel. "Get on the thwart, Dick,
and shout with all your might!" the coxswain says to
the man pulling stroke-oar; "I'll hold you," hauling in
his oar, and catching it under the seat; the man springs
upon the thwart, and balancing himself for a second,
hails with all his force.

"The man is moving, he hears us; hurrah!" is the
glad cry in the boat. They can see that he is looking

about in astonishment, wondering from where the voice
from the sea came.   They all shout together; he sees
them, waves his arm, and hurries along the poop; other
men come hastening up, called by him, and look with
astonishment at the little boat so full of men, being
tossed about in that wild sea.   The boat drifts by the
ship, they venture a pull or two and get her under the
stern of the vessel, shooting her a little across the seas;
they then pull a little harder to try and keep her position, risking a little more to keep near the ship—indeed
the vessel somewhat protects them from the rush of
the seas.

The coxswain sees a man on the vessel throw something overboard—it is a coil of rope with a life-buoy
attached; they make it out as it floats near, and
manage to get it on board.   The pilot is the man who
first saw the boat, and has got the life-buoy and thrown
it over to them.   The captain of the vessel is now on
deck; he orders the men to send down a rope from each
quarter of the vessel, and to try and keep the boat
directly astern of the centre of the ship, for if the boat
sheers to one side or the other, and any of the big
waves which are racing by the ship catch her on her
broadside, she must go over at once.

So they shout to the men in the boat, " Hold on—
we will send you another rope," and soon another life-
buoy with a rope attached, comes floating by; they get
it on board, and seeing directly the object for which it
is sent, haul the ropes over each bow, and strive to
keep the boat in position; but still they are in great
danger; their safety hitherto has been in floating with

the waves, yielding to them as they rolled on ; but now as she is moored to the ship, the little boat has to breast the waves, and at times is tossed high with her bow in the air, and again plunged down, smothered with spray, and in danger every moment of being over-turned ; indeed it is only by the skilful manœuvring of the captain that the boat is kept safe at all.   He has stationed six men on each quarter of the ship ; they hold the ropes to which the boat is fastened ; and as the big waves press the boat, the men slacken the rope, and let the boat go with the seas, pulling her up again between the waves, hauling on one rope, and slack-ing the other if the boat sheers too much on one side. The difficulty now is how to get the men out of the boat, for they dare not haul her up closer to the vessel, as she will not ride with a shorter scope of rope.   They send another rope down to the boat, with a bowline knot made in it for the men to sit in, and then shout to the men, " We will haul you on board, one at a time."

There is a moment's question as to the order in which the men shall go, for each feels that at any moment the boat may sink under them ; it is quickly decided that the men shall leave the boat in the order in which they sit, and one after another, they plunge into the waves, and are hauled on board through the seas.

All safe at last ! and very soon the boat fills and turns over, and hangs there held by the ropes till the morning.   As soon as the men have shaken the water a little from their clothes, and have wiped their eyes and faces somewhat clear, the captain says, "I suppose you have come from the barque that was riding near at the beginning of the gale, and which I missed after a squall, and which must have foundered." (It was supposed that two or three ships went down with all hands that night). "No, sir; we have come from no barque, we were blown away from a wreck some hours ago, near the North Sands Head, and have drifted right over the Goodwin."

"Impossible! impossible! no boat could live in such a sea, and over the Sands, impossible!"—"It is true, sir; we are Ramsgate boatmen and belong to a lugger; we went in from her on to the Sands to a wreck, and could not get back to her again." And the captain declares that their escape has been wonderful indeed. The feelings of the men at finding themselves safe are perfectly overwhelming; the reaction after those long hours of almost hopeless and constant struggle; it is too much for them, especially added, as it is, to the condition of physical exhaustion to which they are reduced. Some of them can scarcely speak; one of them, realizing the almost miracle by which they have been saved, leans against the boom, repeating in a broken voice, "What, I saved! I saved—I saved! one of the worst! one of the worst!" Another can only think of the words he had so often repeated to one of his mates, who had seemed almost dying during the night. "Come, cheer up! come, cheer up! stick to your oar, keep up your heart, man," and he continues for some time repeating these words in a strange dreamy way.

The coxswain, upon whom the chief anxiety and greatest stress of mind had fallen, for he had hour, after hour, to sit watching every sea as it rolled to them and meet it with the tiller, felt more than the others the effect of the night's work ; he soon after fell very ill, was nigh to death's door, and did not recover his strength for a twelvemonth. The captain, officers, and crew of the American ship are full of sympathy and kindness.

The captain takes the men into his cabin, and gives them each a little brandy, then offers them dry clothes, and orders beds to be made up for them in the cabin : the clothes and the bed the men think too kind, but the beef-steak supper and the glass of grog all round, as soon as they have eaten a little, is not to be refused ; and the hardy fellows are soon sound asleep on the cabin-floor, with all their perils for a time forgotten. In the morning the gale has greatly abated ; the men have a hearty breakfast provided by the hospitable captain : their boat is by his orders hauled up, baled out, and as everything has been washed out of her, the captain lends them oars, and they start for Ramsgate, giving their most hearty thanks for the great skill with which they were got on board the ship and saved, and for the kindness they have received on board.

When the crew of the *Champion* lugger had put the men she had saved from the wreck on board the life-boat, they found that they could not well get back to Ramsgate in the then state of the wind and tide, and they were forced to run for Dover.

The men on board the *Princess Alice* remained in
the greatest state of anxiety as to the fate of their
comrades who went into the wreck in their little boat,
and waited on, and on, in the position in which the
boat must come to them, if she clears the Sands ; hour
after hour she cruises backwards and forwards, her
crew keeping most anxious watch, and then runs
down the back of the Sands, thinking it possible the boat
might get out somewhere there ; the gale increases ;
the night comes on ; the high tide has swept over the
whole of the Sands with its wild seas long before this,
and they can only conclude, which they do most posi-
tively and sorrowfully, that their companions in many a
hard struggle—their friends since childhood—have
been lost, overwhelmed in the rage of the sea on the
Goodwin. They therefore give up the search, and now
regard their own safety, and they also find that they
cannot reach Ramsgate, but must make away for
Dover.

Arriving there, they at once telegraph the sad news
to Ramsgate, that they have lost six hands ; news
that creates the greatest excitement in the town. The
next morning the *Princess Alice* starts at daylight for
another cruise round the Sands, hardly with the hope
of finding their lost comrades, but possibly fragments
of the boat may be found ; but they search in vain, and
feeling their fears to be altogether confirmed, they
steer for Ramsgate. There the arrival of the lugger
is most anxiously awaited, and the report of the men
increases the excitement, and sorrow, and sympathy,
which had been created by the telegraph sent the

night before, and now that the names of the missing men are known, there is sad, sad, grief among
their supposed widows, and orphans, and their
friends.

In the meanwhile the boatmen, having left the
American ship, row steadily toward Ramsgate. They
see a lugger making for the harbour ; this proves to be
the *Champion.* The lugger takes the men on board, and
the boat in tow, her crew rejoicing over their friends
whom they had supposed to be drowned. They hoist
the lugger's flag in token that they are bearers of
good news, and speed towards Ramsgate. The lugger's
approach with her flag flying excites the curiosity of
the men on the harbour, and a crowd hurries down
the pier to watch her arrival. And, as soon as the
men missing from the *Princess Alice* are recognised,
the cheers and excitement are wild in the extreme, and
men speed off at their hardest to bear the good news.
One poor woman in the midst of her agony and
mourning for her husband, and surrounded by her
weeping friends, is surprised by her door being burst
violently open, and at seeing a boatman almost dropping with breathlessness, gasping, and gesticulating,
and nodding, but trying in vain to speak ; and it is
some seconds before he can stammer out " All right !
all right ! your husband is safe, coming now !"

A little subscription was got up by the men and
their friends, in order to give to the captain of the
American ship and the pilot a small testimonial of the
appreciation of their skill and hospitality. The men
took the borrowed oars back and presented their

thankofferings, in the shape of a silver cigar case each, to the captain and pilot.

And as the men told the story of the despair and grief that had existed among the wives and children at home—of the tears of sorrow that were turned into tears of gladness—of the rejoicings that took place upon their return, the brave and feeling American captain shared the emotion of the men as they told their tale, and was much overcome as he thanked them for their present, saying,—he should value it as long as he lived, and ever be deeply grateful that he had in any way been the instrument of saving such honest and brave fellows, and of restoring them to their wives and families.

CHAPTER XX.

THE SAVING OF "LA MARGUERITE"—(A HOVEL).

> " The spirit of the storm pursued
>   Their long and toilsome way ;
> At length, in ocean solitude,
>   He sprang upon his prey.
> ' Havoc !' the shipwreck-demon cried,
> Loos'd all his tempests on the tide,
>   Gave all his lightnings play."
>
> *J. Montgomery.*

THE case of *La Marguerite*, a small French brig that was rescued from great peril by a Margate lugger, assisted by the Ramsgate steamer and life-boat, will perhaps convey a sufficient idea of the difficulty and danger that frequently occur in rescuing vessels from positions of peril, and in bringing them in their damaged condition safely into port.

La Marguerite, a small French brig of 187 tons, is owned by her captain, an honest and brave French seaman, and represents to him a great part of the savings of many years' hard work and economy.

She is bound from Christiana to Dieppe with a cargo of deals ; her hold is full, and her deck piled up and hampered with cargo almost to the level of her gunwale.

But on she goes rolling through the seas, with a
fair wind and fine weather, and her crew suffer only
that amount of discomfort which must always be the
case when the deck of a vessel is so crowded with
cargo.

The fresh breeze increases in force, and threatens a
storm ; the men close reef the topsails and speed on
their way ; they make the Orfordness light on the
Essex coast, and then, correcting their course, steer for
the Knock and Galloper lights, which are stationed
to guard sands so named, and which are situated
about eighteen miles from the North Foreland. The
breeze lulls a little, and they shake out a reef in the
sails ; it is now getting somewhat thick—they soon
make out a couple of lights, but they shine so dimly
through the mists that the crew conclude that they
are only fishermen's lights, and shaking out another
reef, they run fast before the wind, carefully steering
their course by the compass ; but all this time a strong
set of tide has been carrying them to the northward
and westward ; this they have not discovered, and are
quite unaware that they are getting into a dangerous
neighbourhood.

The captain is on deck ; he is well-pleased at the
prospect of making a rapid voyage, and seeing that
the night is likely to be wet and squally, he gives his
crew an extra glass of grog all round and goes below,
taking a last look at the compass, and feeling fully
assured that they are steering a straight course home.

In an hour or two the men on deck have their
attention aroused by a hoarse murmur which seems

right a head of them, and which sounds like the noise of waves breaking upon the shore. They look at the compass, their course is correct, they cannot account for it; a couple of men run forward, and soon see distinctly a white line of foam gleaming out in the darkness, and make out the flash of the breakers as they leap high in the air; they are terror-stricken at the sight, and, with a loud cry of "Breakers ahead! breakers ahead!" they rush to the hatchway and shout to the captain to come on deck at once; he, poor man, rushes up and hurries to the wheel, round it flies, but before he can get the brig's head round, she mounts upon a breaker, is thrown forward and grounds heavily upon the Sands.

Where are they? Where can they be? What horrible mistake have they made? they think they must have run somewhere on the mainland, on the Kent coast; one man proposes to swim ashore with a rope, but the seas come sweeping over them with a degree of violence, that quite does away with any thought of making such an attempt. They hurry to the long boat to try and get it out, but it and the only other boat which is in the brig are speedily swept over board by the seas. The vessel is on the edge of the sands and feels all the force of the waves as they roll in and leap and break upon the bank; with every in-rush of the seas she lifts high and pitches, crashing her bow down on the sands, each time with a thump that makes her timbers groan, and almost sends the men flying from the deck.

As the big waves recoil and leap against her in all

directions she rolls heavily, while her masts sway, and her yard-arms almost touch the water on either side.

The tide is rising, and as she lifts she beats each time a yard or two over the Sands; the timbers, piled upon her decks, speedily break loose and are washed away; the hull is writhing and working very badly—her seams open; and so heavily does she strike, that time after time the captain thinks that she must soon break up. This thrashing over the Sands lasts for about twenty minutes, when they find that she is in deep water, but completely water-logged, and torn and wrenched almost to pieces; her rudder is knocked away, and if her cargo were anything but deals she would sink at once, and all would be instantly drowned; as it is, so long as her timbers will hold together her cargo will keep her afloat, and her crew are comparatively safe. But she is by no means a strongly-built vessel, and could not by any possibility stand much more of the thumping and wrenching which she has just gone through, while beating over the Sands.

The captain is still unable to make out where they are; they get a heave of the lead, and find that they are in thirteen fathoms of water; it must be a sand-bank in the middle of a channel that they have just beaten over—they had better anchor at once for fear the ship should be driven upon another bank.

"Is the anchor clear?"

"No," cries the mate. (It is neglect of such matters as these that loses many a fine ship.)

"Get the anchor and cable clear, then, as quickly as
S

you can, or we shall be on the sands again; for although the brig is water-logged, the wind is driving her fast, and the tide is running with great speed." After some delay they get the anchor overboard, and the brig rides to it, head to wind.

The men gather together in the stern of the vessel, and group round the captain, and as there is no work to be done to keep up their excitement, they the more fully realize their danger, and begin to express their fears.

They speak of their wives and children, and bemoan their own probable fate.

The captain is the greatest sufferer, and the bravest hearted of them all.

"Look at me!" he replies. "Have not I got a wife? Have I not got six children? Do I want to be taken from them, any more than you do from yours? Besides, this is my own ship, you know that, and you know that she is all I have got—all I have worked and saved for; if I lose her, I lose all I have, and am a poor man again; you may be sure I'll do all I can to save the ship and our lives too."

But the men watch how severely the brig pitches in the heavy seas. The cable strains as if it would tear itself out of the ship, and the men are afraid it will part, or the anchor drag, and think the ship would ride more easily if her masts were cut away; they urge the captain to have it done; but the ship is not insured, and he, poor man, knows how great must be the expense of repairing her if she is saved, and naturally does not wish to increase that expense

by losing her masts, so for some time he resists
their entreaties ; but at last is forced to give an
unwilling consent to have the foremast cut away.
The carpenter seizes the hatchet, a few heavy blows,
and a great notch gapes in the mast, they cut the
weather shrouds, and after the ship has given two or
three heavy rolls, the mast goes over with a loud
crash, falling well over the side clear of the vessel ;
one man receives a nasty gash in the cheek, from a
splinter from the falling mast, but is not much hurt.
They cut the rigging of the mast from the vessel, and
the mast is speedily carried astern by the tide.

The brig certainly now rides more easily; the night
passes on, and very long and weary the hours seem.
The vessel sinks lower and lower in the water, right
down, indeed, to her deck lining.   The captain and
the crew know how weak she is (like some of the small
timber ships, she has no lower hold beams), and they
fear that as she is full of water, the buoyancy of the
timber cargo may break up her deck, for she is almost
all to pieces already, and if the deck bursts, she will
break up at once.

All hands, therefore, watch eagerly for the daylight,
and as soon as they are able to see, begin to make a
raft ; there are a goodly number of eleven-feet deals
stowed on deck which have been jambed too tight to
be washed away by the seas, and the crew begin to
lash these together as rapidly as they can, although,
from the rolling and pitching of the vessel and from
the seas washing so frequently over the deck, it is a
matter of great difficulty to do so.

As soon as it is daylight the wreck is seen from
Margate, and all is at once astir down by the jetty and
the pier; the life-boat is speedily manned and gets
under weigh, and two fine luggers race with her to get
first to the vessel.

But it is a long beat to windward, and against a
fresh gale and strong tide, and it is doubtful whether
either of the boats will be able to reach the wreck, at
all events, before the turn of the tide, or at the least,
slack water. The luggers have, as a matter of course,
a sufficient amount of ballast on board, and are in
good sailing trim. The life-boat cannot be so heavily
ballasted, or she would sink when filled with water, or
beat to pieces when grounding on the Sands among
the broken seas; the luggers therefore, make to windward much better than the life-boat can, and leave
her astern, the life-boat crew soon find that it will be
impossible for them to reach the wreck, and return to
Margate; the luggers persevere, and one of them runs
alongside the brig in fine style; the men on board
the other lugger think that the brig is drifting and not
at anchor, they therefore make too far to leeward,
astern of her, and cannot beat up into position again.

The men from the first lugger spring on board the
wreck; they find that she is greatly damaged, and
working very heavily as she rolls gunwale under;
they think she would ride easier with her remaining
mast gone, and try to persuade the captain to let
them cut it away, but he stoutly refuses his permission, and the Margate men make the best of it,
as it is.

They get the anchor up, and passing a hawser on board the lugger, seek to tow the brig away from the Sands; knowing the Sands as well as they do, they hope to be able to get clear of them and get the brig into deep water; but it is very difficult work, for with her rudder gone there is no power of steering her, and the weight of the lugger is scarcely sufficient to keep her head straight: they make a little progress, however, the tide being somewhat in their favour, but the tide is on the turn, and they will soon be driven back into their old position, if not in worse, and the men begin almost to despair of saving the vessel, when to their great satisfaction they see the Ramsgate steamboat and life-boat making their way round the North Foreland.

The coastguard officer at Margate, when he saw that the Margate life-boat could not reach the brig, and knowing that if any sea got up where the vessel was, that the luggers could be of no use, telegraphed to Ramsgate that a vessel was on the Knock Sands.

The steamer and life-boat get under weigh at once, and proceed as fast as possible to the rescue; there is a nasty sea running off Ramsgate, but it is not until they get to the North Foreland that they feel the full force of the gale—here the sea is tremendous, and as the steamer pitches to it, the waves that break upon her bows fly right over her funnel—indeed she buries herself so much in the seas that they have to ease her speed considerably to prevent her being completely overrun by them.

No one on board the boat knows where they are being towed; "a telegram from Margate," was the first news "the life-boat wanted;" and then in the hurry and excitement to get under weigh with all possible speed, no one on board had thought of asking for further particulars.

The life-boat plunges on, and her crew are ready for the work whatever it is, and wherever it is. As they round the North Foreland they see a brig, with her foremast gone, in tow of a lugger.

The boatmen cast off the steamer's tow-rope and make for the brig; they run in close under her lee, and venture too near to her; she is rolling so heavily that her yard-arm comes right over the boat, and the loose ropes swaying about catch in the boat's mast; they cannot get the mast down, and the brig hangs so heavily they fear that she is going to capsize right upon them; an active fellow severs the entangled rope with a hatchet, the brig slowly rolls up again, and the life-boat drops astern.

The boatmen get on board the brig; there are six of the lugger's men on board; they find that the lugger is quite unable to make any way with the wreck, and as the tide is on the turn, the vessel is in great peril, for the Sands are just under her lee; no time must be lost, they signal to the steamer to come at once, the life-boatmen take a hawser on board her, and she begins to tow the brig away from the Sands; but the brig's rudder is gone, and she is sheering right and left, jerking the hawser at the end of each sheer with a strain hard enough to break it, and the foremast being cut away, the men cannot carry sail to steady her; she must be steered by the boats.

The life-boat and lugger drop astern, each having a rope from the opposite quarter of the wreck. The steamer moves ahead, and as the brig begins to sheer in one direction, both boats steer in the opposite direction, and turning their broadsides to the vessel as much as possible, hang with all their weight, and try and keep her stern straight ; then as the vessel sheers again in the other direction, away the boats immediately make across her stern, to check her on the other side.

It is difficult and perilous work, this swiftly sheering across the brig's stern in the heavy tumble of sea and strong gale, for the boats can carry no sails to steady them, or they would not be able to sheer quickly from one direction to the other ; and thus they are in constant danger of coming into violent collision with each other, and once they strike together very heavily.

The French crew on board the brig are utterly exhausted with fatigue and excitement, and are quite ready to leave their vessel in the hands of the English boatmen. The men get the anchor and cable clear and ready for use if wanted ; it is of no good attempting anything with the pumps, for the wreck is waterlogged ; and away the brig goes plunging and rolling with the seas washing over her decks, which are scarcely out of the water, and the two boats sheering and tossing astern, all being towed by the gallant little steamer.

As the brig gets good way on her, it is easier to steer her by means of the boats ; but still they do not dare attempt to take her through the narrow Cud channel, they therefore find their way through the Gull stream, and round the small Brake-buoy, and then make up for the entrance of Ramsgate harbour. But the tide has not been long on the flood, and the strong northerly wind is checking it; and so they doubt whether there is water enough to take her into the harbour, and wait until they can see the red light showing on the west pier-head; this is the signal that there is ten feet of water at the harbour mouth; the weather is so thick that they cannot for some time see the light, and it has been up for at least an hour before they can make it out.

They regret every moment's delay, for although it is of no use attempting to enter the harbour before there is abundance of depth of water, yet the tide is making more and more strongly every minute, and it will be a matter of increasing difficulty to steer the brig, in her present helpless condition, across the strong tide, and through the heavy seas, into the narrow entrance of the harbour.

CHAPTER XXI.

THE WRECK BROUGHT IN.

"God keep those cheery mariners !
   And temper all the gales,
That sweep against the rocky coast
   To their storm-shattered sails."

P. Benjamin.

As they tow the wreck near to the harbour they shorten the steamer's hawser to give the brig less scope for sheering ; and as there is not room for both the lugger and the life-boat to hang astern and help the brig steer, the life-boat casts off and makes in to the harbour.

In spite of the rough cold night, the interest in life-boat work is too great for all sympathisers to be driven away from the pier-head ; and there is a crowd there ready to watch the boat's return, and to welcome the men with a cheer.

The steamer approaches cautiously, the brig's head is straight, and she seems well under command ; a couple of minutes more and all will be safe, when suddenly the rush of tide catches the wreck on the

bow ; she overpowers the lugger which is towing astern ;
round her head flies ; she lurches heavily forward, and
strikes the east pier-head just outside the bend ; crash
goes her jibboom ; in vain the steamer tows its hardest,
she is in the grasp of a strong tide and leaping sea,
and again she pitches and plunges heavily against the
pier : with a terrible wrench her bowsprit breaks off
short ; again, and again, she strikes as she drifts round
the pier ; her figurehead is crushed, her stem broken
and twisted, her forefoot torn off, and sweeping round
she grounds on the Sands almost alongside the pier,
on the outer side, grinding and rubbing her sides
against the massive granite walls at each heave and
work of the sea.

The change of scene on the pier is very sudden,
and very great ; at one moment the people were
cheering the crews of the life-boat and steamer upon
the apparently successful ending of their labours ; the
next, and the work of the brave fellows seems
almost more than undone ; and there is quick dread
peril, and deadly strife, and a wild outcry of fear,
and a very wildness of excitement, in the place of
apparent safety and congratulation.   The people on
the pier can look down upon the men on board the
brig, can see them clinging to the wreck as the seas
break over them, can hear the brig grinding and
thumping against the pier as if she would at once
break up.

Some of the lookers-on run for the life-buoys, which
are hanging upon the parapet of the pier and on the
pier-house, and throw them down to the men on board

the brig, others get ropes, and throwing one end down, shout to the men to make themselves fast, that they will haul them up.

The poor Frenchmen are almost paralysed by the scene and by excitement—they cannot make it out; the harbour-master, Captain Braine, has enough to do; he sees the danger of the men on board the brig, but he sees more than this, he sees the danger of the crowd at the pier-head, for the brig's mainmast is swaying backwards and forwards, coming right over the pier as the vessel rolls, and threatens to break and come down upon the people as the brig strikes the pier; and if it does, it will certainly kill some, perhaps many.

The women are shrieking, men shouting, some running about here and there, all anxious to do something, and yet not able to render any assistance.

The French sailors are making themselves fast to the end of the ropes that have been thrown on board, but the harbour-master sees the great danger the men will be in, of being crushed between the wreck and the pier, if they make the attempt to be hauled up, the vessel is rolling so quickly, and the seas are so heavy, he therefore shouts to them not to try it, and the boatmen hold them back.

But still the French sailors struggle to get hold of the ropes, crying out, " Much danger, much danger! What shall we do ? what shall we do ?" The outcry of the people on the pier naturally adding greatly to their excitement.

During this time, which has occupied but very few

minutes, the steamer still keeps hold of the hawser.
She has been swung against the inside of the pier by
the strain of the wreck upon her cable, and by the
eddy of the tide, while the wreck has been beating
against the outside; now she steams out again with
all speed, gets her head round, brings a gradual strain
upon the hawser, and makes every effort to tow the
brig away from the pier and off the Sands; after a
few seconds of hard tugging the brig begins to move,
and they get her into deep water again.

But during this time the crew of the Margate lugger
have been in equal, if not greater, danger than the
men on board the brig.

As soon as the men on board the lugger saw the
brig sweep and crash against the pier, they cast off their
tow rope, but before they could hoist any sail, the way
they had on the boat, and the rush of the tide, carried
the lugger almost between the vessel, as she swung
round, and the pier; the men, however, escaped that
danger, and indeed death, but the boat was swept to the
back of the pier, and in the eddy of the tide was
carried into the broken water; there she rolls in the
trough of the sea; wave after wave catches and sweeps
her up towards the pier as if to crush her against it;
but each time the rebound of the water from the pier
acts as a fender, and saves her from destruction;
but she is an open boat, and if one big wave leaps on
board it will fill her, and she must sink at once; and
the seas around her are very wild, the surf from their
crests breaks into her continually; the people on the
pier see her extreme peril; some run to the life-boat

men who are preparing to moor the boat, and shout to them to hasten out—that the brig is breaking up, and that the lugger will be swamped ; before, however, the life-boat can get out, the brig is towed clear of the pier, and the lugger having gradually drifted to the end of the pier, the men are able to get up a corner of the fore-sail ; it cants the lugger's head round ; the men get the fore-sail well up ; it fills, she draws away from the pier, and away from the broken water, and is clear.

The steamer has the brig in tow, but now the wreck has no boats to help her steer, and she therefore yaws about with tremendous lurches.

The boatmen have all this time been working their utmost ; their danger and the scene of excitement around them having no other effect upon them, than to make them the more cool and determined to do everything they can to save the vessel and themselves.

They rig up a stay-sail upon the tottering mainmast, and as soon as the steamer gets a little way on the brig, they try and steer by it, raising and lowering the sail as the brig sheers one way or the other, and doing their utmost to keep her head straight.

A very heavy sea strikes her on the bow, and she lurches right across the tide ; at that moment the steamer's hawser tightens and strains, and the whole weight of the brig as she lies broadside to the seas dragging upon the rope, it breaks in a weak place, where it has got chafed against the pier.

The brig falls into the trough of the sea ; the waves begin to make a clean breach over her ; water-logged and helpless as she is, with her deck down almost to the level of the sea ; the men on board can now do but little, for time after time, as the seas sweep her decks, they have enough to do to hold on ; still the boatmen on board work when they can, for they see that their lives depend upon getting the vessel in tow of the steamer before she can strike the Dyke Bank, which is just under her lee.

They make all haste to haul in the broken end of the cable ; they already have a good part of the cable on board, which they hauled in when they were about making for the harbour.

They tell the French captain to get all his men to work, and have the ship's hawser ready, but the brig rapidly drifts before the heavy gale and with the tide towards the Dyke Bank, over which the seas are running with fearful violence, the poor shattered wreck must indeed be very soon broken up altogether if she once strikes amid that terrible rage of waters, and there, too, the waves will sweep over her with a violence sufficient to sweep the men from her decks ; they must expect the tottering mast to go at the first shock ; there would be no refuge in the rigging, and the deck would be virtually under water ; it is doubtful indeed if she strikes whether the men will be able to hold on, even while the life-boat, which is close at hand, can reach them.

The life-boatmen had made out to the rescue of the lugger, but when they saw that she was out of danger, and that the brig was under tow of the steamer, they put back, but directly the harbour-master sees that

the brig is again adrift, he hastens to order the life-
boat out once more to the rescue.   Many of the excited
people on the pier throng round the harbour-master,
and entreat him to order the life-boatmen to take all
the boatmen and the crew off the wreck at once.

But the harbour-master knows the boatmen too well
to think that they will be content to leave the wreck,
whatever the danger may be, while there remains a
single chance of saving her ; he therefore tells the
life-boatmen to keep as near to the wreck as possible.

The captain of the steamer, directly he sees the
hawser break, realizes the deadly peril the wreck and
those on board it are in ; without a moment's delay,
he orders his crew to haul in the broken end of the
hawser, and as speedily as possible to back the steamer
down to the wreck, which is now within one hundred
yards of the Dyke Sand.   She is rolling heavily,
broadside to the seas, which are making a clean sweep
over her ; the men on board are scarcely able to keep
the deck for the wash of water, a few minutes more—two
or three—and she will be right in upon the breakers ;
round the pier-head dashes the life-boat, leaping the
seas as she is carried swiftly before the gale, she makes
for the wreck, and is ready to plunge into the surf to
the rescue of the crew directly the unfortunate vessel
touches the Sands. But the steamer may yet be in time
to save her: now she is close to her, and they throw
the end of a rope on board the wreck ; the boatmen on
board fasten a cable to it, the steamer's crew haul it
in with all possible speed, the steamer moves slowly
a-head, the cable gets taught, the steamer tugs and

strains, but it is with the greatest difficulty she can get the brig's head straight ; now it comes slowly round, but as the wreck faces the tide, she sheers right and left ; they see that the wreckage of her bowsprit and jibboom are right across her bow entangled in her cutwater ; it is this that causes her to sheer so much, and to hang so heavily that the steamer cannot make any way with her, or keep her head straight for one moment.

The English boatmen stand ready to hoist the staysail, as soon as the steamer can move her ahead, and keep her at all to the wind.

The poor French sailors give way to much excitement in the wildness and peril of the scene ; clasping their hands and shouting ; and there is little wonder that their fears should be so aroused. " Hold ! hold, good rope, for if you break, nothing can save the ship ; in a short time she must be torn utterly to pieces by the waves now breaking so wildly, almost directly under her lee !"

Each time the brig sheers heavily to one side or the other, she is brought up with a jerk that makes the steamer tremble from stem to stern, and tries the strength of the cable to the utmost.

The life-boat continues to cruise round the brig, keeping as near as possible, but taking care to avoid her, as she sheers swiftly from side to side.

Suddenly the wreckage clears itself from across the vessel's bow, and to the joy of all, the vessel ceases to sheer so violently, and rests for a minute straight in her course.

The boatmen on board at once hoist the stay-sail ;

it steadies her, and she forges ahead, and they battle
their way through the waves, round the west pier-head,
and a little out of the rush of the worst of the seas;
here, five brave fellows come off in a small boat, and
bring a line to her from the pier; with this they haul
the second hawser from the vessel to the pier; they
get another hawser from the pier to the wreck, and as
the tide is setting her in a direction away from the
pier, they can hold her fast by these hawsers; the
steamer now moves round the wreck, and gets a rope
from her stern, but in the meantime they have made
the life-boat's cable fast to the stern of the wreck, and
passed it on to the pier; the crowd of people on the
pier lay hold of it, and begin to pull their hardest, and
succeed in moving the wreck fast astern; with such
energy do they pull that the small cable breaks in
their hands, but the steamer has by this time again
got hold of the vessel, and tows her safely into the
harbour, and the long hours of peril and of struggling
against the storm are at an end.

A miserable figure the poor wreck looks, when she
is hauled up on the slip-way for repairs. Her masts
are out of her, her bow crushed, her stern twisted and
broken, the oakum is streaming out of her seams, her
timbers are started, her rudder is gone, she looks truly
the very wreck she is. Indeed, it was nothing but the
fact of her being timber laden that prevented her going
down immediately after striking the first time upon the
Margate Sands, or has kept her afloat during any one
of the many terrible struggles with the seas, that she
has had since to endure. The brig was ultimately

T

repaired, and sent to sea ; but to whatever extent the general average upon the insured cargo contributed to the bill, the balance required must have made a sad hole in the poor brave-hearted captain's savings.

The Margate and Ramsgate men got some few pounds each for salvage : the ship and cargo were not very valuable, and there were many to share the small amount awarded, so there was not much for each one. But the men were thankful, on account of the captain, as well as on their own account, to have saved the vessel through so much peril, and as a result, to have anything at all to share.

CHAPTER XXII.

THE WRECK OF THE "PROVIDENTIA."

"What dangers press'd, when seas ran mountain high,
When tempests raved, and horrors veiled the sky;
When prudence fail'd, when courage grew dismayed,
When the strong fainted, and the wicked prayed;—
Then in the yawning gulf far down we drove,
And gazed upon the billowy mount above;
Till up that mountain swinging with the gale,
We view'd the horrors of the watery vale!"

Crabbe.

A DARK stormy December night had been followed by a gloomy morning, a heavy gale had been blowing for some hours from the north-east, and thick drifting snow-squalls still further threw heavy shadows over the sea, and added greatly to the perils of the dangerous navigation around the Goodwin.

The men on Ramsgate pier said to each other, "It is *likely weather.*" Likely for disaster and for the need of their services; they therefore keep a careful watch, but the snow and drifting fog-clouds shut out the Goodwin Sands and the light-vessels from their view, and so the men can only wait on, speculating upon the

T 2

possibility of some unseen tragedy being worked out amid the darkness and the wrath of waters that surround the Goodwin.

It is now after breakfast-time, about nine o'clock, the weather is too bad for much ordinary work to be going on, and so a large number of boatmen assemble in the look-out houses and at the head of the pier watching the storm.

Many are the spy-glasses which are every now and then pointed seaward, scanning any break in the storm-drift ; three or four men are at the end of the pier by the watch-house ; one of them fancies that he can make out a dark line 'mid the grey gloom ; he watches carefully, a sheet of fog lifts for a moment ; "Yes, there is ! I see a ship on the Goodwin !"

"Where ? Where ?" and another man looks at the direction of his spy-glass, and points his own the same way. No ; he can see nothing ; and the man himself can now see nothing ; it was just a glimpse, that was all, and the cloud closed in upon the Sands and wrapt them in darkness again.

"But are you positive you saw anything ?" they ask the man.

"I am just as sure of it as I am that I am standing here."

"What was she like ?"

"She seemed a large ship with only two masts standing, and high up on the Sands."

"Well, if you saw her once, and are certain of it, once is as good as fifty times. Away then for the life-boat."

Hurrying up the pier to give the alarm, they shout
to some boatmen who are at work helping to stow
cargo on board a Dutch steamer—the *Orient:* "A
vessel on the Goodwin; Life-boat! Life-boat!" Immediately the men throw down whatever they have in
their hands, spring to the gunwale, and are out of the
ship, up the steps, on the pier, and running for the
life-boat in a moment; and this to the intense astonishment of the Dutch mate, who had not heard the cry
of life-boat. He runs along the deck on to the poop, and
shakes his fist at the men, shouting after them, "You
be bad men you! You be bad men! What for you
run away? You come here work no more!"

The honest-hearted fellow was, however, more
than appeased, when he was told that it was to rush
on board the life-boat; to go out in that wild dark
storm and terrible sea to the rescue of life, that the
men had so suddenly deserted their work and fled
from the vessel.

One of the pier men runs to the harbour-master,
and reports that a large ship has been seen ashore on
the Goodwin; the harbour-master hurries to the pier-
head, but the lift in the storm has settled down thicker
than ever; he can see nothing; he, and all with him,
listen attentively for any report of a gun from the
Goodwin light-vessels, but can hear nothing; they
cross-question the man who saw the wreck. The
harbour-master thinks he may have been mistaken—
that it was probably a ship sailing through the Gull
Channel that he saw. No! the man is positive that it
was a ship on the Goodwin, and nothing else; and so

the harbour-master, although they can hear no signal from the light-vessels, decides upon sending the life-boat, and orders the coxswain to proceed to sea.

Rapid preparation for the start has been going on all this time; and very speedily steamer and life-boat are away in the dark storm speeding their way to the Goodwin Sands. They get to the North Sand light-ship about eleven o'clock, and find a very heavy sea running in the neighbourhood of the Sands, with frequent snow-squalls sweeping along.

The men on board the light-vessel say that both they, and the men on board the Gull light-ship, have been making signals since daylight. (The roar of the storm, and the wind not being on shore, the guns were not heard, and the weather was too thick for any signals to be seen). They report that they had seen a ship on shore on the South-East Spit of the Sands.

Away go steamer and life-boat, the crew of both alike eager to make up for lost time, and they soon discover the vessel they are in search of looming out in the mist.

They see that she is a complete wreck, and that she is settled down upon the Sands, with her bow to the seas; her mizen-mast is gone close to the deck; the seas are running quite over her as they break upon her bow; they mount up and fly over her fore-yard, and race along her deck, breaking again upon her deck-house, which they smother in foam.

There are no sailors to be seen lashed to the rigging, and it is doubtful whether they can have found shelter anywhere on deck, so great is the rush of water over the ship. Indeed, the life-boat men think that it is very improbable that any of the crew can be left on board. Nevertheless, they determine to get on board the vessel, and see if they can find any poor exhausted seaman still clinging to some portion of the wreck.

There is a very heavy sea running, and they have a short consultation as to the best method of getting alongside the vessel; they determine to go in upon the lee quarter, and make preparation for so doing. Now they make in for the wreck; they sail in swiftly; plunge in through the broken water; their anchor is all ready; they watch their distance. Over with it; lower the foresail; and they are about to run the life-boat right alongside the vessel, when the man in the bow shouts, "Up with your helm; up with it hard; sheer off, sheer off!" Up the helm is; swiftly the boat answers, and bears away from the vessel.

The mizen-mast, which had been broken off short, has fallen over the quarter of the vessel, and become entangled in the Sands, and with the ship's side, and is standing out at right angles to the wreck, right in the way the life-boat was steering. If it had been night-time the boat would have been steered in right upon the wreck of the mast and yards, when in every probability she would have been stove and rolled over by the seas; the men would then have been washed out of her, and it would have been impossible for them to have got back to her again, against the rush of sea and tide and entangled as she would have been in the wreckage of the mast, she could not have floated down to them; as it is, this very catastrophe nearly happens, for the men hardly see the danger in time; it is a moment of great peril,. for the boat is being tossed about violently in the broken water, and becomes somewhat entangled in the wreckage; the men lay hold of the cable, and haul upon it with all their strength, and do what they can to check the way of the boat, and help her head round; now they get a good cant out, they throw out some coils of the cable in one cast, they sheer out well, and get clear of the wreck of the mizen-mast; the seas catch the boat and drive it astern of the vessel, the cable runs out its full length and brings the boat up with a strong jerk. The men, on looking at the wreck, are glad to find that there are some of her crew still alive; they can see three men and a boy crouching down, under the shelter of the deck-house, but they must be but a small proportion of the original crew of the ship, for she is a large vessel, and must have had a crew of certainly not fewer than fifteen or sixteen men. "Thank God," say the life-boat men, "that they are not all gone, and that we are here in time to try and save some."

The shipwrecked men have been crouching there for some hours, and have been getting more and more wretched, cold, wet, exhausted, and hopeless; every now and then they heard the loud boom of a gun from one of the light-vessels, but no life-boat came, and the wreck might at any moment break up; they at first felt confident that a life-boat would certainly soon come to their rescue, and had prepared for her coming by getting a life-buoy with a long line fastened to it, ready to throw overboard.

But the hours passed by, the seas broke over the vessel with increasing violence, the storm grew more and more wild, they could not understand why the life-boat did not come, but she did not, and they began to despair of being saved.

Suddenly, as they crouch under the deck-house in their hopeless misery, they see the life-boat swing round on the tide, and come up to her cable just astern of the ship; never were men more agreeably surprised; it is as a reprieve from death; and they feel their blood course again through their veins, their strength returns, and they start up ready for action; the life-boat men give them a cheer, which they answer with glad cries of welcome.

The men on board the wreck throw the life-buoy and line to the life-boat men; there is a tremendous tumble of sea, the life-boat is flying about in all directions, and it is not for some time, and not until after much trouble, that they succeed in getting the life-buoy on board the boat.

All hands lay hold of the rope, and do their utmost to haul the life-boat nearer to the wreck; but the heavy gale, the rush of the sea, and the strong tide, are all directly against her, her cable is straining to the utmost, and they cannot get her to move in the least; they struggle on, and on, but it is all in vain.

" Pull, men, pull! now all together, as the seas pass;

now, try and get a foot or two ahead." Not an inch, strain and pull as they will.

"Look out ! look out ! let go ; take care of yourselves !"

Too late ; a tremendous sea comes rushing over the vessel, right over the life-boat, beats her back with a wrench and jerk that tears one of the timber heads, to which the rope is fastened, right out of her, knocks down by its great weight five or six of the men, who are holding on to the rope, hurts two or three of them somewhat severely, and buries the boat in its very flood of water ; for a moment she is swamped, and beaten right away from the wreck ; she lifts again, in a few seconds rises to her water-line ; she frees herself of water, the men spring to their feet.

"Are all there ? Are any washed out of her ?" "All right ! all right !" "Thank God ! Now at it again, my men."

Happily the anchor still holds, and the boat's cable brings the boat up. But what is to be done to save the poor crew ? They feel that it is quite impossible for them to haul the boat any nearer to the ship.

To their great surprise, they see the captain spring up from the lee of the deck-house, hurriedly take off his oilskin coat, throw it into the water, and then jumping on the gunwale, grasp the hawser that holds the boat, and slide down it into the boiling sea. A huge wave breaks over him, and washes him away from the rope ; he now tries to swim to the boat, but the life-boat is not directly astern, the sheer she has to her cable that is fastened to the anchor which was

thrown over some distance to the side of vessel,
prevents her dropping right astern ; and although
the captain has but to swim a few yards out of the
direction of the sweep of sea and tide, it is impossible
for him to manage it.   He is perfectly overwhelmed
by the boil of sea, tossed wildly up and down,
wave after wave beating over him, it is all that he can
do to keep his head above water, and cannot guide
his course in the least ; the boatmen try all they can
to make the boat sheer towards him, so as to reach
him, or to throw him a rope, but it is impossible, they
cannot get sufficiently near ; and in a few seconds
they see him swept rapidly by in the swift tide ;
Jarman, the coxswain of the boat, seizes a life-buoy,
and throws it with all his force towards him ; the
wind catches it and helps the throw ; it falls near him ;
he makes a spring forward and reaches it ; the men
gladly see that he has got it ; they see him put his
two hands upon one side as if to get upon it ; as he
leans forward it falls over his head like a hoop ; he
gets his arms through it, and shouting to the boatmen
"All right," he waves his hand as if to beckon to them
to follow him, and goes floating down in the strong
tide and among the raging leaping seas in a strange
wild dance, that threatens indeed to be a dance of
death.
    It is with deep feelings of dismay and sorrow that
the boatmen see him thus drifting away, sea after sea
breaking over him ; they think it impossible that he
can live long ; they watch him as far as they can see
him ; he rises now and again on a sea, and waves his

hand to them, but soon disappears from their view, and they seem to have wished him for ever good-bye, for if they go after him at once they will not be able to get back to the ship again, perhaps for hours; and there are two men and a boy still on board whom they must not desert; they must do what they can for these poor fellows first, and then they will hasten away in search of the poor captain, although they have but little hope of then finding him alive, even if they find him at all.

At once they are reminded of the dread peril the men on board the ship are in; for a tremendous crash like a peal of thunder startles them all; and looking round they see the tall mainmast of the ship fall swiftly over on the port side of the vessel.

The men on board give a loud cry—the terrible crash and rend and shock of the falling mast appals them to the uttermost; it is as if the wreck was breaking to pieces in one vast wrench beneath their feet. The chief mate springs wildly to the starboard quarter, and seizes the end of the mainbrace, which is hanging there; he makes it fast round his waist; and with a rapid spring, and with arms outstretched towards the boat, he jumps into the sea; he is a fine powerful young man, and a very good swimmer; but what can he do in a tide and sea so tremendous that twelve strong men cannot haul the boat one foot against them? and so a fearful tragedy is worked out before the boatmen's eyes; they make every effort to sheer the boat towards the man, but in vain; the tide sweeps him at once away on the lee-bow of the boat;

he struggles fearfully hard for his life ; the sea takes
him and throws him away to the full extent of the
rope, which tightens round his waist ; the strain of the
rope draws him back a little ; he falls in the trough of
the sea ; he is just in the thick of the surf, in the break
of the waves, and they curl over him and beat him
down beneath their weight, and then again the next
rushing wave catches him and flings him out, till he
is brought up with a jerk as the rope tightens, that
seems almost to tear him in pieces ; now he is thrown
high in the air on the crest of a wave, now he is
buried in a sea, rolled over and over ; sheering here
and there, as the tangled waves catch him, first
on one side, then on the other, but never nearer
the life-boat ; every now and then he strikes out
wildly as if to make a last effort, and cries aloud
in his agony and despair.   It is indeed a most piteous
sight, and it moves the boatmen to the very heart ;
the poor drowning fellow so near and they unable
to render him the least help.

They cannot remain doing nothing, although they
feel fully assured that all they attempt must be in
vain ; they haul with all their power on the cable
to try and get nearer to the ship when they might
sheer down upon the poor fellow ; but the sea is
raging over them as much as ever, and they cannot
get the boat to move at all ; the waves rush over the
boat in rapid succession, and as they do so the men
have to crouch down and cling with all their force to
the thwarts, and struggle hard to prevent being washed
out of her.   As each sea passes, up they spring and

again try to haul in the cable; the poor drowning
sailor is ahead of the boat, on the starboard bow;
if the line which he has round his waist were only
a few fathoms longer he might be saved; it would be
madness for any of the boatmen to jump overboard
to get at him, they would be instantly swept astern
of the boat, without a hope of saving him, and at
great and useless risk of their own lives; they try and
throw the lead-line over the rope which holds the poor
fellow; hoping that if they can succeed in doing so,
that he may manage to get hold of it, and loosing
himself from the rope which fastens him to the ship,
be hauled on board the boat; but the boat is pitching
and tossing so much that it is hard work attempting
to throw the line, but again and again they make the
effort. "Now he rises on a wave: now try; heave
with a will, well clear of his head. Ah! missed
again; look out, hold on all;" a wave rushes over them,
boat and all; another half-minute and they make
another attempt; no! all in vain, each time it falls
short; the struggle cannot last long; strong and
young as the man is, his strength cannot possibly
endure long in such a conflict; his cries grow more
feeble and soon cease; they see him try and get back
to the ship, climbing up the rope, but his strength
fails, and he falls back; his arms and legs are still
tossed wildly about, but it is by the action of the
waves; his head drops and sinks; yes! it is all over!
—all over! with him; and it is with intense sorrow
that the boatmen realize that all hope of saving him
is at an end—that he is dead.

CHAPTER XXIII.

HARDLY SAVED.

"Much would it please you sometimes to explore
The peaceful dwellings of our borough poor;
To view a sailor just returned from sea,
His wife beside, a child on either knee,
And others crowding near, that none may lose
The smallest portion of the welcome news. . . .
The trembling children look with steadfast eyes,
And panting, sob involuntary sighs;
And sleep awhile his torpid touch delays,
And all is joy, and piety, and praise."

Crabbe.

THE second mate and cabin-boy still remain on board
the wreck; they have watched with the greatest horror
and dread the terrible death of the chief mate, and are
themselves almost in absolute despair.

The seas continue to wash over the ship with great
violence; the deck-house, under the protection of which
the sailors have been crouching, begins to break up,
and wrench, and tear, and is carried away piecemeal;
the second mate, as the wreck wrestles and writhes
beneath him, under the rush of a huge wave, fears that
it is going to break up altogether, that the ship's last

moment is come, and he throws himself upon the rope
by which the life-boat is made fast to the ship, and
begins to make his way along it ; it is almost level with
the water, for the wreck has so worked herself down
in the Sands that her gunwale is but four or five feet
above the sea ; the breakers rush over the poor fellow
as he painfully struggles on ; he is again and again
buried by the waves, but he clings on ; and half
working his way, half carried by the seas and tide, he
reaches the high bow of the life-boat, which is leaping,
and falling, and jerking, tearing the hawser to which the
sailor is clinging, up and down through the seas, as if
trying its utmost violence to jerk him from his hold.

But still he holds on, his hands convulsively clutching
the rope as his body is being swayed and thrown
violently about ; he is exhausted, and breathless—he
is half drowned ; his face is pale as death, his jaw
drops, he seems about to swoon ; in another moment
he will be gone ; he gives a wild despairing look at the
life-boat, and as the waves dash him against it, makes
an effort to grasp it ; the man in the bow of the boat
has been watching his every movement, has shuddered
with dismay as he saw the seas wash over him, expecting him to be carried away in the strong tide.
No ! he still grasps the rope, and at last is within
reach ; in one spring, and with a cry to his mates,
" Hold me ! hold me !" the boatman throws himself
upon the raised foredeck of the life-boat, and with his
body half stretched over the stem, he grasps the collar
of the sailor ; the drowning man throws his arm
around the boatman's neck, and clings to him con-

vulsively, by his weight dragging the man's head down
and burying it in the water ; but the brave fellow
clings as hard to the half-dead sailor as the sailor
does to him ; the seas wash bodily over them and over
the bow of the boat ; up and down the boat plunges
them both, but he still holds on ; three or four of the
boatmen have hold of his legs, and are doing their
utmost to pull him back into the boat, but they
cannot do so, and so the struggle goes on ; it is only
as the boat rises on a wave and throws her bow up in
the air that the men can breathe.

Now a shout of horror, and a cry—" Look-out ! look
out ! sheer the boat, quick ! quick ! port—port your
helm !" For right down upon the bow of the boat,
tossing on the huge seas, and borne swiftly by the
tide comes the wreck of one of the ship's largest and
heaviest boats ; it has been entangled in the mast,
which is hanging over the side of the ship, but it
has now washed free, and comes driving down as
if to stave in the bow of the boat, and crush to
death the two poor fellows hanging on to the side :—
the boat sheers a little ; a cross wave catches the
wreckage, and it just sweeps clear. Thank God ! is
the cry of every man in the boat.

The boatmen cannot get the two men in over the
high bow of the boat, and the poor fellows are drowning fast ; and so they drag the life-boatman by his legs
along the side of the boat, he still clinging to the
sailor, and get him to the waist of the boat where the
gunwale is very low ; some of the men can now catch
hold of the sailor, they drag him on board, and the

U

boatman is pulled in by his legs. The brave fellow is very exhausted by his great and gallant exertions; but he has saved the man's life, and that is every consolation to him; the mate of the vessel is almost unconscious. If the boatman had not clung to him as the seas broke over them both, he must have let go his hold and soon have been beaten under by the waves, for he was quite incapable of any further exertion.

The boatmen again turn their attention to the wreck; they have been so much engaged with the two men struggling in the water, that they have not been able to think of the poor boy still clinging to the vessel in loneliness and fear.

The deck-house has by this time been completely washed away, and no longer affords him any protection. The poor little fellow is clinging to the gunwale, holding on to the cleats; and he is calling out in good English, and in the most piteous tones, O save me! O save me! O do save me! He is only thirteen years old. The boatmen answer him back; and much as they have passed through, it affects them very deeply to see the poor child in his fear, and misery, and danger, to hear his cries and sobs, and not to know how to help him. Continually he is completely buried in the seas, and it seems wonderful that he can hold on; each time the waves rush over the wreck, the boatmen expect to find him washed away like a cork, but he still holds on, and again and again his piteous pleading voice is heard 'mid the roar of the storm—"O save me! O save me! O be quick and save me!"—

"What can we do ? What can we do ?" the boatmen
ask each other in tones of real sorrow and dismay ;
there is not a man among them who is not ready to
risk his own life to save the boy, but nothing can be
done. It is impossible for them to climb on board the
wreck by the rope with which the life-boat is fastened
to the vessel, for the wreck is now so overrun by the
tide that the bend of the rope is continually under
water, and the wreckage of the vessel's masts is
washing over it ; moreover, although it was possible
for a man to come down the rope, the sea and tide
making with him, it would be impossible for a man to
work his way up the rope against such a tremendous
rush of water and breaking surf as are continually
sweeping over it. The steamer is not in sight, or they
might be tempted to go to her, get towed to windward again, and try to run in upon the wreck and
grapple her closer ; but this would be almost impossible, so wild is the sea on the weather side, and on
the lee side the wreck of one of the masts is flying
about in the broken water in a way, which would at
once prove fatal to the life-boat if she got entangled
with it.

And so all they can do is to wait on, till the tide
slackens, when perhaps they will be able to haul the
life-boat up to the wreck, and save the boy. But
while the tide runs so fiercely they can only wait, and
watch the poor little lad. They do not forget the captain
of the vessel, they will go in search of him by-and-by,
but they conclude that all life must have been beaten
out of him long since ; and they must not leave the

U 2

living to go and search for the body of one whom they think must very certainly be by this time dead.

A short time, and the tide rapidly slackens, an eddy comes rushing through some channel in the Sands, and the boat begins to sheer about wildly; and is soon in danger of being crushed against the wreckage of the masts, which is heaving and tossing about among the very heaviest of the seas.

"We must make an effort soon," the coxswain cries; "make ready, my men; try and keep the wreckage clear; haul the boat up to the ship sharp, when I tell you: we will soon have the poor little chap."

Scarcely are the words shouted out by the coxswain when some of the men give a cry—"What's that! look out! yes, he is overboard, washed over by that big sea. Where is he? where is he? There he is! No! only his cap, there he lifts on that sea—he is coming straight for the boat."—From the change and eddy of the tide, the rush of the sea past the boat is not nearly as rapid as it was, and the poor boy comes floating slowly from the ship; once or twice he has been rolled under by the waves, now he is on the surface again, and near the boat. "Here he comes! look! on that wave! Lost! no, he floats again; slacken the hawsers; now he is within reach, carefully, quick; now you have got him; he is making no effort, and floating with his head under water;" a boatman manages to hook his jacket with a long boat-hook, and pulls him towards the boat—gently the men lift him in, sorrowfully; and tears are in the eyes of more than one, as they look upon the small face. "Poor little chap! too late!

too late! he is gone," they say—and think that the
delicate little face and slender childlike form suggest
that he is fitted rather for quiet home scenes, and home
care, than for such scenes of hardship and peril as he
has had to endure.

"Now, my men," shouts the coxswain ; "stations all !
put the poor boy down here in the stern-sheets. If
we do not look sharp we shall be driven upon the
wreck, and likely enough all lost."

"Ay! ay! all right. Get the foresail clear! All
clear,—hoist as the boat sheers ; stand by to cut the
cable, and ship's ropes ; hoist away ! Now she pays
round ; cut the cable ; all gone ; round the boat flies ;
away she goes before the wind. Make all fast. Now
come and look to the poor lad again ; and some of
the boatmen with tender fatherly pity in their hearts,
take up the little fellow. They chafe his hands and
rub his back and limbs, and his chest over his heart,
with strong rum, put a little rum to his lips, and
persevering as well as they can, following the instructions given to all life-boat men, for recovering
the apparently drowned, after about half an hour they
have the joy of seeing him show signs of life ; the men
who can be spared from working the boat continue
their care of him ; his circulation returns, and he can
drink a little water ; some of the men take off their
jackets which have been kept dry by their waterproof
overalls, and wrap him up in them ; they then spread
the mizen sail above him, to prevent the seas breaking over him ; and the poor lad lies quiet, gradually
recovering his strength.

During this time, the coxswain and the men have been consulting about the poor captain, who floated away with the life-buoy round him some two hours before ; and they determine to run down the Stream-reach in search of him, dead or alive. But alive scarcely for one moment can they hope to find him.

The Stream-reach or Stream-wreckage, as it is called, is where the currents setting down on either side of the Sands meet on the highest part.

Most of the wreckage is washed up into it, and what remains of a lost ship or cargo will often be kept in this stream, and float away in one long line some miles to leeward. Along this Stream-reach, and in the heaviest of the seas, the men steer the ·life-boat, all keeping a keen look-out for the body of the lost captain.

They look back at the wreck several times as they speed away ; and they soon see the foremast of the vessel go over the side ; the hull of the vessel seems also to heave over, and that is the last that is seen of the *Providentia*, for by the next morning her hull is completely torn to pieces, the lower part buried in the Sands, and the remaining portion utterly swept away.

They run down the Stream-reach for about two miles ; when one of the men fancies that he can see an arm waving. All look in the direction pointed out ; and to their astonishment they see the captain in the life-buoy ; as he rises on the sea, he shouts to them and again waves his arm.

The coxswain at once steers the boat for him, but the seas are so heavy that they knock the boat to leeward, and they just miss him.

The brave fellow shouts, " All right !" as they pass a few yards from him.

The boatmen lose no time ; they take the mizen-sail which covers the mate and lad, set it with all possible haste, shake out all reefs in the foresail, head the boat round, and sail well to windward of the captain ; almost capsizing the boat under her press of canvas, so eager are they; they keep a good-look out for him, for the seas are leaping so violently that it is a hard thing to keep the poor fellow in view, and at last they lose sight of him altogether. As soon as the boat is well to windward they make across the Stream-reach, then sail down it, and soon catch sight of the captain again ; they lower the mizen and run straight for him ; soon they down with the foresail to lessen the speed of the boat, for fear they should over run him, and manage to drop gently down by his side.

They lay hold of him and drag him into the boat ; the exertion of being pulled in over the side of the boat, and the reaction after his fearful time of suffering and suspense, is too much for his remaining strength, and he seems dying in the men's hands ; they try and get him to swallow a little rum, but he cannot do so, and faints.

The men now set sail and make for the Gull light-ship ; they see the steamer coming round the South Sands Head in search of them ; she takes the boat in tow, and they proceed towards Ramsgate. In the meanwhile some of the men have been doing all they can for the captain, rubbing his back and limbs, and doing all they possibly can to restore his circulation ;

he soon gets a little better, and is able to tell them
that his ship was a Russian ship, the *Providentia*,
from Finland, and that he is a Russian Fin ; this last
fact enables the men to account for his wonderful
powers of endurance in his long exposure to the beating
of the waves and to the coldness of the water, for the
Finlanders are the hardiest of all sailors. He also
tells the men, that the *Providentia* was a full rigged
ship of 700 tons, bound from Newcastle to the Mediterranean with coals. That they had run ashore about
eleven or twelve o'clock the night before, in thick
weather. That they made signals, which the light-
vessels answered. That they had seen the light-
vessels signal to the shore ; and as he knew that he
was near Ramsgate, he felt sure that the life-boat
would come out to their rescue ; he therefore tried to
persuade the crew, eleven in number, to remain by the
ship ; but that they took the big boat, and left the
ship in so heavy a sea that he feared they must all bo
lost (they were blown over on the French coast, and
at last got into Boulogne). Upon reaching Ramsgate
the captain, mate, and the boy were carried to the
Sailors' Home, being too weak to walk, and were well
cared for.

The captain made a long statement as to the gallant
services of the life-boat men, and of his deep gratitude
to them.

We may as well add, that as some of the men, who
had run away so suddenly from their work on board
the Dutch steamer, to make a rush for the life-boat,
were walking upon the pier, they saw the Dutch

mate hurrying to them, evidently in a state of excitement.   Halloo!   What's up now? think the men, re-
membering how the mate had shouted after them as
they left the vessel.   Halloo!   What's up now? but
the honest fellow comes to them, and shaking them
heartily by the hands, says with deep feeling,—"Me
sorry me called you bad men for running away from
the steamer.   You good men! you good men! *Me give
you* more work if me can."

CHAPTER XXIV.

SAVED AT LAST.
THE FATAL GOODWIN SANDS.

> " There are to whom that ship was dear
>   For love and kindred's sake,
> When these the voice of rumour hear,
>   Their inmost heart shall quake,
> Shall doubt, and fear, and wish, and grieve,
> Believe, and long to unbelieve,
>   But never cease to ache ;
> Still doom'd, in sad suspense, to bear
> The hope that keeps alive despair."
>
> *J. Montgomery.*

Do we not often find in the winter evening that our
warm rooms seem more cosy, and the flames to lap
more brightly and closely round the half-consumed
log, as a blast of wind moans in the chimney, and
perhaps the cry of some poor street hawker tells its
plain tale of toiling misery as it goes shiveringly
along the streets? Do we not find our sensations of
personal comfort increased, and our sympathy for the
sufferer quickened, as the wintry gale and slashing
rain beat against our well-shuttered windows, and

suggest the hardships we should have to endure if we were less cared for and less protected ?

But if we may learn the deeper to realize our blessings, and the more to enlarge our sympathies, as we contrast our respective positions with such as are endured by many of the poor toilers on shore, truly still more may we do so as we consider the trials and hardships endured by many of the toilers at sea. Jamb down the window harder to prevent those few drops of rain bubbling in, draw the curtain closer and check that one breath of draught ; and now think of those of your fellow-men who are breasting the storm in its wildest rage, out in the full perils and dense darkness of the night, where cruel winds and mad seas attack them in all their dread force ; but neither daunt their courage, check their efforts, nor frustrate their skill ; their errand is to save, and all personal considerations are lost in the grandness and hope of their enterprise.

Thinking of these things, we shall not fail again and again to render our ready and full-hearted sympathy, not only for the shipwrecked, crying aloud in their quick peril and deep agony for rescue, but also for the poor brave-hearted boatmen of our coasts, who never hesitate to do all and to dare all when the prospect before them is that of saving life.

Let us recall again some of the features in the lives of those whom we may well call the " Storm Warriors " of seafaring life, who not only find their bread upon the waters, but upon the most troubled waters

of the most storm-lashed seas; who, the darker
the night, the sterner the tempest, the more blinding
the snowdrift, are the more full of expectation that
their services will be required, and are therefore the
more determined to urge their way out into the storm,
to be ready to render aid at the first call for assistance,
and perhaps to pluck a harvest of saved lives off the
very edge of the scythe of death.

Yes, my readers, I would once again carry you
in thought far away from quiet home scenes and
peaceful associations, from the pleasant nooks and
sunny corners of memories which you delight to
recall, upon which you love to let your thoughts half
consciously ponder; but I ask you to take the joy of
your home peace—the gladness of your blessings—
with you, that you may be quickened in every chord of
sympathy as you let me draw your thoughts away into
the dread darkness, which is only broken by spectral
sheens of light shed by flying foam, there to picture
the rolling sea-mountains hurling along their ava-
lanches of white spray; to listen to the dread discords
of a howling tempest; to hover in fancy mid a scene of
fierce turmoil and strife, where the elements in their
rage seem to have cast off all bonds to their fury, and
to have determined to sweep from their path every
vestige of man and his works; and now to let your
eyes centre upon a shattered wreck, to which are
clinging a few storm-beaten sailors trembling upon
the very verge of a grave.

Are you practically interested in life-boat work,
then you have a message to them in their hour of

agony; you would have a message to many a loving
wife and innocent child if they could now realize the
danger of those they love, upon whom they depend.
And your whisper is of rescue and of hope. Look
where a fitful light gleams in the darkness ; now rides
high on the crest of a huge wave, now falls buried in
the trough of the sea, shines out again, is hidden in a
cloud of spray, but pressing on and on, getting nearer
each moment to the shipwrecked.

The light gleams from a life-boat in which a small
band of men are battling,—battling on in the teeth of
the fierce storm.   No terrors stay them, no failures
quell their courage and their zeal ; are not fellow-men
held captive and threatened with death by fierce and
cruel seas? and shall they, the Storm Warriors, not
be ready at every peril, and at every hardship, and
against all difficulties to make in to their rescue.
In such scenes we see the men actually at their work
in their efforts to save life and property ; but the life-
boat work does not merely consist in doing the work
at the moment of its necessity, but also in the
unwearying watch and readiness for when that time
of emergency shall come. Many a Ramsgate boatman leaves his poor, but warm and comfortable home,
his humble and loving home circle, to pace Ramsgate
pier for hours, and this, night after night, for many
winter months, and for the mere chance of being
among the first to make a rush for the life-boat when
the signal is given to man her,—a chance that may not
come a dozen times in the season, and which, when it
does come, may afford indeed a grand opportunity

for daring all and doing all for the saving of life, but not for doing much in the way of refilling the half-empty cupboards at home, or rubbing off the debts that have been gradually growing during the winter season.

And in this, the last tale, I propose telling of the doing of the Storm Warriors, the Life Savers, who watch and struggle mid the fierce seas of the Goodwin Sands, I have deeds to relate done by our brave boatmen—acts of daring and determination—for which I claim a place amid the records of the bravest, grandest deeds of heroism of the age; a tale to tell which, unless I fail utterly in the telling—and this God forbid—I reverently pray, and pray it for the sake of noble deeds done, and for the sake of the good life-boat cause—a tale which must excite sympathy for those in suffering and in peril from the dangers of the sea; and sympathy and high esteem for the daring and unselfish workers of brave works ;—a tale, the echoes of which may well stir, as a trumpet peal, stout hearts to perseverance and brave deeds, to do and dare all in God's name, and for the right, whatever storms of opposition may impede their onward course, and stand between them and their high and holy aim.

The early days of the new year were bleak and cold ; strong northerly and easterly winds swept over land and sea ; people on shore spoke of the weather as being seasonable, but shuddered over the word.

At Ramsgate, on the 5th of January, it was a fresh breeze from the east-south-east, and the anxious

boatmen were as usual keeping a good look-out.
About half-past eight in the morning, the booming of
signal guns was heard ; the signals came from both
the Goodwin and the Gull light-ships.

The boatmen, who had been watching all night in
momentary expectation of such a signal, speedily
manned the life-boat.

The steamer, the *Aid,* was soon ready, with her
brave crew full of courage and hardihood, and full of
zeal as ever to second every effort made by the life-
boat men in saving life. The steamer is steered for the
North Sands Head light-vessel. As they were making
their way across the Gull stream, they saw what
proved to be a shipwrecked crew in their own boat ;
they took them on board the steamer, and found that
they were the crew, eight in number, of the schooner
Mispah, of Brixham. The schooner had stranded on
the Goodwin in a thick fog the night previously ; the
weather was still thick, and the men could give no
account of the position of their vessel, and thought that
it was hopeless to try and find her, and that it would be
useless to try and get her off if they did find her, and
so the steamer took the boat in tow and returned to
Ramsgate.

It proved afterwards that the vessel floated off the
Sands at high water. A Broadstairs hovelling-lugger,
while cruising about, fell in with her, and succeeded
in bringing her into Ramsgate. The vessel and cargo
were worth £6000 or £7000 ; the Broadstairs men
obtained £350 as salvage. The life-boatmen were
glad to take a few hours' rest after their night's watch

and morning's work, they therefore found their way
homewards, leaving, however, plenty of ready and
able boatmen to watch on the pier, eager to make up
another crew should a call for their services be made.
The cold became hour by hour more intense, and the
fresh breeze steadily grew ; as the tide made, the sea
broke over the pier in heavy clouds of spray, thundered
down upon it, and poured over it in foaming cascades
into the harbour.

The evening grew on, the gale became terrific ;
heavy snow-storms went sweeping by, showers of
freezing sleet rushed on before the wind, and the
night was as dreary and dismal, as dark and cold, as
night could well be.

At about half-past ten the storm was in its full
fury, and the sea a very howling wilderness of raging
waters.

At that moment the boom of a signal gun made
itself heard, in spite of the roar of the wind and sea,
and rockets were soon seen streaming up from the
Gull light-ship.

" The life-boat was manned with despatch," would
be the short report the coxswain would afterwards
make to the harbour-master. This means, that
directly the signal was given, all was astir at the
pier-head, the harbour-men on watch hurried themselves to lose no moment in getting the life-boat
ready for sea ; that the crew of the steamer also made
all zealous speed ; that the boatmen, in spite of the
piercing cold and terrific gale, rush along the pier,
hurry down the harbour steps, spring into the boat,

and at once set to work in preparing her for sea, as
readily as schoolboys bound down the school stairs
and out on to the common for the joy of a summer
holiday.

It takes the steamer and life-boat about one hour
and a half to urge their way through the terrible
storm into the neighbourhood of the Gull light-ship ;
the crews speak her about one in the morning, and
are told that the men on board saw, some time since,
a large light burning south-east by south, but they
had lost sight of it for about twenty minutes.

The steamer at once tows the boat in the direction
described ; a careful look-out is kept ; the snow-storms
come down more darkly than ever, and the men find
it bitterly cold, as they are continually overrun by
the foam and spray, and by the broken crests of the
waves, which are very wild and running mountains
high ; still on and on the brave fellows battle their
way, but they can discover no signs of any signal-
light.   The crew hold a consultation as to what is
best to be done ; there appears no possibility of any
of the crew of the vessel which gave the signals of
distress being still alive ; she must have broken up
at once, in so tremendous a sea, and it would be
impossible for any poor fellow to float clinging to any
piece of wreckage in the midst of such a terrific
turmoil of water.   Still some other vessel may be in
danger ; the night is wild and dark enough for disaster
after disaster to occur ; and so the men determine to
wait and watch for any signal of distress, and not
seeing one, to remain in the neighbourhood of the

X

Sands at all events until daylight, that they may feel sure before they leave the Sands that they are not turning their backs upon any whom they might leave to perish in the storm for want of their aid.

And so, my readers, while most of you, if not all, were quietly in your beds (the wakeful ones of you perchance listening wistfully to the storm, and perhaps having your hearts moved to great pity and deep prayer for the poor fellows at sea), these brave boatmen, from choice, and not for the hope of money reward, but for the far dearer hope of saving life, waited on and on, by those gloomy storm-beaten Sands, a prey to all the fierceness of the gale, the raging seas, and deadly cold.

Time after time the mad rushing waves break over the boat, burying her in clouds of spray and foam, or, coming in heavier volume still, bury her and the men for a moment or two completely under water. It is to the crew something more than intense discomfort; their sufferings become very great, yet they will not give in; they do all that they can to encourage each other, and still let the boat lay to.

Willing as every man is to endure to the utmost, they soon find that it is getting beyond their strength; they feel as if frozen through and through, and are rapidly getting numbed and exhausted with the continual wash and beating over them of the heavy seas. There is no help for it, and unwillingly they make a signal for the steamer, and are towed back to Ramsgate, arriving between four and five in the morning.

The name of the vessel that was lost during that terrible night was never known ; the greedy Sands soon swallowed up every vestige of the ship ; her name may perhaps be found among the missing ships at Lloyds'. Hope, doubtless, long lingered, may still linger, in many mournful homes ; still the story be told to wondering children, how their father or their brother sailed on such a day from a foreign port, and has not since been heard of ; but no clue has ever yet been found as to which of the many missing vessels it was that came to such sudden destruction in that dread night on the Goodwin Sands.

Shall we linger another moment or two in thought over the poor fellows thus lost in the fierce seas. We fancy that the bronzing of a tropical sun was still ruddy upon their cheeks ; a few weeks since they were ready to rest 'neath the shadow of the sails, and lie about the deck at night ; and then speeding north they were met in the chops of the Channel by the rough welcome of a strong adverse wind, against which they sought, day and night, to beat their way, while the sails and cordage grew hard and stiff with frozen rain and spray.

Favoured at last with a slant of wind, the vessel finds her way up Channel ; the crew already feel the hardship and dangers of their voyage at an end, as they begin to count the hours until they shall be in dock ; night falls as they pass the South Foreland. The wind goes moaningly back to the old direction ; hour after hour it increases, a gale sweeps along in dread force, the blinding snow bewilders the pilot, who can now see no guiding light, and soon in the darkness of the night, the force of the wind, and the swirl of the tide, the vessel is driven through the raging surf on to the Sands.

The crew make a rush for the boats ; useless ; they would not live a moment in such a boil of sea. The waves fly over the vessel, now lift her, and then let her crash with the force of all her weight down upon the Sands ; now they beat with tremendous force against her, and shake her each moment to her keel ; the captain burns a blue light, the spray washes it out, the men hasten to get a tar-barrel on deck, knock in the top, fill it with combustibles, and light it ; it flares up, and for a time resists the rush of spray with which the air is full ; the light-vessel sees the signal, fires a gun and a rocket ; the life-boat starts upon her mission, but the waves close in upon the doomed ship in fierce hungry strife, lifting and crashing her down time after time ; the decks are soon swept of everything that the force of water can tear from them, the tar-barrel is washed out ; the men can no longer remain on the deck, but have to take refuge in the rigging, where they lash themselves to the shrouds, and they wait on in darkness and despair ; a tremendous wave comes boiling along, it lifts the vessel, and almost rolls her over ; the strong masts snap like reeds ; the ship fills and sinks in the hole she has worked by her rolling and beating in the quicksand. Another half-hour, perhaps, and the life-boat is there ; too late ! only the tangled spars and cordage and broken pieces of wreck float near—tokens

of the death and destruction that have been wrought :
and a fine ship has been thus utterly and speedily
destroyed—and all living things on board being
swiftly engulfed, have found their graves in the
strife of that deadly sea.

CHAPTER XXV.

SAVED AT LAST.

WE WILL NOT GO HOME WITHOUT THEM.

"O, the most piteous cry of the poor souls!
  Sometimes to see 'em, and not to see 'em; now
  The ship boring the moon with her mainmast,
  And anon swallowed with yest and froth;
  How the poor souls roared, and the sea
  Mocked them."
                                    Winter's Tale.

As soon as it is daylight the coxswain of the life-boat
and others of the boatmen feel very anxious; they
fear that, when driven in by exhaustion on the previous
night, they may, after all, have left some poor fellows
clinging to a remnant of wreck; or perhaps have left
a ship on the Sands, lost in the darkness of the night,
and unable to make any signal of distress; the men
cannot rest, and although the life-boat has only been
in a few hours, the coxswain of the boat and the mate
of the steamer go to the harbour-master, tell him their
fears, and ask his permission to put to sea again and
to search round the Sands.

The permission is readily given—"Go by all means,"
and the men are encouraged to make their search.

Ten fresh hands join the coxswain and the bowman
of the life-boat ; and soon after daylight they start on
their dangerous and merciful mission.

They are towed again by the steamer *Aid*, and
make for the North Sands Head light-vessel, keeping
a good look-out for the faintest signal of distress. The
men discover nothing on the north side of the Sands,
and they determine to work their way to the back of
the Sands, on the French side, and there pursue their
search.

Soon they see in the misty distance what seems
to be a large vessel on the south-east spit of the
Sands ; they tow with all speed in her direction ;
they are proceeding along the edge of the Sand, just
outside the broken water.

The waves are rolling along in all their fury, and
beat down upon the Sands with tremendous force ;
the surf flying up in great sheets of foam, and the
roar of the breakers is like loud quivering thunder ;
the scene is enough to make the stoutest heart quail ;
but, without one thought of flinching from whatever
lies before them, the men cling to the life-boat as the
seas break over them, and patiently bear all the cold
and storm, and wash of water, as they are towed on
nearer and nearer to the wreck.

One of the men said afterwards, in answer to
questions as to what his feelings were as he watched
the tremendous seas, and knew that shortly he
would be battling for his life in the midst of them,
"Well, Sir, I think that at all such times a man
must naturally have his inward feelings ; soldiers say

that they have theirs, and I am very sure that we have
ours ; a man can't help knowing the danger, and
thinking about it, and feeling about it too; but we
are not going to be made cold-hearted about it, or
we shouldn't be out there.   We can't help seeing that
we've got hard work before us, and we determine by
God's help to do it, and we won't flinch.   We hope
to save others, and feel that we shall do our best to
do so, but at the same time we know that we may
lose our own lives in making the attempt.   We think
about this sometimes as we are sitting in the boat,
holding on against the wash of the seas, but when we
get to the wreck we forget all about ourselves, and
only think about saving the others."

The seas become still heavier and heavier as they
get nearer to the wreck and approach a more exposed
part of the Sands; they now have to encounter one
great rush of water, which, urged by the hurricane of
wind and the strong tide, comes raging along in
unbroken course through the Straits of Dover.

At last they get within a short distance of the
wreck, and find her to be a large barque.   She has
settled down somewhat on the Sands, has heeled over
a good deal, and huge waves are foaming over her.
The men look at the awful rage of sea, hear the
tremendous roar with which the mountainous waves
break upon the Sand, and say to each other, "We
have indeed our work cut out for us."

The boatmen can see no signs of any of the crew
of the vessel being left on board.   They may have
been swept from the wreck, or have been lost in some

vain effort to get to land in their own boat. The
flag of distress is still flying, and the steamer tows
the boat nearer to the wreck ; they can now make out
that the crew are crouching down under cover of the
deck-house ; while the huge waves make a complete
breach over the vessel, and threaten every moment
to wash the deck-house and the crew away.

The steamer tows the boat up to windward.
The life-boatmen feel their turn for the battle has
come, and make every preparation ; they get their
sails ready to hoist, make the cable up all clear for
paying out ; the coxswain sees that they are now far
enough to windward, the steamer's tow-rope is cast
off ; the boat lifts on a huge wave as the strain of the
rope is taken off her, they hoist the sail, round she
flies in answer to her helm, and she makes in for the
wreck ; they mount on the top of huge seas, go
plunging down into the trough of the waves ; the
spray flies over them as the gale catches the crests of
the towering breakers, and fills the air with clouds of
flying foam ; a minute more and they are in broken
water ; the seas rush and leap and recoil, fly high and
fall in tangled volumes over the boat ; she is tossed in
all directions by the wild broken waves, and as she
fills again and again with water, becomes almost
unmanageable.

The men have to cling with all their strength to the
thwarts, but still the wind drives the boat on, and
they get within about sixty yards of the wreck ; the
anchor is thrown out, the cable payed out swiftly ;
the sea is rushing with tremendous force over the

ship; the boat sheers in under her lee-quarter; the boatmen cheer to the poor half-dead sailors who are crouching and clinging under shelter of the deck-house. All is hope; "A minute or two more," they think, "and we shall have saved them." A shout from the coxswain of the boat—"Hold on! hold on!" a glance upwards, a huge mountain of a wave comes rolling swiftly on, its crest curls over, breaks, falls upon the boat, the men and the boat are carried down by the tremendous weight of water. Some of the men seem almost crushed by the blow and pressure of the falling wave; they do not know whether the boat is upset or not, so is she rolled about in the whirl of the broken wave; they cling convulsively to her, she soon floats, lifted by her air-tight compartments, and she frees herself. The men breathe again; they find that the wave that buried them has taken the boat in its irresistible flood, and dragging the anchor with it, has carried it more than one hundred yards away from the ship.

The men lift themselves up, clear their faces from the water, shake it from their clothes, and look at the vessel; they determine that, please God, they will yet save the crew. They give a cheer to encourage and give hope to the poor fellows, and without further thought of the dread danger they have but just escaped, prepare for another attempt.

They hoist the sail quickly and get the boat's head round, and try and sheer her into the ship; but all their efforts are in vain, wave after wave breaks over them, the boat is tossed in all directions by the

broken seas—sometimes the coxswain feels as if he
would be thrown bodily forward on the men, as the
waves lift the boat almost end on end.

Again and again are boat and men overrun bodily by
the rush of the waves, but the boat behaves splendidly,
lifts buoyantly from under the weight of water ; her
undaunted crew bear up bravely, and all are once
more ready for another struggle. They labour on, but
without success ; they cannot make their way back to
the ship : they get the oars out, the waves and wind
take them and send them leaping from the rowlocks,
and out of the men's hands ; they must give it up for
this time.

All their thoughts are for the poor shipwrecked
crew, and the bitter—bitter disappointment they must
feel. Again they cheer to them, and shout to
them, to keep their hearts up—they will soon be at
them again ; and they make the best of their way
back to the steamer. They have failed in their first
attempt.

The steamer again tows them into position, and
they make for the second time boldly in for the wreck ;
the coxswain steers as near to the stern as possible,
avoiding the danger of being washed over it on to the
deck of the vessel, and thus crushed to pieces ; they
get nearer to the vessel than they did before ; the
shipwrecked crew begin to stir themselves, the
boatmen are about to run the boat alongside, when
again they are overwhelmed in the rush of a fearful
sea, buried in its deluge of broken water, and the
boat is again hurled away by the force of the waves,

and carried many fathoms from the vessel; the anchor holds, but the tide is running more strongly than ever, and in the direction to carry them right away from the wreck; and so it is hopeless for them to try to get any nearer to her from where they are.

The tide has risen and is nearly at its height; the vessel has fallen still more over upon her side; the lee side of the deck is completely under water, the top of the deck-house is just above the sea; the crew have been driven from their old place of shelter, they have lashed a spar across the mizen shrouds, and are all clinging to it, while the heavy waves beat continually over the poor fellows.

It is with terrible agony that the crew on board the wreck witness the second failure of the life-boat: "She will never come again," the captain says, in a voice of despair; "the men cannot do it, the very life must have been washed and beaten out of them." Great is their astonishment to find that no sooner does the life-boat clear herself of the water that seems almost to drown her, no sooner do the men free themselves from the rush of the foam, which has for a time overwhelmed them, than they begin to cheer again, as if only rendered the more determined by their second defeat; the more courageous by the difficulties and dangers they had already endured; and the shipwrecked crew, encouraged by the hoarse cheers of the exhausted half-drowned boatmen, do not lose all hope.

The boat is again towed into position, and for the third time makes in for the wreck.

This time they throw the anchor overboard farther from the vessel than before, give longer scope to the cable, sail in well under the ship's stern, and again steer as near as possible to the vessel's lee-quarter, and lower the foresail.

They are within a dozen yards of the ship; the bowman heaves a rope with all his force; it falls short of the men in the shrouds to whom he throws it, and the boat sweeps on; they check her with the cable, and bring her head to the ship abreast of her, but unhappily some distance off.

The captain of the shipwrecked vessel had despaired of the boat being able to come in the third time; but when he saw her coming, he felt fully convinced that it was their last opportunity of being saved, and determined that if the boat were again swept from the wreck, that he would jump into the sea and try and swim to her.

The boat comes and misses, and the crew of the boat see the captain hastily throw off his sea-boots, seize a life-buoy, and prepare to plunge into the sea: they shout to him not to do so, and to the crew to hold him back. "The tide in its set off the Sands would sweep him away; the seas would beat his life out of him: they will be back again soon, and won't go home without them."

The steamer has followed the boat as closely as possible, running down close to the edge of the Sands, just clear of the broken water. The life-boat has swung out to the full length of her cable, and is in deep water; the men upon being beaten away from the wreck for the third time, look round for the steamer, and to their astonishment see her making in straight towards them.

The men on board the steamer had watched with increasing anxiety and dismay the defeat of the successive gallant attempts made by the life-boat crew. They had grown more and more excited each time that the life-boat had returned to them, and feel now prepared to run almost any risk whatever to further help the life-boatmen in their brave but as yet unsuccessful efforts to save the crew.

And so the steamer makes right in across the broken water, straight for the life-boat; a rope is thrown from the steamer, and is made fast in the life-boat; they now hope, with the steamer's help, to be able to sheer the boat right in upon the wreck.

The boatmen have hold of their own cable, to which their anchor is fast; they gradually draw in upon this cable, and the steamer tries to tow the boat nearer and nearer to the vessel, and for the fourth time the life-boat makes in 'mid the wild raging seas for the rescue of the crew.

The steamer ventures into the rage of the sea, and her position becomes one of very great peril; she rolls in the trough of the tremendous waves till her gunwales are right under water; the foam and spray dash completely over her, and tons and tons of water deluge her deck. They gradually approach the vessel; the life-boat sheers in; the seas and tide and wind catch her in their full power, and whirl her away again.

A huge wave sweeps bodily over the steamer—she is in extreme danger ; the life-boatmen watch her in the greatest alarm, fearing each moment that a wave will swamp her—but rolling, plunging, burying herself in the foaming seas, the steamer bravely holds her own, until to remain longer is certain death to all on board ; and sorrowfully the crew of the steamer abandon their most gallant attempt, and make out of the rage of broken water.

The life-boatmen rejoice to see the steamer get clear of the deadly peril, but they are scarcely in less peril themselves ; they cut the steamer's tow-rope, and then find that they must cut their own cable, to avoid being dashed over the wreck ; and away they go again driven on before the gale. They look at each other, but only read courage and determination in each other's countenances. Beaten off for the fourth time, not one heart fails, not one speaks of giving up the attempt, not one of the brave fellows has any such thought for an instant ; their one consideration is what next shall be attempted to save the poor fellows from a speedy and terrible death, which indeed threatens them every minute. Thus the only question is, what they shall try next ? and weak and exhausted, and almost frozen with cold, but determined, and full of courage and zeal as ever, their one anxiety is for the poor shipwrecked crew, whose peril increases each minute, and they prepare for a fifth effort for their rescue, strong still in their old determination—" that they will not go home without them."

CHAPTER XXVI.

SAVED AT LAST.
VICTORY OR DEATH.

"'Tis done—despite the winds—the roll
   Of that storm-maddened fearful sea ;
Bravery hath snatched each shivering soul,
   O greedy death ! from thee.
Then the rough seamen's hands they wring,
   And some, o'erpowered by bursting feeling,
Their arms around them wildly fling,
   While tears down many a cheek are stealing ;
They bless them for their noble deed,
True saviours sent in hour of need."

N. Michell.

THE ship's hull has now been for some time under
water, and it is evident that the wreck is breaking
up fast. She has coals and iron on board ; this dead
weight keeps her steady on the Sands, and prevents
the waves lifting her and crashing her down, or she
would long since have been torn and broken to fragments. As it is, the decks have burst, and the lighter
portions of her cargo are being rapidly washed out of
her ; the sea in some places is black with coal-dust,

and much wreckage, pieces of her deck and forecastle
are being swept away by the tide.

Each time that the men on board the steamer and
life-boat look at the vessel, count the crew still in
the rigging, and find that not any are missing, they
think it indeed a wondrous mercy that all should still
be safe, and get each moment more impressed with
feelings of deep sympathy for the poor fellows, and
with the greater eagerness to dare all to save them.

Daniel Reading, the brave, skilful, and long-tried
master of the steamer, is ill on shore, and so she is in
charge of John Simpson, the mate; he and William
Wharrier, the engineer, consult as to the possibility of
making another effort with the steamer, for the tide is
setting off the Sands with such force that they do
not see how it is possible for the life-boat to get in
to the wreck and save the crew, and they find that
all the men on board the steamer are perfectly prepared to second them in any effort that they decide
upon making.

They get the mortar-apparatus ready, and again
urge the steamer through the seas in the direction of
the wreck; they hope to get near enough to the vessel
to fire a line from the mortar into the rigging, to
which the shipwrecked crew will attach a rope, and
then hauling this rope on board the steamer, they
will take it to the life-boat's men, who will by it be
able to haul the boat through the seas to the wreck.
Cautiously the steamer approaches; the tide has been
for some time rising fast; the steamer does not draw
much water; they are almost within firing distance;

Y

the waves come rushing along and nearly overrun the steamer; at last a breaker larger than the rest catches her, lifts her high upon its crest, and letting her fall down into its trough as down the side of a wall, she strikes the Sands heavily; the engines are instantly reversed, she lifts with the next wave, and being a very quick and handy boat, at once moves astern before she can thump again, and they are saved from shipwreck; and thus the fifth effort to save the shipwrecked crew fails.

No time is lost; at once the steamer heads for the life-boat, and makes ready to tow her into position. Again not a word—scarcely a thought—about past failures, only eagerness to commence without delay a fresh attempt; the steamer is alongside the life-boat.

"Look out, my men, here is another rope for you." "All right!" the boatmen answer as they catch the line, and haul the hawser into the boat.

"All right! tow us well to windward, give us a good position, plenty of room, we must have them this time. All fast! away you go, hurrah!" The men watch the wreck as they are towed past her. "Oh! the poor fellows! to think we have not got them yet. Well, we have had a hard struggle for it, but, please God, we will save them yet—we will save them yet!"

"Ah! look how that wave buries them all; there they are again, let us give them a cheer, it will help them to keep their hearts up." And as the boat rose upon a sea, they shouted and waved to the shipwrecked crew.

" There, another breaker has gone right over her ;
how she heaves and works to it ! Yes, and do you see
how her masts are swinging about, and in different
directions ? they are getting unstepped and loose ; she
is breaking up fast, working all over—all of a quiver
and tremble ! Poor fellows ! poor fellows ! we have
not a moment to spare. It must soon be all over, one
way or the other !" Thus the men speak to each other ;
they are in a glow of eagerness and excitement, and
can scarcely restrain themselves to get quietly to
work. For as they watch the poor fellows, and time
after time see the waves wash over them in quick
succession—and as each wave passes, see them still
clinging on—they almost feel as if they could jump at
them to try and save them, and in their noble and
gallant sympathy and determination lose all sense of
weakness, and cold, and exhaustion.

When describing their feelings, one of the men said,
" We were thoroughly warm at our work, and felt like
lions, as if nothing could stop us."

It is in this spirit that they now consult together, as
to the plan upon which they shall make their next
effort. First one scheme is suggested, and then
another, but these seem to give no better prospect
of success than those that have been already tried in
vain.

At last one of the men proposes a plan which
must indeed either prove rescue to the shipwrecked or
death to all.

" I tell you what, my men, if we are going to save
those poor fellows, there is only one way of doing it ;

it must be a case of save all, or lose all, that is just it. We must go in upon the vessel straight, hit her between the masts, and throw our anchor over right upon her decks."

"What a mad-brained trick!" says one.

"Why, the boat would be smashed to pieces."

"Likely enough; but there is one thing certain, is there not? and that is that we are never going home to leave those poor fellows to perish, and I do not believe that there is any other way of saving them, and so we must just try it. And God help us, and them!"

Not a single word against it now!

What, charge in upon the vessel in that mad rage of sea! Victory, or death, indeed!

Most of the men on board the life-boat are married men with families—loved wives, and loved little ones dependent upon them. Thoughts of this, tender heart-felt thoughts of home, come to them.

"Well, and so we have, and have not those poor perishing fellows also got wives and little ones, and are they not thinking of their homes, and loved ones, as much as we are thinking of ours; and shall we go home, having turned back from even the greatest danger, without having tried all it is possible to try; go home to our wives and little ones, and leave them to perish thinking of theirs? No! please God, that shall never be said of us."

Such thoughts as these pass through the minds of some of the boatmen. And what think the poor nearly drowned crew of the unfortunate vessel.

There they are clinging to the loose and shaking
rigging ; a few feet above the boil of the hungry and
raging sea.   They have seen effort after effort made,
and effort after effort fail ; they have watched the men
do more than they ever dreamt it was possible for men
to do ; and they have watched the life-boat live, and
battle with seas with which they never thought it
possible a boat could for one moment contend ; time
after time they have thought that the boatmen were
drowned, as they saw the huge curling waves break
over the boat, swamp it, bury it in the weight of their
falling volume of water, and for some seconds hide all
from view ; they have been watching the men persevere
in attempt after attempt, when they thought that from
sheer exhaustion it would be impossible for them to
make another effort for their rescue.

With equal wonder and admiration they watched the
noble efforts of the steamer, marked how nearly she was
wrecked, and when she failed, gave up all as lost ; de-
ciding in their minds that in such a rush of broken sea,
strength of tide and gale of wind, that it is impossible
for the boat to reach them, or for them to be saved, and
all but one give up all hope.   When the captain says in
despair, " The life-boat can never make another effort,"
this man answers, " I have sailed in English ships ; I
have often heard about life-boat work, and I know that
they never leave any one to perish as long as they can
see them, and they will not leave us."

"And look, here she comes again.   O God help
them ! God help them !"

Yes, here she comes again ; the steamer had

hastened to tow her well into position, well to windward of the wreck. "And here she comes again."

Once more the boat heads for the wreck—this time to do, or to die ; each man knows it, each man feels it. They are crossing the stern of the vessel ; " Look at that breaker—look at that breaker—hold on, hold on, it will be all over with us if it catches us, we shall be thrown high into the masts of the vessel, and shaken out into the sea in a moment! Hold on all, hold on ! Now it comes ! No, thank God, it breaks ahead of us, and we have escaped. Now, men, be ready, be ready!" Thus shouts the coxswain. Every man is at his station, some with the ropes in hand ready to lower the sails ; others by the anchor prepared to throw it overboard at the right moment ; round, past the stern of the vessel the boat flies, round in the blast of the gale and the swell of the sea ; down helm, round she comes ; down foresail ; the ship's lee gunwale is under water, the boat shoots forward straight for the wreck, and hits the lee rail with a shock that almost throws all the men from their posts, and then, still forward, she literally leaps on board the wreck. Over ! over with the anchor ; it falls on the vessel's deck ; all the crew of the vessel are in the mizen shrouds, but they cannot get to the boat, a fearful rush of sea is chasing over the vessel, and between them and it. Again and again the boat thumps on the wreck as on a rock, with a shock that almost shakes the men from their hold.

The waves soon lift the boat off the deck, and carry her away from the vessel. " Is even this attempt to be

a failure? No, thank God! the anchor holds; veer
out the cable; steadily, my men, steadily; do not
disturb the anchor more than you can help; we shall
have them now! we shall have them, all will be well;
ease her a bit, ease her, see how she plunges, a little
more cable; now for the grappling-iron; quick, throw
it over that line; there you have it;" and they haul
on board a line which had been made fast to a cork-
fender, and thrown overboard from the wreck early in
the day, but which the boatmen had never before
been able to reach.

They get the boat straight, haul in slowly upon
both ropes; cheer to the crew: "Hurrah! mates,
hurrah!" All is joy and excitement, but at the same
time steady attention to orders; now the boat is
abreast the mizen rigging, opposite to where the men
are clinging. "Down helm, the boat sheers in; haul
in upon the ropes, men, handsomely, handsomely;"
the boat jumps forward, hits the ship heavily with her
stern, crashes off a large piece of her fore-foot. The
men are for a moment thrown down with the shock;
two of the boatmen spring on to the raised bow
gunwale, and seize hold of the captain of the vessel,
who seems nearly dead, drag him in over the bows;
two of the sailors jump on board; "Hold on all, hold
on!"

A fearful sea rolls over them, the boat is washed
away from the vessel; the anchor still holds; they
sheer the boat in again; they make the ropes fast, and
lash the boat to the shrouds of the wreck, thus verily
nailing their colours to the mast. No! they will not

be washed away again until they have all the crew on
board.

A sailor jumps from the rigging, the boat sinks in
the trough of the sea, the man falls between the boat
and the wreck; a second more and the boat will be
on the top of him, crushing him against the rail of the
vessel, upon which the keel of the boat strikes and
grinds cruelly; two boatmen seize him, leaning right
over the gunwale to do so, they are almost dragged
into the water; they are seized in turn by the men in
the boat, and all are with difficulty got on board.

Up the boat flies and crashes against the spar
lashed to the rigging. " Jump in, men, jump in all of
you. Now! Now!" In they spring, and tumble, falling
upon the men, and all rolling over into the bottom of
the boat. All are now on board—all on board!
" Hurrah! cut the lashings, there, she falls away from
the wreck; cut the cable, quick with the hatchet; all
gone! all gone! up foresail." The seas catch the
boat and bear her away from the wreck; away she
goes with a bound, flying through the broken water;
the heavy wind fills the sail; they are fairly under
weigh, and with the precious freight for which they
had fought so long and so gallantly, safely on board.
Thank God! thank God! all are saved at last—*saved
at last.*

Now the boat is through the broken seas away
from the terrible Sands, out in the deep water; the
men have time to look at each other; and how gladly,
and yes, how fondly, they do so. Strangers though
they be, yet at that moment their hearts are warm to

each other with more than a brother's love—all is
gladness and thankfulness; they shake hands, the
rescuers and the rescued, time after time.

The saved crew are ten in number. They are
Danes, and the wreck the Danish barque *Aurora
Borealis.*

Some of the sailors can speak a little broken
English, and in such terms as they are able the poor
fellows express the depth of their gratitude, and their
wonder at being saved.

The boat makes for the steamer, which is coming
down rapidly to meet her; the crew of the steamer
greet the life-boatmen with cheers! Who can describe the joy they all feel at the successful ending of
their long battle with terrible danger and threatened
death! and great indeed is their sympathy with the
saved from death, for whom they and the boatmen
have so willingly, and to the very utmost, risked their
own lives.

They lift the captain on board the steamer; he is
thoroughly exhausted; they carry him into the engine-
room, and in the warmth there, do their best to revive
him, and he soon recovers. The Danish seamen will
not leave the boat; the life-boat crew tell the mate
that his men would be much more comfortable on
board the steamer, that the seas will be washing over
the boat all the way in; but no, as so frequently
happens on such occasions, and as has been before
noticed, the rescued men feel so grateful to the life-
boatmen, that they are not content to leave the boat
until they get to land. And the mate replies, "No!

you saved us, you saved us ; we thought you never, never do it ; you had plenty trouble ; we stop with you." And they would not desert their friends, their brothers indeed, who had done so much to save them.

In Ramsgate the anxiety is very great.

The steamer and life-boat have been out many hours, nothing can be seen of them in the mist that hangs over the Goodwin Sands.

"Can anything have happened ?" is the question that is restlessly put from one to another.

It might well be so, in the terrific sea that must have been raging on the Goodwin in so fearful a storm.

At about half-past two, hundreds of people are collected on the pier ; for the news that the life-boat is out always spreads like wildfire through the town ; and if there is any cause for anxiety on her account, the whole town soon shares the apprehension, and throngs of anxious men crowd the pier and harbour. Now the men who are anxiously on the watch make out something looming in the mist ; and speedily the steamer and life-boat are seen, their flags are flying, glad sign of successful effort, of rescue effected ; and great is the joy of all the lookers-on ; steamer and life-boat speed between the massive granite heads of the two piers, and the crowd that looks down upon them as they come pitching and rolling along, greet them with cheer after cheer.

The saved crew land, they are many of them very weak, and worn, and exhausted ; but all around is welcome, and sympathy, and active service.

They are taken to the Sailors' Home, where warm clothing, and beds, and goodly fare are ready for them, and the poor fellows soon recover ; some of them before they attempt to take any rest insist upon writing to the loved ones at home, to tell of their safety, and of their rescue from apparently almost certain death.

Doubtless these letters contain simple expressions of gratitude to God, and of deep love for the dear wife, of many many kisses for the sturdy little boy, or the laughing girl, for the children whose bright eyes seemed so often staring at them so wistfully out of the storm, and whom they never thought to see again ; and doubtless contain also expressions of great admiration and thankfulness for the untiring courage of the English life-boatmen ; and their full belief in the expression of one of their number who told them in the height of their danger, and in the very depth of their despair, " to take courage, for the life-boatmen will never leave us while they can see us."

The Board of Trade, in recognition of the gallant services of the men, presented them with one pound each. The King of Denmark forwarded two hundred rix-dollars to be divided among them.

The boatmen are all poor men, and these presents proved very acceptable ; but the joy with all was, and will be while life lasts, that God had in His providence and mercy so crowned their perseverance with success, and enabled them to save their drowning brother sailors. While all who heard of the circumstances, declared that never by land or by sea was more gallant

service rendered than was accomplished by these brave
boatmen, who in the face of all danger, and of all
hardship, determined to persevere to the death—
determined that while the shipwrecked crew still
remained alive, "They would not go home without
them."

CHAPTER XXVII.

OF SOME OF THE LIFE-BOAT MEN.

" The rank is but the guinea-stamp ;
The man 's the gold for a' that."
Burns.

IT may be that some of my readers who have
followed the adventures of our Storm Warriors
through their varied struggles and heroic deeds,
and have felt sympathy more or less deep for the
gallant life-savers, would like to know a little of one
or two of the leading men among those who, during
the last twenty years, or more, have done such good
work in the Ramsgate life-boat on the Goodwin
Sands.

Gallant men who, time after time, have plunged
their boat into the thickest of the fray, and heedless
of hardship, heedless of peril, forgetful of self, intent
only upon rescuing the distressed, have laboured on
through the dark stormy nights, 'mid the rush of the
waves, the howling winds, the fierce hurricane blasts,
the spray, and sleet, and snow—encountering all
dangers, and persevering through all difficulties, and

repaid for all as they have brought home in the morning's light the brother sailors, or the passengers, whom they have been instrumental in saving from swift and terrible deaths.

Quiet, broad-chested, steadfast-eyed men, who, by all the scenes they have witnessed, and by all the hardships they have suffered, and by all the thoughts of the shipwrecked ones that they have brought safely home, have it deeply written in upon their hearts : that (to use their own simple and noble expression) *they have a call to save life.*

Well indeed would it be for the world if more of those to whom talents are given, and to whom stewardships are intrusted, and who stand watching the many who are in danger, overrun by the dark troubled waters of social life—wrecked in poverty, in misery, in ignorance—wrecked for want of true teaching, true guidance, true sympathy, true love—well would it be if more of these stewards of God's loans might have the same noble conviction written in upon their hearts : that they have *a call to save life!* Then would more lives grow noble by noble work, and become happy in the consciousness of the happy results, which God grants to the efforts of all those who humbly seek to live and labour for the good of others ; grants to those who would sooner put to sea 'mid toil and peril, 'mid self-sacrifice and opposition, rather than let the life-boats God has given for their use rot and canker upon the banks, while the cries of the despairing and the lost plead in vain from the dark storms and troubled waters at their feet.

Yes, surely; the humble boatmen of our coasts, our
"Storm Warriors," afford a lesson by which many
may well profit, in the noble self-sacrificing way in
which they realize their mission—*that they have a call
to save life.*

"Who shall be the first coxswain of our new
Northumberland Prize Life-boat?" was the question
asked by the Ramsgate Harbour Trustees some two
and twenty years ago; and it was an important and
anxious question; for the good boat required skilful
handling to do efficient service, and if she failed in
what was required and expected of her, the life-boat
cause would receive a serious check.

"No man better than James Hogben for the first
coxswain; no man among them all holds a higher
character for cool courage, and skill, and experience;"
such was the answer. Hogben had been to sea since
he was a lad; for some years he was sailing in a
small vessel that traded between London and Ostend;
then he sailed a little bit of a boat, of about fifteen
tons, between Ramsgate and Dunkirk and Boulogne,
winter and summer. Ask him about it now, and the
dangers he used to run; and he shakes his head, and
with a quiet smile tells you that, "He met with a
good many very *whole* breezes, very!" in that little
craft of his.

After that, he had nearly twenty years of hovelling;
cruising about the Goodwin Sands in open luggers in
the stormiest winter weather, till he almost knew the
Sands by heart; and so James Hogben was appointed
first coxswain of the Ramsgate life-boat.

Each time that he and his crew went out in her they gained fresh confidence in her powers; and noble work the good boat did under his command; indeed from the time the *Northumberland* life-boat began her career at Ramsgate to the time she was broken up, from December 1851 to July 1865, no fewer than two hundred and sixty-one lives were saved by her and the gallant Storm Warriors who sailed her, from vessels that were utterly lost; and nineteen vessels, with their crews, were extricated from the Goodwin Sands and brought safely into harbour.

For nine years Hogben was coxswain of the life-boat, and then came that dread New Year's Eve, when doubts were thrown upon the telegram that came from Deal; and there was delay; and the life-boat got out to the south of the Goodwin Sands only in time for her crew to see the *Gottenburg* over-whelmed by the waves, and to hear the last cries of the drowning men.

Hogben had been out in the life-boat once before that day, and was exhausted and unwell; and he had a nasty fall in the boat, and hurt his knee badly, and soon fell seriously ill; his nerves were, for a time, utterly shattered, and he who had been remarkable for his dauntless courage became too nervous to walk even down the pier for fear of falling over.

And although, after a while, he so far recovered as to be able to be employed as a boatman in the harbour, and as a watchman on the pier, yet he was never able to go to sea again; his iron constitution broken down by some thirty years of Storm Warrior life, during the last nine years of which he had been coxswain of the famous Ramsgate life-boat.

Isaac Jarman was appointed coxswain in Hogben's room.

Who among Ramsgate boatmen has been better known in his time than Isaac Jarman—or Mr. Jarman, as I suppose I ought to call him now? for is he not master of a thriving public-house, which he will take good care to keep respectable? and it will not be his fault if any of his customers wreck themselves by taking too much drink.

But a yarn on Ramsgate pier with the life-boat coxswain, Jarman, was for some years quite an institution with many a visitor to Ramsgate, as well as with many an inhabitant.

When I have known Jarman (it does not seem quite natural *Mistering* my old boatman friend) to be out in the life-boat, enduring all the rage of the storm, and I have imagined the wild scenes 'mid the strife of waters through which he has been passing, another picture, one in very vivid contrast, has often presented itself to my mind.

I have remembered the scene I saw one evening when I called upon him, and found him with his family at tea.

"Come in, sir, come in; you won't disturb us: glad to see you."

His wife and, I think, five little daughters were there, and the baby boy, the only son, was taken out of the cradle to be shown to me.

Z

And as Jarman dandled the little fellow in his
strong arms he said, "Bless the boy! Bless the boy!
he will make a life-boat coxswain some day, that he
will;" and I felt that all the thoughts of the danger of
the work was lost in the joy of saving life; I glanced
at the mother, half expecting some expression of
dissent; no, her smile showed that she was proud of
her husband, and that all her sympathies were with
him in his noble work, and that she was quite content
that her only boy should in his day follow in his
father's steps and be, like him, one of the gallant band
of life-savers who guard our coasts.

And I have often felt, that however much such
pictures of happy home-circles dwelt in the heart of
Jarman, and of his comrades, as they have struggled
out through the dark storms, and rushed into conflict
with the wild seas, yet that they have never caused
them to turn back from any danger, or to lessen one
single effort in their warfare to save life.

Isaac Jarman was turned out into the North Sea
almost from his cradle.

His father, a boatman, got severely hurt on board a
hovelling-lugger, so much so, that he was never fit for
work again; as a matter of course, the family became
very poor.

Many hungry children to feed, and the arms once so
strong now powerless to labour for them, no wonder
that the cupboard was often empty, and the growing
lads forced to do something for themselves as soon as
they were able.

And so Isaac Jarman, when a boy of twelve years

old, was sent away to sea on board a small fishing-smack called the *Pledge;* she was only twenty-five tons, but used to sail long distances away to fish in the North Sea, in all weathers, summer and winter.

The poor lad had all the clothing his parents could supply him with, but that was little more than he stood up in ; no waterproof overalls, no sea-boots, the almost child had to rough it hardly enough ; in bad weather wet through day and night, with no bed to lie upon, and no change of dry clothes ; he used to throw himself down on the floor of the small cabin, and lie coiled up before the little fire that glimmered in the stove ; the spray oftentimes washing down the hatchway and surging up against his back, so that he had to be content with being dry one side at a time ; but strangely enough it agreed with him ; as that rough life, with all its strong sea-breezes, and its abundance of good fish diet, does agree with many a little urchin, who, for sturdiness, is not to be sur-passed by any luxury-lapped little fellow in the land.

After Jarman had finished his apprenticeship in the fishing-smack, he was for some years in a collier, during which time he was twice wrecked. And after that for seven or eight years he worked as a Ramsgate boatman, always on the look-out in rough weather, day and night, with but short intervals for sleep, for a signal of distress from the Goodwin Sands, and a call for the life-boat ; and so all his training well fitted him for the post of life-boat coxswain ; and when the vacancy was made by Hogben's illness

Z 2

Jarman was well chosen to fill the post. For ten years he continued coxswain of the life-boat, going out in her no fewer than one hundred and thirty-two times, and helping to save between three and four hundred lives.

You may see many a medal that has been well won—and that is worthily worn—by veteran soldier or sailor, but you will find few that have been better won, or that are more worthily worn, than are the four medals and a clasp that our Storm Warrior Jarman has to show as records of his brave and self-sacrificing services; or the three medals that Hogben can display on high days and holidays; or those given to Reading, the brave master of the steam-tug *Aid*, and those worn by many another gallant boatman or sailor, who, at Ramsgate, or at other stations round the coast, have done true warrior service in saving life from shipwreck.

After holding his post of coxswain for ten years, Jarman found the exposure too much for him: he was out nine times in one fortnight, five times in one week; he was seized with a very severe attack of bronchitis, from which he never thoroughly recovered, and had shortly to give up going to sea, and resign his position of coxswain.

He had three brothers and a nephew brought up as sailors, all of whom have been drowned; well do I remember the night when his last brother was drowned.

It had been blowing a heavy gale for three days and nights, with continual snowstorms; the vessels at

sea were in terrible peril : they had no help for it but
to drive blindly before the gale, unable to see any
of the lights or buoys which mark the sands and
shoals. I had heard that a Ramsgate collier was
known to have sailed from the North some days since,
and could not be far off; and it was with a sad heart
and deep anxiety that I lingered on the pier that
afternoon watching the storm. I saw the boatmen
all ready on the look-out for any signal, but I felt,
as they felt, that there could be but little hope of any
vessels being able to run the gauntlet of the many
sandbanks in that dark storm, or of being able
to make any signals heard, or seen, if they got into
danger.

It was with a deep feeling of dread and apprehension that I left Jarman and his fellow-boatmen to
their dreary and almost hopeless watch ; and they
watched on through the long dark hours of the night,
ready at any moment to man the life-boat ; but they
could discover no signal—the roar of the storm was
too great, the fall of snow too continuous. And yet
during those sad hours while the boatmen crouched,
sheltering themselves as well as they could—watching,
and listening, and waiting, but in vain—the terrible
tragedy was worked out ; at daylight they saw a
wreck in Pegwell Bay. Man the life-boat ! No, too
late, she is bottom up, her masts are gone ; she must
have been wrecked on the Brake Sand, and been
rolled over and over by the tremendous sweep of
the sea, and the tide. Yes, it is the Ramsgate collier that was expected, and that Jarman's brother

commanded ; and he and all his crew have miserably perished—perished within sight of home, and within half a mile or so of the life-boat men who were so eagerly watching and waiting for a call to their rescue, and to whom they could not make their danger known.

And to this day you may see the sad record of the disaster in the remains of the hull of the wreck, washed high up on the shore in Pegwell Bay, and there half buried in the sand.

A great grief to Jarman this sad loss of his brother ; and the poor man left a widow and a large family of children ; and when fine weather came, in the early summer, many a friend who had had pleasant chats with the life-boat coxswain on Ramsgate pier, was surprised to find him diligently cruising in and out of offices in London ; he was canvassing for votes for the Merchant Seamen's Orphan Asylum, and he laboured on until he succeeded in getting two of his late brother's children into that famous institution.

Charles Fish was appointed to succeed Jarman as coxswain, and the life-boat under his guidance continues to do good service ; many times has he been out in her, and many times has he, through much hardship and danger, brought saved lives home. And may God in His mercy continue to shield and bless him and the brave men who sail with him, and aid them in their gallant efforts to pluck the shipwrecked and the drowning from all the mighty strife of waters, that battles with such deadly fury when the storms rage round the fatal Goodwin Sands.

I cannot refrain from bearing my tribute of admiration to worthy Daniel Reading, a brave, skilful,
modest sailor, the master of the steam-tug *Aid;*
many and many a time has he rendered service,
which for daring and skill could not be well sur-
passed, threading in and out of the Goodwin Sands
'mid terrible storms while seeking for the position
of wrecked vessels, or making short cuts to tow the
life-boat into position, that no time should be lost in
her efforts to save the drowning crews.

Yes! Reading, and James Simpson, the mate of
the *Aid*, and William Wharrier, the engineer, who
have been together more than twenty years, and have
been out on almost every occasion that the life-boat
has been called for, have all three of them done noble
and gallant service time after time, and are indeed
well worthy to be ranked among the Storm Warriors
who have nobly fought in the great and good cause
of saving life.

And many another gallant fellow might I mention,
whose name stands worthily on the Ramsgate life-
boat roll-call ; famous specimens of what a British
sailor should be—full of daring and determination, and
skill, and hardihood ; men who are ready to encounter
all danger, and to endure any amount of hardship, in
answer to the holy call : to go forth and seek to save
the shipwrecked and the perishing.

CHAPTER XXVIII.

THE NATIONAL LIFE-BOAT INSTITUTION.

"The quality of mercy is not strain'd ;
It droppeth as the gentle rain from heaven
Upon the place beneath : it is twice bless'd ;
It blesseth him that gives, and him that takes :
'Tis mightiest in the mightiest ; it becomes
The throned monarch better than his crown ; . . ."

WHATEVER interest my readers may have felt in the narrative of gallant deeds wrought at one life-boat station on the coast, must be intensified at the thought of the noble work that is going on all round our sea-girt land—that, at almost all dangerous places where vessels are likely to be in distress, or lives in peril, there are life-boats ready to be manned, and brave fellows ever anxious promptly to launch forth 'mid the wind and sea, and battle their way to the rescue of the perishing. Yes, thank God, the gallant old Anglo-Saxon blood is still to the fore ; the spirit of our ancestors has not died out, and we may well believe, from abundant evidence continually arising from very diversified fields, that it has not even in the least degenerated ; for at all times can men be found

ready to go forth either by sea or land, to dare all
that men should dare, and to do all that men can do,
when duty calls them to labours of self-sacrifice,
endurance, and courage.

And to the old bravery is now added modern
science and organization, and the British coasts are
guarded by a volunteer navy, equipped and marshalled
by the Royal National Life-boat Institution.

Two hundred and thirty-three life-boats form, at
present, the great storm fleet of the Institution ; the
boats are stationed at the most dangerous places on
the coast, and are kept always ready for service.

Those who are living inland may often notice how
fast the high clouds are flying overhead, and may
listen to the soughing of the rising wind among the
branches of the trees ; but no dread conflict is pictured
by the swift onsweep of the clouds, and the murmur of
the wind, fitful and angry though it at times is, scarcely
seems to suggest scenes of terrible peril, and of warfare
unto life or death ; but watch the direction in which the
clouds are flying ; consider on what part of our coast
it is that this fierce gale strikes ; imagine the heavy
sea that rolls in there, the foaming breakers, the air
thick with spray, the sound of the deep-voiced waves
as they thunder down upon the rocks over which they
break ; yes ! and fancy that you can make out through
the low flying mist that several vessels are in the
distance trying to beat their way against the growing
gale, and off the dangerous lee-shore, and then rejoice
as you feel fully assured, if any of those struggling
vessels are overwhelmed by the storm, that it shall not

be without a gallant effort for their safety that the poor fellows who form their crews shall be left to perish, for you are convinced that there are, if a life-boat station is near, storm warriors keenly watching the scene, and that they are ready at any moment to launch the life-boat and do battle with the storm and seas for the lives of their brother-sailors. Yes! and it is one of old England's many glories that it should be so.

"It is the soul that makes us rich or poor;" so the old philosopher tells us, and we feel that it is as true of a nation as of an individual. And we count a nation rich with a true glory, that can point to many good works organized and carried out for great and good ends by the loving heartedness, generosity, un-selfishness, and courage of its people. And among such works is life-boat work; there are the rich in soul who have the means and the open hand, and there are the many who are rich in soul and have the courageous and strong hand; and the hand generous with its wealth, clasps the hand generous with its labour and readiness for peril, and together they work out those noble results in which we all rejoice, and which the records of the Life-boat Institution so fully declare.

And we should be less proud of our country if it were not so; indeed we are almost inclined to think it a matter of necessity that in our island home, where the history of our country is so interwoven with the triumphs of our sailors, either in contests with our enemies, in pursuit of discovery, or in the development of commerce, that our sympathies with our sailors should indeed be deep and practical, and that while we rejoice in the safety and the comfort afforded by their labours, that we shall ever be prepared to help them in the hour of their distress ; and that there can be therefore little room for wonder that those who realize the enormous traffic that is carried on around our shores, the dangerous nature of our coasts, and the constant casualties that are occurring, should earnestly desire the welfare of the life-boat cause, and be ready to labour for its development.

The history of the life-boat movement, and of the foundation and gradual development of the Life-boat Institution, are given in the earlier pages of this book. The present condition of the Society tells abundantly of the success it has enjoyed, and of the sympathy it has gained, until now it is able almost to girdle our land with life-boat stations.

Every year there is published by the Board of Trade, a register of the number of wrecks that have taken place in the British Isles during the previous year ; the Life-boat Institution publishes a wreck-chart compiled from these returns ; each wreck is denoted by a black dot which marks on the map the place at which the wreck occurred ; and a truly dismal appearance the map has. See how plentifully these black dots are sprinkled round the coast-line, here one, and there two, at other places half-a-dozen side by side, or growing in number to ten or twelve, and then increasing still more rapidly at the more exposed parts of the coast, or where dangerous sands are more directly in the highway of vessels, so that in such places there may be found twenty, thirty, or forty such marks, and at some localities even more than these, as at the Sands off Yarmouth, the Goodwin Sands, the Bristol Channel, and others, where line after line is required to find room for the number of wrecks to be thus recorded.   For the past year no fewer than 1958 such marks are necessary to complete the dismal list, for such was the number of the wrecks that took place, within that time, in the seas that surround the British Isles.   The months of November and December were especially fatal, heavy gales, thick weather, shifting winds, worked terrible havoc among the shipping ; the coasts were strewn with wrecks ; and the wreck-chart grew proportionally darker in its outline ; and is it not a terrible picture that it presents, as we recognise that almost every mark speaks of a dismal scene of destruction and of peril, of ships with wild seas breaking ruthlessly over them, and of men clinging on, being, perhaps, beaten slowly to death by the constant rush of the heavy waves, until, unless rescued, the shattered wreck breaks up beneath their feet, and they are at once launched into eternity ?

But let us look again at the chart, and we find red marks on the coast lines opposite to the black dots which stud the sea ; and wherever the sea is more dark with the signs of wrecks, there do we find the coast line opposite to such places pencilled the more abundantly with the thin red lines which mark the life-boat stations ; and thank God that the red marks on this wreck-chart do now so often confront the black ! for if the black colour speaks of death, the red

colour speaks of life ; if the one tells of terrible danger
the other tells of gallant rescue; if the one pictures
sailors clinging to a few spars, expecting death at
every moment ; the other pictures the Storm Warriors
ready at their various stations to man the life-boat,
and launch forth to wrestle nobly with the cruel seas,
to snatch from them their intended prey.

And moreover, if the one set of signs tells us of the
dangers incurred by the tens of thousands of sailors
who are helping to minister to the necessities, and
comfort, and luxury of the population of England
the other tells of men and women with warm hearts
and generous hands, who let their sympathies go out
towards their sailor brethren, and plant our storm-
ridden shores with life-boats that shall be for the
rescue of those in peril ; and who are glad also to
encourage and reward the brave men who so often risk
their own lives in their efforts to save the lives of others.

And so famously has its work gone on, that the
Life-boat Society can now report that the number of
lives saved, either by the life-boats of the Institution,
or by especial exertions for which the Society has
granted rewards, presents the grand total of more
than 22,000 ; and we are told that for these services
the Society has granted 91 gold medals, 842 silver
medals, and more than £40,000 in money, so that
now we may well say, that the Institution has truly
become one of national importance, as it has ever
been one of national necessity.

Well indeed was it that Lionel Luken nearly a
century ago, " In the morning sowed the seed, and

in the evening withheld not his hand ;" for although it was not given him to see the results of his labours, yet he commenced a work which has grown into its present noble proportions ; while in contrast to all the apathy he met with, we can now point to a wide-spread and positive affection that the people of England feel for the life-boat cause ; and in evidence of the hold that the work of the Society has now obtained upon the public mind we can point to its meetings, when its friends assembled have been found to rank among all classes of society, when those who are among the chief of the Royal personages of the land have been present, and have been surrounded by some of the first repre-sentatives of our aristocracy, of our army, of our navy, and of our commerce. Among the most memorable of such meetings was one held in the Mansion House in the year 1867, when the Prince of Wales occupied the chair—and the testimony he gave in favour of the Society found an echo, I am sure, in the hearts of all present. It was to the following effect : "My Lord Mayor, my lords, ladies and gentlemen. It affords me great pleasure to occupy the chair upon so interest-ing an occasion as the present. Among the many benevolent and charitable institutions of this country there are, I think, few which more demand our sym-pathy and support, and in which we can feel more interest, than the National Life-boat Institution. An institution of this kind is an absolute necessity in a great maritime country like ours. It is wholly dif-ferent in one respect to many other institutions, because, although lives are to be saved, they can in

those cases, in which this society operates, only be
saved at the risk of the loss of other lives. I am
happy to be able to congratulate the Institution upon
its high state of efficiency at the present moment, and
on the fact that by its means nearly 1000 lives have
been saved during the past year.

" I am happy also to be able to say, that life-boats
exist not only upon our coasts, but that our example
in this matter has been emulated by many foreign
maritime countries, some of which have chosen to
model their Institutions upon our own. . . . Half a
century ago this Institution originated in this city.
In 1852, the late Duke of Northumberland became
its president. My lamented father was also the vice-
president, and took the warmest interest in its pros-
perity. I am happy to say that the respected secretary, Mr. Lewis, occupied that position in 1850. He
has held it ever since, and much of the success of
the Institution is owing to his long experience; and
the energetic manner in which he has directed its
working has raised the Institution to its present high
state of efficiency.

" Before concluding my brief remarks, I call upon
you once more to offer your support to so excellent
an Institution. I congratulate you that it has arrived
at so excellent a state, and I feel sure that you would
be the last to wish it to decay for the want of support
to its funds."

Thus spake His Royal Highness, in 1867, and since
then the Institution has developed more and more,
completing its organization, perfecting its system, and

yearly in its noble results increasing its hold upon the affections of the country.

And now, as I write the concluding lines of my book, the reality of the work related is deeply impressed upon my mind, for this morning my two little boys came running downstairs making the house ring with their cries of " The life-boat! the life-boat!" they had seen it from their nursery window. Yes, there she was, being towed by the steamer, the rough seas lashing over her; her flag was flying in triumph. I could see through my glass that there were about a dozen saved men on board the steamer; and as I have since learned, seldom have men more narrowly escaped than did those poor fellows, and seldom have men been saved by a greater exhibition of courage and perseverance than was displayed by our life-boat men while effecting their rescue.

The *Scot*, a barque of 345 tons, bound from Sunderland to Algiers with a cargo of coals, after experiencing much stormy and thick weather, ran on the Kentish Knock Sand at five o'clock in the morning; the seas immediately began to break over her; the carpenter sounded the well and found two feet and a half of water in her hold, but as the waves lifted her, and plunged her down upon the Sands, she filled at once with water. The captain sent the steward into the cabin for the ship's papers; he found the water up to the cabin floor; he seized the box in which the papers were, and ran up on deck; a wave rushed over the vessel and swept him along the deck; he caught hold of a rope with one hand, but one of the sailors,

overwhelmed by the same wave, threw his legs around
his neck and nearly tore him from his hold ; the wave
passed and the two men were enabled to spring into
the rigging : all hands had to take refuge there, for
within five minutes of the vessel's striking she began
to break up ; the boats were washed away, the deck-
house was torn to fragments and carried away piecemeal ; the deck began to twist, and buckle, and open,
and then was speedily ripped up by the force of the
seas, and torn away plank after plank. The vessel
broke her back and' heeled over on the starboard side,
and settled down upon the Sands ; the men could
not make any signal of distress, and if they could
have done so, they were miles away from any life-
boat, and at any moment the masts might give and
they be plunged into the boiling sea. If the weather
moderated some passing vessel might see them and
be able to send a boat in to their rescue, but not
while the gale lasted. The day grew on ; many vessels
passed the Sands, but not near enough to be able to
make out the men in the rigging of the masts, which
were only just above water ; the weather grew worse
and worse, the day was wearing away, and the night
coming on ; it was all very, very hopeless.

At last a brig passed nearer to them than any
other vessels had come ; the mate said, " If they are
looking at the wreck with a good glass, they may,
perhaps, see us," and he stood up and waved to them.
At that moment, most providentially, the pilot on
board the vessel looked at the wreck through a glass,
and saw the mate waving his south-wester cap. The

2 A

brig soon after spoke a smack that was making in for the land, and the smack proceeded to Broadstairs and reported a wreck on the Kentish Knock, with the crew in the rigging, and that a life-boat was wanted for their rescue, for that no ordinary boat could live through the sea that was running over the Sands. At Broadstairs they felt that their own boat could never get there in time without the assistance of a steamer, and they telegraphed to Ramsgate. It was about six o'clock in the evening, the steamer *Aid*, with Reading in command, and the life-boat *Bradford*, with Fish as coxswain, and R. Goldsmith as second coxswain, at once made their way out into the gale and tremendous sea to the rescue of the shipwrecked crew.

In the meantime the poor fellows on board the wreck waited on almost in despair, the ship each moment yielding to the force of the storm till the whole deck was washed away, and the masts were working more and more loose; happily she had wire rigging, which stood the heavy swaying and lurching of the masts better than the ordinary rope rigging would have done.

It was piteous in talking to the men to hear them describe the condition of utter despair that they were in, and how little ground they could find for any hope whatever; piteous to hear the captain say, "There were just two planks of the deck left floating entangled in a rope, and I kept watching them, thinking that if the mast went I would try and swim to them, and float on them for the chance of being

picked up by some vessel;" to hear the mate answer,
"But I was just watching them too, with the same
idea;" and the carpenter adds, "That was just the
plan I had in my mind."

And thus the ten men clung to the rigging and
to each other, standing on the small crosstrees of one
tottering mast, hour after hour. The day passed, still
no signs of rescue; it became quite dark; it seemed impossible that they could ever see another day's dawn.

They might perish at any moment! at any
moment! and all ten of them. This was the conviction of each one. They told me how endless the
dark hours of that terrible night seemed; and one
man said, "That the thought that seemed ever
present with him, was the bitter way that his little
boy sobbed and cried when he bid him good-bye, and
how he would cry again when he heard that "Dadda
was gone." At last there was a streak of dawn, but
the mast had fallen over almost to a level with the
water and seemed still yielding rapidly; they might
see the sunrise again, but that was all; when one of
the sailors cried out, "A steamer!" "What good can
that be to us?" and they watch her without interest,
for there seems little chance of her coming in their
direction. "Ah! she is running down the edge of the
Sands, and comes nearer, and nearer!"—"Well she
can't help us if she does; no boat can come across the
Sands to us in this surf—No! no." Shortly, a man
cries, "She has a large boat in tow;"—"What!
perhaps a life-boat! it may be that some passing
vessel made us out yesterday and has sent a life-boat;"

Oh, what a thought of hope, of joy, of life! "Can it be so? it is—it is! thank God it is—it is! Look, she has left the steamer and is coming in through the breakers straight towards us!"

It is something to remember, the way in which one man said to me, as if almost unnerved by the remembrance, "Oh, what a beauty she looked! what a beauty she looked coming over those seas!"

The steamer and life-boat had got out to the Sands after battling with the storm for a distance of twenty-six miles. At about 11 o'clock the night before, they spoke the Lightship on the Kentish Knock, and learnt the bearings of the wreck; but they found that it was impossible to discover her in the darkness of the night and storm, so after several vain efforts they lay to until the morning. As soon as it was light they went in search of the wreck, and the life-boat made in across the Sands, and it was then truly a great matter of heartfelt congratulation to the life-boat men that all their labour and perseverance had not been in vain; for to their great joy they could see the crew in the rigging. They anchored the boat as near to the wreck as they could venture, and then let the cable veer out until the boat was under the vessel's jib-boom. It was low-tide—the seas were not breaking over the wreck so violently as they had been; and the men were able to work their way out on to the bowsprit, and drop into the boat, and thus the ten men were saved, after being twenty-six hours holding on in the maintop of the wreck.

The flood-tide was just making; all felt, that as

soon as it rose and the wreck began to heave and work again, the mast would speedily go, and they realized to the full that they had only been saved just in time.

The life-boat returned to the steamer as speedily as possible, and put the rescued men on board her. The shipwrecked men had not tasted anything for nearly thirty-six hours, as it was before breakfast time that they had run ashore, and they had been in the rigging for twenty-six hours. The life-boat got back to the harbour at 11 o'clock in the morning; the life-boat men had been in the open boat exposed to all the fury of the storm for nearly seventeen hours, and their exhaustion was very great The kindness of some friends provided the weary and famished men with a good dinner at the house of their old comrade and friend, Jarman, and soon after a telegram came from Mr. Lewis, of the Life-boat Institution, to whom tidings of the rescue had been telegraphed, that the life-boatmen were to have a sovereign each, and a good dinner; but by that time they were all resting at home after their long hours of fatigue. Other friends made recognition by subscription of their noble services; and comfort was thus carried into the homes of our Storm Warriors after their gallant and triumphant efforts in saving life.

The shipwrecked men were cared for in our Sailors' Home, and speedily recovered their fatigues. The captain told me he did not think they would have been alive one hour longer, if the life-boat had not come just when she did; and speaking of the life-boat, said with deep feeling, "Oh! she is a noble boat, and nobly manned ; there could not be a kinder set of men !" And with these words of the brave and grateful sailor so recently and unexpectedly saved with all his crew, from that which seemed most certain death, I feel inclined to finish my book. But I will add one wish, namely, that we had a better Sailors' Home in which to receive the poor fellows who are brought ashore; 156 wrecked men were received into the Home at Ramsgate last year, 40 in one day ; and a little house of £25, or so, rent, and its one sitting-room for the use of the men, only about sixteen feet by fourteen, and eighteen beds crowded together in small rooms is, of course, quite inadequate to afford the accommodation that we would wish to provide for the poor fellows brought in half dead with cold, with exhaustion, and with hunger, plucked by the Storm Warriors from the very jaws of death 'mid the rage of waters on the Goodwin Sands.

God speed the life-boat ! God guard the Storm Warriors !

THE END.

LONDON : PRINTED BY WILLIAM CLOWES AND SONS, STAMFORD STREET AND CHARING CROSS.

Second Edition, Crown 8vo., price 5s.

THE HISTORY

OF

THE LIFE-BOAT AND ITS WORK.

By RICHARD LEWIS,

BARRISTER-AT-LAW, SECRETARY TO THE ROYAL NATIONAL
LIFE-BOAT INSTITUTION.

With Illustrations, and Wreck Chart.

" To tell the story of a noble work — the work of the
Life-boat, — was almost the privilege of Mr. Lewis, and he
has told it admirably."—*Standard.*

" Though the book perforce contains many matters of
sheer science, and a multitude of statistics, it is not by any
means dry reading, and even the frivolously inclined will
read with deep interest some of the chapters, more especially
that of the Ramsgate Life-boat above alluded to."—*Land
and Water.*

MACMILLAN AND CO., LONDON.

BOOKS OF TRAVEL.

SIR SAMUEL W. BAKER'S "ISMAILIA."
A Narrative of the Expedition to Central Africa for the Suppression of the Slave Trade. Organized by ISMAIL, Khedive of Egypt. With Maps, Portraits, and numerous Illustrations. Two Vols., 8vo., 36s.

THE ALBERT N'YANZA GREAT BASIN of the
NILE, and Exploration of the Nile Sources. By Sir SAMUEL BAKER. With Maps and numerous Illustrations. Fourth Edition. Crown 8vo., 6s.

THE NILE TRIBUTARIES OF ABYSSINIA, and
the Sword Hunters of the HAMRAN ARABS. By Sir SAMUEL BAKER. With Maps and numerous Illustrations. Fifth Edition. Crown 8vo., 6s.

AT LAST: a Christmas in the West Indies.
By the Rev. CHARLES KINGSLEY, Canon of Westminster. With numerous Illustrations. Fourth Edition. Crown 8vo., 6s.

THE MALAY ARCHIPELAGO: the Land of the
Orang-Utan and the Bird of Paradise. A Narrative of Travel. By ALFRED RUSSEL WALLACE. With Maps and numerous Illustrations. Fourth Edition. Crown 8vo., 7s. 6d.

GREATER BRITAIN. A Record of Travel in English-speaking Countries. By Sir CHARLES W. DILKE, M.P. With Illustrations. Sixth Edition. Crown 8vo., 6s.

A YEAR'S JOURNEY THROUGH CENTRAL and
EASTERN ARABIA, 1862-3. By W. GIFFORD PALGRAVE. Sixth Edition. Crown 8vo., 6s.

A RAMBLE ROUND THE WORLD, 1871.
By M. le Baron de HÜBNER, formerly Ambassador and Minister. Translated by Lady HERBERT. Two Vols., 8vo., 25s.

HOLIDAYS ON HIGH LANDS; or, Rambles and
Incidents in Search of Alpine Plants. By the Rev. HUGH MACMILLAN, LL.D., F.R.S.E.

BY SEA AND LAND. Being a Trip through Egypt, India, Ceylon, Australia, New Zealand, America—All Round the World. By H. A. MEREWETHER, one of Her Majesty's Council. Crown 8vo., 8s. 6d.

STATION LIFE IN NEW ZEALAND.
By Lady BARKER. Third Edition. Crown 8vo., 3s. 6d.

MR. PISISTRATUS BROWN, M.P., in the Highlands.
New Edition. With Illustrations. Crown 8vo., 3s. 6d.

MACMILLAN AND CO., LONDON.

MACMILLAN & CO.'S CATALOGUE of Works in BELLES LETTRES, including Poetry, Fiction, etc.

Allingham.—LAURENCE BLOOMFIELD IN IRELAND; or, the New Landlord. By WILLIAM ALLINGHAM. New and Cheaper Issue, with a Preface. Fcap. 8vo. cloth. 4s. 6d.

> "*It is vital with the national character. . . . . It has something of Pope's point and Goldsmith's simplicity, touched to a more modern issue.*"—ATHENÆUM.

An Ancient City, and other Poems.—By A NATIVE OF SURREY. Extra fcap. 8vo. 6s.

Archer.—CHRISTINA NORTH. By E. M. ARCHER. Two vols. Crown 8vo. 21s.

> "*The work of a clever, cultivated person, wielding a practised pen. The characters are drawn with force and precision, the dialogue is easy: the whole book displays powers of pathos and humour, and a shrewd knowledge of men and things.*"—SPECTATOR.

Arnold. — THE COMPLETE POETICAL WORKS. Vol. I. NARRATIVE AND ELEGIAC POEMS. Vol. II. DRAMATIC AND LYRIC POEMS. By MATTHEW ARNOLD. Extra fcap. 8vo. Price 6s. each.

> The two volumes comprehend the First and Second Series of the Poems, and the New Poems. "*Thyrsis is a poem of perfect delight, exquisite in grave tenderness of reminiscence, rich in breadth of western light, breathing full the spirit of gray and ancient Oxford.*"—SATURDAY REVIEW.

Atkinson. — AN ART TOUR TO THE NORTHERN CAPITALS OF EUROPE. By J. BEAVINGTON ATKINSON. 8vo. 12s.

> "*We can highly recommend it; not only for the valuable information it gives on the special subjects to which it is dedicated, but also for the interesting episodes of travel which are interwoven with, and lighten, the weightier matters of judicious and varied criticism on art and artists in northern capitals.*"—ART JOURNAL.

Baker.—CAST UP BY THE SEA; OR, THE ADVENTURES OF NED GREY. By SIR SAMUEL BAKER, M.A., F.R.G.S. With Illustrations by HUARD. Fifth Edition. Crown 8vo. cloth gilt. 7s. 6d.

> "*An admirable tale of adventure, of marvellous incidents, wild exploits, and terrible dénouements.*"—DAILY NEWS. "*A story of adventure by sea and land in the good old style.*"—PALL MALL GAZETTE.

Baring-Gould.—Works by S. BARING-GOULD, M.A.:—

IN EXITU ISRAEL. An Historical Novel. Two Vols. 8vo. 21s.

> "*Full of the most exciting incidents and ably portrayed characters,*

Baring-Gould—*continued.*

abounding in beautifully attractive legends, and relieved by descriptions fresh, vivid, and truth-like."—WESTMINSTER REVIEW.

LEGENDS OF OLD TESTAMENT CHARACTERS, from the Talmud and other sources. Two vols. Crown 8vo. 16s. Vol. I. Adam to Abraham. Vol. II. Melchizedek to Zachariah.

"*These volumes contain much that is very strange, and, to the ordinary English reader, very novel."*—DAILY NEWS.

Barker.—Works by LADY BARKER:—

"*Lady Barker is an unrivalled story-teller."*—GUARDIAN.

STATION LIFE IN NEW ZEALAND. New and Cheaper Edition. Crown 8vo. 3s. 6d.

"*We have never read a more truthful or a pleasanter little book."*—ATHENÆUM.

SPRING COMEDIES. STORIES.

CONTENTS:—A Wedding Story—A Stupid Story—A Scotch Story —A Man's Story. Crown 8vo. 7s. 6d.

"*Lady Barker is endowed with a rare and delicate gift for narrating stories,—she has the faculty of throwing even into her printed narrative a soft and pleasant tone, which goes far to make the reader think the subject or the matter immaterial, so long as the author will go on telling stories for his benefit."*—ATHENÆUM.

STORIES ABOUT:— With Six Illustrations. Third Edition. Extra fcap. 8vo. 4s. 6d.

This volume contains several entertaining stories about Monkeys, Jamaica, Camp Life, Dogs, Boys, &c. "*There is not a tale in the book which can fail to please children as well as their elders."* —PALL MALL GAZETTE.

A CHRISTMAS CAKE IN FOUR QUARTERS. With Illustrations by JELLICOE. Second Edition. Ex. fcap. 8vo. cloth gilt. 4s. 6d.

"*Contains just the stories that children should be told. 'Christmas Cake' is a delightful Christmas book."*—GLOBE.

RIBBON STORIES. With Illustrations by C. O. MURRAY. Second Edition. Extra fcap. 8vo. cloth gilt. 4s. 6d.

"*We cannot too highly commend. It is exceedingly happy and original in the plan, and the graceful fancies of its pages, merry and pathetic turns, will be found the best reading by girls of all ages, and by boys too."*—TIMES.

SYBIL'S BOOK. Illustrated by S. E. WALLER. Second Edition. Globe 8vo. gilt. 4s. 6d.

"*Another of Lady Barker's delightful stories, and one of the most thoroughly original books for girls that has been written for many years. Grown-up readers will like it quite as much as young people, and will even better understand the rarity of such simple, natural, and unaffected writing . . . . That no one can read the story without interest is not its highest praise, for no one ought to be able to lay it down without being the better girl or boy, or man or woman, for the reading of it. Lady Barker has never turned her fertile and fascinating pen to better account, and for the sake of all readers we wish 'Sybil's Book' a wide success."*—TIMES.

Bell.—ROMANCES AND MINOR POEMS. By HENRY
GLASSFORD BELL. Fcap. 8vo. 6s.
" *Full of life and genius.*"—COURT CIRCULAR.

Besant.—STUDIES IN EARLY FRENCH POETRY. By
WALTER BESANT, M.A. Crown 8vo. 8s. 6d.

*The present work aims to afford information and direction touching
the early efforts of France in poetical literature. " In one moderately sized volume he has contrived to introduce us to the very
best, if not to all of the early French poets.*"—ATHENÆUM.

Betsy Lee ; A FO'C'S'LE YARN. Extra fcap. 8vo. 3s. 6d.
" *There is great vigour and much pathos in this poem.*"—MORNING
POST.
" *We can at least say that it is the work of a true poet.*"—ATHE-
NÆUM.

Black (W.)—Works by W. BLACK, Author of "A Daughter of
Heth."

THE STRANGE ADVENTURES OF A PHAETON.
Seventh and Cheaper Edition. Crown 8vo. 6s. Also, Illustrated
by S. E. WALLER, 8vo. cloth gilt. 10s. 6d.

" *The book is a really charming description of a thousand English
landscapes and of the emergencies and the fun and the delight of a
picnic journey through them by a party determined to enjoy themselves, and as well matched as the pair of horses which drew the
phaeton they sat in. The real charm and purpose of the book is
its open-air life among hills and dales.*"—TIMES. " *The great
charm of Mr. Black's book is that there is nothing hackneyed
about it, nothing overdrawn,—all is bright and lifelike.*"—MORNING
POST.

A PRINCESS OF THULE. Three vols. Sixth and cheaper
Edition. Crown 8vo. 6s.

The SATURDAY REVIEW says :—"*A novel which is both romantic
and natural, which has much feeling, without any touch of
mawkishness, which goes deep into character without any suggestion
of painful analysis—this is a rare gem to find amongst the débris of
current literature, and this, or nearly this, Mr. Black has given
us in the ' Princess of Thule.'*" " *It has, for one thing, the great
charm of novelty. . . . There is a picturesqueness in all that
Mr. Black writes, but scarcely even in the ' Adventures of a
Phaeton' are there the freshness and sweetness and perfect sense
of natural beauty we find in this last book.*"—PALL MALL
GAZETTE. " *A beautiful and nearly perfect story.*"—SPEC-
TATOR.

Borland Hall.—By the Author of "Olrig Grange." Crown
8vo. 7s.

Brooke.—THE FOOL OF QUALITY ; OR, THE HISTORY
OF HENRY, EARL OF MORELAND. By HENRY BROOKE.
Newly revised, with a Biographical Preface by the Rev. CHARLES
KINGSLEY, M.A., Rector of Eversley. Crown 8vo. 6s.

Broome.—THE STRANGER OF SERIPHOS. A Dramatic Poem. By FREDERICK NAPIER BROOME. Fcap. 8vo. 5s.
Founded on the Greek legend of Danaë and Perseus. "Grace and beauty of expression are Mr. Broome's characteristics; and these qualities are displayed in many passages."—ATHENÆUM. *"The story is rendered with consummate beauty."*—LITERARY CHURCHMAN.

Buist.—BIRDS, THEIR CAGES AND THEIR KEEP : Being a Practical Manual of Bird-Keeping and Bird-Rearing. By K. A. BUIST. With Coloured Frontispiece and other Illustrations. Crown 8vo. 5s.

Burnand.—MY TIME, AND WHAT I'VE DONE WITH IT. By F. C. BURNAND. Crown 8vo. 6s.

Cabinet Pictures.—Oblong folio, price 42s.
CONTENTS :—*" Childe Harold's Pilgrimage" and " The Fighting Téméraire," by J. M. W. Turner; " Crossing the Bridge," by Sir W. A. Callcott; " The Cornfield," by John Constable; and " A Landscape," by Birket Foster. The* DAILY NEWS *says of them, " They are very beautifully executed, and might be framed and hung up on the wall, as creditable substitutes for the originals."*

CABINET PICTURES. A Second Series.
Containing:—" The Baths of Caligula" and " The Golden Bough," by J. W. M. Turner; " The Little Brigand," by T. Uwins; " The Lake of Lucerne," by Percival Skelton; " Evening Rest," by E. M. Wimperis. Oblong folio. 42s.

Carroll.—Works by "LEWIS CARROLL :"—

ALICE'S ADVENTURES IN WONDERLAND. With Forty-two Illustrations by TENNIEL. 46th Thousand. Crown 8vo. cloth. 6s.

A GERMAN TRANSLATION OF THE SAME. With TENNIEL's Illustrations. Crown 8vo. gilt. 6s.

A FRENCH TRANSLATION OF THE SAME. With TENNIEL's Illustrations. Crown 8vo. gilt. 6s.

AN ITALIAN TRANSLATION OF THE SAME. By T. P. ROSSETTE. With TENNIEL's Illustrations. Crown 8vo. 6s.
" Beyond question supreme among modern books for children."—SPECTATOR. *" One of the choicest and most charming books ever composed for a child's reading."*—PALL MALL GAZETTE. *" A very pretty and highly original book, sure to delight the little world of wondering minds, and which may well please those who have unfortunately passed the years of wondering."*—TIMES.

THROUGH THE LOOKING-GLASS, AND WHAT ALICE FOUND THERE. With Fifty Illustrations by TENNIEL. Crown 8vo. gilt. 6s. 35th Thousand.
" Quite as rich in humorous whims of fantasy, quite as laughable

in its queer incidents, as loveable for its pleasant spirit and grace-
ful manner, as the wondrous tale of Alice's former adventures."—
ILLUSTRATED LONDON NEWS. *" If this had been given to the*
world first it would have enjoyed a success at least equal to ' Alice
*in Wonderland.' "—*STANDARD.

Children's (The) Garland, FROM THE BEST POETS.
Selected and arranged by COVENTRY PATMORE. New Edition.
With Illustrations by J. LAWSON. Crown 8vo. Cloth extra. 6s.

Christmas Carol (A). Printed in Colours from Original
Designs by Mr. and Mrs. TREVOR CRISPIN, with Illuminated
Borders from MSS. of the 14th and 15th Centuries. Imp. 4to. cloth
inlaid, gilt edges, £3 3s. Also a Cheaper Edition, 21s.
"A most exquisitely got up volume. Legend, carol, and text are
preciously enshrined in its emblazoned pages, and the illuminated
borders are far and away the best example of their art we have seen
this Christmas. The pictures and borders are harmonious in their
colouring, the dyes are brilliant without being raw, and the volume
is a trophy of colour-printing. The binding by Burn is in the very
*best taste."—*TIMES.

Church (A. J.)—HORÆ TENNYSONIANÆ, Sive Eclogæ
e Tennysono Latine redditæ. Cura A. J. CHURCH, A.M.
Extra fcap. 8vo. 6s.
"Of Mr. Church's ode we may speak in almost unqualified praise,
*and the same may be said of the contributions generally."—*PALL
MALL GAZETTE.

Clough (Arthur Hugh).—THE POEMS AND PROSE
REMAINS OF ARTHUR HUGH CLOUGH. With a
Selection from his Letters and a Memoir. Edited by his Wife.
With Portrait. Two Vols. Crown 8vo. 21s.
"Taken as a whole," the SPECTATOR *says, "these volumes cannot*
fail to be a lasting monument of one of the most original men of
our age." "Full of charming letters from Rome," says the
MORNING STAR, *"from Greece, from America, from Oxford,*
and from Rugby."

THE POEMS OF ARTHUR HUGH CLOUGH, sometime Fellow
of Oriel College, Oxford. Fourth Edition. Fcap. 8vo. 6s.
"From the higher mind of cultivated, all-questioning, but still conser-
vative England, in this our puzzled generation, we do not know
of any utterance in literature so characteristic as the poems of
*Arthur Hugh Clough."—*FRASER'S MAGAZINE.

Clunes.—THE STORY OF PAULINE: an Autobiography.
By G. C. CLUNES. Crown 8vo. 6s.
"Both for vivid delineation of character and fluent lucidity of style,
' The Story of Pauline' is in the first rank of modern fiction."—
GLOBE. *"Told with delightful vivacity, thorough appreciation of*
*life, and a complete knowledge of character."—*MANCHESTER
EXAMINER.

Collects of the Church of England. With a beautifully Coloured Floral Design to each Collect, and Illuminated Cover. Crown 8vo. 12s. Also kept in various styles of morocco.

"*This is beyond question," the* ART JOURNAL *says, "the most beautiful book of the season." The* GUARDIAN *thinks it "a successful attempt to associate in a natural and unforced manner the flowers of our fields and gardens with the course of the Christian year.*"

Cox.—RECOLLECTIONS OF OXFORD. By G. V. Cox, M.A., late Esquire Bedel and Coroner in the University of Oxford. Second and cheaper Edition. Crown 8vo. 6s.

The TIMES *says that it "will pleasantly recall in many a country parsonage the memory of youthful days."*

Culmshire Folk.—By IGNOTUS. Three vols. Crown 8vo. 31s. 6d.

"*Its sparkling pleasantness, its drollery, its shrewdness, the charming little bits of character which frequently come in, its easy liveliness, and a certain chattiness which, while it is never vulgar, brings the writer very near, and makes one feel as if the story were being told in lazy confidence in an hour of idleness by a man who, while thoroughly good-natured, is strongly humorous, and has an ever-present perception of the absurdities of people and things."*—SPECTATOR.

Dante.—DANTE'S COMEDY, THE HELL. Translated by W. M. ROSSETTI. Fcap 8vo. cloth. 5s.

"*The aim of this translation of Dante may be summed up in one word—Literality. To follow Dante sentence for sentence, line for line, word for word—neither more nor less, has been my strenuous endeavour."*—AUTHOR'S PREFACE.

Days of Old; STORIES FROM OLD ENGLISH HISTORY. By the Author of "Ruth and her Friends." New Edition. 18mo. cloth, extra. 2s. 6d.

"*Full of truthful and charming historic pictures, is everywhere vital with moral and religious principles, and is written with a brightness of description, and with a dramatic force in the representation of character, that have made, and will always make, it one of the greatest favourites with reading boys."*—NONCONFORMIST.

Deane.—MARJORY. By MILLY DEANE. Third Edition. With Frontispiece and Vignette. Crown 8vo. 4s. 6d.

The TIMES *of September* 11th *says it is "A very touching story, full of promise for the after career of the authoress. It is so tenderly drawn, and so full of life and grace, that any attempt to analyse or describe it falls sadly short of the original. We will venture to say that few readers of any natural feeling or sensibility will take up 'Marjory' without reading it through at a sitting, and we hope we shall see more stories by the same hand." The* MORNING POST *calls it "A deliciously fresh and charming little love story."*

De Vere.—THE INFANT BRIDAL, and other Poems. By AUBREY DE VERE. Fcap. 8vo. 7s. 6d.

"Mr. De Vere has taken his place among the poets of the day. Pure and tender feeling, and that polished restraint of style which is called classical, are the charms of the volume."—SPECTATOR.

Doyle (Sir F. H.)—LECTURES ON POETRY, delivered before the University of Oxford in 1868. By Sir FRANCIS HASTINGS DOYLE, Professor of Poetry in the University of Oxford. Crown 8vo. 3s. 6d.
"Full of thoughtful discrimination and fine insight: the lecture on 'Provincial Poetry' seems to us singularly true, eloquent, and instructive."—SPECTATOR.

Estelle Russell.—By the Author of "The Private Life of Galileo." New Edition. Crown 8vo. 6s.
Full of bright pictures of French life. The English family, whose fortunes form the main drift of the story, reside mostly in France, but there are also many English characters and scenes of great interest. It is certainly the work of a fresh, vigorous, and most interesting writer, with a dash of sarcastic humour which is refreshing and not too bitter. "We can send our readers to it with confidence."—SPECTATOR.

Evans.—BROTHER FABIAN'S MANUSCRIPT, AND OTHER POEMS. By SEBASTIAN EVANS. Fcap. 8vo. cloth. 6s.
"In this volume we have full assurance that he has 'the vision and the faculty divine.' . . . Clever and full of kindly humour."—GLOBE.

Evans.—THE CURSE OF IMMORTALITY. By A. EUBULE EVANS. Crown 8vo. 6s.
"Never, probably, has the legend of the Wandering Jew been more ably and poetically handled. The author writes as a true poet, and with the skill of a true artist. The plot of this remarkable drama is not only well contrived, but worked out with a degree of simplicity and truthful vigour altogether unusual in modern poetry. In fact, since the date of Byron's 'Cain,' we can scarcely recall any verse at once so terse, so powerful, and so masterly."—STANDARD.

Fairy Book.—The Best Popular Fairy Stories. Selected and Rendered anew by the Author of "John Halifax, Gentleman." With Coloured Illustrations and Ornamental Borders by J. E. ROGERS, Author of "Ridicula Rediviva." Crown 8vo. cloth, extra gilt. 6s. (Golden Treasury Edition. 18mo. 4s. 6d.)
"A delightful selection, in a delightful external form."—SPECTATOR.
"A book which will prove delightful to children all the year round."—PALL MALL GAZETTE.

Fletcher.—THOUGHTS FROM A GIRL'S LIFE. By LUCY FLETCHER. Second Edition. Fcap. 8vo. 4s. 6d.
"The poems are all graceful; they are marked throughout by an accent of reality; the thoughts and emotions are genuine."—ATHENÆUM.

Garnett.—IDYLLS AND EPIGRAMS. Chiefly from the Greek Anthology. By RICHARD GARNETT. Fcap. 8vo. 2s. 6d.
"A charming little book. For English readers, Mr. Garnett's

translations will open a new world of thought."—WESTMINSTER
REVIEW.

Gilmore.—STORM WARRIORS ; OR, LIFE-BOAT WORK
ON THE GOODWIN SANDS. By the Rev. JOHN GILMORE,
M.A., Rector of Holy Trinity, Ramsgate, Author of "The
Ramsgate Life-Boat," in *Macmillan's Magazine.* Crown 8vo. 6*s.*
*" The stories, which are said to be literally exact, are more thrilling
than anything in fiction. Mr. Gilmore has done a good work as
well as written a good book."*—DAILY NEWS.

Gladstone.—JUVENTUS MUNDI. The Gods and Men of the
Heroic Age. By the Right Hon. W. E. GLADSTONE, M.P.
Crown 8vo. cloth extra. With Map. 10*s.* 6*d.* Second Edition.
" To read these brilliant details," says the ATHENÆUM, *"is like
standing on the Olympian threshold and gazing at the ineffable
brightness within." According to the* WESTMINSTER REVIEW, *"it
would be difficult to point out a book that contains so much fulness
of knowledge along with so much freshness of perception and
clearness of presentation."*

Gray.—THE POETICAL WORKS OF DAVID GRAY. New
and Enlarged Edition. Edited by HENRY GLASSFORD BELL, late
Sheriff of Lanarkshire. Crown 8vo. 6*s.*

Guesses at Truth.—By TWO BROTHERS. With Vignette
Title and Frontispiece. New Edition, with Memoir. Fcap. 8vo.
6*s.* Also see Golden Treasury Series.

Halifax.—AFTER LONG YEARS. By M. C. HALIFAX.
Crown 8vo. 10*s.* 6*d.*
*" A story of very unusual merit. The entire story is well conceived,
well written, and well carried out ; and the reader will look
forward with pleasure to meeting this clever author again."*—
DAILY NEWS. *" This is a very pretty, simple love story. . . . :
The author possesses a very graceful, womanly pen, and tells the
story with a rare tender simplicity which well befits it."*—
STANDARD.

Hamerton.—A PAINTER'S CAMP. Second Edition, revised.
Extra fcap. 8vo. 6*s.*
BOOK I. *In England;* BOOK II. *In Scotland;* BOOK III. *In France.*
*" These pages, written with infinite spirit and humour, bring into
close rooms, back upon tired heads, the breezy airs of Lancashire
moors and Highland lochs, with a freshness which no recent
novelist has succeeded in preserving."*—NONCONFORMIST.

Heaton.—HAPPY SPRING TIME. Illustrated by OSCAR
PLETSCH. With Rhymes for Mothers and Children. By MRS.
CHARLES HEATON. Crown 8vo. cloth extra, gilt edges. 3*s.* 6*d.*
" The pictures in this book are capital."—ATHENÆUM.

Hervey.—DUKE ERNEST, a Tragedy ; and other Poems.
Fcap. 8vo. 6*s.*
" Conceived in pure taste and true historic feeling, and presented with

much dramatic force. . . . . Thoroughly original."—BRITISH QUARTERLY.

Higginson.—MALBONE: An Oldport Romance. By T. W. HIGGINSON. Fcap. 8vo. 2s. 6d.
The DAILY NEWS *says: " Who likes a quiet story, full of mature thought, of clear, humorous surprises, of artistic studious design ? 'Malbone' is a rare work, possessing these characteristics, and replete, too, with honest literary effort."*

Hillside Rhymes.—Extra fcap. 8vo. 5s.

Home.—BLANCHE LISLE, and other Poems. By CECIL HOME. Fcap. 8vo. 4s. 6d.

Hood (Tom).—THE PLEASANT TALE OF PUSS AND ROBIN AND THEIR FRIENDS, KITTY AND BOB. Told in Pictures by L. FRÖLICH, and in Rhymes by TOM HOOD. Crown 8vo. gilt. 3s. 6d.
" The volume is prettily got up, and is sure to be a favourite in the nursery."—SCOTSMAN. *" Herr Frölich has outdone himself in his pictures of this dramatic chase."*—MORNING POST.

Keary (A.)—Works by Miss A. KEARY :—
JANET'S HOME. New Edition. Globe 8vo. 2s. 6d.
" Never did a more charming family appear upon the canvas ; and most skilfully and felicitously have their characters been portrayed. Each individual of the fireside is a finished portrait, distinct and lifelike. . . . The future before her as a novelist is that of becoming the Miss Austin of her generation."—SUN.
CLEMENCY FRANKLYN. New Edition. Globe 8vo. 2s. 6d.
"Full of wisdom and goodness, simple, truthful, and artistic. . . It is capital as a story; better still in its pure tone and wholesome influence."—GLOBE.
OLDBURY. Three vols. Crown 8vo. 31s. 6d.
"This is a very powerfully written story."—GLOBE. *"This is a really excellent novel."*—ILLUSTRATED LONDON NEWS. *" The sketches of society in Oldbury are excellent. The pictures of child life are full of truth."*—WESTMINSTER REVIEW.

Keary (A. and E.)—Works by A. and E. KEARY :—
THE LITTLE WANDERLIN, and other Fairy Tales. 18mo. 2s. 6d.
" The tales are fanciful and well written, and they are sure to win favour amongst little readers."—ATHENÆUM.
THE HEROES OF ASGARD. Tales from Scandinavian Mythology. New and Revised Edition, Illustrated by HUARD. Extra fcap. 8vo. 4s. 6d.
" Told in a light and amusing style, which, in its drollery and quaintness, reminds us of our old favourite Grimm."—TIMES.

Kingsley.—Works by the Rev. CHARLES KINGSLEY, M.A., Rector of Eversley, and Canon of Westminster :—
"WESTWARD HO !" or, The Voyages and Adventures of Sir Amyas Leigh. Ninth Edition. Crown 8vo. 6s.

Kingsley (C.)—*continued.*

Fraser's Magazine *calls it "almost the best historical novel of the day."*

TWO YEARS AGO. Fifth Edition. Crown 8vo. 6s.

"*Mr. Kingsley has provided us all along with such pleasant diversions —such rich and brightly tinted glimpses of natural history, such suggestive remarks on mankind, society, and all sorts of topics, that amidst the pleasure of the way, the circuit to be made will be by most forgotten.*"—Guardian.

HYPATIA; or, New Foes with an Old Face. Seventh Edition. Crown 8vo. 6s.

HEREWARD THE WAKE—LAST OF THE ENGLISH. Second Edition. Crown 8vo. 6s.

YEAST: A Problem. Sixth Edition. Crown 8vo. 5s.

ALTON LOCKE. New Edition. With a New Preface. Crown 8vo. 4s. 6d.

The author shows, to quote the Spectator, "*what it is that constitutes the true Christian, God-fearing, man-living gentleman.*"

THE WATER BABIES. A Fairy Tale for a Land Baby. New Edition, with additional Illustrations by Sir Noel Paton, R.S.A., and P. Skelton. Crown 8vo. cloth, extra gilt. 5s.

"*In fun, in humour, and in innocent imagination, as a child's book we do not know its equal.*"—London Review. "*Mr. Kingsley must have the credit of revealing to us a new order of life. . . . There is in the 'Water Babies' an abundance of wit, fun, good humour, geniality, élan, go.*"—Times.

THE HEROES; or, Greek Fairy Tales for my Children. With Coloured Illustrations. New Edition. 18mo. 4s. 6d.

"*We do not think these heroic stories have ever been more attractively told. . . There is a deep under-current of religious feeling traceable throughout its pages which is sure to influence young readers powerfully.*"—London Review. "*One of the children's books that will surely become a classic.*"—Nonconformist.

PHAETHON; or, Loose Thoughts for Loose Thinkers. Third Edition. Crown 8vo. 2s.

"*The dialogue of 'Phaethon' has striking beauties, and its suggestions may meet half-way many a latent doubt, and, like a light breeze, lift from the soul clouds that are gathering heavily, and threatening to settle down in misty gloom on the summer of many a fair and promising young life.*"—Spectator.

POEMS; including The Saint's Tragedy, Andromeda, Songs, Ballads, etc. Complete Collected Edition. Extra fcap. 8vo. 6s.

The Spectator *calls "Andromeda" "the finest piece of English hexameter verse that has ever been written. It is a volume which many readers will be glad to possess.*"

PROSE IDYLLS. NEW AND OLD. Second Edition. Crown 8vo. 5s.

Contents:—*A Charm of Birds; Chalk-Stream Studies; The Fens; My Winter-Garden; From Ocean to Sea; North Devon.*

"*Altogether a delightful book. . . . . It exhibits the author's best traits, and cannot fail to infect the reader with a love of nature and of out-door life and its enjoyments. It is well calculated to bring a gleam of summer with its pleasant associations, into the bleak winter-time ; while a better companion for a summer ramble could hardly be found.*"—BRITISH QUARTERLY REVIEW.

Kingsley (H.)—Works by HENRY KINGSLEY :—

TALES OF OLD TRAVEL. Re-narrated. With Eight full-page Illustrations by HUARD. Fourth Edition. Crown 8vo. cloth, extra gilt. 5s.

"*We know no better book for those who want knowledge or seek to refresh it. As for the 'sensational,' most novels are tame compared with these narratives.*"—ATHENÆUM. "*Exactly the book to interest and to do good to intelligent and high-spirited boys.*"—LITERARY CHURCHMAN.

THE LOST CHILD. With Eight Illustrations by FRÖLICH. Crown 4to. cloth gilt. 3s. 6d.

"*A pathetic story, and told so as to give children an interest in Australian ways and scenery.*"—GLOBE. "*Very charmingly and very touchingly told.*"—SATURDAY REVIEW.

OAKSHOTT CASTLE. 3 Vols. Crown 8vo. 31s. 6d.

"*No one who takes up 'Oakshott Castle' will willingly put it down until the last page is turned. . . . It may fairly be considered a capital story, full of go, and abounding in word pictures of storms and wrecks.*"—OBSERVER.

Knatchbull-Hugessen.—Works by E. H. KNATCHBULL-HUGESSEN, M.P. :—

Mr. Knatchbull-Hugessen has won for himself a reputation as a teller of fairy-tales. "*His powers,*" *says the* TIMES, "*are of a very high order ; light and brilliant narrative flows from his pen, and is fed by an invention as graceful as it is inexhaustible.*" "*Children reading his stories,*" *the* SCOTSMAN *says,* "*or hearing them read, will have their minds refreshed and invigorated as much as their bodies would be by abundance of fresh air and exercise.*"

STORIES FOR MY CHILDREN. With Illustrations. Fourth Edition. Crown 8vo. 5s.

"*The stories are charming, and full of life and fun.*"—STANDARD. "*The author has an imagination as fanciful as Grimm himself, while some of his stories are superior to anything that Hans Christian Andersen has written.*"—NONCONFORMIST.

CRACKERS FOR CHRISTMAS. More Stories. With Illustrations by JELLICOE and ELWES. Fourth Edition. Crown 8vo. 5s.

"*A fascinating little volume, which will make him friends in every household in which there are children.*"—DAILY NEWS.

MOONSHINE : Fairy Tales. With Illustrations by W. BRUNTON. Sixth Edition. Crown 8vo. cloth gilt. 5s.

"*A volume of fairy tales, written not only for ungrown children,*

Knatchbull-Hugessen (E. H.)—*continued.*

but for bigger, and if you are nearly worn out, or sick, or sorry, you will find it good reading."—GRAPHIC. *"The most charming volume of fairy tales which we have ever read. . . . We cannot quit this very pleasant book without a word of praise to its illustrator. Mr. Brunton from first to last has done admirably."*—TIMES.

TALES AT TEA-TIME. Fairy Stories. With Seven Illustrations by W. BRUNTON. Fifth Edition. Crown 8vo. cloth gilt. 5s.
" Capitally illustrated by W. Brunton. . . . In frolic and fancy they are quite equal to his other books. The author knows how to write fairy stories as they should be written. The whole book is full of the most delightful drolleries."—TIMES.

QUEER FOLK. FAIRY STORIES. Illustrated by S. E. WALLER. Fourth Edition. Crown 8vo. Cloth gilt. 5s.
" Decidedly the author's happiest effort. . . . One of the best story books of the year."—HOUR.

Knatchbull-Hugessen (Louisa).—THE HISTORY OF PRINCE PERRYPETS. A Fairy Tale. By LOUISA KNATCHBULL-HUGESSEN. With Eight Illustrations by WEIGAND. New Edition. Crown 4to. cloth gilt. 3s. 6d.
"A grand and exciting fairy tale."—MORNING POST. *"A delicious piece of fairy nonsense."*—ILLUSTRATED LONDON NEWS.

Knox.—SONGS OF CONSOLATION. By ISA CRAIG KNOX. Extra fcap. 8vo. Cloth extra, gilt edges. 4s. 6d.
" The verses are truly sweet ; there is in them not only much genuine poetic quality, but an ardent, flowing devotedness, and a peculiar skill in propounding theological tenets in the most graceful way, which any divine might envy."—SCOTSMAN.

Latham.—SERTUM SHAKSPERIANUM, Subnexis aliquot aliunde excerptis floribus. Latine reddidit Rev. H. LATHAM, M.A. Extra fcap. 8vo. 5s.

Lemon.—THE LEGENDS OF NUMBER NIP. By MARK LEMON. With Illustrations by C. KEENE. New Edition. Extra fcap. 8vo. 2s. 6d.

Life and Times of Conrad the Squirrel. A Story for Children. By the Author of "Wandering Willie," "Effie's Friends," &c. With a Frontispiece by R. FARREN. Second Edition. Crown 8vo. 3s. 6d.
" Having commenced on the first page, we were compelled to go on to the conclusion, and this we predict will be the case with every one who opens the book."—PALL MALL GAZETTE.

Little Estella, and other FAIRY TALES FOR THE YOUNG. 18mo. cloth extra. 2s. 6d.
" This is a fine story, and we thank heaven for not being too wise to enjoy it."—DAILY NEWS.

Lowell.—Works by J. Russell LOWELL :—
AMONG MY BOOKS. Six Essays. Dryden — Witchcraft —

Lowell—*continued.*
Shakespeare once More—New England Two Centuries Ago—
Lessing—Rousseau and the Sentimentalists. Crown 8vo. 7*s.* 6*d.*
*"We may safely say the volume is one of which our chief complaint
must be that there is not more of it. There are good sense and lively
feeling forcibly and tersely expressed in every page of his writing."*
—PALL MALL GAZETTE.
COMPLETE POETICAL WORKS of JAMES RUSSELL LOWELL.
With Portrait, engraved by Jeens. 18mo. cloth extra. 4*s.* 6*d.*
*"All readers who are able to recognise and appreciate genuine verse
will give a glad welcome to this beautiful little volume."*—PALL
MALL GAZETTE.

Lyttelton.—Works by LORD LYTTELTON :—
THE "COMUS" OF MILTON, rendered into **Greek Verse.**
Extra fcap. 8vo. 5*s.*
THE "SAMSON AGONISTES" OF MILTON, rendered into
Greek Verse. Extra fcap. 8vo. 6*s.* 6*d.*
"Classical in spirit, full of force, and true to the original."
—GUARDIAN.

Maclaren.—THE FAIRY FAMILY. A series of Ballads and
Metrical Tales illustrating the Fairy Mythology of Europe. By
ARCHIBALD MACLAREN. With Frontispiece, Illustrated Title,
and Vignette. Crown 8vo. gilt. 5*s.*
*"A successful attempt to translate into the vernacular some of the
Fairy Mythology of Europe. The verses are very good. There is
no shirking difficulties of rhyme, and the ballad metre which is
oftenest employed has a great deal of the kind of 'go' which we find
so seldom outside the pages of Scott. The book is of permanent
value."*—GUARDIAN.

Macmillan's Magazine.—Published Monthly. Price 1*s.*
Volumes I. to XXIX. are now ready. 7*s.* 6*d.* each.

Macquoid.—PATTY. By KATHARINE S. MACQUOID. Third
and Cheaper Edition. Crown 8vo. 6*s.*
"A book to be read."—STANDARD. *"A powerful and fascinating
story."*—DAILY TELEGRAPH. *The* GLOBE *considers it "well-
written, amusing, and interesting, and has the merit of being out
of the ordinary run of novels."*

Maguire.—YOUNG PRINCE MARIGOLD, AND OTHER
FAIRY STORIES. By the late JOHN FRANCIS MAGUIRE, M.P.
Illustrated by S. E. WALLER. Globe 8vo. gilt. 4*s.* 6*d.*
*"The author has evidently studied the ways and tastes of children and
got at the secret of amusing them; and has succeeded in what is not
so easy a task as it may seem—in producing a really good children's
book."*—DAILY TELEGRAPH.

Marlitt (E.)—THE COUNTESS GISELA. Translated from
the German of E. MARLITT. Crown 8vo. 7*s.* 6*d.*
"A very beautiful story of German country life."—LITERARY
CHURCHMAN.

Masson (Professor).—Works by DAVID MASSON, M.A., Professor of Rhetoric and English Literature in the University of Edinburgh.

BRITISH NOVELISTS AND THEIR STYLES. Being a Critical Sketch of the History of British Prose Fiction. Crown 8vo. 7s. 6d.

WORDSWORTH, SHELLEY, KEATS, AND OTHER ESSAYS. Crown 8vo. 5s.

CHATTERTON : A Story of the Year 1770. Crown 8vo. 5s.

THE THREE DEVILS : LUTHER'S, MILTON'S, and GOETHE'S ; and other Essays. Crown 8vo. 5s.

Mazini.—IN THE GOLDEN SHELL ; A Story of Palermo. By LINDA MAZINI. With Illustrations. Globe 8vo. cloth gilt. 4s. 6d.

" *As beautiful and bright and fresh as the scenes to which it wafts us over the blue Mediterranean, and as pure and innocent, but piquant and sprightly as the little girl who plays the part of its heroine, is this admirable little book.*"—ILLUSTRATED LONDON NEWS.

Merivale.—KEATS' HYPERION, rendered into Latin Verse. By C. MERIVALE, B.D. Second Edition. Extra fcap. 8vo. 3s. 6d.

Milner.—THE LILY OF LUMLEY. By EDITH MILNER. Crown 8vo. 7s. 6d.

" *The novel is a good one and decidedly worth the reading.*"— EXAMINER. "*A pretty, brightly-written story.*" — LITERARY CHURCHMAN. "*A tale possessing the deepest interest.*"—COURT JOURNAL.

Milton's Poetical Works.—Edited with Text collated from the best Authorities, with Introduction and Notes by DAVID MASSON. Three vols. 8vo. With Three Portraits engraved by C. H. JEENS and RADCLIFFE. (Uniform with the Cambridge Shakespeare.)

Mistral (F.)—MIRELLE, a Pastoral Epic of Provence. Translated by H. CRICHTON. Extra fcap. 8vo. 6s.

" *It would be hard to overpraise the sweetness and pleasing freshness of this charming epic.*"—ATHENÆUM. "*A good translation of a poem that deserves to be known by all students of literature and friends of old-world simplicity in story-telling.*"—NONCONFORMIST.

Mitford (A. B.)—TALES OF OLD JAPAN. By A. B. MITFORD, Second Secretary to the British Legation in Japan. With Illustrations drawn and cut on Wood by Japanese Artists. New and Cheaper Edition. Crown 8vo. 6s.

" *They will always be interesting as memorials of a most exceptional society ; while, regarded simply as tales, they are sparkling, sensational, and dramatic, and the originality of their ideas and the quaintness of their language give them a most captivating piquancy.*

The illustrations are extremely interesting, and for the curious in such matters have a special and particular value."—PALL MALL GAZETTE.

Mr. Pisistratus Brown, M.P., IN THE HIGHLANDS.
New Edition, with Illustrations. Crown 8vo. 3s. 6d.

" *The book is calculated to recall pleasant memories of holidays well spent, and scenes not easily to be forgotten. To those who have never been in the Western Highlands, or sailed along the Frith of Clyde and on the Western Coast, it will seem almost like a fairy story. There is a charm in the volume which makes it anything but easy for a reader who has opened it to put it down until the last page has been read.*"—SCOTSMAN.

Mrs. Jerningham's Journal. A Poem purporting to be the
Journal of a newly-married Lady. Second Edition. Fcap. 8vo. 3s. 6d.

"*It is nearly a perfect gem. We have had nothing so good for a long time, and those who neglect to read it are neglecting one of the jewels of contemporary history.*"—EDINBURGH DAILY REVIEW. "*One quality in the piece, sufficient of itself to claim a moment's attention, is that it is unique—original, indeed, is not too strong a word—in the manner of its conception and execution.*"
—PALL MALL GAZETTE.

Mudie.—STRAY LEAVES. By C. E. MUDIE. New Edition.
Extra fcap. 8vo. 3s. 6d. Contents :—"His and Mine"— "Night and Day"—"One of Many," &c.

This little volume consists of a number of poems, mostly of a genuinely devotional character. "They are for the most part so exquisitely sweet and delicate as to be quite a marvel of composition. They are worthy of being laid up in the recesses of the heart, and recalled to memory from time to time."—ILLUSTRATED LONDON NEWS.

Murray.—THE BALLADS AND SONGS OF SCOTLAND,
in View of their Influence on the Character of the People. By J. CLARK MURRAY, LL.D., Professor of Mental and Moral Philosophy in McGill College, Montreal. Crown 8vo. 6s.

"*Independently of the lucidity of the style in which the whole book is written, the selection of the examples alone would recommend it to favour, while the geniality of the criticism upon those examples cannot fail to make them highly appreciated and valued.*"— MORNING POST.

Myers (Ernest).—THE PURITANS. By ERNEST MYERS.
Extra fcap. 8vo. cloth. 2s. 6d.

"*It is not too much to call it a really grand poem, stately and dignified, and showing not only a high poetic mind, but also great power over poetic expression.*"—LITERARY CHURCHMAN.

Myers (F. W. H.)—POEMS. By F. W. H. MYERS. Containing "St. Paul," "St. John," and others. Extra fcap. 8vo. 4s. 6d.

"*It is rare to find a writer who combines to such an extent the faculty of communicating feelings with the faculty of euphonious expression."*—SPECTATOR. *" 'St. Paul' stands without a rival as the noblest religious poem which has been written in an age which beyond any other has been prolific in this class of poetry. The sublimest conceptions are expressed in language which, for richness, taste, and purity, we have never seen excelled."*—JOHN BULL.

Nichol.—HANNIBAL, A HISTORICAL DRAMA. By JOHN NICHOL, B.A. Oxon., Regius Professor of English Language and Literature in the University of Glasgow. Extra fcap. 8vo. 7s. 6d.
" The poem combines in no ordinary degree firmness and workmanship. After the lapse of many centuries, an English poet is found paying to the great Carthagenian the worthiest poetical tribute which has as yet, to our knowledge, been afforded to his noble and stainless name."—SATURDAY REVIEW.

Nine Years Old.—By the Author of "St. Olave's," "When I was a Little Girl," &c. Illustrated by FRÖLICH. Third Edition. Extra fcap. 8vo. cloth gilt. 4s. 6d.
It is believed that this story, by the favourably known author of " St. Olave's," will be found both highly interesting and instructive to the young. The volume contains eight graphic illustrations by Mr. L. Frölich. The EXAMINER *says: "Whether the readers are nine years old, or twice, or seven times as old, they must enjoy this pretty volume."*

Noel.—BEATRICE, AND OTHER POEMS. By the Hon. RODEN NOEL. Fcap. 8vo. 6s.
"It is impossible to read the poem through without being powerfully moved. There are passages in it which for intensity and tenderness, clear and vivid vision, spontaneous and delicate sympathy, may be compared with the best efforts of our best living writers." —SPECTATOR.

Norton.—Works by the Hon. Mrs. NORTON :—

THE LADY OF LA GARAYE. With Vignette and Frontispiece. New Edition. Fcap. 8vo. 4s. 6d.
" Full of thought well expressed, and may be classed among her best efforts."—TIMES.

OLD SIR DOUGLAS. Cheap Edition. Globe 8vo. 2s. 6d.
" This varied and lively novel—this clever novel so full of character, and of fine incidental remark." — SCOTSMAN. *" One of the pleasantest and healthiest stories of modern fiction."*—GLOBE.

Oliphant.—Works by Mrs. OLIPHANT :—

AGNES HOPETOUN'S SCHOOLS AND HOLIDAYS. New Edition with Illustrations. Royal 16mo. gilt leaves. 4s. 6d.
" There are few books of late years more fitted to touch the heart, purify the feeling, and quicken and sustain right principles."— NONCONFORMIST. *" A more gracefully written story it is impossible to desire."*—DAILY NEWS.

A SON OF THE SOIL. New Edition. Globe 8vo. 2s. 6d.
"It is a very different work from the ordinary run of novels.

The whole life of a man is portrayed in it, worked out with subtlety and insight."—ATHENÆUM.

Our Year. A Child's Book, in Prose and Verse. By the Author of "John Halifax, Gentleman." Illustrated by CLARENCE DOBELL. Royal 16mo. 3s. 6d.
"It is just the book we could wish to see in the hands of every child."
—ENGLISH CHURCHMAN.

Olrig Grange. Edited by HERMANN KUNST, Philol. Professor. Extra fcap. 8vo. 6s. 6d.
"A masterly and original power of impression, pouring itself forth in clear, sweet, strong rhythm. . . . It is a fine poem, full of life, of music and of clear vision."—NORTH BRITISH DAILY MAIL.

Oxford Spectator, The.—Reprinted. Extra fcap. 8vo. 3s. 6d.
"There is," the SATURDAY REVIEW *says, "all the old fun, the old sense of social ease and brightness and freedom, the old medley of work and indolence, of jest and earnest, that made Oxford life so picturesque."*

Palgrave.—Works by FRANCIS TURNER PALGRAVE, M.A., late Fellow of Exeter College, Oxford :—
THE FIVE DAYS' ENTERTAINMENTS AT WENTWORTH GRANGE. A Book for Children. With Illustrations by ARTHUR HUGHES, and Engraved Title-page by JEENS. Small 4to. cloth extra. 6s.
"If you want a really good book for both sexes and all ages, buy this, as handsome a volume of tales as you'll find in all the market."—ATHENÆUM. *"Exquisite both in form and substance."*
—GUARDIAN.

LYRICAL POEMS. Extra fcap. 8vo. 6s.
"A volume of pure quiet verse, sparkling with tender melodies, and alive with thoughts of genuine poetry. . . . Turn where we will throughout the volume, we find traces of beauty, tenderness, and truth; true poet's work, touched and refined by the master-hand of a real artist, who shows his genius even in trifles."—STANDARD.

ORIGINAL HYMNS. Third Edition, enlarged, 18mo. 1s. 6d.
"So choice, so perfect, and so refined, so tender in feeling, and so scholarly in expression, that we look with special interest to everything that he gives us."—LITERARY CHURCHMAN.

GOLDEN TREASURY OF THE BEST SONGS AND LYRICS. Edited by F. T. PALGRAVE. See GOLDEN TREASURY SERIES.

SHAKESPEARE'S SONNETS AND SONGS. Edited by F. T. PALGRAVE. Gem Edition. With Vignette Title by JEENS. 3s. 6d.
"For minute elegance no volume could possibly excel the 'Gem Edition.'"—SCOTSMAN.

Parables.—TWELVE PARABLES OF OUR LORD. Illustrated in Colours from Sketches taken in the East by McENIRY with Frontispiece from a Picture by JOHN JELLICOE, and Illuminated Texts and Borders. Royal 4to. in Ornamental Binding. 16s.

B

The TIMES *calls it "one of the most beautiful of modern pictorial works;" while the* GRAPHIC *says "nothing in this style, so good, has ever before been published."*

Patmore.—THE CHILDREN'S GARLAND, from the Best Poets. Selected and arranged by COVENTRY PATMORE. New Edition. With Illustrations by J. LAWSON. Crown 8vo. gilt. 6s. Golden Treasury Edition. 18mo. 4s. 6d.

"*The charming illustrations added to many of the poems will add greatly to their value in the eyes of children.*"—DAILY NEWS.

Pember.—THE TRAGEDY OF LESBOS. A Dramatic Poem. By E. H. PEMBER. Fcap. 8vo. 4s. 6d.

Founded upon the story of Sappho. "He tells his story with dramatic force, and in language that often rises almost to grandeur."—ATHENÆUM.

Poole.—PICTURES OF COTTAGE LIFE IN THE WEST OF ENGLAND. By MARGARET E. POOLE. New and Cheaper Edition. With Frontispiece by R. Farren. Crown 8vo. 3s. 6d.

"*Charming stories of peasant life, written in something of George Eliot's style. . . . Her stories could not be other than they are, as literal as truth, as romantic as fiction, full of pathetic touches and strokes of genuine humour. . . . All the stories are studies of actual life, executed with no mean art.*"—TIMES.

Population of an Old Pear Tree. From the French of E. VAN BRUYSSEL. Edited by the Author of "The Heir of Redclyffe." With Illustrations by BECKER. Cheaper Edition. Crown 8vo. gilt. 4s. 6d.

"*This is not a regular book of natural history, but a description of all the living creatures that came and went in a summer's day beneath an old pear tree, observed by eyes that had for the nonce become microscopic, recorded by a pen that finds dramas in everything, and illustrated by a dainty pencil. . . . We can hardly fancy anyone with a moderate turn for the curiosities of insect life, or for delicate French esprit, not being taken by these clever sketches.*"—GUARDIAN. "*A whimsical and charming little book.*"—ATHENÆUM.

Prince Florestan of Monaco, The Fall of. By HIMSELF. New Edition, with Illustration and Map. 8vo. cloth. Extra gilt edges, 5s. A French Translation, 5s. Also an Edition for the People. Crown 8vo. 1s.

"*Those who have read only the extracts given, will not need to be told how amusing and happily touched it is. Those who read it for other purposes than amusement can hardly miss the sober and sound political lessons with which its light pages abound, and which are as much needed in England as by the nation to whom the author directly addresses his moral.*"—PALL MALL GAZETTE. "*This little book is very clever, wild with animal spirits, but showing plenty of good sense, amid all the heedless nonsense which fills so many of its pages.*"—DAILY NEWS. "*In an age little remarkable for powers of political satire, the sparkle of the pages gives them every claim to welcome.*"—STANDARD.

Rankine.—SONGS AND FABLES. By W. J. McQUORN RANKINE, late Professor of Civil Engineering and Mechanics at Glasgow. With Illustrations. Crown 8vo. 6s.

"*A lively volume of verses, full of a fine manly spirit, much humour and geniality. The illustrations are admirably conceived, and executed with fidelity and talent.*"—MORNING POST.

Realmah.—By the Author of "Friends in Council." Crown 8vo. 6s.

Rhoades.—POEMS. By JAMES RHOADES. Fcap. 8vo. 4s. 6d.

Richardson.—THE ILIAD OF THE EAST. A Selection of Legends drawn from Valmiki's Sanskrit Poem, "The Ramayana." By FREDERIKA RICHARDSON. Crown 8vo. 7s. 6d.

"*It is impossible to read it without recognizing the value and interest of the Eastern epic. It is as fascinating as a fairy tale, this romantic poem of India.*"—GLOBE. "*A charming volume, which at once enmeshes the reader in its snares.*"—ATHENÆUM.

Roby.—STORY OF A HOUSEHOLD, AND OTHER POEMS. By MARY K. ROBY. Fcap. 8vo. 5s.

Rogers.—Works by J. E. ROGERS:—
RIDICULA REDIVIVA. Old Nursery Rhymes. Illustrated in Colours, with Ornamental Cover. Crown 4to. 3s. 6d.

"*The most splendid, and at the same time the most really meritorious of the books specially intended for children, that we have seen.*"— SPECTATOR. "*These large bright pictures will attract children to really good and honest artistic work, and that ought not to be an indifferent consideration with parents who propose to educate their children.*"—PALL MALL GAZETTE.

MORES RIDICULI. Old Nursery Rhymes. Illustrated in Colours, with Ornamental Cover. Crown 4to. 3s. 6d.

"*These world-old rhymes have never had and need never wish for a better pictorial setting than Mr. Rogers has given them.*"— TIMES. "*Nothing could be quainter or more absurdly comical than most of the pictures, which are all carefully executed and beautifully coloured.*"—GLOBE.

Rossetti.—GOBLIN MARKET, AND OTHER POEMS. By CHRISTINA ROSSETTI. With two Designs by D. G. ROSSETTI. Second Edition. Fcap. 8vo. 5s.

"*She handles her little marvel with that rare poetic discrimination which neither exhausts it of its simple wonders by pushing symbolism too far, nor keeps those wonders in the merely fabulous and capricious stage. In fact, she has produced a true children's poem, which is far more delightful to the mature than to children, though it would be delightful to all.*"—SPECTATOR.

Runaway (The). A Story for the Young. By the Author of "Mrs. Jerningham's Journal." With Illustrations by J. LAWSON. Globe 8vo. gilt. 4s. 6d.

"*This is one of the best, if not indeed the very best, of all the stories that has come before us this Christmas. The heroines are both charming, and, unlike heroines, they are as full of fun as of charms. It is an admirable book to read aloud to the young folk when they are all gathered round the fire, and nurses and other apparitions are still far away."*—SATURDAY REVIEW.

Ruth and her Friends. A Story for Girls. With a Frontispiece. Fourth Edition. 18mo. Cloth extra. 2s. 6d.

" We wish all the school girls and home-taught girls in the land had the opportunity of reading it."—NONCONFORMIST.

Scouring of the White Horse; or, the Long VACATION RAMBLE OF A LONDON CLERK. Illustrated by DOYLE. Imp. 16mo. Cheaper Issue. 3s. 6d.

"A glorious tale of summer joy."—FREEMAN. *" There is a genial hearty life about the book."*—JOHN BULL. *" The execution is excellent. . . . Like 'Tom Brown's School Days,' the 'White Horse' gives the reader a feeling of gratitude and personal esteem towards the author."*—SATURDAY REVIEW.

Shairp (Principal).—KILMAHOE, a Highland Pastoral, with other Poems. By JOHN CAMPBELL SHAIRP, Principal of the United College, St. Andrews. Fcap. 8vo. 5s.

" Kilmahoe is a Highland Pastoral, redolent of the warm soft air of the western lochs and moors, sketched out with remarkable grace and picturesqueness."—SATURDAY REVIEW.

Shakespeare.—The Works of WILLIAM SHAKESPEARE. Cambridge Edition. Edited by W. GEORGE CLARK, M.A. and W. ALDIS WRIGHT, M.A. Nine vols. 8vo. Cloth. 4l. 14s. 6d.

The GUARDIAN *calls it an "excellent, and, to the student, almost indispensable edition ;" and the* EXAMINER *calls it "an unrivalled edition."*

Shakespeare's Tempest. Edited with Glossarial and Explanatory Notes, by the Rev. J. M. JEPHSON. New Edition. 18mo. 1s.

Slip (A) in the Fens.—Illustrated by the Author. Crown 8vo. 6s.

"An artistic little volume, for every page is a picture."—TIMES. *"It will be read with pleasure, and with a pleasure that is altogether innocent."*—SATURDAY REVIEW.

Smith.—POEMS. By CATHERINE BARNARD SMITH. Fcap. 8vo. 5s.

"Wealthy in feeling, meaning, finish, and grace ; not without passion, which is suppressed, but the keener for that."—ATHENÆUM.

Smith (Rev. Walter).—HYMNS OF CHRIST AND THE CHRISTIAN LIFE. By the Rev. WALTER C. SMITH, M.A. Fcap. 8vo. 6s.

" These are among the sweetest sacred poems we have read for a long time. With no profuse imagery, expressing a range of feeling and expression by no means uncommon, they are true and elevated, and their pathos is profound and simple."—NONCONFORMIST.

Spring Songs. By a WEST HIGHLANDER. With a Vignette Illustration by GOURLAY STEELE. Fcap. 8vo. 1s. 6d.

"*Without a trace of affectation or sentimentalism, these utterances are perfectly simple and natural, profoundly human and profoundly true.*"—DAILY NEWS.

Stanley.—TRUE TO LIFE.—A SIMPLE STORY. By MARY STANLEY. Crown 8vo. 10s. 6d.

"*For many a long day we have not met with a more simple, healthy, and unpretending story.*"—STANDARD.

Stephen (C. E.)—THE SERVICE OF THE POOR; being an Inquiry into the Reasons for and against the Establishment of Religious Sisterhoods for Charitable Purposes. By CAROLINE EMILIA STEPHEN. Crown 8vo. 6s. 6d.

"*It touches incidentally and with much wisdom and tenderness on so many of the relations of women, particularly of single women, with society, that it may be read with advantage by many who have never thought of entering a Sisterhood.*"—SPECTATOR.

Stephens (J. B.)—CONVICT ONCE. A Poem. By J. BRUNTON STEPHENS. Extra fcap. 8vo. 3s. 6d.

"*It is as far more interesting than ninety-nine novels out of a hundred, as it is superior to them in power, worth, and beauty. We should most strongly advise everybody to read 'Convict Once.'*"—WESTMINSTER REVIEW.

Streets and Lanes of a City: Being the Reminiscences of AMY DUTTON. With a Preface by the BISHOP OF SALISBURY. Second and Cheaper Edition. Globe 8vo. 2s. 6d.

"*One of the most really striking books that has ever come before us.*"—LITERARY CHURCHMAN.

Thring.—SCHOOL SONGS. A Collection of Songs for Schools. With the Music arranged for four Voices. Edited by the Rev. E. THRING and H. RICCIUS. Folio. 7s. 6d.

The collection includes the "Agnus Dei," Tennyson's "Light Brigade," Macaulay's "Ivry," etc. among other pieces.

Tom Brown's School Days.—By AN OLD BOY. Golden Treasury Edition, 4s. 6d. People's Edition, 2s. With Seven Illustrations by A. HUGHES and SYDNEY HALL. Crown 8vo. 6s.

"*The most famous boy's book in the language.*"—DAILY NEWS.

Tom Brown at Oxford.—New Edition. With Illustrations. Crown 8vo. 6s.

"*In no other work that we can call to mind are the finer qualities of the English gentleman more happily portrayed.*"—DAILY NEWS.
"*A book of great power and truth.*"—NATIONAL REVIEW.

Trench.—Works by R. CHENEVIX TRENCH, D.D., Archbishop of Dublin. (For other Works by this Author, see THEOLOGICAL, HISTORICAL, and PHILOSOPHICAL CATALOGUES.)

POEMS. Collected and arranged anew. Fcap. 8vo. 7s. 6d.

Trench (Archbishop)—*continued.*
ELEGIAC POEMS. Third Edition. Fcap. 8vo. 2*s.* 6*d.*

CALDERON'S LIFE'S A DREAM : The Great Theatre of the
World. With an Essay on his Life and Genius. Fcap. 8vo. 4*s.* 6*d.*

HOUSEHOLD BOOK OF ENGLISH POETRY. Selected and
arranged, with Notes, by Archbishop TRENCH. Second Edition.
Extra fcap. 8vo. 5*s.* 6*d.*
" *The Archbishop has conferred in this delightful volume an important
gift on the whole English-speaking population of the world.*"—
PALL MALL GAZETTE.

SACRED LATIN POETRY, Chiefly Lyrical. Selected and
arranged for Use. By Archbishop TRENCH. Third Edition,
Corrected and Improved. Fcap. 8vo. 7*s.*

JUSTIN MARTYR, AND OTHER POEMS. Fifth Edition.
Fcap. 8vo. 6*s.*

Trollope (Anthony). — SIR HARRY HOTSPUR OF
HUMBLETHWAITE. By ANTHONY TROLLOPE, Author of
"Framley Parsonage," etc. Cheap Edition. Globe 8vo. 2*s.* 6*d.*
The ATHENÆUM *remarks :* " *No reader who begins to read this book
is likely to lay it down until the last page is turned. This brilliant
novel appears to us decidedly more successful than any other of Mr.
Trollope's shorter stories.*"

Turner.—Works by the Rev. CHARLES TENNYSON TURNER :—
SONNETS. Dedicated to his Brother, the Poet Laureate. Fcap.
8vo. 4*s.* 6*d.*
SMALL TABLEAUX. Fcap. 8vo. 4*s.* 6*d.*

Under the Limes.—By the Author of "Christina North."
Second Edition. Crown 8vo. 6*s.*
" *The readers of ' Christina North' are not likely to have forgotten
that bright, fresh, picturesque story, nor will they be slow to
welcome so pleasant a companion to it as this. It abounds in
happy touches of description, of pathos, and insight into the life
and passion of true love.*"—STANDARD. " *One of the prettiest
and best told stories which it has been our good fortune to read for
a long time.*"—PALL MALL GAZETTE.

Vittoria Colonna.—LIFE AND POEMS. By MRS. HENRY
ROSCOE. Crown 8vo. 9*s.*
" *It is written with good taste, with quick and intelligent sympathy,
occasionally with a real freshness and charm of style.*"—PALL
MALL GAZETTE.

Waller.—SIX WEEKS IN THE SADDLE : A Painter's Journal
in Iceland. By S. E. WALLER. Illustrated by the Author.
Crown 8vo. 6*s.*
" *An exceedingly pleasant and naturally written little book. . . Mr.
Waller has a clever pencil, and the text is well illustrated with his
own sketches.*"—TIMES.

Wandering Willie. By the Author of "Effie's Friends," and
"John Hatherton." Third Edition. Crown 8vo. 6*s.*

"*This is an idyll of rare truth and beauty. . . . The story is simple and touching, the style of extraordinary delicacy, precision, and picturesqueness. . . . A charming gift-book for young ladies not yet promoted to novels, and will amply repay those of their elders who may give an hour to its perusal.*"—DAILY NEWS.

Webster.—Works by AUGUSTA WEBSTER :—

"*If Mrs. Webster only remains true to herself, she will assuredly take a higher rank as a poet than any woman has yet done.*"—WESTMINSTER REVIEW.

DRAMATIC STUDIES. Extra fcap. 8vo. 5s.
"*A volume as strongly marked by perfect taste as by poetic power.*"—NONCONFORMIST.

A WOMAN SOLD, AND OTHER POEMS. Crown 8vo. 7s. 6d.
"*Mrs. Webster has shown us that she is able to draw admirably from the life; that she can observe with subtlety, and render her observations with delicacy; that she can impersonate complex conceptions and venture into which few living writers can follow her.*"—GUARDIAN.

PORTRAITS. Second Edition. Extra fcap. 8vo. 3s. 6d.
"*Mrs. Webster's poems exhibit simplicity and tenderness . . . her taste is perfect . . . This simplicity is combined with a subtlety of thought, feeling, and observation which demand that attention which only real lovers of poetry are apt to bestow.*"—WESTMINSTER REVIEW.

PROMETHEUS BOUND OF ÆSCHYLUS. Literally translated into English Verse. Extra fcap. 8vo. 3s. 6d.
"*Closeness and simplicity combined with literary skill.*" — ATHENÆUM. "*Mrs. Webster's 'Dramatic Studies' and 'Translation of Prometheus' have won for her an honourable place among our female poets. She writes with remarkable vigour and dramatic realization, and bids fair to be the most successful claimant of Mrs. Browning's mantle.*"—BRITISH QUARTERLY REVIEW.

MEDEA OF EURIPIDES. Literally translated into English Verse. Extra fcap. 8vo. 3s. 6d.
"*Mrs. Webster's translation surpasses our utmost expectations. It is a photograph of the original without any of that harshness which so often accompanies a photograph.*"—WESTMINSTER REVIEW.

THE AUSPICIOUS DAY. A Dramatic Poem. Extra fcap. 8vo. 5s.
"*The 'Auspicious Day' shows a marked advance, not only in art, but, in what is of far more importance, in breadth of thought and intellectual grasp.*"—WESTMINSTER REVIEW. "*This drama is a manifestation of high dramatic power on the part of the gifted writer, and entitled to our warmest admiration, as a worthy piece of work.*"—STANDARD.

YU-PE-YA'S LUTE. A Chinese Tale in English Verse. Extra fcap. 8vo. 3s. 6d.
"*A very charming tale, charmingly told in dainty verse, with occasional lyrics of tender beauty.*"—STANDARD. "*We close the*

Webster—*continued.*

> *book with the renewed conviction that in Mrs. Webster we have a profound and original poet. The book is marked not by mere sweetness of melody—rare as that gift is—but by the infinitely rarer gifts of dramatic power, of passion, and sympathetic insight."* —WESTMINSTER REVIEW.

When I was a Little Girl. STORIES FOR CHILDREN.

By the Author of "St. Olave's." Fourth Edition. Extra fcap. 8vo. 4s. 6d. With Eight Illustrations by L. FRÖLICH.

> *"At the head, and a long way ahead, of all books for girls, we place 'When I was a Little Girl.'"*—TIMES. *"It is one of the choicest morsels of child-biography which we have met with."*—NONCONFORMIST.

White.—RHYMES BY WALTER WHITE. 8vo. 7s. 6d.

Whittier.—JOHN GREENLEAF WHITTIER'S POETICAL WORKS. Complete Edition, with Portrait engraved by C. H. JEENS. 18mo. 4s. 6d.

> *"Mr. Whittier has all the smooth melody and the pathos of the author of 'Hiawatha,' with a greater nicety of description and a quainter fancy."*—GRAPHIC.

Wolf.—THE LIFE AND HABITS OF WILD ANIMALS. Twenty Illustrations by JOSEPH WOLF, engraved by J. W. and E. WHYMPER. With descriptive Letter-press, by D. G. ELLIOT, F.L.S. Super royal 4to, cloth extra, gilt edges. 21s.

> *This is the last series of drawings which will be made by Mr. Wolf, either upon wood or stone.* The PALL MALL GAZETTE *says:* *" The fierce, untameable side of brute nature has never received a more robust and vigorous interpretation, and the various incidents in which particular character is shown are set forth with rare dramatic power. For excellence that will endure, we incline to place this very near the top of the list of Christmas books." And the* ART JOURNAL *observes, " Rarely, if ever, have we seen animal life more forcibly and beautifully depicted than in this really splendid volume."*

Also, an Edition in royal folio, handsomely bound in Morocco elegant, Proofs before Letters, each Proof signed by the Engravers. Price 8l. 8s.

Wollaston.—LYRA DEVONIENSIS. By T. V. WOLLASTON, M.A. Fcap. 8vo. 3s. 6d.

> *"It is the work of a man of refined taste, of deep religious sentiment, a true artist, and a good Christian."*—CHURCH TIMES.

Woolner.—MY BEAUTIFUL LADY. By THOMAS WOOLNER. With a Vignette by ARTHUR HUGHES. Third Edition. Fcap. 8vo. 5s.

> *" No man can read this poem without being struck by the fitness and finish of the workmanship, so to speak, as well as by the chastened and unpretending loftiness of thought which pervades the whole."* —GLOBE.

Words from the Poets. Selected by the Editor of " Rays of Sunlight." With a Vignette and Frontispiece. 18mo. limp.,˙1s.
" *The selection aims at popularity, and deserves it.*"—GUARDIAN.

Yonge (C. M.)—Works by CHARLOTTE M. YONGE.
THE HEIR OF REDCLYFFE. Twentieth Edition. With Illustrations. Crown 8vo. 6s.
HEARTSEASE. Thirteenth Edition. With Illustrations. Crown 8vo. 6s.
THE DAISY CHAIN. Twelfth Edition. With Illustrations. Crown 8vo. 6s.
THE TRIAL: MORE LINKS OF THE DAISY CHAIN. Twelfth Edition. With Illustrations. Crown 8vo. 6s.
DYNEVOR TERRACE. Sixth Edition. Crown 8vo. 6s.
HOPES AND FEARS. Fourth Edition. Crown 8vo. 6s.
THE YOUNG STEPMOTHER. Fifth Edition. Crown 8vo. 6s.
CLEVER WOMAN OF THE FAMILY. Third Edition. Crown 8vo. 6s.
THE DOVE IN THE EAGLE'S NEST. Fourth Edition. Crown 8vo. 6s.
" *We think the authoress of ' The Heir of Redclyffe' has surpassed her previous efforts in this illuminated chronicle of the olden time.*" —BRITISH QUARTERLY.
THE CAGED LION. Illustrated. Third Edition. Crown 8vo. 6s.
" *Prettily and tenderly written, and will with young people especially be a great favourite.*"—DAILY NEWS. " *Everybody should read this.*"—LITERARY CHURCHMAN.
THE CHAPLET OF PEARLS; OR, THE WHITE AND BLACK RIBAUMONT. Crown 8vo. 6s. New Edition.
" *Miss Yonge has brought a lofty aim as well as high art to the construction of a story which may claim a place among the best efforts in historical romance.*"—MORNING POST. " *The plot, in truth, is of the very first order of merit.*"—SPECTATOR. " *We have seldom read a more charming story.*"—GUARDIAN.
THE PRINCE AND THE PAGE. A Tale of the Last Crusade. Illustrated. 18mo. 2s. 6d.
" *A tale which, we are sure, will give pleasure to many others besides the young people for whom it is specially intended. . . . This extremely prettily-told story does not require the guarantee afforded by the name of the author of ' The Heir of Redclyffe' on the title-page to ensure its becoming a universal favourite.*"—DUBLIN EVENING MAIL.
THE LANCES OF LYNWOOD. New Edition, with Coloured Illustrations. 18mo. 4s. 6d.
" *The illustrations are very spirited and rich in colour, and the story can hardly fail to charm the youthful reader.*" —MANCHESTER EXAMINER.
THE LITTLE DUKE: RICHARD THE FEARLESS. New Edition. Illustrated. 18mo. 2s. 6d.

Yonge (C. M.)—*continued.*

A STOREHOUSE OF STORIES. First and Second Series. Globe 8vo. 3*s.* 6*d.* each.

CONTENTS OF FIRST SERIES :—History of Philip Quarll—Goody Twoshoes—The Governess—Jemima Placid—The Perambulations of a Mouse—The Village School—The Little Queen—History of Little Jack.

"*Miss Yonge has done great service to the infantry of this generation by putting these eleven stories of sage simplicity within their reach.*"—BRITISH QUARTERLY REVIEW.

CONTENTS OF SECOND SERIES :—Family Stories—Elements of Morality—A Puzzle for a Curious Girl—Blossoms of Morality.

A BOOK OF GOLDEN DEEDS OF ALL TIMES AND ALL COUNTRIES. Gathered and Narrated Anew. New Edition, with Twenty Illustrations by FRÖLICH. Crown 8vo. cloth gilt. 6*s.* (See also GOLDEN TREASURY SERIES). Cheap Edition. 1*s.*

" *We have seen no prettier gift-book for a long time, and none which, both for its cheapness and the spirit in which it has been compiled, is more deserving of praise.*"—ATHENÆUM.

LITTLE LUCY'S WONDERFUL GLOBE. Pictured by FRÖLICH, and narrated by CHARLOTTE M. YONGE. Second Edition. Crown 4to. cloth gilt. 6*s.*

"'*Lucy's Wonderful Globe*' *is capital, and will give its youthful readers more idea of foreign countries and customs than any number of books of geography or travel.*"—GRAPHIC.

CAMEOS FROM ENGLISH HISTORY. From ROLLO to EDWARD II. Extra fcap. 8vo. 5*s.* Second Edition, enlarged. 5*s.*

A SECOND SERIES. THE WARS IN FRANCE. Extra fcap. 8vo. 5*s.*

"*Instead of dry details,*" *says the* NONCONFORMIST, "*we have living pictures, faithful, vivid, and striking.*"

P's AND Q's ; OR, THE QUESTION OF PUTTING UPON. With Illustrations by C. O. MURRAY. Second Edition. Globe 8vo. cloth gilt. 4*s.* 6*d.*

" *One of her most successful little pieces . . . . just what a narrative should be, each incident simply and naturally related, no preaching or moralizing, and yet the moral coming out most powerfully, and the whole story not too long, or with the least appearance of being spun out.*"—LITERARY CHURCHMAN.

THE PILLARS OF THE HOUSE ; OR, UNDER WODE, UNDER RODE. Second Edition. Four vols. crown 8vo. 20*s.*

" *A domestic story of English professional life, which for sweetness of tone and absorbing interest from first to last has never been rivalled.*"—STANDARD. " *Miss Yonge has certainly added to her already high reputation by this charming book, which, although in four volumes, is not a single page too long, but keeps the reader's attention fixed to the end. Indeed we are only sorry there is not another volume to come, and part with the Underwood family with sincere regret.*"—COURT CIRCULAR.

Yonge (C. M.)—*continued.*

LADY HESTER; OR, URSULA'S NARRATIVE. Second
Edition. Crown 8vo. 6s.

"*We shall not anticipate the interest by epitomizing the plot, but we
shall only say that readers will find in it all the gracefulness, right
feeling, and delicate perception which they have been long accustomed
to look for in Miss Yonge's writings.*"—GUARDIAN.

MACMILLAN'S GOLDEN TREASURY SERIES.

UNIFORMLY printed in 18mo., with Vignette Titles by Sir
NOEL PATON, T. WOOLNER, W. HOLMAN HUNT, J. E.
MILLAIS, ARTHUR HUGHES, &c. Engraved on Steel by
JEENS. Bound in extra cloth, 4s. 6d. each volume. Also
kept in morocco and calf bindings.

"*Messrs. Macmillan have, in their Golden Treasury Series, especially
provided editions of standard works, volumes of selected poetry, and
original compositions, which entitle this series to be called classical.
Nothing can be better than the literary execution, nothing more
elegant than the material workmanship.*"—BRITISH QUARTERLY
REVIEW.

The Golden Treasury of the Best Songs and
LYRICAL POEMS IN THE ENGLISH LANGUAGE.
Selected and arranged, with Notes, by FRANCIS TURNER
PALGRAVE.

"*This delightful little volume, the Golden Treasury, which contains
many of the best original lyrical pieces and songs in our language,
grouped with care and skill, so as to illustrate each other like the
pictures in a well-arranged gallery.*"—QUARTERLY REVIEW.

The Children's Garland from the best Poets.
Selected and arranged by COVENTRY PATMORE.

"*It includes specimens of all the great masters in the art of poetry,
selected with the matured judgment of a man concentrated on
obtaining insight into the feelings and tastes of childhood, and
desirous to awaken its finest impulses, to cultivate its keenest sensi-
bilities.*"—MORNING POST.

The Book of Praise. From the Best English Hymn Writers.
Selected and arranged by LORD SELBOURNE. *A New and Enlarged Edition.*

"*All previous compilations of this kind must undeniably for the
present give place to the Book of Praise. . . . The selection has
been made throughout with sound judgment and critical taste. The
pains involved in this compilation must have been immense, embracing, as it does, every writer of note in this special province of
English literature, and ranging over the most widely divergent
tracks of religious thought.*"—SATURDAY REVIEW.

The Fairy Book; the Best Popular Fairy Stories. Selected and rendered anew by the Author of "JOHN HALIFAX, GENTLEMAN."

"*A delightful selection, in a delightful external form; full of the physical splendour and vast opulence of proper fairy tales.*"—SPECTATOR.

The Ballad Book. A Selection of the Choicest British Ballads. Edited by WILLIAM ALLINGHAM.

"*His taste as a judge of old poetry will be found, by all acquainted with the various readings of old English ballads, true enough to justify his undertaking so critical a task.*"—SATURDAY REVIEW.

The Jest Book. The Choicest Anecdotes and Sayings. Selected and arranged by MARK LEMON.

"*The fullest and best jest book that has yet appeared.*"—SATURDAY REVIEW.

Bacon's Essays and Colours of Good and Evil. With Notes and Glossarial Index. By W. ALDIS WRIGHT, M.A.

"*The beautiful little edition of Bacon's Essays, now before us, does credit to the taste and scholarship of Mr. Aldis Wright. . . . Is puts the reader in possession of all the essential literary facts and chronology necessary for reading the Essays in connection with Bacon's life and times.*"—SPECTATOR.

The Pilgrim's Progress from this World to that which is to come. By JOHN BUNYAN.

"*A beautiful and scholarly reprint.*"—SPECTATOR.

The Sunday Book of Poetry for the Young. Selected and arranged by C. F. ALEXANDER.

"*A well-selected volume of Sacred Poetry.*"—SPECTATOR.

A Book of Golden Deeds of All Times and All Countries. Gathered and narrated anew. By the Author of "THE HEIR OF REDCLYFFE."

"*. . . To the young, for whom it is especially intended, as a most interesting collection of thrilling tales well told; and to their elders, as a useful handbook of reference, and a pleasant one to take up when their wish is to while away a weary half-hour. We have seen no prettier gift-book for a long time.*"—ATHENÆUM.

The Poetical Works of Robert Burns. Edited, with Biographical Memoir, Notes, and Glossary, by ALEXANDER SMITH. Two Vols.

"*Beyond all question this is the most beautiful edition of Burns yet out.*"—EDINBURGH DAILY REVIEW.

The Adventures of Robinson Crusoe. Edited from the Original Edition by J. W. CLARK, M.A. Fellow of Trinity College, Cambridge.

"*Mutilated and modified editions of this English classic are so much the rule, that a cheap and pretty copy of it, rigidly exact to the original, will be a prize to many book-buyers."*—EXAMINER.

The Republic of Plato. TRANSLATED into ENGLISH, with Notes by J. Ll. DAVIES, M.A. and D. J. VAUGHAN, M.A.
"A dainty and cheap little edition."—EXAMINER.

The Song Book. Words and Tunes from the best Poets and Musicians. Selected and arranged by JOHN HULLAH, Professor of Vocal Music in King's College, London.
"A choice collection of the sterling songs of England, Scotland, and Ireland, with the music of each prefixed to the Words. How much true wholesome pleasure such a book can diffuse, and will diffuse, we trust through many thousand families."—EXAMINER.

La Lyre Française. Selected and arranged, with Notes, by GUSTAVE MASSON, French Master in Harrow School.
A selection of the best French songs and lyrical pieces.

Tom Brown's School Days. By AN OLD BOY.
"A perfect gem of a book. The best and most healthy book about boys for boys that ever was written."—ILLUSTRATED TIMES.

A Book of Worthies. Gathered from the Old Histories and written anew by the Author of "THE HEIR OF REDCLYFFE." With Vignette.
"An admirable addition to an admirable series."—WESTMINSTER REVIEW.

A Book of Golden Thoughts. By HENRY ATTWELL, Knight of the Order of the Oak Crown.
"Mr. Attwell has produced a book of rare value . . . . Happily it is small enough to be carried about in the pocket, and of such a companion it would be difficult to weary."—PALL MALL GAZETTE.

Guesses at Truth. By TWO BROTHERS. New Edition.

The Cavalier and his Lady. Selections from the Works of the First Duke and Duchess of Newcastle. With an Introductory Essay by EDWARD JENKINS, Author of "Ginx's Baby," &c. 18mo. 4s. 6d.
"A charming little volume."—STANDARD.

Theologia Germanica.—Which setteth forth many fair Lineaments of Divine Truth, and saith very lofty and lovely things touching a Perfect Life. Edited by DR. PFEIFFER, from the only complete manuscript yet known. Translated from the German, by SUSANNA WINKWORTH. With a Preface by the REV. CHARLES KINGSLEY, and a Letter to the Translator by the Chevalier Bunsen, D.D.

Milton's Poetical Works.—Edited, with Notes, &c., by PROFESSOR MASSON. Two vols. 18mo. 9s.

Scottish Song. A Selection of the Choicest Lyrics of Scotland. Compiled and arranged, with brief Notes, by MARY CARLYLE AITKIN. 18mo. 4s. 6d.

" Miss Aitken's exquisite collection of Scottish Song is so alluring, and suggests so many topics, that we find it difficult to lay it down. The book is one that should find a place in every library, we had almost said in every pocket, and the summer tourist who wishes to carry with him into the country a volume of genuine poetry, will find it difficult to select one containing within so small a compass so much of rarest value."—SPECTATOR.

MACMILLAN'S GLOBE LIBRARY.

Beautifully printed on toned paper and bound in cloth extra, gilt edges, price 4s. 6d. each; in cloth plain, 3s. 6d. Also kept in a variety of calf and morocco bindings at moderate prices.

BOOKS, Wordsworth says, are
"the spirit breathed
By dead men to their kind;"
and the aim of the publishers of the Globe Library has been to make it possible for the universal kin of English-speaking men to hold communion with the loftiest "spirits of the mighty dead;" to put within the reach of all classes *complete* and *accurate* editions, carefully and clearly printed upon the best paper, in a convenient form, at a moderate price, of the works of the MASTER-MINDS OF ENGLISH LITERATURE, and occasionally of foreign literature in an attractive English dress.

The Editors, by their scholarship and special study of their authors, are competent to afford every assistance to readers of all kinds : this assistance is rendered by original biographies, glossaries of unusual or obsolete words, and critical and explanatory notes.

The publishers hope, therefore, that these Globe Editions may prove worthy of acceptance by all classes wherever the English Language is spoken, and by their universal circulation justify their distinctive epithet; while at the same time they spread and nourish a common sympathy with nature's most "finely touched" spirits, and thus help a little to "make the whole world kin."

The SATURDAY REVIEW *says:* " *The Globe Editions are admirable for their scholarly editing, their typographical excellence, their compendious form, and their cheapness.*" *The* BRITISH QUARTERLY REVIEW *says:* " *In compendiousness, elegance, and scholarliness, the Globe Editions of Messrs. Macmillan surpass any popular series*

*of our classics hitherto given to the public. As near an approach
to miniature perfection as has ever been made."*

Shakespeare's Complete Works. Edited by W. G, CLARK, M.A., and W. ALDIS WRIGHT, M.A., of Trinity College. Cambridge, Editors of the "Cambridge Shakespeare." With Glossary. pp. 1,075.

The ATHENÆUM *says this edition is "a marvel of beauty, cheapness,
and compactness. . . . For the busy \[man, above all for the
working student, this is the best of all existing Shakespeares."
And the* PALL MALL GAZETTE *observes: "To have produced
the complete works of the world's greatest poet in such a form,
and at a price within the reach of every one, is of itself almost
sufficient to give the publishers a claim to be considered public bene-
factors."*

Spenser's Complete Works. Edited from the Original Editions and Manuscripts, by R. MORRIS, with a Memoir by J. W. HALES, M.A. With Glossary. pp. lv., 736.

*"Worthy—and higher praise it needs not—of the beautiful 'Globe
Series.' The work is edited with all the care so noble a poet
deserves."*—DAILY NEWS.

Sir Walter Scott's Poetical Works. Edited with a Biographical and Critical Memoir by FRANCIS TURNER PALGRAVE, and copious Notes. pp. xliii., 559.

*"We can almost sympathise with a middle-aged grumbler, who, after
reading Mr. Palgrave's memoir and introduction, should exclaim
—'Why was there not such an edition of Scott when I was a school-
boy?'"*—GUARDIAN.

Complete Works of Robert Burns.—THE POEMS, SONGS, AND LETTERS, edited from the best Printed and Manuscript Authorities, with Glossarial Index, Notes, and a Biographical Memoir by ALEXANDER SMITH. pp. lxii., 636.

"Admirable in all respects."—SPECTATOR. *"The cheapest, the
most perfect, and the most interesting edition which has ever been
published."*—BELL'S MESSENGER.

Robinson Crusoe. Edited after the Original Editions, with a Biographical Introduction by HENRY KINGSLEY. pp. xxxi., 607.

"A most excellent and in every way desirable edition."—COURT
CIRCULAR. *"Macmillan's 'Globe' Robinson Crusoe is a book to
have and to keep."*—MORNING STAR.

Goldsmith's Miscellaneous Works. Edited, with Biographical Introduction, by Professor MASSON. pp. lx., 695.

*"Such an admirable compendium of the facts of Goldsmith's life,
and so careful and minute a delineation of the mixed traits of his
peculiar character as to be a very model of a literary biography
in little."*—SCOTSMAN.

Pope's Poetical Works. Edited, with Notes and Intro-ductory Memoir, by ADOLPHUS WILLIAM WARD, M.A., Fellow

of St. Peter's College, Cambridge, and Professor of History in Owens College, Manchester. pp. lii., 508.

The LITERARY CHURCHMAN *remarks :* "*The editor's own notes and introductory memoir are excellent, the memoir alone would be cheap and well worth buying at the price of the whole volume.*"

Dryden's Poetical Works. Edited, with a Memoir, Revised Text, and Notes, by W. D. CHRISTIE, M.A., of Trinity College, Cambridge. pp. lxxxvii., 662.

"*An admirable edition, the result of great research and of a careful revision of the text. The memoir prefixed contains, within less than ninety pages, as much sound criticism and as comprehensive a biography as the student of Dryden need desire.*"—PALL MALL GAZETTE.

Cowper's Poetical Works. Edited, with Notes and Biographical Introduction, by WILLIAM BENHAM, Vicar of Addington and Professor of Modern History in Queen's College, London. pp. lxxiii., 536.

"*Mr. Benham's edition of Cowper is one of permanent value. The biographical introduction is excellent, full of information, singularly neat and readable and modest—indeed too modest in its comments. The notes are concise and accurate, and the editor has been able to discover and introduce some hitherto unprinted matter. Altogether the book is a very excellent one.*"—SATURDAY REVIEW.

Morte d'Arthur.—SIR THOMAS MALORY'S BOOK OF KING ARTHUR AND OF HIS NOBLE KNIGHTS OF THE ROUND TABLE. The original Edition of CAXTON, revised for Modern Use. With an Introduction by Sir EDWARD STRACHEY, Bart. pp. xxxvii., 509.

"*It is with perfect confidence that we recommend this edition of the old romance to every class of readers.*"—PALL MALL GAZETTE.

The Works of Virgil. Rendered into English Prose, with Introductions, Notes, Running Analysis, and an Index. By JAMES LONSDALE, M.A., late Fellow and Tutor of Balliol College, Oxford, and Classical Professor in King's College, London ; and SAMUEL LEE, M.A., Latin Lecturer at University College, London. pp. 288.

"*A more complete edition of Virgil in English it is scarcely possible to conceive than the scholarly work before us.*"—GLOBE.

The Works of Horace. Rendered into English Prose, with Introductions, Running Analysis, Notes, and Index. By JOHN LONSDALE, M.A., and SAMUEL LEE, M.A.

The STANDARD *says*, "*To classical and non-classical readers it will be invaluable as a faithful interpretation of the mind and meaning of the poet, enriched as it is with notes and dissertations of the highest value in the way of criticism, illustration, and explanation.*"

LONDON : R. CLAY, SONS, AND TAYLOR, PRINTERS.

www.ingramcontent.com/pod-product-compliance
Lightning Source LLC
Chambersburg PA
CBHW051509100726
47898CB00005B/1385